Praise for Steve Cavanagh

'This guy is the real deal. Trust me'   Lee Child

'A terrific writer. He has talent to burn'   Don Winslow

'A brilliant, twisty, ingeniously constructed puzzle'   Ruth Ware

'If you read a thriller as good this year, it's only because you've read this one twice'   Mark Billingham

'Trust me – it will keep you guessing until the very end'
                                                         Ian Rankin

'Steve Cavanagh must have sold his soul to the devil at the crossroads outside of Rosedale, Mississippi in exchange for becoming one of the world's best crime writers. Steve is 5/5'
                                                         Adrian McKinty

'What a great read – an absolute page turner'   Shari Lapena

'A dead bang beast of a book expertly combining his authority on the law with an absolutely great thrill ride. Books this ingenious don't come along very often'   Michael Connelly

'Unpredictable, daring and completely compelling. Top notch writing'   Alex North

'Eddie's back! Steve Cavanagh writes the best hooks in the business'
Mick Herron

'A great read' Martina Cole

'Smart and original. A belter of a book' Clare Mackintosh

'Steve Cavanagh's writing is intelligent, sophisticated and tense, his plots executed with forensic attention to detail. I can't get enough of Eddie Flynn' Mari Hannah

'Steve Cavanagh stands head and shoulders above the competition with his skilfully plotted, action-packed and big-hearted Eddie Flynn novels . . . highly intelligent, twist-laden and absolutely unput-downable' Eva Dolan

'A fantastic read. Guaranteed to be one of the big books of 2019. You won't be able to put this down' Luca Veste

'A corkscrewing rollercoaster of thrills, switchbacks, loop-de-loops and screaming good fun' Mark Edwards

'Very clever, darkly funny, moving, fast-paced, and Eddie Flynn is a terrific character' Jane Casey

Steve Cavanagh was born and raised in Belfast before leaving for Dublin at the age of eighteen to study Law. He practiced civil rights law and was involved in several high-profile cases; in 2010 he represented a factory worker who suffered racial abuse in the workplace and won the largest award of damages for race discrimination in Northern Ireland legal history. He holds a certificate in Advanced Advocacy and lectures on various legal subjects (but really he just likes to tell jokes). His novel *The Liar* won the 2018 CWA Gold Dagger award while his follow-up novel *Thirteen* won the Theakston Old Peculier Crime Novel of the Year Award in 2019. *Twisted* and *Fifty-Fifty* were both *Sunday Times* Top 10 bestsellers. He is married with two young children.

To find out more, visit Steve's website or
follow him on Facebook and Twitter.

www.stevecavanaghauthor.com

 /SSCav1

 @SSCav

THE DEVIL'S ADVOCATE

An Eddie Flynn Thriller

Steve Cavanagh

ORION

First published in Great Britain in 2021 by Orion Fiction,
an imprint of The Orion Publishing Group Ltd.,
Carmelite House, 50 Victoria Embankment
London EC4Y 0DZ

An Hachette UK company

1 3 5 7 9 10 8 6 4 2

A CIP catalogue record for this book
is available from the British Library.

ISBN (Hardback) 978 1 3987 0017 8
ISBN (Trade Paperback) 978 1 4091 8589 5
ISBN (eBook) 978 1 4091 8591 8

Typeset by Born Group
Printed and bound in Great Britain by Clays Ltd, Elcograf S.p.A.

MIX
Paper from
responsible sources
FSC® C104740

www.orionbooks.co.uk

To John, Matt and Alan.

For friendship.

PROLOGUE

Holman Correctional Facility, Escambia County, Alabama

Randal Korn had waited for this moment for four long years.

He stood in the death chamber, arms folded, staring at the chair. It was almost one hundred years old. Constructed from mahogany and then painted bright yellow with highway-line paint borrowed from the State Highway Department, just down a ways from Holman Correctional. They called the chair Yellow Mama.

One hundred and forty-nine people had sat in that chair, never to stand again.

The digital clock on the wall read 23:45.

It was almost time. He exited the brick chamber and found himself in a cinderblock hallway. Unpainted. A door to the left led to the control room for the chair – the hot box. He didn't go inside, instead he went straight to the enclave at the end of the hall. Two couches faced each other. On one sat a priest, on the other were the execution team. Four corrections officers, trained to get the prisoner from his death cell to the chair, and strap him in, all in under two minutes.

Korn waved a hand at the death team, and the lead officer nodded back. He ignored the priest. Beyond the couches, a narrow corridor broke left. At the end of that corridor a small, barred cell and inside it, sitting on the cot, watching TV, was Darius Robinson. He'd eaten his last meal – chicken-fried steak, cornbread and a Pepsi. The last rites had been given by the priest. His head and left calf had been freshly shaved. One man stood between Darius and Yellow Mama.

His name was Cody Warren.

Cody was outside the cell, using the phone fixed to the wall. Korn knew exactly what Cody was doing. He was on the phone

I

to the Governor's Office, waiting while Governor Chris Patchett looked over the papers Cody had sent through appealing for a stay of execution. As a defense lawyer with experience of death-penalty cases in Alabama, Cody was the one person who could persuade the governor to save his client's life.

Korn stood very still. A tall, thin man with little musculature over his frame and no body fat. Not that he kept in shape. He ate little and it showed. High cheekbones that could slice a New York strip. No age lines visible, anywhere. Some said his face was that of a peculiar porcelain doll. With his dark hair parted to one side, his wire-rimmed glasses perched carefully on his nose, he looked like a much older man who had stolen a younger body to inhabit. Korn had small, black eyes that were hooded by his brow, as if to conceal his gaze. His mouth was just a dark slit in his face. That six-foot-seven-inch tall body could have been an advantage if it had ever taken up sports, but instead it stayed inside, in the dark, reading, learning and thinking. Like an old spider, spinning a web that only it could see.

Darius Robinson, twenty-five years old, had been convicted of murder four years ago, and sentenced to death. His appeals were quickly exhausted. The victim was a used-car salesman who'd been shot in the chest during a robbery. A man named Porter shot the salesman while relieving him of five grand in cash. Robinson had driven Porter to the lot and driven him away after the robbery. He maintained that he hadn't known Porter was armed, and all he was doing was giving him a ride to the lot to pick up a new car. Porter had been shot dead by police twenty-four hours after the robbery. Robinson told the jury he hadn't been armed, he hadn't even set foot on the lot, he was in the car the whole time and hadn't known Porter intended to rob anyone until he heard the shot. He even said that Porter threatened to shoot him if he didn't drive him away from the scene after the robbery.

That didn't matter in Sunville County. Randal Korn, the district attorney for the county, convinced the jury Robinson was in on the robbery and he had known Porter was armed. Under party laws, that was enough to put Robinson on death row and treat him as if he had been the one who fired the gun. All executions in Alabama are carried out at Holman, in Escambia County, the next county over from Sunville.

Korn knew that because Porter had been the one who actually pulled the trigger, there was always a very good chance Darius could have his death penalty commuted.

Cody was older than Korn and wore every year of his sixty-three on his face. Deep lines creased his forehead. Crow's feet crowded his eyes, but they remained bright – hopeful. His suit jacket lay on the painted concrete floor, along with his tie. He rubbed sweat off his forehead into his gray hair, then pressed the phone back to his ear. Cody Warren was a good lawyer, and he was confident of saving Darius's life, even if he couldn't set him free.

'Any word from the Governor's Office yet?' asked Korn.

Cody turned, shook his head, then checked his watch. Ten minutes to midnight. Ten minutes until Darius Robinson took his last steps to the chair. The wall phone was a dedicated line to the Governor's Office, but most lawyers sat on hold. Like Cody. Listening to dead air, and waiting for an act of mercy.

'He's gonna commute my sentence. I know it. I'm an innocent man,' said a voice. Korn turned to see Darius in the death cell, holding onto the iron bars, almost dancing from foot to foot, his teeth were in his lips, biting down in anticipation. Sweat covered his face, even though the hallway was cool. Waiting on a phone call to decide if you're going to live or die can tear a man apart, and the mental strain was showing on Darius.

Korn took his cell phone from his jacket, swiped, tapped and placed the device to his ear.

'Lieutenant Governor Patchett,' said Korn. 'I'm here with Cody Warren and the man of the hour, Mr. Robinson. I believe Mr. Warren has been on hold for some time trying to get through to the office.'

The Governor of Alabama was in the middle of an impeachment hearing, which had been adjourned on account of the governor taking leave due to illness. He was currently recovering in a hospital in Arkansas. As he was out of the state, the lieutenant governor was acting up.

3

Korn tapped the screen again for speaker, so Cody and Darius could hear.

'I'm still considering the decision. Wanted to ask your opinion first,' said Patchett.

'Sure, let me discuss the position with Mr. Warren. I'll just put you on hold.'

Warren slammed down the phone in its cradle. He'd been on hold to the Governor's Office for almost an hour, and Korn liked letting him know that he could get the governor instantly. These little power plays gave Korn a momentary thrill.

'Look, Korn. He had a lesser role in that robbery, no matter what way you dice this. He doesn't deserve to die, and you know it. He's still a young man. He can still have a life and I'm convinced there's new evidence out there that's going to clear his name one day. Please, just give him a chance,' said Warren, his voice cracked and shrill – he'd been working flat out to save Darius Robinson from the chair for five days straight.

Korn's expression remained impassive. That blank, doll face. He said nothing in reply and took enjoyment from watching Warren's eyes search his own, looking for an answer, searching for hope, holding his breath.

No one spoke. No one dared breathe. Korn could stand very still when he wanted to, one of the other traits that made him seem at times inanimate. A portentous silence enveloped them. It was filled with possibility and dread. And Korn luxuriated in that ominous quiet as if he were bathing in dead water.

And then, the silence was broken. Darius took a breath. He inhaled deeply. Like the momentary vacuum in space as the core of a star collapses, drawing everything inside its fractured heart, right before it explodes.

'Porter held a gun on me after the robbery! If I hadn't driven him away, he woulda killed me. I didn't know he was gonna shoot somebody and rob 'em. I swear I didn't know!' shouted Darius, the fear and desperation dripping from every single word.

'I believe you,' said Korn.

'You what?' asked Warren.

'I believe him. And the acting governor will do whatever I tell him. I'll get him back on the phone right now. Give me a second, and it will all be over soon,' said Korn.

Tears began to run down Darius Robinson's cheeks.

Cody Warren's shoulders slumped, as if five hundred pounds had just been lifted off his back. He looked to the ceiling, whispered a *thank you* to the heavens and closed his eyes. He had saved a young man's life. And right then, nothing could be as sweet as that relief.

He strode up to the death cell, put his forearms through the bars and held his client's face. 'It's going to be okay,' he said.

Korn pressed the screen on his cell with this thumb. 'Governor, are you still there?'

'I'm here. We're cutting this fine, Randal. What do you want me to do? I'm inclined to commute the sentence based on Mr. Warren's submission, but I won't go against my district attorney – not if you have strong views. What's your attitude?'

Korn took a step back, admiring the scene in front of him. Warren and Robinson were hugging each other through the bars of the cell. Both of them were crying now.

'I've spoken to Mr. Warren. He is very persuasive. He has a strong argument for commuting Robinson's sentence. I understand that is your preference too. It's not easy to take a life in the name of justice,' said Korn.

Warren and Robinson were now smiling through their tears, laughing. The vast, unfathomable fear that had held them for weeks had gone, and the relief was total.

'But that's why we *must* go through with the sentence in this case,' said Korn.

Warren was the first to register what Korn had just said. His head snapped to the side, his eyes locking on the district attorney.

'A jury convicted Mr. Robinson of murder and sentenced him to death. We are dishonoring that jury, and dishonoring Mr. Robinson's victim, if we allow him to live. No, in my opinion, Darius Robinson dies tonight.'

Warren started toward Korn, but two guards stepped in between them, grabbing hold of Warren and forcing him back.

'Like I said, Randal, I'm not going to go against your wishes. The execution will proceed as planned. Appeal denied,' said Patchett.

The Department of Corrections staff had performed training drills for weeks leading to this day, making sure the straps were tight, the sponge on his head held enough saline, the electrodes securely attached. They finished their well-practiced work in under two minutes, and stepped out of the death chamber leaving Robinson strapped into Yellow Mama and blindfolded.

The chamber itself was relatively small. The chair was in the center of the brick-walled room, facing the large viewing window. The controls for the electric current were in a separate room. It was through the glass pane in the control-room door that Korn would watch the execution.

Robinson's blue prison-issue uniform had been altered somewhat. His left pant leg had been cut away just above the knee. An electrode strapped to that calf, which had been smeared with a conductor gel. Both legs were secured to the chair by thick leather straps with bright silver buckles around his ankles. More straps around his stomach, chest, arms and forehead. A sponge containing exactly three fluid ounces of saline sat ready on the electrode emanating from what they called the 'helmet', the cap which delivered most of the current into Korn's body. If there was too much saline in the sponge, the electrode would short. Too little, and Darius's head would catch fire.

The prisoner's uniform had damp patches on it. Under the arms and on the chest. Robinson was sweating through his uniform. Even strapped down tightly, he was still shaking like a pistol in a child's hand.

A lever in the control room pulled open the curtain in the death chamber to reveal the glass wall, and the people beyond. Half a dozen witnesses. None of them related to the dead used-car salesmen who'd been murdered by Porter. No, these were professional witnesses and reporters. Cody Warren was not present. He had been removed from the building. Korn could see the witnesses, but they could not see him. His viewing pane was one-way glass.

The condemned man was offered his final words.

'I'm innocent and they all know it.'

Korn knew it. And he didn't care. He didn't become a prosecutor in a death-penalty state to concern himself with guilt or innocence. It was the system that appealed to him. Justice was simply a cloak he wore to disguise his true nature.

All was quiet now. Then, he heard the sound of the machine kick to life.

Korn heard something else, a low hum, which suddenly became louder as Robinson's left shoulder jerked and then slammed back against the chair.

Yellow Mama had begun her first cycle.

Almost two-and-a-half-thousand volts were now coursing through Robinson. Korn's eye's widened, his lips parted. He could taste something metallic in his mouth. The air was thick with static.

For the first two seconds, Robinson appeared as if an invisible force had pinned his shoulder to the back of the chair. Another two seconds passed with his body jerking wildly, like a jackhammer was buried in his stomach. This first jolt was supposed to knock him out, stop his heart.

It did neither of those things. The human skull is a poor conductor.

After another five seconds the current was shut off. When it reconnected, it was much lower – just seven hundred volts. This would remain on for thirty seconds and then the machine would shut down automatically. If Robinson wasn't dead in that time, then the whole process would be repeated.

Korn stood at the window and watched the entire time, never taking his eyes from Robinson.

His gaze did not break from the man in the chair.

Not even when his skin began to smoke. Not even when the current fractured his left shinbone. Not even when the bloody foam erupted from his mouth.

All the while, Korn felt as if there was electricity flowing in his own veins. An elemental power that coursed through him. As district attorney, he had the power of life and death in his long, crooked hands. And he loved it. He had killed this man as surely as putting a bullet through his head, and the thought was intoxicating. Shooting or stabbing someone wasn't the same for Korn. Too animalistic. Korn killed using the power of his office, and his mind, and his skill. And that gave him more pleasure than he could ever have imagined. All the while he was willing Robinson to stay alive, just a little longer.

Long enough for the suffering to last.

When it was done, a cloud of smoke sat above Yellow Mama, and Korn was breathless.

It took nine minutes for Darius Robinson to die.

And in those nine excruciating minutes, Randal Korn felt truly alive.

FIVE MONTHS LATER

SKYLAR EDWARDS

Skylar Edwards sheltered in the corner of the kitchen in Hogg's Bar and used both thumbs to type the message on her phone. The clicks that she heard with every tap on the screen were just effects, mimicking the noise from an old keyboard, but even those sounds carried the anger she'd just put into the text. She finished the message, hit send, stuffed the phone in the pocket of her jeans before the bar owner came looking for her.

It was almost midnight, the kitchen had closed hours ago and the chef, who wore that title loosely, had left shortly after wiping down the grill with a dirty cloth. There was no good reason for her to be in here, other than to get five minutes' privacy with her phone. It wouldn't take long to get a reply. Her boyfriend, Gary Stroud, never sent long messages. He used emojis, or GIFS, to hide his bad spelling. But Skylar didn't have time to wait. She pushed through the double doors, into the hallway, past the bathrooms and through another door into the bar.

Just three customers left. Locals from Buckstown. Soft rock still played on the speaker at one corner of the bar, but the customers were ignoring it. Instead, they were looking at the TV.

'Say, Ryan, can you turn that up?' asked the big man at the end of the counter. He'd sat there most of the night, after he'd finished his meal, and drank club sodas and ginger beer while he worked. She'd seen him here before. He usually came in when it was quiet, did some paperwork and watched a game. Not a handsome man, but he was well built and he always tipped well.

'Sure, Tom,' said Ryan as he put down two full beers in front of the other customers.

Tom. That was his name. She knew he worked as a prosecutor in the district attorney's office. Seen him on TV, and they'd even discussed one of his cases, about five months back. The man who got executed up in Escambia County. Tom had helped convict the man. He said very little about it, but then again, Tom didn't talk much. Ryan Hogg, the bar owner, was always extra nice to him.

She glanced up at the TV as Ryan turned down the stereo and turned up the volume on the flatscreen on the wall above the bar. The new governor, Pratchett, was on the news, talking about the plant again.

'. . . *I will do whatever it takes to save those jobs at Solant Chemicals . . .*'

'They closing the plant?' asked Ryan.

'They've been threatening to do it for years,' said Tom. 'Looks serious this time if the governor's involved.'

Skylar began collecting glasses from the tables, keeping an eye on the TV. Her father, Francis, worked at the plant. He drove trucks for them. Had done so for twenty years and he was earning enough to help Skylar with college. While Skylar was smart, she wasn't able to secure a scholarship, and her father was paying her tuition fees. If he lost that job, she might have to drop out. Just something else to worry about.

Her phone buzzed in her pocket. She turned away from Ryan as she slid it out of her jeans. Ryan Hogg wasn't a bad boss. He paid a little more than most, and he didn't skim her tips. While he never said anything inappropriate, and he certainly never put a hand on her, she sometimes caught him looking at her. And not in a way that a boss checks that their employee isn't wasting time texting her boyfriend. It was only a look, but it still made her feel a little sick in her stomach.

She opened the text message. A heart emoji and *Please come over soon.* Gary's sister, Tori, was having a party that night and he'd begged her to call in sick. She'd told him she had to work and he'd been sour about it. Bugging her to quit early and join him. Skylar didn't want to give Gary false hope. She was tired and didn't feel much like partying. He'd been going on about the party for days, and so she texted Tori and asked if the party would still be on when she finished her shift.

'Is that a double-thumb conversation?' asked Andy.

She knew his voice and turned to smile at him. Andy had a handful of dirty beer glasses. He'd cleared the rest of the tables while she had been distracted.

'What do you mean, a double-thumb conversation?' she asked.

'When you and Gary are fighting you use both thumbs to text. Sometimes I think you're gonna break that screen, you type so fast,' he said.

She smiled, warmly. Andy Dubois made working at Hogg's Bar much more tolerable. He was younger than her, just a little. Starting college in September. A smart kid, with a warm heart. Smarter than Skylar, because he'd won a full scholarship. She didn't begrudge him, because that was the only way Andy could go to college. It was just Andy and his mom, and in Buckstown there were the white middle classes, like Skylar's folks, who got by and had enough to put money away, and then on the other side of town were the poor black and immigrant families who seemed to have it harder than most. Once Skylar graduated college, she was going to get the hell out of this town. She knew Andy would too, and he'd bring his mom with him.

Andy turned away with a smile and returned the dirty glasses to the bar. She saw a paperback novel sticking out the back pocket of his jeans. Any spare moment on the job, and Andy was reading. He didn't have a cell phone. Skylar thought that if she spent as much time reading as Andy, instead of staring at her phone, she might have gotten that scholarship after all. Still, it reminded her she could upgrade her phone next month. She had already decided to give her old model to Andy, with some credit.

Skylar collected the last of the glasses and Ryan made a discreet suggestion to the two customers in front of him, on bar stools, that it was about time he closed up.

They were large men. One tall, one average height, but every one of their limbs were thick with muscle.

Two cops. Both in plain clothes, off duty.

The tall one was Deputy Leonard. He had red hair, a moustache and an attitude. Especially when it came to Andy. The other was

Deputy Shipley. He had small, dark eyes that seemed to catch the light at strange angles – almost like there was a fire behind his eyeballs that could occasionally be glimpsed. He wasn't as hotheaded as Leonard, but Skylar suspected he was more dangerous.

They were regulars and they always sat up front on bar stools so they didn't have to tip the waitress. Ryan didn't share any bar tips. What was on the tables was for Skylar and Andy, whatever green got slapped on the bar was for him.

'Hey, Sky, your old man still work at the plant?' asked Leonard.

He called her Sky. No one else did, but she smiled and answered like always.

'Sure does,' she said.

'Hard times for a lot of folks,' said Shipley, and then they returned to their own conversation. Skylar loaded the dishwasher as Tom gathered up his papers, settled his tab and strode out the front door. Ryan started turning off the lights, and then Shipley and Leonard got the message and left. They cleaned up the bar, and then Ryan told Skylar and Andy they could go.

They left together, stepping into the warmth of the evening at around twelve-fifteen. She waved goodnight to Andy as he started his long walk home. Her phone buzzed. A text message.

A reply from Tori that said, *What party?*

Raking her fingers through her hair, Skylar swore. She took a screenshot of Tori's message, and was about to send it to Gary with a *WTF? You lied about a party?* when her phone rang. It was Tori. She answered the call.

'Oh my God, I'm so sorry. Please come over, I've messed up,' said Tori, over loud rock music in the background.

'What the hell's going on? Gary has been pressuring me for weeks to go this big party at your house.'

'Yeah, just come over,' she said, hesitantly.

Skylar had been friends with Tori before she'd even met Gary. She knew her well, and could tell when she was holding back.

'What's going on? Tell me, right now or I'm going to call Gary and—'

Tori cut her off.

'I'm in Buddy's Bar. Gary is at my house. Alone. You need to go—'

'Tell me what the hell is happening or I'm—'

'He's bought a ring,' said Tori.

Skylar's hand covered her mouth just as she gasped a lungful of air and her fingers shut her lips tightly, as if she dare not let a single breath escape. She stayed like that for a moment.

'I'm sorry, I messed up so bad. Please just go over there now. He's waiting to surprise you. So act goddamned *surprised* and don't tell him I told you.'

'I can't believe he did this . . .'

'He's been planning it for weeks. It's five years to the day since you met him. At my house. He wanted to make it special.'

There was warmth in Tori's voice now and Skylar felt the tears welling up in her eyes, her joy erupting through her stomach, moving up to cloy at her throat. She and Gary had an anniversary – marked by their first date. She hadn't even remembered when they first met, but it was incredibly sweet that he had, and that he'd gone to all this trouble.

'We're going to be sisters,' said Skylar. 'Like, for real.'

'This means you're gonna say yes!' said Tori.

'Of course I'm going to say yes.'

They talked a little more, then Skylar hung up the call. She had to go and meet Gary and she could hardly contain her excitement.

Hogg's Bar was on Union Highway, two miles outside of Buckstown, beside a gas station.

Skylar stood by the highway, thinking about what to do.

She could walk into town. She'd done it before. But it was hot tonight, and she'd been on her feet for ten hours straight. The highway always had traffic, and it slowed here coming into Buckstown to thirty-five miles an hour. She could get a lift, easy.

She'd done it before. There was one cab company in town. None of the digital taxi companies had made it this far into Alabama just yet. People drove around here, even when they were drunk.

Skylar stood by the side of the road, waiting for a sober, friendly driver.

She started typing a text message to her father, telling him not to wait up, when a semi-truck began to slow down. It flashed its lights, stopped beside her and the passenger door opened. Skylar took hold of the handle on the door, climbed the steps so she could see into the dark cab.

The driver wore a cap, so it was hard to see his face. He had one hand on the wheel, the other on his thigh.

'Need a lift, little lady?' he said.

There was something off about this man. A smell in the cab. Her father was a truck driver, so she was used to the odor of sweat, chewing tobacco and coffee. It wasn't that. It was something else. Something foul.

Her father hated her doing this. He worried about her a lot. Said she was too trusting. She would need to toughen up or folks would walk all over her, or worse. Of course, Skylar dismissed this, but right about now she thought her father may have a point. She could imagine getting into the truck, and then, in the few minutes it would take to get into town, a hand moving across the seat toward her. And then the truck not stopping in the town, and she wouldn't get to meet Gary, and she would never get engaged, and her face would end up on a milk carton. Then again, she wasn't sure if people her age got their faces on milk cartons. Maybe they didn't do that anymore, or maybe it was just for kids.

Then the analytical part of her brain kicked in. The odds of something happening to her on a short trip with a stranger were low. Very low. Like, a million-to-one. She had to stop worrying, and just get into the goddamn cab.

The driver reached out a hand to help her inside.

His skin was ingrained with dirt, and she could see the sweat on his palm, and the slight shaking, perhaps with excitement of having a young woman in his cab. And a pretty one, too.

Something inside her yelled *NO*.

'You know what, it's fine. I'm sorry, sir, I just got a message from my boyfriend, he's gonna pick me up,' she said as she stepped back down onto the blacktop at the side of the road.

The driver swore, but she didn't catch it as she shut the door to his cab. He gunned the engine and took off as Skylar got her breathing under control.

And then she heard a vehicle pull up, right where the semi had stopped. She looked inside, saw the driver.

This was okay. This wasn't a stranger. It was perhaps the last person she expected to meet. And there was no worry about getting into this car. She knew the driver. She'd heard him talking in Hogg's Bar not twenty minutes ago, while she collected the dirty glasses.

Of course, he offered her a ride.

Skylar got into the passenger seat, said she was just going into town, and began texting her father.

Don't wait up for me. I got a ride into town with

Skylar didn't finish the message.

As the driver punched her in the face, her phone slid down into the gap between the passenger seat and the console of the vehicle. And there it stayed.

Skylar didn't get time to scream, or think, or feel.

She would never reach Tori's house. Would never get to kiss Gary again, or hear his proposal, or give him her answer and her heart.

THREE MONTHS LATER

CHAPTER ONE

EDDIE

I don't go looking for trouble. I don't need to.

It has a way of finding me all by itself.

If only money came with it, maybe then it wouldn't be so bad. Some people become lawyers with the hope of making a lot of money. Money is nice, don't get me wrong. I like having a roll in my pocket as much as the next guy, but I like being able to sleep at night too. The more cash in your pocket, and the more scumbags you put back on the street, the harder it is to sleep. A criminal attorney's wealth can be measured by their bank account and the weight they carry on their souls. Until that day, that magical day when they just stop giving a shit. Then, there's just the money and it can be enjoyed without a conscience getting in the way.

I never rode that path. Getting a guilty client off was against the rules. My rules. This makes me either the worst defense attorney in the world, or the best, depending on how you looked at it. While I occasionally looked at it, if I was *really* short on cash, I could always hit the tables at Vegas for a weekend and that would be enough to get me over. A previous life as a con artist comes in handy when criminal work dries up for a spell. For now, I was doing just fine. My new partner, Kate Brooks, was a rainmaker. Mostly she was raining shit on big law firms and businesses in class-action sexual harassment suits. And she was damn good at it. Our investigator, Bloch, who'd come with Kate to the business, was just about the most resourceful PI I'd ever met. Bloch and Kate were childhood friends and it sure helped melt the ice on Bloch's tongue. She didn't talk much. Mostly she talked to Kate. That didn't mean she was unfriendly – she spoke when she had something to say and it paid to listen.

My criminal practice was thriving. Harry Ford, retired New York Justice, and now my consultant, was able to take appointments in the office with clients while I wore my shoe leather thin in Center Street and the Brooklyn courthouse. Harry preferred to stay in the office so he could be with his dog, Clarence, who was now pretty much the office dog.

The only thing we lacked as a new firm was a good secretary to take calls, type and organize our asses. A lawyer is only as good as his administrative support – and usually only half as smart.

Kate had put an ad online for a legal secretary and was fielding the applications. There was someone due in sometime this morning for an interview, and Kate wanted me to sit in. We were joint part-ners, everything fifty-fifty, including decisions, good or bad. It was coming up on nine-fifteen. Our office was in Tribeca, just above a tattoo parlor. Kate had wanted offices in a shiny tower close to Wall Street – all glass, pine and leather. I couldn't work in that kind of place, and Kate took pity on me by letting us rent a fleapit above a tattoo parlor called Stinkin' Ink.

Kate and Bloch were shuffling bundles of papers around the Xerox machine, Harry was on the couch in the small reception area with Clarence. He'd bought Clarence a fancy new collar with a GPS locator. He'd been trying to activate the collar for the past ten minutes without success. I was trying to get the coffee machine to produce something that didn't wipe three layers of skin off the roof of my mouth, when the buzzer rang downstairs.

'Eddie, can you get that? I bet that's Denise,' said Kate.

'Who?'

'Denise Brown, the applicant for the secretary's position. Didn't you read her resume?'

'You gave me a resume?'

'Last week. It's probably still on your desk.'

I couldn't remember reading it. That's not to say I didn't get it. Administration is my weak spot.

I pressed the button to open the front door and waited at the top of the stairs.

Heavy footsteps made me wonder if Denise wore boots. I leaned over the rail. There, coming up the stairs, was the last man on earth I wanted to see.

He wore a trilby hat, an old gray raincoat that must've been a gift from a now deceased spouse because that was about the only excuse you could have for wearing it. Beneath the coat was a bespoke suit, and inside the suit was one hundred and eighty-five pounds of serious trouble.

'Unless you're here about the secretarial job, I'm afraid you'll have to leave,' I said.

He got to the top of the stairs, tipped his hat and smiled at me in a way that reminded me of a crocodile about to take a bite out of my ass.

'My secretarial skills are not what they used to be,' he said.

'Can you type and make coffee? If so, you're in. The pay is bad, but the work is lousy.'

'I'm here about a job, Eddie. But it's got nothing to do with typing. May I come in?'

His name was Alexander Berlin. When I last saw him, he was working for the State Department. I'd heard he'd moved around since – CIA, NSA, Justice Department. He was a fixer, and a black-ops man who bent the laws to get a result for whatever limb of federal government that happened to employ him at the time. He knew where all the government's bodies were buried. And if he had a job for me, then I wasn't interested.

'I don't need a job. Whatever it is, it's going to be a *no* from me.'

'You haven't heard what it is yet. Let me in for ten minutes and a hot cup of coffee. You don't want this? Fine, I'll walk out straight after. No hard feelings. No grudges.'

'I think it's premature to say you won't hold a grudge, you haven't tasted my coffee yet. And you won't like my answer. I'm not interested, Berlin.'

It had been raining out. His old coat was soaked through and he was dripping on the stair carpet. We hadn't had time to get the carpets cleaned yet, and his dripping coat was beginning to make a clean spot among the stains.

'Hear me out, Eddie. Please,' said Berlin.

'Give me one good reason why I should listen to you.'

Berlin removed his hat, looked at me with heavy, wet eyes and said, 'Because, if you don't, a nineteen-year-old kid is going to be murdered.'

'Murdered? Murdered by who?'

'Technically, me.'

CHAPTER TWO

EDDIE

Berlin's coat dripped water onto the floor of my office while it hung on the coat rack in the corner.

He took out a pair of glasses from his pocket and began wiping them clean with the wide end of his tie. If the old coat was a treasured gift from a loved one, the tie looked like a present from a mortal enemy. I let him settle, closed the file that was open on my desk and gave him my attention.

'Who's the kid, and why are you going to be responsible for their death?'

'That's a long story. Do you know what I do in government?' he asked.

'Can't say that I do, exactly.'

'Neither can I. Not without divulging classified information and thereby committing treason. All I can tell you is that I move around government departments solving problems.'

'I knew you were a fixer of some kind. What type of problems do you solve?'

'The kind of problems that Fortune 500 companies have with government policy, the kind of problems that law enforcement have when their hands are tied, and the kind of problems that we had two years ago.'

I'd first met Berlin in upstate New York, after a fed had been shot. Berlin helped us clear up the mess.

'One of your dogs gone wild again?' I asked.

He shook his head, said, 'Let's say part of my role is to keep the status quo. Government doesn't like change. Doesn't matter who's in the White House, the day-to-day tasks of policing and justice need order and consistency. This is on a state and federal level. We're not limited in our scope. There's a district attorney in Sunville County, Alabama, named Randal Korn, and it was made clear to me that he was to be re-elected.'

'You rigged a local district attorney election?'

Berlin rolled his eyes.

'Please, Eddie. We've rigged national elections in more countries than I can count. This was small potatoes. There are businesses that finance our politicians, and they always have a hand in local elections. Someone with credibility and cash was running against Korn, and I made a few calls to the youngblood's backers – got them to pull their checkbooks. That's all it took. You win elections in the US by spending money. Usually, whoever spends the most wins.'

'Okay, so then what?'

'Then I got a little curious. Korn has been DA of Sunville County for the past seventeen years. In his tenure he has brought most crime statistics to record lows in the county. That's why we liked him. Good for business, good for property prices in the area, good for investors. Maintain the status quo. I should've left it alone after the election, but there was something wrong about this guy. I went deeper, what I found was disturbing.'

'What was that?'

Before Berlin could answer, he hesitated, distracted by the noise outside my office. The usual commotion. I got up and opened my door a crack to see what was happening. Harry was swearing at the new digital dog collar he'd bought for Clarence, still unable to activate the GPS signal through his phone and his agitation was wearing on the dog, who barked every time Harry used a cuss word. The Xerox machine had jammed again, and Bloch was banging the side of the copier with her fist. The phone was ringing, which Kate then answered, holding a laptop in the other hand and her cell phone cradled on her shoulder. Organized chaos. I closed the door. Sat down. Gestured for Berlin to continue.

'It sounds busy out there,' he said.

He was stalling. There was something he needed to say, but he didn't feel able to do it. Not yet.

'Just tell me the whole thing. You're under client confidentiality here. This is a safe room.'

Berlin glanced at pictures on my desk. My daughter, Amy, at summer camp, paddling a canoe. I had since stopped putting up pictures of my ex-wife. She had moved on with another man.

'Cute kid,' said Berlin. 'How old?'

'Fifteen. Come on, you worked up enough spit to get this thing out yet?'

His eyes flicked to mine. They were troubled and red. The bags underneath them seemed heavier all of a sudden.

'Sunville County leads the US in death-penalty convictions. The county encompasses a few big towns, but no cities. Randal Korn has sent more people to death row than any other district attorney in history. Currently, one in every twenty of the death-row population for the whole of the United States was put there by Korn. One hundred and fifteen convictions in seventeen years.'

I said nothing. I'd heard about zealous prosecutors in the South who valued marriage, church, family, assault weapons and the death penalty above all things. Even so, those figures couldn't possibly be accurate.

'Around two to three percent of the counties in the United States are responsible for convicting the vast majority of death-row inmates. Sunville County is top of the league. When I discovered this, I thought exactly the same as you're thinking right now – bullshit. This can't be true. Eddie, it's one hundred percent accurate. I checked the records myself.'

'There has to be a mistake.'

'Look, you know a prosecutor has huge discretion on whether to make a serious felony a capital case. Korn has never prosecuted a murder without calling for the death penalty. He's never been successfully appealed, and he's never lost a case.'

'Why does he go for the death penalty every damn time? And why has no one noticed this before?'

'Oh, it's been noticed. When I was checking out Korn I found a few breadcrumbs left behind by previous investigations. All of them came to nothing because Korn is still district attorney, thanks to me. You asked why this guy goes after the death penalty? Isn't it obvious?'

'Not to me,' I said.

'Why do people join the army? Most say they want to serve their country, a lot of them join because of family, more still because of pay or training, and then there's the tiny percentage of people, the two percent, who join the army for one simple reason – they want to kill somebody.'

'You're saying this guy, Korn, became a district attorney so he could kill people?'

'No, that's not what *I* say, that's what *he* says – all the damn time. He's the king of death row. Wears it like a medal. I've dealt with bad people before. After a while, you can see it in their eyes. Korn is a killer. And he's doing it on my watch.'

'Who is this kid who's going to be executed?'

'His name is Andy Dubois, he goes on trial for murder in a week. He's innocent and Korn just wants to watch the kid fry. When I found out about Korn, I had someone keep an eye on his cases. This kid is accused of murdering a young waitress from a dive bar on the highway. Andy couldn't swat a fly on a dog's ass. There's nothing I can do to get rid of Korn now. I had my chance. So I hired a lawyer in Sunville to represent Andy. His name is Cody Warren. He copied me in on the case files. They're in my car right now. I haven't heard from Warren in a week. His secretary reported him missing three days ago. I think he's dead.'

'Woah, that's quite a leap. A lawyer goes missing and you think he's dead? What? You think Korn killed him?'

I didn't know if it was a trick of the light from the shades on my window, but Berlin's features seemed to darken, and his voice dropped low as he said, 'Korn runs the biggest town in Sunville – Buckstown. And he's tight with the county sheriff. He's bloodthirsty, crooked and ruthless. It was only a matter of time before a defense attorney mysteriously disappeared on his patch. If Korn didn't do it himself, he had help. I think Korn could've arranged for Warren to disappear, and he wouldn't even have blinked.'

'So call the FBI,' I said.

'The feds would swamp that town, spend six months tearing the place apart and end up with nothing. I don't need a sledgehammer here. I need someone smart enough to take on Korn in the courtroom, get the kid off. If something bad has happened to Warren, no one will ever find him. Korn is too careful. Warren is beyond my help now. What I want to know is will you go to Alabama and save this kid's life?'

'I know nothing about the case. What if the kid is guilty? I'm no friend of the death penalty, but I won't get someone off just to save their life. Not if they're guilty.'

'Didn't you hear me? I checked it out. I believe he's innocent. I think you will too. They're keeping him in the county lock-up. Isolating him. Eddie, this is your wheelhouse.'

The cacophony of noise outside the office rose even louder.

'I need to think about it, but I want to know why you're doing this. The kind of work you do means you checked your conscience at the door when you joined up. No offense.'

Berlin stared off into the distance, his eyes were twenty years and a thousand miles away when he said, 'I didn't know who Korn was when I buried his opponent. There's a line for everyone. When a sadist has the power of life and death and I helped give him that power, then there's a personal responsibility. I took an oath once. A long time ago when I first strapped on a gun. His current tenure is down to me, so our fortunes are partially linked. I need evidence, something juicy enough to let me make the right phone calls and quietly retire him.'

'This is about self-preservation,' I said.

'It's not just that. If I had the time, I would build a case against Korn. Slow, solid – brick by friggin' brick. There's a ticking clock now. I can't wait. I have to do something before he sends this kid to death row. If I can save one life . . .'

Berlin swung his gaze at me, leveled it and kept it there.

I knew the look.

People make mistakes, other people get hurt. There comes a time when you realize you drove past the exit a long time ago, and you can't roll back the years, but you can damn sure do everything in your power to stop one more soul getting hurt or killed. Berlin's conscience was getting to him. There's a price to be paid for his kind of work, and it was almost time to collect. Everyone seeks redemption in the end. That's how the song goes. I had been singing that same song for a long time.

'I need to talk to my partner and the rest of the firm,' I said.

'I'll wait,' said Berlin.

He wasn't going to leave and come back. He wanted an answer, right then. Maybe he figured he had me on the ropes and he didn't want to risk losing his advantage. I got up and opened the door to my office, then stopped. There was something wrong. For a second I didn't know what it was, then it hit me.

There was no sound from the outer office. No shouting. No banging. No swearing or barking.

I pulled open the door, fully expecting the place to be empty.

Clarence's new leash was attached, Harry was gazing happily at his phone. The photocopier was humming as it merrily produced paper, Bloch stood beside it with a contented smile. Kate was sitting quietly in her office tapping on the keys of her laptop, and a lady I didn't recognize sat at the desk we used for a reception. She was in her forties, blond hair cut short, smiling as she arranged papers on the desk and occasionally looked at the computer screen in front of her.

Clarence padded over to her, and she bent low and said, 'I love your new leash. Do you need any more help with the app, Harry?'

Harry said, 'No thank you, ma'am. You've worked enough miracles for one morning. Oh, Eddie, this is Denise. She works here now.'

She turned away from Clarence, stood and approached me. She held out a hand and I shook it.

'I'm Denise. I love your office.'

'I'm beginning to like it too,' I said as I heard Kate coming over.

'Eddie, I know we said we would discuss candidates for the secretarial post but Denise here—'

'Let me guess. She fixed Clarence's leash, mended the copier and arranged all your papers for your case.'

'And I fixed the coffee machine,' said Denise, brightly.

I took a moment and looked at the faces present. For the first time since we'd set foot in the new building everyone was calm and happy.

'Denise,' I said, 'you're not only hired, but you are forbidden from ever leaving this place.'

'Things will be running smoothly from now on,' said Kate.

'Well, I guess this is the time to tell you all I'm thinking of going away for a while. We've got a potential case out of state. A capital murder. I might need some help with it too.'

'I've got my big divorce case coming up next week,' said Kate.

'Don't worry, Harry and I can handle this.'

'What's the case?' said Harry.

'Young kid about to be sent to death row for a murder he didn't commit. We'd be working pro-bono, but a friend will cover expenses.'

'Do you know the kid?' asked Kate.

'Never met him before.'

'So you're going to go out of state to do a capital murder case for free, for a kid you've never met?' asked Bloch, from the kitchen.

'Yep. This job isn't about helping people you know. It's about helping the people you *don't* know.'

'Do it, I think we've got everything covered here,' said Kate.

I looked at Denise and said, 'I think you have now. Look, there's something else, this kid's attorney has gone missing. This could be dangerous.'

'It wouldn't be your goddamn case if it wasn't,' said Harry. 'There's just one problem, Eddie. You're not licensed to practice outside of New York.'

Berlin stepped onto the office floor, whipped a brown envelope from his jacket and said, 'He will be by three o'clock this afternoon.'

THE FIRST DAY

CHAPTER THREE

KORN

At 9:01 in the a.m., limping slightly, Randal Korn threw open the doors to the Sunville County District Attorney's Office and made his way, silently, through the rows of desks occupied by secretaries and assistant DAs. No morning greetings were exchanged. There was work to be done. And besides, he didn't need to say anything.

His presence was felt.

The door to Korn's private office was half glass and at least seventy years old. The names of the respective district attorneys for Sunville had been painted on the window, removed and then repainted as their tenures came and went. By the time Randal put a hand on the door, he was already being trailed by one of the assistants with a binder of documents in his hand. Sinking into a green leather studded chair behind a wide mahogany desk, Korn gazed up at the assistant DA, a man of thirty in a white, short-sleeved button-down shirt with a blue tie. Tom Wingfield was Korn's number one ADA. He handed Korn the binder.

'This is the index for the jury bundle in the Dubois case?'

Tom nodded.

'Where are we with Andy Dubois?' asked Korn. 'And no bullshit, Tom, I want to know the lie of the land. We're picking a jury in three days.'

Tom pulled at the knot in his tie, tightening it. He was putting on weight recently. Bulking up by pouring protein shakes down his throat at every opportunity. He wasn't exactly small to begin with, but now his arms and shoulders looked as though they were filled with helium. When Tom wasn't in the office, he was in the gym hauling weights. His shirt was old enough to remember when

Tom was slimmer and had less strain on the sleeves and the buttons around his chest.

'Forensics are ready. Reports complete, witnesses primed. The photographer is blowing up the photographs of the murder victim nice and big, just like you asked . . .'

'How big?'

'Life-sized, or thereabouts. The jury will think they're looking at the actual body.'

'Remember I asked for the colors to be pumped up, remind him to do that. I want that blood on her face to look *bright* red. These photos have to shock this jury. That's the first step, remember?'

Tom nodded.

Korn took time to school his assistant DAs on how to get a conviction in a capital murder case. Picking a jury and convincing them to send a man to his death is no easy thing. The jury would seek to preserve life as it's the default human reaction. The first job was to shock them as much as possible, preferably using images that would stay with the jurors for the rest of their lives. The more visceral and bloody, the better.

Next, give them someone to hate. A defendant who was the cause of that vile, bloody mess. Part of this step was to elevate the victim to near sainthood. Paint them as a real person – a good, honest, God-fearing member of the community. Make the victim sit on the jury, make them familiar and relatable to each juror as a spouse, child or parent.

The more a jury loves the victim, the more they hate the defendant.

The last step was the most difficult. There were two approaches. The more Christian the jury, the more Korn relied on select retributive passages from the Bible which he had memorized over the years – an eye for an eye – all the hits. Alongside the Bible was the personal. Make the jury think that their child, spouse, partner or parent would be next if they didn't take action to protect society and send this demon to death row.

Conducting a death penalty case was an exercise in dehumanizing a defendant – turning them into a monster to be feared and put to death. Once a jury was convinced of these elements, it was simple to show that it was this defendant who was guilty. As long as the jury feared the defendant they would convict. Hate is a great motivator, but it's not enough to make a jury kill. Fear was much better. Fear is a powerful weapon. One Korn learned to wield a long time ago.

'What about Dubois' attorney, Cody Warren? Any sign of him showing up?' asked Korn.

'I got no clue. His secretary hasn't seen him for days now. Judge Chandler says the case goes ahead whether he turns up or not.'

'Good,' said Korn.

'There's just one more thing,' said Tom. He hesitated, raised a forefinger to his lips and closed his eyes. It was as if some unseen force was preventing Tom from speaking. A sense of duty, perhaps. Something else that Korn would need to train out of him.

'I heard some of the clerks talking in the judge's chambers last night. It seems there's been an approval for a guest bar certification.'

'Some lawyer from out of state shopping around for class-action lawsuits?'

'No,' said Tom. 'At least, I don't think so. The way I heard it, this guy is coming down here from New York to defend Andy Dubois.'

'When did you hear about this?' snapped Korn.

'Late last night. I heard them talking when I locked up the office to go home.'

'A lawyer from New York? Who?'

'Some guy named Eddie Flynn.'

A small brush fire burst into life behind Korn's eyes. He licked his lips, said, 'Find out all you can. Flynn is a serious player. I've read about some of his cases. I want to know everything. There's got to be some connection between Dubois and Flynn. Dubois doesn't have a cent to his name, he couldn't afford an attorney. The ACLU wouldn't fund Flynn either; they'd just get one of their own lawyers down here. Could be some connection with Cody Warren's office, but that doesn't seem likely. Go and talk to the clerks, the judges, whoever you have to, just find out why Flynn is here representing a two-bit killer,' said Korn, then looked back at the binder, leafing through the pages.

'No problem, I'll find out all I can. Who is he? I never heard of Eddie Flynn.'

'He's a hand grenade is what he is. There are rumors about him. Some say he used to be a con artist before he was a lawyer, and he's been conning juries in Manhattan ever since.'

Wingfield nodded, backed out of the room, leaving Korn to his thoughts.

It was a plain office, with filing cabinets on one side, some framed pictures of Korn with various mayors and state politicians on the other. Whirling his chair around, he gazed at the one hundred and fifteen individually framed mug shots that hung on the wall behind his chair. Men in various states of dishevelment, their eyes either wide in fear, or low and booze-sleepy. Looking at the wall made him sit up straighter, his heart lifting. This was his legacy. His life's work. These were the men he'd sent to death row. He'd gotten to watch seventy-nine of them die. It was not enough, not by a long shot.

His father had been a man consumed with thoughts of the family name, who had built a fortune on the stock market, and handed most of it to Korn in his will. But Korn wasn't interested in his father's money. Nor anyone else's. There had always been plenty of cash around, and so it held no fascination for him. With thirty million in his bank account now, it still didn't concern him. What Korn had taken to heart was his father's talk of family legacy. That was more important.

It doesn't matter how much money you've got when you die, son. A man is not measured by the stack of dollars in his vault. It's the corpses of broken enemies that you leave in your wake. That's how you measure your life. When you're still standing at the end, and you've put all your competitors down. That's when you know who is best.

Korn drew strength from the faces of the dead and those he had condemned to die. Darius Robinson was the last to give him that personal pleasure. Andy Dubois would be the next face on the wall.

He picked up the phone, called the Sheriff's Department and asked for Sheriff Lomax. After a small delay, his call was transferred.

'Good morning to ya,' said Lomax, in a low, country drawl.

'I wanted to check if there's been any progress on our missing attorney?'

'Nothing, I'm sorry to say. We'll keep looking, keep making calls. I've got some of my best officers working this one hard.'

'I'm glad to hear it. So, how was the fishing this weekend?'

'Pretty good. Got me a catfish that damn near broke the rod.'

'Keep on Cody Warren, I want to know the instant he's found. I'm praying for his safe return.'

'We all are, Randal.'

'Have yourself a fine day, Sheriff,' said Korn, and hung up.

Ten minutes later Korn was working the wheel of his Jaguar around the tight corners of the country roads on the outskirts of Buckstown. He made a series of turns along narrower and narrower roads, until he was on a dirt road that didn't look like it went anywhere. Another ten minutes on this road and the thick trees on either side parted, just briefly, as the road curled toward the Luxahatchee River. Buckstown stood in the center of Sunville County. To the north was the bottom of the Talladega Forest – half a million acres of pinewood. To the south, swampland from the overflow of the Luxahatchee. East of Buckstown lay rich farmland, and to the west lay the industrial side of the county occupied by a steel mill and a large chemical processing plant that was ever on the verge of closure.

Korn stopped the car, got out and made his way through the thinning tree line. The trees were very old and draped in Spanish moss. The Luxahatchee narrowed here, before reaching full flow a few miles further south. Its banks were brimming with brown, fast-moving water. Korn had grown up in an apartment in Lower Manhattan with a view of the East River. He would often watch the dark water from his bedroom window, a curious teenager, wondering what secrets lay at the bottom of that river. He wondered how the river grew so muddy and black. And how many men his father had sent tumbling into those freezing depths from the top of the Brooklyn Bridge.

The bubble and rumble of flowing water brought his thoughts back to the present and provided the baseline to the crickets and cicadas that were still singing in the early morning sun. Another sound joined the orchestra. A V8, gurgling to a slow crawl. The engine died, a car door squeaked open and slammed closed. Footsteps rustled through the brush.

CHAPTER FOUR

LOMAX

Sheriff Colt Lomax could smell something foul as he approached the riverbank. He'd parked the department cruiser on the dirt road and was making his way to the meeting point. During the phone call with Korn, he'd been asked about fishing – a code that meant they had to meet here. If he'd been asked how his bowling arm felt, they would meet in the bowling alley parking lot. Similar meeting points had been arranged for the diner parking lot, the boathouse on the lake and the old mill. Fishing meant the river, so that's where he had come.

Korn was a cautious man.

The vegetation rotting in the heat and humidity did not account for the odor that grew stronger as Lomax came through the brush. The sweet decay that comes from the moss and the river is quite pleasant. This was different. He sometimes thought he caught the scent from Korn, as if the man was rotting from the inside out. When that happened, he told himself it was just his imagination – no one could smell that bad, not unless they'd been lying in the river for a few days, dead and filling with gas.

He came into a small clearing at the bank and caught sight of Korn's tall frame, sheltering from the sun beneath the branches of a pine tree.

'It's hotter than all hell,' said Korn.

The accent was muddled. Sometimes he was pure Sunville County, born and bred, but at odd times some of his Manhattan accent would peep through in a word, just enough to remind Lomax that Korn was not from around here. Lomax wondered whether Korn spent his life affecting the Sunville accent – that it was a permanent role he was playing for an unseeing crowd, and at times, just for a second, the veil dropped to reveal the real Korn.

The DA was pale and sweating. He was not overweight, far from it. Korn looked thin and ill, all the time. A fine veneer of sweat seemed to permanently coat his bone-china skin. Korn liked to stay out of the sun. He took a handkerchief from his top pocket, wiped his neck and forehead.

'You should be used to the heat by now,' said Lomax.

'I hate it. Always have, always will.'

'What's the problem? I already told you Cody Warren is on ice. No one is going to find him.'

'This isn't about Warren. Well, not all of it.'

There it was again, that smell, hitting Lomax like a brick wall falling on his head.

'No, this is about his replacement. I hear there's some hotshot from New York coming down here to kick our asses in the Dubois case.'

'I wouldn't worry. Dubois is sewn up nice and tight. Don't matter how good a lawyer this city boy is, he can't get an acquittal, not with the confession.'

'That's not my concern. Dubois doesn't have any family or connections in New York, and his momma ain't got a dime. My concern is how the hell this lawyer got hired in the first place. There's something we don't know. Something we're missing.'

'You want me to speak to Dubois?'

'You do that. Maybe let Dubois know the last thing he needs is a fancy lawyer making things worse for him. That reminds me. I still need to prep Dubois' old cell mate, Lawson, for trial.'

'With Lawson's testimony, and the rest, that should be enough to get us over the line with any jury. Don't sweat this city boy.'

Korn moved quickly out of the shade to stand over the sheriff. Lomax took a step back, his heart quickening. Korn could move fast when he needed to. Like a spider when it feels a fly land on its web. That's how Lomax felt – as if he'd just caused a tremor on a thin wire and awakened something hungry that could devour him at any moment. Sweat flooded his face, and his mouth felt like he'd been sucking on a dry stone.

When Korn spoke, his voice was lower, like he was training a dog.

'You think I'm scared of Mr. New York? I grew up there, I know those guys. I can beat them any damn day in a courtroom. Don't you dare think otherwise, not for a second.'

'No offense intended, Mr. Korn,' said Lomax, averting his stare so he didn't have to look into Korn's dead eyes. 'I just meant there's no need to be hasty. If two lawyers working the same case go missing, this town will be crawling with FBI.'

Korn nodded, said, 'I can see your point, but the FBI won't find anything. Same as last time. If I think Flynn needs to go on ice you'll oblige me, won't you, Sheriff? We've talked about this. An enemy of justice is *our* enemy. You saw what Dubois did to Skylar Edwards. He can't get away with this. And if someone stands in our way . . .'

Lomax nodded. His eyes were far away. He had been the first officer on scene when the victim's body was found. He had seen, first hand, the horrors inflicted on her body. It didn't take long to pick up Andy Dubois, and Lomax got a confession out of him pretty fast. Then the damn medical examiner's report came in and Dubois didn't look so good for this one anymore. It was too late though. He'd already been charged and Korn had made up his mind that Dubois was the killer. There had been a short discussion about further investigations into alternative suspects, but Korn wouldn't hear of it. Dubois' confession would automatically weaken any case against another suspect.

'We're not going to let anything stop us from getting the death penalty for Dubois. Until then, see what you can find out about Flynn. Call me when you're done. Oh, and one more thing . . .'

Lomax swallowed, his throat dry and painful.

'Make sure Flynn gets a warm welcome when he arrives in town.'

And with that, Korn turned away and walked back to his car. Lomax breathed out, the sweat coming off his moustache sent a fine spray into the air. He took off his hat, and found he'd sweated right through it.

Before he left, Lomax took a last view of the river. Nothing but crocs, turtles and dead things out there. A low mist hung over the marshes and moss-lined trees, as if fine spiderwebs had been strung over the land.

The smell of corruption grew fainter the further Korn moved away. Taking his time, Lomax walked back to his car, opened the door and got in. As he turned the ignition key, his radio blared to life. A classic rock station was having a special week of Rolling Stones tracks. He threw his right arm over the passenger seat back, looked out the rear windshield and reversed back up the dirt track as Mick Jagger asked politely if he could introduce himself.

As he reversed back up the lane toward an area where he could turn the car, Lomax took his foot from the accelerator. He could smell the clutch burning, but that wasn't what had stopped him.

It was a thought that dragged him to a dead stop.

He took the keys from the ignition, turned them over in his thick, red fingers. A rabbit's foot hung from his keychain. A gift from his wife, Lucy, the first day on the job. She said it would be lucky, for both of them. Sure enough, Lomax had always come home, safe and sound, at the end of every shift. The same could not be said for Lucy.

Feeling that soft fur between his fingers allowed his breathing to ease and he began to feel cool. He put the keys back into the ignition switch, fired the V8, and spun the wheels to turn around. Some days he wished he could reverse a lot more than just the car. There were some roads he'd been down which were all one-way. You can't stop. And you can't back up.

Some things could not be undone.

Within a few minutes he was on the outskirts of Buckstown. He took the exit before the first traffic light and drove home. His house was an old colonial, refurbished in the last few years. Every wooden panel had been replaced and repainted. It was a picture-postcard house, with four bedrooms, only one of which he used. He parked in the driveway, got out and saw Lucy sitting on the porch. New screens protected her from the worst of the insects. She sat on her Adirondack chair, her knitting needles idle in her lap, her pattern by her feet with a roll of fresh red wool.

'Hot out. I was passing, thought I'd come home and get some lemonade,' he said.

Lucy was in her early sixties and knew her husband too well. She smiled up at him, or at least put on a smile as she raised her head.

'Bullshit, Colt. But go on. Get yourself a cold drink from the fridge. Get me one, too.'

He placed an arm gently on her shoulder, as if it were made of glass, and said, 'You sure you're up to it?'

She nodded.

Inside, the kitchen was as he had left it that morning. Her oatmeal untouched on the table. Glass still full of orange juice beside her pills. Some of the smaller pills lay on the plate, others had been crushed and set on spoons. Her wig, freshly brushed by him that morning, lay perched on the back of her kitchen chair. He poured two glasses of lemonade and returned to the heat outside. He handed one to Lucy, took a seat next to her.

'You didn't take your pills, darlin',' he said.

'I sure haven't,' she said, softly.

Every morning and evening, Lomax carefully laid out Lucy's pills. A dozen of them. Some she couldn't swallow. The larger pills he would crush between two spoons, or the flat blade of a kitchen knife. The others he cut in half. Swallowing was becoming a bigger problem.

'You should take the pills. Lucy, the doc said—'

'The doc said six months, Colt. That was six months ago. I've had my time,' she said, running her fingers over her scalp. Some threads of hair remained, drawn back over her pale skull, failing to hide the worms of blue veins that now stood out against her skin.

'We talked about this,' said Lomax.

'We did. It's my decision. We tried the chemo. It didn't work, and I ain't going through that again. The pills are making me dumb and sicker than I already am. I want to knit. I can't when the drugs make me shake so. Either I'm stumbling around, or I'm being sick or sleeping. The pain ain't so bad. It lets me know I'm still alive.'

She reached out, touched his hand, lightly. It was as if a breeze fell on his skin, her touch was so soft and cold.

'I want to be a wife again. For a little while at least.'

'But there are always new drugs, new treatments. We could get another opinion—'

'No,' said Lucy, louder than he'd heard her say anything for a long time. 'We've spent too much money already. Hundreds of thousands of dollars, and what for? I'm dying, Colt. It's my time. And it's time you understood that. And accepted that. For me, please?'

Lomax didn't hear his glass of lemonade fall from his grasp and smash on the porch boards. He heard his wife's soft voice, and felt her touch. He wanted to cry, but he couldn't. Not in front of her. He'd sworn that he would not do that. Not ever. It only made it harder for her. He gulped back the loss that was coming for him.

He had always known this day would come.

He knew the bad things he'd done had caused this. That God was punishing him for his sins. That the lies he'd told in his job and the people he had hurt, and the money he'd taken from Korn, which had paid for the house, had also made Lucy sick. It then paid for her treatment. It wasn't Karma, that was some Buddhist bullshit to Lomax. No, this was God sending him a message. And he hated him for it.

Lomax wished he'd kept to the road. Used his rabbit's foot to get home safe every night, like he should've done. Looked after his wife in their old house in Buckstown, and never taken a dime from Randal Korn.

The wind blew, and he caught the scent of death on the air. It reminded him of Cody Warren. A .22 Smyth and Wesson had done the job. He'd pressed the muzzle to the lawyer's skull, caught the look of fear in his eyes, then pulled the trigger, locking that expression of terror on Warren's face forever. It was the hardest thing Lomax had ever done. He'd been sick afterwards. And he had not slept well since.

When Korn decided to proceed with the prosecution of Andy Dubois, it put in motion a series of events. Each one following on, inevitably, from the other. The forensics undermined the case against Dubois, and so Korn altered the reports. Lomax couldn't let Dubois go after beating a confession out of him, either. And when Cody Warren got too close to the truth, he had to be dealt with too.

Unlike other cases, the murder of Skylar Edwards haunted Lomax.

The brutality and the strangeness of the killing unnerved him. And so he had ignored Korn's suggestion to stick with Dubois for the murder. Unknown to Korn, Lomax had continued his investigation.

He knew what would've happened if he had brought the results of those investigations to Korn. It would be buried, possibly along with Lomax himself for disobeying Korn's order. He couldn't risk taking his investigation results to the US Attorney's office either. Korn had enough dirt on Lomax to put him away for a long time, and then who would look after Lucy? He was trapped in this lie, and it caused him to take the life of a lawyer. Andy Dubois would soon be another dead body weighing on Lomax's heart. Another consequence of a simple cover-up. Because that's what happens when you make one compromise. It's never about the first time evidence goes missing. It's the efforts to cover up that original sin that will corrupt your soul, utterly.

He knew the guilt and the shame of what he'd done would ease eventually. Just like it had done last time, and the time before that. Until then he would live with it. He had no choice but to follow the path. Even if that meant, down the line, more lawyers would have to die.

CHAPTER FIVE

EDDIE

I hate flying.

I hate airports. It's the AC, and the overpricing, and the rattle of luggage wheels on tile.

It was two hours from LaGuardia to Charlotte, North Carolina, a short layover and then another two-hour flight to Mobile. I read the case during the flights. Soon as the doors on the plane closed and the cabin started to pressurize, I opened the files, and Harry's head began to nod. By the time the wheels were up, he was snoring.

Berlin had given me the files from the trunk of his car. Harry had read them yesterday while I passed some cases to Kate to look after while we were gone.

Altogether there were around five hundred pages. There were a number of depositions and as I read, I built up a picture of Andy Dubois in Sunville County.

Andy was the son of Patricia and Franco Dubois, but not for long. By the time Andy was walking and talking, Franco was out of his life. Andy's father had tried to turn over a gas station in Tucson and got a shoulder full of buckshot and fifteen years in the state penn for his trouble. Inside, Franco's fortunes didn't fare any better. He was found, a year into his sentence, partially beheaded in the exercise yard. The other inmates had given him *the weight*. Four guys held Franco down on the weight bench, while at least another two maneuvered a barbell loaded with three hundred pounds over him and dropped it on his throat.

The state paid for Franco's burial, in the grounds of the penitentiary. Patricia refused to take his body. She had cut ties with him and didn't want the man costing her a dime more. Patricia believed the best thing Franco ever did for his son was get himself killed. She didn't want Andy growing up around alcohol, drugs and all the lies, bitterness and pain that came with them.

She knew, from the day he was born, Andy would be a good boy.

Reading Patricia's extensive deposition, prepared by Andy's attorney, Cody Warren, I knew this case would take something from me. Some cases just cost a piece of you, something you won't ever get back. Sometimes it's a little piece. Sometimes it's a big piece. The more I read, the more I was willing to pay the price.

Patricia Dubois

My Andy wasn't much good at catching a ball, or throwing one, he sure wasn't big enough to tackle, but boy he loved to read. He read everything he could get his hands on from no age. He is a good boy, my big southern gentleman. Book smart, that's what I call him. That boy has read damn near every book in the library on Chapel Avenue, but he can't remember to look both ways crossing the street. No sense. Head in the clouds, my boy. But he worked hard at school, graduated second in his class and got himself a scholarship to Montevallo University. I still can't believe my boy was going to college. He was working so hard in that bar, every day he could get. Saving every cent. Then this happens. My boy didn't kill that girl. He says his prayers in church on Sunday, and he ain't never hurt no one. He ain't never even been in a fight. And I can tell you another thing, Andy would never, ever harm no woman.

I flicked forward to find out about the victim in this case.

Her name was Skylar Edwards. Twenty years old, student at the University of Alabama. She was studying chemistry, commuting to college from home every day. Her parents were not wealthy, and I wondered how they were managing to pay her tuition as there was no mention of a scholarship and it would be damn hard for a blue-collar worker to put their kid through college. She was working at a bar, part time. Her father, Francis Edwards, drove trucks long haul.

Her mother, Esther, was a homemaker. I couldn't find a statement from her. Francis described the night of the fourteenth of May.

Francis Edwards
She was working at Hogg's Bar. It's a trucker's bar. She was waiting tables, serving beer and saving her tips for college. She worked four nights a week. Seven till one a.m. Sometimes later if the bar was busy. Skylar couldn't afford a car, so she would call me when she was about done and I would drive out and pick her up. Take her home. Usually, she would be waiting with that boy, Andy. I gave him a ride a couple times. Dropped him off at his maw's when it was raining. But it was out of our way, you know? He wasn't my problem, so most times I didn't bother. Anyways, that night, Skylar didn't call. It was past midnight. Her mom, Esther, don't sleep too good. She was up and fussing over somethin' in the kitchen. She told me I should call Skylar. I figured the bar must've been busy and I would give her more time. Jesus, the nights I've spent since wishing I'd called. Maybe it would've made a difference, you know? Maybe that boy wouldn't a beat her and killed her if her phone started ringing? Esther still hasn't forgiven me. I drove out at one-thirty, and the bar was closed up. No one around. I called Skylar but she didn't pick up. I drove all over town, in case she hitched into Main Street for a late-night drink.

It wasn't like Skylar. She always let us know where she was. Esther called the sheriff. I looked for her all day. Then, that night we got the call saying she'd been found.

I don't think you'll get much out of Esther. Doc had to sedate her when she got the news from you boys, the Sheriff's Department, I mean. She's just been crying, crying, crying. She ain't come out of Skylar's room in days. Esther never worked, you see. Skylar was Esther's life. She lived for that little girl. Now she's gone I don't know what she'll do. It's not right, our little girl being taken like that. Murdered. That boy, Andy, I hope they fry his ass for what he done to my little girl.

*

I flicked through the pages, saw a statement from Ryan Hogg, the bar owner.

<u>Ryan Hogg</u>
Skylar worked for me for three years waiting tables. She was a good worker. Always showed up on time, good with the customers – even the rowdy ones. She could handle herself, you know? Anyway, I closed up the bar around twelve. She cleaned up, with Andy, and they left just after midnight. They left together, as I recall. That's not unusual. Sometimes Skylar's daddy would give him a ride home if it was raining. Most times he just waited with her until her ride arrived. That night they were arguing about something before they left. Don't ask me what. I don't know. I didn't hear. But Andy raised his voice to her. I remember that much. It wasn't like Andy to do that. He's a quiet kid. Always had his head in a book when he should've been mopping the floor. Anyway, Skylar looked scared. They left together and I never saw her again.

Skylar was missing for twenty-four hours before her body was found.

His name was Ted Buxton. A local truck driver. He'd parked his rig at Hogg's Bar on the fourteen of May, the night Skylar disappeared, and had left it there for a day while he took some R & R. When he returned to the rig on the night of the fifteenth of May, he saw something in the marshland just beyond the gravel and dirt lot.

At first it looked like someone bent over in the tall grass, crawling along. He grabbed a flashlight and went to take a closer look. That's when he found a couple of turtles investigating the corpse of Skylar Edwards. At first, he didn't know it was Skylar. All he saw were the soles of her feet sticking up out of the ground. He called the cops, who dug her out.

Skylar had been buried vertically. She had gone into a deep, narrow grave head first. But it wasn't deep enough, nor wide enough for her legs to fold, and so her feet protruded from the ground. The earth compacted around her ankles. She had been buried upside down.

I skipped to the autopsy report. The injuries were savage in their intensity. She had been burned. Her face, torso, legs, but just the front of her body, not the back. The medical examiner, Miss Price, guessed that it was sunburn. Price found two of her fingers broken on her left hand, bruising on her forearms where she'd tried to defend herself and contusions to her face. There were ligature marks on her wrist and ankles. The coroner listed cause of death as strangulation. She described the force involved as massive, given the damage done to the throat and neck bones.

I was careful not to let anyone else on the plane see the photographs. Wide shots of a partially burned and bloodied corpse.

There was a log of the crime scene, detailing the time of arrival of the first officer on scene through to the arrival of the ME, the sheriff, all the officers and then eventually the time logged the closure of the scene. It was like a rough diary of the investigation. At two a.m. the sheriff noted the possible ID of the victim as Skylar Edwards. They'd found a purse not far from the body.

Purse – contents of same:
One set of keys (three keys), wallet (forty-nine dollars and twenty-five cents in cash. ATM card Bank of America, ATM card Wells Fargo, Buckstown Library Card all in the name of Skylar Edwards. University of Alabama Student ID in the name of Skylar Edwards, driver's license in the name of Skylar Edwards), lip balm, hand mirror, foundation, gum.

Not much to have at the end of a life. I flicked over the page, found more pictures. The first was a picture of Skylar at her prom. Blond hair swept back in a tight ponytail. A big smile on her face. A blue dress that looked inexpensive, but still pretty. She looked excited, filled with life and energy. Her date for the prom was Gary Stroud. High school football team quarterback. He looked like he'd been hitting the steroids. His tuxedo bulged with muscle, acne covered his face and he smiled as he stood next to Skylar. There were a few more pictures of Skylar at home, with family.

A hole opened somewhere in my chest and I found it hard to swallow. The usual thoughts came to me. How could a human being do that to an innocent girl?

The Sunville County Sheriff's Department were quick to make an arrest after the body was discovered. The statement from Ryan Hogg that he had seen them arguing late that night was probably a big part of the reason for Andy's initial arrest. There was a short statement from her boyfriend, Gary, who was going to propose to her that night. She never got to meet him.

I shut the file for a second to collect my thoughts. There wasn't much evidence here against Andy. It was circumstantial at best. So far.

I opened it and read on.

Shit.

I put the case file away, lay back in my seat and closed my eyes for the last hour of the flight.

They had more than enough to convict Andy.

Andy's blood was found under Skylar's nails. A forensics expert named Cheryl Banbury confirmed the DNA match. Her report was short and devastating.

Doctor Cheryl Banbury FMB,
Lead Analyst, Department of Forensic Biology.
Fingernail clippings taken from the victim's right hand were supplied by Sunville County Sheriff Colt Lomax. He confirmed there was dirt and what appeared to be blood present under the fingernails. I examined the fingernail clippings provided in a sealed evidence bag marked CL12, and found the following:

Blood, skin, general detritus, powder residue.

The powder residue tested as particles of Anticholinergic (four parts), Sertraline (one part), Morphine Sulphate (four parts), Phenothiazine (most likely prochlorperazine) (one part).

Sheriff Colt Lomax also provided a DNA swab taken from suspect Andy Dubois, labeled CL28.

DNA Isolation was carried out on all samples. Genetic characteristics were determined by following PCR single locus technology analysis. Twenty-one PCR characteristic maker comparisons were carried out with both samples, along with a control test, separately isolated. The biostatistical analysis confirmed the markers of DNA from CL12 matched the DNA from CL28 to a probability of 99.9999 percent.

The powder residue didn't cause me much concern – the victim was studying chemistry so I guessed she had contact with all kinds of stuff. The DNA was a killer. There is no such thing as a perfect DNA match. The report said that the DNA of the blood under Skylar's fingernails matched Andy's, as far as science was able to analyze them. Andy had a corresponding finger scratch on his shoulder. Deep enough to draw blood. It looked like Skylar scratched her attacker, and that attacker was Andy.

Andy had given Sheriff Lomax a full and detailed confession on the sixteenth of May. A day after Skylar's body had been found. I couldn't read most of it. What I read didn't sound like it was written by a young man. It sounded like law enforcement. Probably the cop wrote the damn thing and got Andy to sign it.

But that wasn't the only confession. His cellmate would testify that Andy confessed to killing Skylar because she wouldn't sleep with him. I felt sickened, but also strangely hopeful.

There were not one, but two shaky confessions in this case. One written by a cop within hours of Andy's arrest, the other supposedly came a week later and had been given by a jailhouse snitch. Why did they need two confessions?

I needed to talk to Andy. Get a sense of him. I needed to see him, face to face. I had to be sure he was innocent. I would know when I talked to him.

One thing was now beyond any doubt – if I decided I was going to defend Andy, this would be toughest case of my life.

CHAPTER SIX

EDDIE

We arrived at Mobile airport around eight, picked up our bags and I charged a rental car on the office credit card.

The rental company dropped Harry and I at the end of a huge parking lot next to a Prius that had seen better days. Stepping out of the golf buggy, Harry gazed at the Prius like it was a child of his who had just dropped out of Harvard to take up basket weaving.

'I thought we were hiring a car,' he said.

'This is a car,' I said.

'No, it's not. This is a battery on wheels, with a toy car engine. It's got no soul.'

'Neither do you. Let's just put our bags in the trunk and get to Buckstown. I'll drive.'

'No, *I'll* drive. It'll give me an excuse to complain about the car and give you an excuse to complain about my driving. Then we'll both be happy.'

The satellite navigation in the car seemed to operate on astrology and hope more than GPS, but by the time we found the freeway, it was a short enough hop into Sunville County. Harry kept putting his foot down and complaining about the car being broken.

'It's not broken, it's a hybrid.'

'A hybrid with what? A mule? I'm telling you this thing is busted.'

The exit sign for Buckstown sported three bullet holes, rusted around the edges. All of them in the 'O' in Buckstown. We came onto a two-lane stretch of blacktop surrounded by trees on either side. They soon gave way to open fields with low mist covering them. Then the mist moved. Gently undulating, as if there were a thousand ghosts rolling in the soil.

It wasn't mist. It was something I'd never seen before.

'Cotton fields,' said Harry. 'They look strange in the moonlight, don't they?'

'Spooky,' I said.

'My great-grandfather picked Alabama cotton. Back-breaking work. Except it wasn't really work. He didn't get paid.'

His voice grew softer, deeper, as he said, 'Too much blood has been spilled on this land. This place feels . . . poisoned, somehow. My father preached all over Alabama. We were here for five years. Can't say I ever missed the place.'

I felt a shiver worming through my back.

'Soon as this case is done, we're out of here. And we're not coming back,' I said.

The fields stretched for miles in every direction until we came over the brow of a hill, and there was forest ahead of us. The road wound around great oaks and willows, clothed in Spanish moss. Their limbs were a gothic veil, stretched over the blacktop. There were old timber houses along the side of the road. Single story. Not one of them with a decent roof or standing up straight. They looked abandoned, or at least they should have been. There were lights on inside a few of them. Some didn't even have windows, just tar paper that became luminous and strangely beautiful with light behind it.

'You read all the case papers?' asked Harry.

'I did. What do you think?'

'If he says he's innocent, and he might be, we've got a hell of a hill to climb. You've had tough cases in the past. Me too. But never like this. We've got two confessions to throw out before we even get started. One to a cellmate, one to the sheriff,' said Harry.

'We need to talk to him. If he says the police confession was coerced, we need evidence of that. The other confession is to a jailhouse snitch. That might be easier to fight.'

'I don't think the kid murdered that poor girl,' said Harry, bluntly.

'What makes you so sure?' I asked.

'There's something off about this whole thing. I've seen cops bolster poor cases with doctored evidence before, but not like this.

They've got Andy's blood and DNA underneath the victim's finger-nails, and the kid has a scratch on his shoulder. Why get not one, but two false confessions on top of that? It's not right.'

'What's not right is we've got a death-penalty trial coming up in a few days, we're not getting paid, we're in the middle of nowhere and we've got a client who's confessed to murder twice. What's right about it?'

'Not one goddamn thing. The victim is the key to this case. We need to know everything about her. There's not much in the file.'

A gas station marked the beginning of the town. Harry took us down what the GPS told us was Main Street. Apart from a bar and a 7-Eleven, the place was closed for the night. The buildings thinned out. At the edge of the street, the last building had three county sheriff cruisers parked outside. The Sheriff's Department. A long, two-story brick building that stuck out like a sore ass. The second floor was painted white, the bottom half exposed brick. Around halfway along Main Street was a crossing. Buck Street intersected Main Street like the crosshairs on a rifle. I'd checked the internet and found that the only hotels in town were both on Buck Street. There were no websites to book online, and they hadn't picked up the phone when I'd called earlier that day. We would have to wing it.

Harry liked the look of the first hotel we saw, called The Chanterelle, and parked outside.

It was no more than a large colonial house, with faded white paint and a swing chair on the porch. The sign in the window said 'Vacancy'.

Soon as I opened the car door, the Alabama climate splashed my face with sweat. There was eighty-nine percent humidity, and it was baking hot. Hot and wet I was used to, living through New York summers, but this was different. It was thick and sodden with not a breath of wind to move it. Like the air inside a rotten tomb. And there were bugs everywhere.

I followed Harry through the front door to a mahogany reception desk complete with a mahogany receptionist. The name badge on her blue dress said 'Clara' and she would have been white, once, but sixty-plus years of sunbathing and sucking on Camel cigarettes had turned her pallor the same color as the furniture. The desk looked younger, and cleaner.

'Names?' she said, in a dead voice. Her blond hair curled up at the fringe, making it appear as though it was making an effort to avoid skin contact.

'Ford, Harry. Pleased to meet you. This is my colleague, Eddie Flynn.'

Clara took a drag on the Camel, blew a cloud of blue smoke at the 'No Smoking' sign and croaked, 'Sorry, gentlemen. We're fully booked.'

And with that, she screwed the cigarette into the ashtray and pointed her head toward a copy of *Cosmopolitan*.

'Excuse me, ma'am. The sign outside said you have a vacancy,' said Harry.

'The sign don't work here,' she said, never taking her eyes from an article entitled, 'Essential Bikinis'.

Harry gave me a knowing look. The ball had dropped for him. Whatever ball that was, it still eluded me.

'I think I know what the problem is here. Ma'am, we understand this is a traditional town. Eddie and I work together. We're not a couple. Not that there's anything wrong with that, of course. All the same, we would like two separate rooms.'

'We're fully booked,' she said.

Harry leaned forward, I took his arm.

'Let's try the other hotel,' I said.

I wasn't exactly excited at the prospect of staying at The Chanterelle. We stepped outside, and Harry tapped me on the shoulder.

'You think she wouldn't let us stay because she thought we were gay?'

I shook my head, said, 'I don't know.'

'Makes a refreshing change from hotels in Alabama refusing to give me a room because I'm black,' he said.

'Either way, I don't want to stay there. Doesn't matter if it's racism or homophobia, it's all bad. Let's try the one across the street. *I'll* go in this time. I'm Irish Catholic.'

We both made our way across the street. We hadn't seen a single car on the road since we came into town. Even the streetlights looked depressed. The short walk stuck the shirt to my back like hot glue. I wasn't cut out for this climate. Harry waited outside while I ventured into the New Hotel. I suppose it was new once. Probably in the forties. A small red neon signed burned the word vacancy into a passing mosquito's ass. I opened the front door, and a bell rung. Like The Chanterelle, there was already someone behind the reception desk. This receptionist was a young man with black hair that looked as though it had been painted onto his head. He stood up, nodded. Opened the register book.

'May I have your name, sir?'

'Eddie Flynn,' I said, reaching for the pen cradled in the fold of the guest register.

A light bulb went off behind his small, blue eyes. He sucked air through his teeth, closed the book in front of me and said, 'I'm sorry, we're fully booked.'

I stood there in silence, staring at the kid. He couldn't have been more than twenty. He bit his lip and began to tap a rapid beat on the reception desk with his pen.

'Is there a convention in town?' I asked.

'It's summer. Our busy season,' he said, with his head firmly pointed at the floor.

There was no sense in arguing, I left and rejoined Harry on the sidewalk.

'It seems they're fully booked, too. Funny, isn't it? I think someone knew we were coming.'

'Don't be ridiculous. Look, I don't want to stay in either of these dumps anyway. Let's go back to Mobile, get a real hotel,' said Harry.

'Good idea,' I said.

We made our way back across the deserted street toward the Prius. Harry opened the driver's door, put one leg inside and froze.

'What is it?' I said.

I came around to his side of the car, followed his gaze to the flat front tire. I looked at the back tire. It was good. I walked around the car and saw the rear passenger tire was flat too. I knelt down in the light from the porch of The Chanterelle, and ran my finger along the rubber. There was a hole, about an inch wide and two inches above the rim. A knife mark.

'It's my name,' I said. 'Someone knew we were coming and wanted to make sure we got the right kind of welcome.'

Harry blew out his cheeks, said, 'I hate this goddamn town.'

CHAPTER SEVEN

THE PASTOR

The Pastor gazed through the dormer window at the ivory, butter-ball moon that crested the rooftops of Buckstown.

He heard footsteps on the stairs.

He turned and looked around the room. It was a wide-open space. The floor above Buckstown Insurance Services didn't get much use. A row of filing cabinets filled one side of the room. Seven seats had been arranged in a circle in the middle of the wooden floor. A table sat below the window with cups and a coffee dispenser, which the Pastor had filled in the small kitchen in back. The only decoration on the walls were two flags. The first was the Confederate flag, pinned to the eaves. The second was an antique flag that had been framed and hung on the wall opposite the file storage. The flag's colors had faded. A once-vibrant red background now looked rusted. In the middle of that brownish red sat a white flower. An old emblem on age-worn cloth. The flower was a camellia. It had turned from white to yellow. The seven petals fanning out from the center appeared tarnished. Either from age, or urine. It was a flag likely to be pissed on, and probably had been. It was one of only three flags of its type that survived today. The Pastor paid fifty thousand dollars for it in a black-market auction.

No reputable antique dealer would sell the flag in public. It had history. The thin, fraying cloth carried the weight of the sins committed under that banner.

The door opened and a squat, bald man in a tweed jacket entered the room. Professor Gruber was sweating right through that jacket. Even at night, the heat was oppressive and the walk up the flight of stairs had turned Gruber's blue shirt black with perspiration.

Behind him was a tall, lean man with red hair and a beard, softened by flecks of gray. He wore a checkered shirt and blue jeans. They looked incongruous – the two of them.

The Pastor had come to learn that ideas and thoughts brought all kinds of people together.

'Is this the father?' asked the Pastor.

Gruber nodded.

The Pastor headed straight for the man in the working clothes, held out his hand, said, 'Welcome.'

The man glanced at the Pastor's hand, then accepted the greeting. His palms and fingers were rough and dry from heavy work.

'It's an honor to meet you, sir. I—' but before the man could say any more, the Pastor cut him off.

'We don't use names in our meetings. You can call me the Pastor. You already know the professor, here. We think it's safer this way. We sweep this room regularly for listening devices, and it's secure, but to make sure we don't make a slip on the phone, or at a meeting elsewhere, we never use real names in conversation. The FBI have ears everywhere.'

The man nodded.

'I am very sorry for the loss of your daughter,' said the Pastor. 'She was such a life force in this community. We are all feeling that sense of loss quite deeply. Of course, that doesn't compare to the pain you and your wife are experiencing. Please, take a seat.'

The man was Francis Edwards. He released his grip and sent that big hand of his running over his face. The Pastor noticed Francis' eyes were red and wet. His breathing labored. As if he was on the verge of breaking down, and every second was a battle to keep that pain inside.

He took a seat in the circle of chairs, the Pastor and Gruber sat opposite.

'I want to thank you for coming here tonight. The professor told me he had met you in Calhoon's. You were hitting the bottle pretty hard that night. I understand. Alcohol can be a balm, but it soon becomes a crutch. And once it has a grip on you, it's hard to let it go. The best thing is to talk about how you feel.'

'I'm grateful I met Professor Gru— I mean, *the professor*, that night. We . . .' said Francis, halting before he said any more. He bowed his head. His big Adam's apple bobbed up and down in his neck. He cleared his throat, swallowed as he tried to fight down the emotion threatening to overwhelm him.

He settled himself, rubbing his palms together, over and over, as if he was dry-washing his hands.

'We talked about Skylar. It, uh, it was the first time I really spoke to someone about it. The sheriff said I should talk to a doc, or a shrink, but I wasn't brought up that way. You understand?'

A smile spread over the Pastor's features as he nodded. Francis had used his daughter's name, which irritated him somewhat, but he wasn't about to remonstrate with a bereaved parent.

'I understand all too well. It's good that you were able to share. It helps. But we can do a lot more than just talk, can't we, Professor?' said the Pastor.

Gruber nodded as he got to his feet. He approached one of the filing cabinets, pulled out a drawer and lifted clear a large manila envelope. It was five inches thick and unsealed. He gave the envelope to Francis.

'We are given to believe you haven't been able to work since your daughter's murder. You drive long haul, right?' said the Pastor.

Francis looked inside the envelope. His hand shot to his forehead, as if he was struck by what he'd seen inside. It was then that he began to cry. He couldn't keep it at bay any longer and his shoulders looked as though they were pumping the tears out of him.

'There's twenty-five thousand in that envelope. We raised it among the six of us. I know you're struggling, and we want to do what we can. There will be more soon,' said the Pastor.

'No, please, this is already way too much.'

'Don't be ridiculous. Look, you know the professor. And now we've met. There are four more of us in the church. We all have connections to authorities, together with influence and power. And we care about the people of this state. What happened to your daughter was inevitable, in some ways.'

Wiping his face, Francis fixed the Pastor with a questioning look.

'I know how special she was to you. To all of us in this town. She was our homecoming queen not so long ago. I used to see her sitting in Gus's Diner, drinking milkshakes and laughing with her friends. Trust me when I say, if it wasn't her, it would have been someone else. Look there, you see that flag? That's the original flag of the White Camellia. It hung in a church in Louisiana one hundred and fifty years ago. The men and women who stood beneath that flag knew the horrors that would be inflicted on our way of life if we didn't keep those people in check. You understand? Your daughter wasn't killed by a white man. A white man wouldn't do that. We have to look after our families.'

Francis stared at the Pastor, something like disbelief on his face. And confusion.

'I don't want any more white parents to sit where you are right now, weeping for their murdered child. We will help you and your wife, but you've got to wake up and understand you are in a fight for your survival, just like every other white man.'

Francis said nothing.

'Now, go on home. We will speak tomorrow. I know the trial is coming up, and there's a lot to discuss.'

A moment of silence before Francis got to his feet, thanked both of them and left.

Gruber and the Pastor waited until they heard the door closing downstairs.

'I'm not sure about him,' said Gruber. 'We have less than a week until the reckoning. He's not ready for this. Let me—'

'I told you, he is the one. And he will be ready. We have six days. That's plenty—'

'No, there's too much at stake. I'm telling you it's not enough time—'

'You're worried, and I understand. You need to trust me. Is it you're not sure about him, or are you unsure of yourself?' asked the Pastor.

Gruber shook his head.

The Pastor said, 'We've been over this. There is no other way. People will die. A lot of people. I thought you had accepted that?'

'I do, you know I do.'

'In six days he will be ready. You have his email, don't you? Send him some videos. The usual kind – Breitbart, Fox News, One America. He'll soon be convinced.'

'If you say so. I'll drop in on him and the wife tomorrow.'

'Good. Now, tell me, has Flynn arrived in town yet?'

'I don't know. I helped put the word out.'

'Good enough,' said the Pastor.

The two men spoke for another hour, going over their preparations. The Pastor and Gruber wanted the same thing, but they sometimes had different views on how to achieve it. Gruber understood and accepted that sacrifice was necessary. Just as long as he wasn't the one who had to do the sacrificing.

'I'll try to be with him every day of the trial, but I might need one of the others to sit in occasionally,' said Gruber.

'Do you have plans?' asked the Pastor.

'No, it's just I find his grief tiring. I can only be a shoulder to cry on for so long before I become irritated.'

'The others are busy. You're not working at the moment. It only seems right that you do the lion's share. After all, he likes you.'

When Gruber left it was almost two a.m. and the Pastor felt like some fresh air. As Gruber drove away, the Pastor walked the streets. Buckstown was quiet at this time of night. If you avoided the bars, then you could walk the whole length of the town without meeting another soul.

He enjoyed the silence. The warmth from the streetlights burning on the wet blacktop. The temperature didn't bother him. Not since he was a boy, and his father had put him in the box for not finishing his meal. The box may as well have been an oven. Thin traces of light seeped in from the spaces between the pine boards. Enough light to read his Bible, but no more. Anything could warrant some time in the box. Raising his voice, forgetting to brush his teeth, or not praying hard enough. His childhood experiences meant he never complained about the heat, because nothing was as bad as being cooked in that box.

He grew up on a farm outside of Buckstown. The first few years of his life held no firm memories, only a feeling of warmth and protection. His mother passed when he was six, which just left the Pastor and his father, who never recovered from the death of his wife. The Pastor's father blamed himself for her death – that he wasn't pious enough, that in neglecting his devotion to God he had somehow brought divine wrath on the family. He took down all the paintings in the house, all the clocks, and in their stead, he placed thick wooden boards bearing hand-carved passages from the Bible. They went to church every morning, and twice on Sunday. Between the box and the beatings, the Pastor learned the strength of the word of God.

He stopped at the corner of Buck Street. The two hotels that served the town were visible, and there was a car parked outside The Chanterelle that he didn't recognize. He made his way down the street and saw it was a Toyota, and inside, asleep, were two men. The tires on the car had been slashed, and there was no room at the inn for these strangers. The Pastor recognized Eddie Flynn from the picture he'd seen on the internet. The man looked disheveled, sleeping in his clothes. The Pastor's teeth began to grind. Here was the man whose sole purpose was to set Andy Dubois loose. And that was something the Pastor couldn't allow.

There was no one else on the street. No cameras. No cars. No people. Just a light rustle of wind in the young pine tree behind him. One of many new trees that lined the street.

Ten years on his father's farm had slowly tightened the screws in the Pastor's head. Over time, he had learned to spot the signs that would precede one of his episodes. Grinding his teeth was one. The Pastor inhaled, tried to slow his breathing.

But it was no good. His heart was hammering. His fists tight.

He leaned down, brought his face close to the passenger window. His breath fogged the glass with each exhalation – like a great bull with its nose against the rodeo gate, ready to be set loose.

Reaching inside his jacket, he drew his .22 pistol. Pointed it at Flynn's head, the barrel almost touching the window.

If he pulled the trigger now, he would have to kill the man in the driver's seat. That wouldn't be a problem for him. They were all the same, those New York elites. They didn't understand the real America. They weren't patriots, not like the Pastor. He could kill for his country, for his cause. In six days' time, the reckoning would begin.

His finger touched the trigger.

He imagined the shot. The crack of gunfire exploding the dark, silent street, his view of Flynn distorting as the round tore through the glass, leaving only spider-web cracks surrounding a single bullet hole. He would adjust his aim, put two rounds in the black man in the driver's seat, and then he would be gone, into an alley, swallowed by the night.

A pearl of sweat took a run down his cheek.

Killing Flynn would draw more attention. Attention he didn't need.

He put the gun away, bent low to the window and bore his teeth, screaming in silence.

The Pastor backed up from the car, and he heard a *snap*.

He'd stepped on a dry twig that had fallen from the tree.

The sound was familiar. He turned and made his way back to his car, thinking about the last time he'd heard that noise.

That *snap*.

It was the same sound he'd heard as he choked Skylar Edwards to death – the small bones in her neck breaking under his thumbs.

THE SECOND DAY

CHAPTER EIGHT

EDDIE

I don't normally see six-thirty in the morning. People who have seen me at that time normally say I'm not at my best. This morning, I woke to Harry's snoring in the driver's seat beside me. We had no choice but to recline the seats and sleep in the car. There was only one puncture repair kit in the rental, and the nearest road assistance crew said it would be six hours before they got to us. Eight hours later, they still hadn't shown up.

The sun hit me through the windshield. It seemed to bore right through my eyelids directly into my brain. My back was singing a bad song, my head pounded, and I felt like I had a terrible hangover that I didn't deserve. Harry woke up, got out of the car and stretched. I drank some water and joined him.

'I take it all back. That is one comfortable car,' said Harry. 'You look like shit.'

'Thanks. You're not sore or anything?'

'I slept in a wet foxhole for a month in a rat-infested stretch of mean jungle twelve clicks from Saigon. This excuse for a car,' he said, patting the hood of the Prius, 'is luxury compared to that.'

We both remembered seeing a diner on Main Street. In shirt-sleeves, loose ties and crumpled pants we made our way to it on foot before the sun decided to really get to work. The town looked dirtier in the daylight. Most of the buildings lining the streets were low, one or two-story. Some had shabby awnings, pitted with holes. Others had bright yellow, plastic streamers advertising a sale in the window, but no indication of what might be on sale inside. We turned right at Main Street and found Gus's Diner. It was classic Americana. Booths covered in red fake leather, hard plastic tables and a long, chrome-edged counter with tall leather stools screwed to the floor to service it. I pointed toward a booth in the corner.

Old habits. I like to see who is coming in, who is going out, and my back is always against a wall. Hangover from a life as a con man when survival depended on knowing how and when to make an exit. Same as being a trial attorney – the key to cross-examination is knowing the precise moment to shut up and sit your ass back down in that chair.

We took the booth, Harry flipped open the menu with difficulty. The combination of laminated pages, uncharted humidity and cold grease made it sound like someone ripping duct tape off bare skin. The diner wasn't busy. Couple of guys in checked shirts, jeans and ball caps were sending their cholesterol count into orbit with fried chicken and waffles, an elderly man was reading the paper at the counter and a huge guy in a suit sipped coffee in the corner. It was his bulk that stood out, and that the suit was too tight.

A car pulled up outside. It had once been red, but now was mostly rust. There were a couple of holes in the hood, but they were largely obscured by the black cloud of smoke that billowed over the car from the exhaust. A woman in a waitress uniform got out of the car, ran into the diner. She came around the counter, put on an apron, grabbed an order pad and a pen. There was a big guy working the grill, he looked around the restaurant then sent her over to our table. By the look on her face, he hadn't been too polite about it. She had dark hair, sad blue eyes and smelled of hot motor oil. Despite all of this, she put on a smile.

'Hi, I'm Sandy, I'll be your waitress. What can I get for you, gentlemen?'

We both ordered pancakes and coffee.

I watched the big guy in the suit get up, button his suit jacket with some difficulty and make for the counter. He called over the guy at the grill who wiped his hands on his white, cotton apron and leaned over the counter. The man whispered something to him, then they both turned and looked right at us. I waved a friendly greeting.

The grill man said, 'Thanks, Mr. Wingfield,' as the big guy in the suit left.

The grill man came over to the table. He had thick arms, no neck and a bald head filled with bad attitude. On the breast of his white shirt it said, 'Gus'. I fixed him for the owner, but then again, we were in Alabama. Everyone in the diner could've been called Gus, including the rest of the waitresses. Gus wiped his hands on his apron.

'Are you boys the lawyers for Andy Dubois?' he said.

Harry looked at me.

'What if we are?' I asked.

'Then get the hell out of my restaurant. We don't feed folk who help filth like him. He murdered that girl, and he's gonna fry for it.' Without another word he stepped away and started hollering 'Sandy! We're not serving these men. They're leaving.'

Sandy came out from behind the counter with a coffee pot. She looked confused, said, 'But they haven't done anything, have they?'

'They're lawyers for Andy Dubois.'

'So?' she asked.

'So you're fired. Never question me in my own business. And this is your third time late this week. Get your shit and get out.'

Sandy put down the coffee, took off her apron and left before the reddening of her cheeks boiled into tears.

Harry and I followed on her heels.

Outside, the sun had somehow gotten stronger, I felt the back of my neck start to sweat.

'Goddamn piece of shit,' said Sandy, and kicked the rear panel of her car. It left a dent and sent chips of rust into the air like confetti.

'Harry, there's no way that tow truck is coming all the way out here,' I said.

I walked toward the rusting car, saw that it had a Volkswagen badge on the back. The bodywork may be shot but a VW engine will keep going until doomsday.

'Hey, Sandy. Sorry about that,' I said.

Shielding her eyes from the sun, Sandy said, 'Oh, it's not your fault. Gus has been looking for an excuse to get rid of me for weeks. Maybe it's for the best.'

'Say, we need a car. You need money. How much do you want for this . . . automobile?'

'A thousand dollars,' she said, faster than I expected.

'It would cost two-fifty to junk it. What do you say to four hundred?'

'Five and it's yours,' she said, dangling the keys. Any misconceptions I'd had about rural folk in the South being slow was quickly disappearing. If I didn't close the deal now, I had a feeling I would end up losing my shirt.

I counted five one hundred-dollar bills, put them in Sandy's palm and took the keys.

'What model of Volkswagen is this?' I asked.

Sandy was already ten feet away, but she turned and smiled and said, 'It's not a VW. It's got a nice VW *badge*. I don't rightly know what kind it is. But good luck to you.'

Harry snatched the keys, got into the car and started it up. It started just fine. Then a loud bang came from the engine, followed by smoke, but it was still running.

'I need a break from this town. I'll go get us some food and two tires for the mule. What are you going to do?' he asked.

I looked down the street toward the Sheriff's Department.

'I'm going to talk to our client,' I said.

CHAPTER NINE

EDDIE

Berlin had told me Andy was being held in the county lock-up. This is not the norm, even for Alabama. Once the defendant has been charged and brought to court, and bail denied, they head for the state penitentiary like everyone else, to await trial.

Except Andy.

The county lock-up was in the Sheriff's Department headquarters and wasn't much more than a cage. No exercise yard. Little or no sunlight. Surrounded by drunks, junkies and the cops who were trying to get Andy executed.

This couldn't have been worse for him. I tried to think of why Andy would've been denied due process, and why his former lawyer, Cody Warren, hadn't managed to move him out of there.

Then I remembered the warm welcome Harry and I were receiving and didn't much wonder after that. Berlin had warned me to be careful. As I walked toward the Sheriff's Department building, I took out my phone, typed the name of the town into the search bar and hit enter. The first dozen news articles didn't make good reading. They were all about a bomb that had failed to detonate in a gospel hall on the edge of town about a year ago. It was an African American church mostly, although like in all good churches, everyone was welcome no matter the color of their skin. The reverend found the device one Sunday morning under a stack of Bibles and magazines at the back of the church.

Someone upstairs was looking after that church, but it put a bad taste in my mouth. So far, the inhabitants of Buckstown that I'd seen on the street were all white. I didn't hold out much hope for an impartial jury. The rest of the articles were on the convictions of various individuals, and their death sentences. I put the phone away and wiped a layer of sweat off my forehead.

I passed a small law office with the name 'Cody Warren' on the shingle outside. There was a middle-aged lady sitting behind a desk in the window. I decided I would pay a visit on the way back. First, I needed to talk to Andy Dubois.

A small set of steps led up to the public entrance to the Sheriff's Office. Inside, it was a welcome respite from the sun, but not much cooler. Two large desk fans blew at the enquiry desk, but none were pointed at the public area. A thin deputy with a fat red moustache stood behind a tall enquiry desk, the fans trained on his face. His name badge said his name was Leonard. Although he was slim, his arms and chest bulged in all the right places. The moustache helped soften a cruel mouth.

'Can I help you, sir?' he asked, politely, the moustache smiling.

'My name is Eddie Flynn. I'm a lawyer, here to see Andy Dubois.'

Deputy Leonard didn't seem to like this development. Without a word, he walked away toward a room in back, eyeing me suspiciously as he left, like I was about to steal the bell on the counter.

A minute later he returned, and said, 'Andy Dubois doesn't have any visits scheduled. And anyhow, it ain't visiting hours yet.'

My shirt was already sticking to me with sweat. I hadn't had a cup of coffee yet, no breakfast, little sleep, and I wondered how his moustache would look after I broke the nose sitting above it.

'Look, Andy's lawyer is missing. I'm here to represent him. I just need to see him first. Don't make me go see the judge to get a court order. Just let me in.'

'From what I can see, his lawyer is Cody Warren. You can't get a court order to see a man who ain't your client.'

A large man appeared behind Leonard. He was fifty pounds overweight, red-faced and didn't look happy about any of it. He wore a badge on a dark blue shirt, and I guessed he was the sheriff around here. A closer look at his name badge confirmed it. This was Sheriff Colt Lomax, the man who had witnessed Andy's signature on the confession, and probably the same guy who wrote it.

For a few seconds, I took the moment in. The smiles on their faces. They folded their arms. I turned and looked to my left. A double, swing, half-door that came up to my thigh was all that separated me from the office beyond. There were another half-dozen deputies milling around in the open-plan office. At the corner on the left was the sheriff's private office, and in the center of the back wall, a steel door stood open, revealing a dark hallway that I took to be the entrance to the cellblock. I took a step closer to the swing door to get a better look at the holding cells.

'Where do you think you're going?' said Leonard.

I ignored him, narrowed my eyes. There were maybe half a dozen cells in that block, some had cage doors open. It was a relatively small holding area. Most occupants wouldn't be there for more than a few hours until they were brought to court.

'Take one more step, sir, and you'll be under arrest,' said Leonard.

I took a step back, turned and left the building without a word.

The five hundred feet between the Sheriff's Department and the office of Cody Warren burned the back of my neck and my arms. I needed sunblock and a shower. Instead, I opened the door to Warren's legal practice. The air conditioning was just about the best thing that had happened to me that morning.

The middle-aged lady got up from behind her desk and approached me.

'I'm sorry, we can't take on any new clients at the moment,' she said.

'I'm not a client. My name is Eddie Flynn. Alexander Berlin sent me.'

Her polite, upturned mouth and bright customer eyes collapsed into concern.

'Has he found him?'

'Not that I know of. He sent me here to take over Andy Dubois' defense. I need to talk to someone about the case, and I want to try and find out what happened to Mr. Warren.'

Without warning, the lady grabbed me in a bear hug and tight-ened her arms like she was about to fall off a cliff. At that moment I was glad I hadn't eaten breakfast – it might have been squeezed clean out of me, along with all the air in my body.

'Oh, thank you,' she said, and let go.

I took a breath to refill my lungs.

'I'm Betty Maguire, Cody's office manager. And secretary. Well, there's just me and Cody really, but he likes to call me the manager. Oh God, I'm just so glad someone is here that I can talk to. The sheriff is – well, I think he's secretly glad Cody's missing. They never did see eye to eye, and in recent years it's gotten worse. But here I am rambling, please sit down, would you like something? Tea? Lemonade?'

'Some water and coffee would be great,' I said.

She showed me toward a chair, and disappeared into the back, her floral dress and candy-curl hair bouncing along with her step.

I looked around the law office. Two desks. A line of filing cabinets along the other side. Framed certificates and practicing licenses, photographs of Cody and Betty standing with clients holding what I assumed to be large damages checks. Cody was a small man, much smaller than Betty. I assumed as Betty appeared to be wearing the same dress, that this was a recent photograph. Cody had gray hair, large keen eyes and a nice smile. Some say all a small-town lawyer needs is a good smile to go on a highway billboard and a memorable phone number.

Betty came back with a glass of water, and a glass of tea balanced on a tray.

'Sorry, Cody is the only one who drinks coffee. We ran out a week ago.'

'This is fine, thank you.'

I drained the glass of water, took a sip of the iced tea but it was far too sweet for me.

'When did you last see Mr. Warren?'

'Almost a week ago. It's not like Cody to go away and not tell me. He doesn't have family – never married. He's all about the job, you know. And art. He collects paintings. That's his life. I thought maybe he had gone to see someone or lost his cell phone. He's been missing over a week. The last I heard from him was a text. He sent me a message to ask if the letters *F C* meant anything to me.'

'What is that about?'

'I don't know, and no, it didn't mean anything to me at the time. Still doesn't.'

'Does Cody live locally?'

'Sure, I've been to the house. When I pulled into the driveway his car was gone. No one in the house. I tried him on his cell – nothing. I got worried, called the police.'

'Were they able to pin-point his cell phone?'

Betty paused, frowned and said, 'Honey, the Sheriff's Department won't lift a finger. They talk a good talk, but they won't do shit, pardon my French.'

Her bottom lip began to tremble, she took a huge breath, and wiped delicately at her eyes with long fingernails. They were painted bright yellow, with a different colored stone in the center of each nail, and a pattern of smaller stones around them.

'Do you think Cody's disappearance has anything to do with the Dubois case?'

'I can't say for sure. Cody didn't have enemies. The only people who disliked him were the law, and the DA, of course. A tall drink of piss, that one – oh, pardon my—'

'Don't worry,' I said, and took another sip of sweet tea. I could feel it stripping the enamel from my teeth.

'I'll do what I can to find Cody. But I need to get up to speed on the Dubois case. Did Cody have any theories, any prep work I could look at?'

'Our case files were in his trunk. He always took that file home to work on at night. The only thing I might have would be our expert's report.'

'Cody had an expert lined up?'

'Just one, an independent medical examiner.'

'That's unusual.'

'Not for Cody. Doc Farnesworth used to be the medical examiner for the next county over, now retired. Cody always got his own autopsy of the victim in every murder case. Farnesworth is an honest man, I can't say the same for our county medical examiner.'

'Why?'

'Cause the county medical examiner sometimes misses things. Things that might be useful for the defense. I haven't been able to get a hold of Doc Farnesworth. I know Cody tried to talk to him. I don't know if he spoke to him or not before he went missing. I've got a copy of our autopsy on email. I can print that out for you now.'

'Actually, Betty, there's somewhere I have to be, and I don't want to take important papers with me right now. Thank you for the tea. Would it be okay if my colleague, Harry Ford, collected them later?' I asked, getting to my feet.

'Why sure, honey,' she said. 'Where are you going all of a sudden?'

'I'm going to get arrested,' I said.

Outside, it felt like the devil had thrown a few thousand more souls on the fire. I stayed close to the buildings, hugging every available inch of shadow as I made my way back to the Sheriff's Office. Ten feet from the entrance I stopped and called Harry.

'I'll bring back some fried egg sandwiches and coffee. Just getting the tires now,' he said.

'Don't bother about me. I need to go see Andy and they're not letting me in. I have to do it the hard way. Two things I need you to do for me. When you get back to town, pick up a report from Cody Warren's office. I talked to his office manager, Betty. She's helpful. Tell me this, do the letters F and C have any significance for you?'

'No, not off the top of my head. What's that about?'

'Before Cody Warren went missing he texted Betty, asked if the letters F C meant anything to her. She said they didn't ring any bells. Don't worry about it for now, the last thing I need you to do is very important – whatever happens, *don't* bail me out immediately. Give me a few hours.'

'Bail? Eddie, I know you haven't had coffee yet, but what the hell are you talking—'

I ended the call, threw open the doors of the Sheriff's Department and walked straight through the waiting area, past the yelling Leonard to *stop right there*. I pushed through the swing doors.

A buzzer must've been attached to the doors, to let cops know someone had come through. There were three deputies in the office, all behind their desks, all with stupid expressions on their faces as I made my way through the clutter of desks toward the holding cells.

'I said hold it, goddamn it!' cried Leonard. He stood in front of me and put both hands on my shoulders. He was about to push me back out the door, throw my ass on the street.

I didn't dislike Leonard. It wasn't personal. He was standing between me and a client. And that can't happen.

My right hand closed into a fist and I threw it forward. A snap punch. Low. Way low. No one would see it coming. Especially Leonard. He was now only four inches from my face. My fist travelled six inches. That's one of the secrets of putting power into a punch. You've got to aim the blow two inches beyond the target.

The thing about getting punched, hard, in the balls, is the delay. You feel the impact, the sensation of something coming into sharp contact with that tender area, and then there's a second where you think it's not that bad. There's no pain. It was just a glancing blow. You've cheated death.

And then a wave of hot agony shoots into your body, takes away your breath and you collapse. Just like Leonard did.

I stepped over him.

That's when I felt something sharp hit my thigh. Then a nightstick appeared in front of me and I was down on the floor, face in the carpet.

My head ringing.

CHAPTER TEN

EDDIE

I saw boots all around me, felt strong hands cuff my wrists from behind. A knee landed on my back, then I felt the full weight of that sheriff leaning on me while they searched me. They took my cell phone and wallet. They hauled me upright, and I didn't listen as they read me my rights. Something wet trickled down my cheek. Blood, I expected, from the nightstick. There were two of them. The sheriff, Lomax, and a squat, hairy deputy with no neck who looked as though he was mainly made out of butter and muscle.

They took my neck chains – a Saint Christopher's medal, and a crucifix that had belonged to someone I lost. Someone special. They stripped my belt from my pants, took my shoes and sat me down. Lomax pulled out a chair and sat opposite me. Lomax and butterball were breathing hard. Leonard was still rolling around on the floor, both hands on his groin.

'Now that was damn stupid, Flynn,' said Lomax.

'I didn't do anything. I was trying to get to my client when your desk deputy rammed right into me. I hope he's okay,' I said. 'Because I'm going to sue him, and you, for assault and false arrest.'

Lomax let out a wheezy peel of laughter that sounded like a bag of wet kittens.

'Here's what's going to happen. You're going to cool off, and then we'll charge you and take you to court late this afternoon. If there's any more trouble out of you . . .' He waved his nightstick.

'You threatening me, Sheriff?'

'You're goddamn right. I don't know if you've noticed, but you're a long ways from New York City. We do things different around here. You should think about what you're going to tell the judge.

Now, let's get you into the cell, nice and quiet. That's where you wanted to go, isn't that right?'

The butterball came around behind me, used my arms to get me up. I decided to play nice. He walked me through the steel door to a narrow hallway, brick wall on one side, cell bars on the other, the whole way to the end of the hall. A single exterior lamp glowed on the brick wall opposite each cell. I glanced ahead. There were five cells in total. Five lamps. The first had a guest. Single occupant. A man with long, silver, greasy hair, asleep on a bunk. He wore no shoes. The bottom of his pants had been torn up and the soles of his feet were dirty, red and blistered.

I could tell the next two cells were free. The iron bar doors were ajar. The door of the last cell was shut. Andy Dubois' cell.

Lomax stepped in front of me. The Sam Browne around his waist held a Glock, two spare clips, and two sets of keys. He unclipped one set, hauled the cell door wide and stood back. Butterball was behind me, one arm on my shoulder. He rattled with keys as he moved. His belt was a lot wider than the sheriff's. It moved and jangled with every step and every sway of his gut. He pointed me at the open cell door. I stood on the threshold, and just for a second, I pushed back. Part of it was instinct – no human is willingly locked up. Part of me pushing into him was deliberate, and not altogether altruistic. His response was predictable. He gave me an almighty shove in the back, and I knew I was going down, straight onto my face, my hands still cuffed from behind. I twisted to my right, threw myself onto the bunk. I landed awkwardly, but softly on the thin mattress, covered by a sheet and a brown blanket. I gripped the blanket as I stood, balling it, then let it drop back onto the bed.

Lomax slammed the door, locked it.

'Approach the bars, turn around,' said Lomax.

There was an open slot a little below waist height. I walked over, turned, put my wrists through. Lomax unlocked the cuffs. I rubbed at my wrists. They were red, and I'd lost some skin, but it could've been worse.

Butterball walked away. Lomax lingered. Then instead of heading toward the exit, he walked to the end of the hallway. He spoke softly. Not a whisper, not quite conversation level either. The walls amplified it, and I heard every word.

'Andy, don't you be talking to anyone in here. We just put a crazy in the cell down the hallway. Don't listen to him. D'you hear me, boy?'

'Yes, sir,' said Andy.

Lomax walked past my cell without even looking at me, then down the hallway, and out. I heard the steel door squeak, and the wedge of light thrown from the outer office grew wider on the concrete floor. He must've opened the steel door to the cellblock a little wider, keen to hear if I was talking to Andy.

It was around nine-thirty, my first day in Buckstown.

The mattress stank. I tore some of the sheet, used it to staunch the cut on my scalp. It was in the hairline, thankfully. I lay down on the floor, put my back to the wall and waited.

An hour went by. I could hear the distant sounds of a busy office beyond the hallway, and I supposed that things had calmed down and gone back to normal. The man in the cell next to me started to make noise. I could hear the springs in his mattress protest as he tossed around.

I approached the cell bars, getting as close to his cell as possible and whispered.

'Hey, buddy, want to make a hundred bucks?'

His name was Seamus Cohan. Second-generation Irish, originally from Boston. He was an alcoholic with a music problem. He needed to play his guitar on the street to get money for booze. But the more booze he had, the less he was inclined to play music. Seamus did want a hundred bucks.

I wasn't sure if music was a good career move for Seamus. His voice sounded like a man hollering for help from the bottom of a mine. It didn't seem to bother Seamus though. By the time Seamus had murdered 'The Fields of Athenry', the bulkheads of 'The Irish Rover' had turned right over, and Paddy Reilly had come back numerous times to Ballyjamesduff, the Sunville County Sheriff's Department had just about reached their limit of musical appreciation.

'Shut the hell up in there,' called a voice, just before the steel door to the cells slammed shut.

'Keep it up, Seamus. Louder this time,' I said.

While Seamus finished 'Dirty Old Town', I went to the bunk and unfurled the blanket in which I'd hidden Butterball's keys. I'd taken them from his belt just as he was about to push me into the cell. A bump lift. My body colliding with his masked the grab. Thankfully, I'd managed to turn around, and hide them in the bunk blanket before they saw what had happened. I found the key that looked like it fitted the lock on the cell door. It was tricky working through the cell bars, and my wrist was really burning with the strain. The lock clicked. I pulled my door open slowly, quietly, then went down the hallway and put the key in the lock of Andy's cell.

He was lying on the bunk. A young man wearing a dirty white tee, jeans and plastic slippers. There was nothing in his cell. No books. No TV. No newspapers. No spare clothes. It looked like he'd just arrived in that cell ten minutes ago. He gazed up at me, and his eyes grew wide with fear. He scrambled to sit up in the bed as I turned the key in the lock. He drew the blanket up under his chin, and began to tremble, violently.

I stepped into his cell, turned and put the key in the lock on the outside, through the bars.

When I turned around, Andy was in the far corner of the cell. The floor was wet. A trail that led from the bed to the corner. Andy's fear had gotten the better of him. He sat in the corner, with his left hand on his right shoulder. He was patting his shoulder, and rocking gently back and forth, rhythmically.

'Andy, my name is Eddie Flynn. I'm an attorney from New York. Your lawyer, Cody Warren, has gone missing. I'm here to stand in for Cody until he gets back. Don't be afraid, I'm here to help you.'

I stepped back from Andy, giving him space. I stood in the opposite corner, then slid down the wall, onto my knees. Then I sat down, stretching out my legs, and checked my head. I was bleeding again.

Andy's legs were still shaking, and he maintained that rocking rhythm, patting his right shoulder to a beat I couldn't hear.

'I'm not going to hurt you. You're not going to get in trouble for talking to me,' I said.

'I will,' said Andy.

'You will what?'

'I'll get in trouble for talking to you. The sheriff, he-he-he told me. He said, not to. I don't want no trouble.'

I breathed out, long and slow. Kept doing it until Andy started to mimic the breathing exercise himself. Even through the blanket he'd wrapped around his midriff and torso, I could tell he was skinny. His right leg stretched out on the floor, his jeans riding up. I could put my whole hand around his calf muscle. Andy's eyes were large, soft, and filled with fear. His lips were dry, a thin white film covering them, and the top one had split. I'd seen hostages on the news who had just been pulled out of war zones that looked better than Andy. After a few minutes, he'd calmed enough to get his breath back. He kept patting his shoulder, but the rocking stopped.

'I had to get myself arrested, just to get in here to speak to you. The sheriff wouldn't let me in otherwise.'

Andy said nothing. He was still terrified.

'I don't think you killed Skylar Edwards. The sheriff says you did, but I don't believe it.'

'I didn't. I said goodbye to her that night, and I walked home. I never . . .' he said, then caught himself, and clamped a hand over his mouth. His terror returning.

'Andy, the sheriff wants you to be found guilty of murder, in a court, and then executed. The sheriff is *not* your friend.'

'He said he wouldn't,' said Andy, talking his hand away just enough to spit out the sentence, then whipping it back.

I didn't want to speak. I couldn't risk interrupting any kind of exchange I could get going with this kid. He was smart. Great GPA, played chess and read everything in the school library. A smart young man on his way to college. Intelligence doesn't really come into play when you're locked up for a murder you didn't commit. It wouldn't matter if Andy was as smart as Albert Einstein – fear has a way of robbing you of your intellect.

He was struggling to talk. I inclined my head, knotted my eyebrows together and asked, 'What did the sheriff say he wouldn't do?'

Andy took the bait.

'He said I'll just go to jail for a while. I won't get hurt anymore, and he'll take care of my mother.'

'He hurt you?' I asked.

He pulled down the blanket, lifted his tee. I could only see his left side, but there were several vivid lines over his ribs and kidneys. I counted at least three. They were straight, with clearly defined edges, linear and parallel to each other. They looked like fresh bruises. Not more than a couple of days' old.

Nightstick strikes.

'Whupped me till I blacked out. He's done it a couple of times. I don't want anyone hurting my mother. I'll just do what they tell me. Cody Warren got it wrong. The best thing for me to do is plead guilty.'

CHAPTER ELEVEN

EDDIE

I didn't want to push things too far with Andy. Not on our first meet. Not when I was under arrest and had sneaked into his cell. Jury selection was tomorrow. Andy had agreed to let me act as his lawyer until Cody Warren came back. That was enough for now. I couldn't start discussing details of the case, not yet. Andy was too scared. I needed to get him out of there first.

I left his cell, locked him in, returned to my own cell and locked the door. I told Seamus to quiet down, but there was no stopping him. After two renditions of 'The Rising of the Moon' and 'Some Say the Devil is Dead', I was banging on the cell bars myself.

Lomax came in. Butterball in tow. The big man reached for his keys to unlock the door and couldn't find them on his belt. Lomax sighed, unclipped his own keys and opened my cell.

'We don't need cuffs now, do we?' said Lomax.

'I want to apologize for any misunderstanding,' I said.

'You can tell that to the judge,' said Lomax.

I followed them out of the hallway, back into the office, casually placing the cell keys on a desk as I walked past, the move swift and unnoticed, taking the keys out of my hip pocket and reaching behind my back for the dump.

Instead of going out front, Lomax led me to the side door and a small processing office. I gave my prints, had my mug-shot moment, and they took me straight out a side door to a waiting car.

'We need to cuff you for this part,' said Lomax.

I was handcuffed, placed in the back of a patrol car and driven all of ten minutes to a tall, grand old courthouse that sat just outside of the town. The Sunville County Courthouse was painted white, and looked a little like an old church with its clock tower rising in a spire. Like a lot of old courthouses, there was no side door for processing prisoners. I was led in through the front door, down a side hallway and into cells. This was a single courtroom kinda place. Criminal work would take precedence; family and civil law would have to fit in around it.

I wasn't in the cells long.

A deputy took me into court via a side door. The courtroom was straight out of *To Kill A Mockingbird*. The movie, with Gregory Peck, not the book. Two large ceiling fans whirred above my head. A balcony wrapped around the huge room, in a 'U' shape with a central, stained-glass window at the base of the curve, although it didn't give much light. The light came from a beautiful chandelier that hung between the fans. The gallery consisted of walnut church pews, about a half a dozen each side, separated from the action end of the courtroom by a wood panel divider with a swing door in the center. The paneling had been hand-carved, but instead of extracts from the constitution, or legal maxims, or even judicial insignia, the panels themselves represented scenes from the Old Testament.

Two long tables sat parallel to the gallery – one for the defense, one for the prosecution. The judge's bench faced the tables, with the jury box on the right and the witness stand on the left. An American flag hung limply from a pole behind the judge's empty chair. On the wall above the flag was another piece of wood carving. A huge slab of pine, with the scales of justice at the top, and below it, the Ten Commandments, chiseled into the wood.

I wasn't in Kansas anymore.

Religious symbolism isn't allowed in court buildings. The constitution forbids it. And yet, I got the feeling if any defendant or defense attorney complained about it they wouldn't get much of a reception. This wasn't a courthouse, this was a personal fiefdom.

The overgrown guy in the tight suit that I'd seen in the diner that morning came into court, trailing behind a tall, pale man carrying a leather briefcase. I sat down at the defense table still cuffed to the front.

'My name is Randal Korn, I'm the district attorney for Sunville County. This is my deputy DA, Tom Wingfield. I would shake hands, but I fear you're still wearing your jewelry,' said the tall man.

Korn didn't even look at me as he spoke, just fetched papers from his briefcase and set them down on the prosecution table. An odor came to me just then. Something smelled bad, but I couldn't say where it was coming from.

'I wouldn't shake your hand anyway,' I said.

His expression changed, and it took me a second to realize he was smiling. If that's what a smile looked like on his face, I didn't want to see him angry.

'We'll be objecting to bail, unless you agree to my terms,' he said. 'One, you are released on your own recognizance of five hundred dollars. Two, do not enter the city limits of Buckstown except for your next court appearance. Is that agreeable?'

'No can do,' I said. 'I represent Andy Dubois. I'll be staying right here for his trial.'

'Since when did you speak to Andy Dubois?'

'This afternoon. He's innocent. And I'm going make sure he gets an acquittal.'

There was that smile again – like a wound on the face of a corpse.

'Mr. Flynn, you can't even get *yourself* acquitted.'

I was thinking of a pithy reply, when I looked down and saw my shirt was undone and stained with my own blood, I didn't have a tie on, I'd sweated through every inch of clothing, I hadn't shaved, and my head was ringing like a church bell. Maybe I wasn't in the best position to make threats. Korn was a good six inches taller than me – he looked like a point guard for a Halloween basketball team.

'Silence in court, all rise. The Honorable Judge Frederick Chandler presiding,' said the court bailiff.

Judge Chandler swept into court, in black robes over a gray suit. He sat down fast. He was at least in his seventies, with wispy grey hair, a dark red line for a mouth, a thin nose and eyeballs that looked like they didn't want to stay in his skull.

While the bailiff started to call the name of the case, my name, the judge interrupted him. He stared at me like I'd just wiped my ass with his robe.

'I have in front of me papers which confirm your guest status as an advocate in this state. Never in my life have I seen a lawyer, practicing as a guest of the state bar, behave in such a manner as you have, Flynn.'

His complexion darkened as he spoke, like each word was pumping up his blood pressure.

'You are a disgrace to the New York bar, to the Alabama bar, to yourself and to this great profession. You stand here on charges of assaulting a sheriff's deputy, and trespassing on sheriff's property. Just what on earth do you think you're doing? Well? What have you to say for yourself, Flynn?'

As he said my name a fleck of foamy spittle left his lips, and arced over the bench to land on the parquet flooring.

I had remained standing since the judge came in, as had Korn. He was loving every minute of this.

'Your Honor, there are three things I should make clear. One, it's *Mr.* Flynn, to you. Second, I didn't assault anybody. I am entitled to the presumption of innocence. You seem to have already found me guilty. I haven't even been asked to plead. By the way, my plea will be *not guilty*. Third, unless I'm released immediately I'll be filing a lawsuit against the Sheriff's Department, you, Frankenstein's monster over here and anyone else in this town I can think of.'

Judge Chandler's red cheeks began to tremble. He looked like a bowl of old Jell-O.

'Never have I been so insulted from the defense table—' he said.

'You should get out more,' I said.

'Your Honor,' said Korn, 'this is an egregious insult from the defendant. I would ask the court to consider holding Mr. Flynn in contempt. Not only for his insult to this court, but his discourtesy to the office of the district attorney, which I hold.'

'Granted. Mr. Flynn, I take it you are applying for bail. I hope you have some rich friends, otherwise you'll be cooling that hothead in the state penitentiary for a long time.'

I looked at the floor, swore under my breath. I'd let this town, this DA, and this judge get to me. I wasn't playing smart. This was a bad idea and Andy Dubois would suffer if I was going to be stuck in a cell until his trial was over.

I should've called Harry. The man who represents himself has a fool for a client.

Just then I heard the doors behind me swing open. A voice I recognized hollered from the back of the court, and footsteps grew louder as they approached. Half-inch heels. And behind them, boots.

I didn't need to turn around to know the cavalry had arrived.

'Your Honor, Kate Brooks for the defendant,' said the voice, in a north New Jersey accent that I'd missed more than I cared to admit.

'Are you a member of the Alabama Bar Association?' asked the judge.

'My papers were filed this morning. I understand that I can appear as a guest of the bar until my application is granted.'

Kate came across and whispered something to the DA. He let her look at the charge sheet and the statement from the deputy who had to ice his balls. Kate took it all in. Absorbing the details in seconds. Speed reading. And her mind worked just as fast. Kate had the innate skill of being able to assimilate and use new information almost instantly. Bloch was there beside her, in her leather boots, skinny jeans and blue sportscoat.

Neither Kate nor Bloch said a word to me.

'Your Honor, the assault of the officer is minor in nature, and disputed. It's my client who has been assaulted. You can see a cut high on his forehead. We will immediately file suit for assault and battery against the Sunville County Sheriff's Department, seeking one million dollars in damages. Trespass is a misdemeanor and a fairly hopeless charge in these circumstances. Police precincts are public property and unless there are signs clearly delineating the areas of restricted access, a trespassing charge cannot be sustained. In relation to the contempt charge – a judge who is supposedly offended by a possible contempt should have an alternative judge review the facts before proceeding. No one can be a judge in their own cause. It would be unlawful for this court to decide its own case against a defendant. We would ask for the trespassing charge and the contempt charge to be formally withdrawn at this time. In relation to the assault charge, if Mr. Korn wishes to proceed, he will require an alternative prosecutor to present that case in a different jurisdiction because we will be adding the Sunville County District Attorney's Office to our lawsuit for malicious and wrongful prosecution.'

Judge Chandler looked to Korn. For a time, both men stared at one another, sizing up their options. Kate had left them none. There was no sign on the swing doors to the precinct office to say it was private. And if there was security video of the assault, it would show the moustache being aggressive, slamming into me, and then me being beaten to the ground with a nightstick.

Damn, Kate was good.

Finally, Korn nodded and said, 'In the circumstances, we will withdraw the trespass, and the assault charge. It is up to the court to deal with the contempt matter.'

Chandler drew a gray tongue over his teeth. Then spoke slowly, every word coated in venom.

'I will withdraw the contempt if Flynn apologizes to this court, and to the district attorney. Now.'

Kate said nothing.

I said nothing. I flicked my eyes straight ahead at Judge Chandler.

He stared right back. His jaw set.

'Eddie . . .' whispered Kate.

'What are you doing here? I thought you had your big divorce case.'

'We settled late last night. Harry called this morning. Said I needed to get here fast to save your ass. So, I'm here. Saving your ass. Just swallow it down and apologize. It doesn't mean anything. We've got to work smarter here. Not harder.'

'I don't like this town. I don't like this judge. And I hate the DA and his big ass assistant.'

'I know all of that, but this isn't about you. It's about Andy Dubois.'

I nodded. She was right, but it didn't make it any easier.

'Your Honor, I apologize for my earlier remarks,' I said.

'Case dismissed,' said the judge, and he rose and left, his right hand shaking in a tight fist.

Korn picked up his papers, and as he was leaving, he said, 'I hope you don't get any foolish ideas about trying to mount a defense for Andy Dubois.'

'Like I said, Andy is innocent.'

'Andy is going to fry,' said Korn. 'One way or another.'

CHAPTER TWELVE

EDDIE

At five o'clock in the afternoon, sweaty, sore and bleeding, carrying my property in a clear plastic bag, Kate escorted me out of the front door of the courthouse into the last hours of atomic sun.

'Thank you,' I said.

'You and Harry have a capacity for getting yourselves into trouble. I knew this case would bring its fair share, but I didn't think it would happen this quickly. This must be a new record, even for you,' she said.

'I try to better myself at every available opportunity.'

'You should try keeping your head down. Harry has been filling us in on the Andy Dubois case. That kid needs all the help he can get. Royally pissing off the judge who will be presiding over Andy's murder trial isn't the way to do things.'

'I know, but I needed to see Andy. And besides, pissing off judges is kinda my thing. How else am I going to enjoy myself?'

Bloch sat behind the wheel of a dark blue Chevrolet SUV, Harry in the passenger seat beside her. I held the rear door open for Kate, she got in and I followed her inside. The AC in the car wasn't even switched on.

'Could you put the air conditioning on? I don't do well in the heat.'

Bloch said nothing. Harry began adjusting a knob on the dash, turning on the AC. Bloch glared at him, shut off the air conditioning, then pulled a small lever that cracked open my rear window two inches.

'AC is bad for you,' said Bloch. She turned the wheel and took us into the light traffic of Buckstown.

'When did you get in?' I asked.

'About an hour before you were due in court. It was tight. Bloch managed to get us a place in town. Harry tells me you guys had some problems with accommodation.'

'You might say that. Where are we staying?'

'Somewhere close,' said Kate.

'Who is looking after Clarence?' I asked.

'Denise agreed to take him.'

'I got you this,' said Harry, handing me a sandwich wrapped in greaseproof paper.

'Is this my fried egg sandwich from this morning?'

'I didn't think it should go to waste. Cost me two dollars, that sandwich,' said Harry. I opened the sandwich, looked at it, wrapped it up again and buzzed the window all the way down to get some air on my face, and to take away the smell from the egg.

'Did you get the reports from Betty at Cody Warren's office?' I asked.

'Sure did,' said Harry. 'And before you ask, I already talked to Kate and Bloch – we've got no idea what F C might be. They're not initials from any witnesses or persons involved in the case – I just don't know. Maybe Farnesworth knows. His report makes interesting reading. The county medical examiner missed some things on Skylar Edward's autopsy – marks on her forehead. Apparently, Warren's medical examiner took photographs, but Betty didn't have them. They were in Warren's car with the file. The report says there are indentations in the wounds on the forehead. A distinctive bruising pattern.'

'So the murderer maybe used a club of some kind?' I said.

'He thinks the mark is from a pattern on a ring. I think he's right.'

'Is it distinctive?' I asked.

'The report says it's a star shape. Far as I can tell from checking the property record at the time of Andy's arrest, he didn't wear a ring.'

'Things are looking up. This is the foundation of a good defense,' I said, with a smile. 'We just need the photos.'

Silence in the car. Neither Harry nor Kate looked in my direction.

Bloch sighed.

'Do you want to tell him?' asked Kate.

'Tell me what?'

'As you know, Betty didn't have the photos. They were in Warren's car, which is missing, and we can't find the medical examiner. He's not returning calls or emails. I get the impression we're being frozen out,' said Harry.

'Have you asked Betty to call him?'

'Do you think this is our first murder case?' asked Harry. 'She's getting the run around too. I think someone got to our expert. Without seeing the photos or Farnesworth showing up to court, we can't use the report and that means we don't have *any* kind of a defense.'

'Any more good news?' I asked.

Bloch pulled up outside The Chanterelle.

'Perfect,' I said.

The hotel receptionist still had a cigarette in the same corner of her mouth, the nicotine-stained 'No Smoking' sign fluttered in a gust of wind as Block closed the front door. She narrowed her eyes at us as we made our way up the stairs, toward the two rooms Bloch had reserved. Whoever had sent the word out on me had obviously failed to do their homework. Kate Brooks was not on the Buckstown blacklist and it was too late now to repeat the lie about being fully booked. We went in through one door, to a room with a desk, one chair, a lamp, two single beds. They were adjoining rooms, separated by a door so light you could spit through it. The door was open, and Harry had all the case papers laid out on the double bed of the next room. This room only had the bed, a dresser and the bathroom. No desk.

No coffee machine in either room.

'If I don't get a cup of coffee soon I'm going to kill somebody,' I said.

Without a word, Bloch turned to leave.

'Cream, and extra sugar,' I said. Bloch flipped me the bird on the way out, with a smile.

'What do you want to do now?' asked Harry.

'I want to read the whole file again. Then draft a motion for bail. We need to get Andy out of there. We can go see his mom tonight, maybe.'

'I'll read with you,' said Kate.

'When you're done, we need to work on a plan. We've got to save this kid. Right now, I can't see a way to do that.'

'We'll find a way,' said Kate.

Harry nodded, then got to work.

I wanted to be more optimistic, but right then I felt like I was going to sweat out a murder trial, only to watch a sentence of death pass on Andy Dubois. I could just feel it. The room, the whole goddamn town felt like hostile territory. There was a pressure building behind my eyes, and it wasn't from the crack on the head with the stick.

Andy Dubois' life was on the line. And right then I didn't know how to save him.

CHAPTER THIRTEEN

KORN

Korn pulled up outside the Quickies dry cleaners on Fourth Street, turned off the engine to his Jaguar and buzzed the window down. The cicadas beat out a constant rhythm in the heat of the night, their tempo slowly melding with the beating of his heart. The lights were still on inside Quickies. It was almost midnight. Closing time.

The rest of the stores on the block had locked their doors hours ago. A bar, four blocks away, was the only other sign of life. Half a dozen parked cars on either side of the road, but all were dark and unoccupied. Streetlights gave a dull, yellow glow to the blacktop. Korn closed the window, got out of the car just as the light in Quickies went off. He crossed the street, the heels of his Brooks Brothers loafers *clacking* with every step.

The door of the dry cleaners opened. Patricia Dubois produced a set of keys from her apron and locked the door behind her.

'Good evening, Mrs. Dubois,' said Korn.

Still with her back to him, her shoulders flinched. She turned slowly. Her eyes fearful at first, then cold. Her mouth closed tightly, her lips thinned at the pressure and she nodded. It was an acknowledgement of his presence and the threat that came with it. Some people, usually women, could somehow look right into Korn and see the rotten, dark soul inside of him. Yet he knew she could never know the true depth of hatred and darkness within. No one could.

'I'm glad I caught you,' he said.

'You ain't catching me for anything. I haven't broken no laws, mister. Just like my Andy. You here to tell me you're gonna let him go?'

'I'm afraid not. There may be other things I could do for you, your family? Can I give you a ride home?'

It was still over ninety degrees. Hotter in the dry cleaners, probably.

'I think I'll walk,' said Patricia.

'Are you sure? I thought we could talk.'

'You can talk right here, and then you can leave.'

Korn took a step back, making sure his features were not lit by the streetlamp. It wasn't a conscious move on his part. It just felt natural. Some things should only be spoken in the dark.

'Andy murdered that young woman, Mrs. Dubois. The law requires a punishment for that crime. A punishment that will deter others. A life for a life. For that, I'm sorry. I know times have been tough since Andy has been in jail. You're behind on your rent.'

'He didn't hurt no one. My Andy . . . Hey, how do you know about my rent?'

'This is a small town. Word gets around. Your neighbors don't seem as willing to help as they once were. You're in debt for medical bills,' he said, with a quick glance at her ankle.

Patricia Dubois was fifty-five years old, and the twelve-hour shifts, constantly on her feet, had added another twenty years on top. Her right ankle was almost the same size as her calf, her shoe bulging at the side to contain it. Her left knee was heavily strapped. The poor worked hard to stay alive, and that hard work brought pain and disability.

'I am not without sympathy for your position. After all, it's not your fault Andy killed that girl,' he said.

Patricia's breathing became faster. Her lips began to wobble. The streetlight picked up tears glazing her large, sad eyes, her pride stinging them.

When she spoke, her voice was tremulous, and barely above a whisper. And yet, it was all the breath she could muster from her body and with that came a quiet power.

'I don't want charity from *you*. You want to kill my boy. I know. I can see it. I can smell it on you. There's something *wrong* with you.'

The streetlight didn't gutter, but at once Korn was three or four feet from her, and then he wasn't – he had snapped forward, like a bad cut in a movie reel that didn't show him moving, or maybe a trick of the light that didn't catch his step, but whatever it was, he was now suddenly towering over Patricia Dubois, his face inches from hers. He could smell the chemicals on her, the soap powder and cleaning fluids.

Each word he spoke sounded wet – something on the edge of each syllable, like honey laced with arsenic.

'Do not be so hasty, Mrs. Dubois. Think on what I have said. I *can't* save your son. I *can* promise him a quick death. And I can promise you enough money to bury him and clear your debts. The people of this town can be charitable and Christian to those who seek forgiveness. All I ask is one thing. You tell the truth. Tell us how Andy came home that night and told you he killed Skylar Edwards. Make sure he tells the same story to the jury. If he doesn't, I can make both of you suffer. You think this is bad? It can get worse for you. It can get a whole lot worse for him. I'll make sure Andy gets the needle. The good stuff. So he sleeps before they put the poison in his veins. If he doesn't co-operate, we'll be too short on drugs. It'll be the chair for Andy. Think on it, Mrs. Dubois.'

Korn stepped back. Before he turned to his car he said, 'Andy will die. The only question is how. Easy or hard? He can fall asleep, or he can die with his blood boiling in his veins. It's your choice.'

CHAPTER FOURTEEN

EDDIE

I watched Korn limp across the street to his car, leaving the woman on the sidewalk reeling. He got into his Jaguar. The car lit up.

A hand on the back of my head pushed me down. Bloch hunkered down too. Soon as Korn sped past in his car, she let me up.

Bloch opened the driver's door and stepped onto the street, I opened the passenger door. Bloch shook her head, motioned for me to wait in the car.

That was probably wise. From the looks of the conversation Patricia Dubois just had with Korn, she didn't need any more surprise meetings with strangers this evening. Two of us approaching her might be too much. Patricia was leaning against a street lamp, her head bowed, her back heaving air into her body. Korn had not physically touched her, but it looked as though she had been winded. Bloch approached her straight on, not wanting to startle the woman further.

As she got closer, Bloch slowed her approach, raised her open hands. Bloch used words like hundred-dollar bills. She didn't give them out often, but when she did, they were worth every cent.

I stayed in the car. I wouldn't get out until Bloch gave me the thumbs up.

Mrs. Dubois was talking now. Slowly. Struggling to get the words out while wiping her wet cheeks. Whatever Korn had said had shaken her to the core.

Bloch stood still, listening while Mrs. Dubois talked. Then, something happened that I didn't expect. Mrs. Dubois stepped forward, threw her arms around Bloch. I'd never seen Bloch give anyone so much as a handshake. For a few seconds, Bloch froze, her arms outstretched, as if this was something that had never happened before. It was almost alien to her. Then, slowly, she embraced Mrs. Dubois as the woman cried onto Bloch's shoulder.

I could almost sense Bloch's discomfort, but she must've forced it down. This woman needed people to lean on, and not just because of her bad knee and swollen ankle.

I waited a few more minutes, then Bloch approached the car, her arm around Mrs. Dubois. I got out, opened the rear passenger door.

'Mrs. Dubois, my name is Eddie Flynn.'

She released Bloch, took me in a hug. Damn, she was strong.

'Mr. Flynn, Melissa told me you're gonna help save Andy. For that I can't never thank you enough. When Cody went missing, I prayed. I've been praying so hard for so long. I prayed for someone to come help us. Now I got you and Melissa.'

It was unusual to hear anyone calling Bloch by her first name. She didn't use it. She was Bloch to everyone. Maybe she made an exception for women like Mrs. Dubois. She released me from the hug, but kept her hands on my shoulders while she looked at my face.

'God sent you, Mr. Flynn. I know it.'

I didn't tell her it was a corrupt government fixer trying to grow a conscience that had sent me. It just didn't feel like the right time.

'If I'm going to help Andy then I need you, Mrs. Dubois.'

'I'll do anything to get my boy home. Melissa said you saw him, in the cell. How is he? They won't let me talk to him.'

I didn't want to tell her. I couldn't.

'He's holding up, Mrs. Dubois, but we need to get him out.'

'That man, Mr. Korn. There's something cold about him. Something old and bad that hangs around him like a smell. He's evil. He wants to kill my Andy. Said if I made sure Andy plead guilty, he would see to it Andy died asleep, peaceful like. And if I didn't, my boy . . . my boy would suffer somethin' terrible.'

Mrs. Dubois' eyes closed on fresh tears, and she doubled over. Bloch and I got her into the car, and we drove the six miles to Mrs. Dubois' home. On the way I decided the stories about Korn's obsession with the death penalty had more truth than I'd first thought. I also made a pledge – to myself. I wasn't just going to get an acquittal for Andy.

One way or another, Randal Korn was going down.

For good.

CHAPTER FIFTEEN

EDDIE

The one-story timber house that was home to Patricia Dubois lay on the outskirts of Buckstown just off a stretch of two-lane highway. A dirt track led through the old moss-covered trees to a house with a bowed roof. It had a small living space, an even smaller kitchen and a closet that doubled as a second bedroom. The other bedroom wasn't much bigger. There was an outhouse around back, which had a toilet and shower.

Given what she had to work with, Patricia, as she insisted we call her, had given the place a warm and welcoming feeling. Throws covered the old couch. It had three cushions. The one to the far right had collapsed as if there was an invisible person sitting on it. The middle cushion also had a large indentation and I could tell this was where Patricia and Andy sat, together. An old boxy TV perched on a milk crate faced the couch. A blanket covered the milk crate, but not all the way to the bottom. The walls were covered with pictures of Andy. Photos of Andy's first day at school, riding his bike, sitting on his mother's knee, and more from Thanksgiving dinners to birthday parties. There was very little money in this house, but there was more love than most.

'Sit down, make yourselves comfortable,' said Patricia.

Bloch and I took up the couch. With a single lamp lit in the corner, we could just about make out the shape of an old armchair, in which Patricia dumped her apron.

'Y'all like some coffee?'

The thought of it made me feel a little giddy.

'I'd love some, thank you.'

Bloch nodded.

Patricia drew back the curtain that separated the galley kitchen from the living room and busied herself opening cupboards.

'I'm sorry, we out of coffee. Tea okay?'

I hadn't had coffee for almost twenty-four hours, and I wasn't getting any closer. Tea would be fine, for politeness' sake at least.

She came out with two glasses of iced tea. I took the extra sugar, Bloch declined.

Apart from the TV and a sideboard, there were boxes and boxes of old books. Paperbacks, some with their front covers ripped off. Bloch reached into a box on her side of the couch and took out some of the books – romance novels. The box on my side was filled with old detective magazines and dime paperbacks.

'You both like to read. Andy must've gotten the reading bug from you,' I said.

'The TV broke when Andy was eleven. By the time I saved up enough to get us a new one, Andy said he'd rather we spend the money on books. And we did. We sit here at night, and we read. There's nothing good on TV anyhow,' she said.

'When did Andy start working at the truck-stop bar?' I asked.

'Maybe three, four years ago. I wasn't happy about it to begin with, but I spoke to the owner, a nice man, name of Ryan, who told me he would look after my Andy. He did, too. Andy never got no trouble in the bar. He swept the floor, washed glasses, kept the place nice and square. He's a worker, like his momma. He did good, too, and he never let it interfere with his schooling,' she said, unable to stop her pride in Andy from beaming out of her.

'Was he close to Skylar?'

A light that had briefly shone from Patricia's eyes sputtered behind her flickering eyelids, and her brows came together, her lips clamping shut and rolling back to disappear insider her mouth. When she spoke again, her voice was very soft.

'That poor girl. No, he didn't talk about her much. Now and again. He talked about Ryan mostly. And the customers. For a truck-stop bar there were a lot of regulars. This town ain't short on drunks, that's for damn sure.'

'Were they friends? Andy and Skylar?'

'Friendly, I'd say. Not friends. He never met her outside of the job. Not that I know, anyways. But she was good to him. Showed him the ropes at first. Looked after him. Andy can read a novel in a few hours and write a paper on it. But he's not smart in other ways. He doesn't do too well with people. Skylar helped with that, because she was real popular.'

'What did he tell you about Skylar?'

'She was a clever girl. Kindly. I remember him saying they talked about college, and books. That's about it. Andy did mention one time that she'd told him she had some boy trouble.'

'A boyfriend?'

'I think so. She was always talking to some boy on the phone, or texting him when Ryan wasn't looking. The staff weren't supposed to use their phones during their shift. That didn't bother Andy, he didn't have a phone.'

'Do you know the name of this boy? Was it Gary Stroud? That's who she went out with.'

'Yeah, that's him. I'm sorry I can't say more. I didn't know Skylar. I regret that now. I went to—'

She broke off, drew a napkin from her sleeve and dabbed at her eyes with it.

'I went to Skylar's funeral. That man, Mr. Korn, stood beside Skylar's parents the whole time. He was whispering to them, and looking at me. Esther Edwards came over after the service. Everyone looking at me. And you know what she did? She spat in my face. *Right* in my face. Lord, I was so upset. My son didn't kill that girl. I knew it then, I know it now. Aw, I don't blame Esther. She was in pain. I think about what Mr. Korn said, and I remember the look on Esther's face that day. And I know, I'm gonna feel that pain too, when they take Andy away.'

'We'll do our best to make sure that doesn't happen,' I said.

Bloch opened her jacket and drew out the report from Doctor Farnesworth, the pathologist selected by Cody Warren, and placed it in her lap. It was a not-so-subtle hint that I had to get specific information, and we didn't have a lot of time to go softly.

'Did Andy ever wear a ring with a star-shaped pattern on it?' I asked.

'No, Andy never wore rings. I bought him one, once. For his sixteenth birthday. Got it in the pawn shop on Eighth Street. It had two black stones in it. He wore it one day, then said it made his fingers itchy.'

'Could he have had a button, or a badge or something with a star on it?'

'No, Andy's clothes were all plain. What kind of star?'

Bloch turned over a few pages in the report, held it up for me. While we didn't have photographs, there was a good description of the wound.

'A five-pointed star,' I said.

Patricia blessed herself, said, 'Ain't that something to do with devil worship? Andy would never have anything to do with something like that.'

Bloch nodded, satisfied, and let me go on to something else.

'After Andy was arrested, when did you first get to visit with him?' I asked.

'It was in the county jail. He told me he had to tell the sheriff he hurt Skylar or they wouldn't let him out. They told him to sign a piece of paper and then they would let him see me so I could take him home.'

I'd heard of cops leaning on young, frightened suspects. This was not the first time it had happened, and it wouldn't be the last. There was no videotape or audio of Andy's interrogation. The recorder wasn't working, apparently. All we had to go by was the sheriff's word over Andy's that Andy signed the confession of his own free will.

'Andy would have told them anything to get home, Mr. Flynn. He trusted the police. He wasn't smart, not that way. My poor boy, please tell me there's something you can do to help.'

'I'll do my very best, Patricia. Look, there are no guarantees in a trial. I'll do all I can to get Andy an acquittal. I promise you. Just one more thing for now, when did you last see Cody Warren?'

'He came by Quickies, maybe a week ago, said he had found something that could prove Andy was innocent. He didn't tell me what it was, he just said he had to find out a couple more things.

I'm worried about him, too. No one's seen him for days. Do you think . . . ?'

'Do I think something has happened to Cody? Yeah, I do.'

She said, 'I think you're right. And I wouldn't be surprised if the law is behind it. That Sheriff Lomax. He used to be good man. Everyone in the town respected him, and he was good to the poor. Fair, you know. Then this DA came, Korn. And the sheriff's wife got sick. Mrs. Lomax worked in the charity store on Main Street. She was kind. A quiet woman, but you could tell she wanted to help people. The sheriff changed after she got sick. He whupped Andy. When I saw him that day, he was all beat up. My poor son.'

'He'll pay for that,' said Bloch.

'Don't go messing with the sheriff,' said Patricia.

Bloch leaned forward said, 'After what you've told us tonight, I'm coming for him and Korn.'

'You need to be careful. They're dangerous men.'

'That doesn't scare me,' said Bloch.

'How come?'

'Because I'm a dangerous woman.'

CHAPTER SIXTEEN

THE PASTOR

Esther Edwards walked on shaky legs to the kitchen table, coffee slewing over the sides of the cups in her hands. Drops splashed on the dirty tile floor of her kitchen, but she couldn't help it. More spilled with each step. It looked as though those cups weighed twenty pounds. As she set them on the table she mouthed an apology, said it was the meds the doc had given her that made her tremble so. The Pastor nodded, placed his big hand on hers and felt the shakes coursing through her.

It wasn't pain or medication causing her tremors. He smiled up at her and saw the hole behind her eyes. Something had been sucked out of this woman. Life, hope, love, the very meaning of her existence had been torn from her body. That part of her now lay beside her daughter in a cold cheap casket six feet beneath the ground of the old cemetery in Buckstown.

'I saw you at the funeral,' she said, in a cracked voice. 'I'm sorry, I can't remember if we spoke.'

'We spoke,' said the Pastor. 'But don't worry about that. I can't imagine your pain. What you and Francis are going through, it's just terrible.'

Francis lifted the coffee to his lips, but hesitated, then put the cup back down.

'I told Francis I want to help in any way I can. The money we gave to you both, that's just the start. The group I belong to, we are committed to ensuring you and your husband want for nothing in the years ahead.'

She withdrew her hand from his and her eyes, which had been empty, flashed with fear.

'Francis told me about the group. I'm not sure what it is exactly.'

'It's a . . . what did the professor call it? A collective?' asked Francis.

'Something like that. We are group of concerned citizens who have banded together to take certain steps to protect Christian folks in the county,' said the Pastor.

'White folks?' asked Esther.

The Pastor fixed the smile on his lips before he gave it to her and said, 'Yes, white folks. Skylar isn't the only one to have been lost to these people—'

'*These people?* asked Esther. 'We're all people, sir. Ordinary folk, all of us. Not one color better or worse than the other. Our daughter was murdered, and I have nothing but hate for the one who did it, and those who protected him, but we're not prejudiced. It was one man . . .'

'We all know who killed your daughter. We all know what he looks like. This is not an isolated incident, Mrs. Edwards. Esther, if I may—'

'Mrs. Edwards is fine,' she said, straightening up. She wasn't shaking anymore.

'Esther, this man gave us—' said Francis, but didn't get to finish the sentence.

'I know what he gave us,' she said, turning to Francis. 'For that I'm thankful. You know I am, but what he's saying ain't true. It's not right.'

The Pastor felt his phone vibrating in his right-hand jacket pocket. His *other* work phone. The burner that had to be answered immediately.

'I'm afraid I have to go. Duty calls. I'll see myself out, Francis. Maybe you could show Esther, I mean, *Mrs. Edwards*, some of the videos the professor sent to you. They can be enlightening. Thank you for the coffee.'

The Pastor made his way through the hallway, the dust sitting thick on the table bearing the mail with red banners across the envelopes. He knew he could wear Francis down, and money helped. Esther was proving more difficult than anticipated.

As he closed the front door behind him, he heard the beginnings of an argument coming from the kitchen. Their home was one of fifty creole-style one-story houses on the block. Seventy years old, and cheaply built at the time. The Pastor could still hear them as he descended the porch steps.

'*I don't want that man in this house again. He's a racist and—*'

'*He gave us thousands and thousands of dollars, and there's more to come. We need that money and you know what, he might be right—*'

He checked his phone for missed calls, hit dial on the last one.

The number he called was another burner. It was answered immediately. The voice on the other end of the line sounded cold and strange. The accent veered slightly – moved around from rural Alabama to the Upper East Side of Manhattan.

'You didn't pick up. Something wrong?' asked Randal Korn.

'Nothing you need to worry about. What's the emergency?' asked the Pastor.

'Andy Dubois' new lawyer paid a visit to Cody Warren's office today. He was in there for half an hour.'

The Pastor reached his black SUV, popped open the car, got inside and closed the door.

'Are you concerned?'

'His partner, Harry Ford, went in later and came out with a thin binder of documents.'

'Farnesworth's autopsy report?'

'That's my suspicion.'

The Pastor's teeth ground together, squeaking under the strain. Korn had sought advice from the Pastor about the case and the difficulties presented by the injuries found on Skylar Edwards's body. This amused the Pastor. The symmetry of it all. Korn didn't know, and couldn't know, that the Pastor himself had murdered Skylar Edwards. And he wanted to keep it that way. So he had given advice on how best to deal with the problems created for the prosecutor by the autopsy.

The Pastor's advice had been to remove the defense attorney and his secretary, and threaten Doctor Farnesworth. He could not take the chance that a lawyer might discover the true killer. It was in both their interests that Andy Dubois receive a swift and clear conviction. Korn would get another body to burn in that chair, and the Pastor would have a black man convicted of killing a white girl, just as he had planned.

'At least they won't have the photographs. That's one good thing, but remember Randal, I told you Betty Maguire should've disappeared along with Cody Warren. It would've been a more convincing story. They're both about the same age, both single. They elope in the night with client money. Tell me again why that didn't happen . . .' said the Pastor.

'I'm not a trigger man. You know that. And it took all my powers of persuasion to get Lomax to deal with Warren. He wouldn't kill a woman. It's not in him,' said Korn.

'I remember you telling me that, and I remember saying I would take care of it. Betty has seen those photographs. She could describe them to Dubois' lawyers. We can't take any more chances with this case. Betty has to—'

'No, I don't want that. It could distract the media from the trial.'

'That won't happen. Leave it to me.'

'What are you going to do?'

'I'm going to have a little talk with Betty and make sure Flynn doesn't get any more help. This is important. Dubois has to die for what he did. There are only two sides in this. Those who stand for justice, and the ones who would tear down our courts and set the murderers free. *You* told me that, Randal.'

Korn sighed, said, 'Just be careful. The trial is so close now.'

'I won't do anything to damage the trial. I know how important it is to you, and to all of us.'

As the Pastor hung up the call, he wondered for a second what Korn would do if he knew for a fact that Dubois was innocent. The answer was obvious. Korn didn't care about justice. He only cared about power. The Pastor knew Korn well enough to understand his appetites – that it didn't matter who was strapped into Yellow Mama after the trial. The Pastor had sought out the DA some years ago. His record spoke for itself, but it wasn't until they met that the Pastor realized he had found a true kindred spirit.

Korn was a monster – a terrible angel. Just like him. He sometimes wondered if he hadn't sought out the prosecutor, would Korn have found him anyway? He knew his own kind – those who were unburdened by conscience, who were held to a higher morality. God kills millions and a follower had to be prepared to kill in his name. For the cause. For the purity of his country. At times, while the Pastor lay alone in the dark, he wondered what he would've become if his father had not given him these gifts. Monsters were not born, they were created. The Pastor realized that it was God working through his father's quick, rough hands. He was suffering for his god. And he would answer the call.

The Pastor knew Korn's father had passed down his gifts to his son. Korn senior had been a legend on Wall Street not for the vastness of his wealth – but for what he was willing to do to his enemies. For a man who was so rich, money meant nothing. Power meant everything. And that taste for power had passed to the son along with the will and strength to use it.

He recalled one of their meetings, in Korn's home in Buckstown some years ago, while they sipped lemonade on his back porch and looked out at a frenzy of starlings barreling through the dying light, swooping black Rorschach patterns against a violet sky.

'Why do you kill them all?' asked the Pastor.

'It's what the law demands,' said Korn, without hesitation.

The Pastor laughed, but there was no mirth in the sound.

'You and I both know that's not true. You can keep the facade for Lomax and the others, but you don't fool me. You don't care about justice.'

'I suppose not. There are no innocents. Not really. What matters is order.'

'Order doesn't cut it. I know you've executed innocent men. So drop the act. Tell me why you do it.'

Korn put down his lemonade and stared at the birds.

'You know, no one understands why the starlings fly together like that. Maybe it's to do with defending themselves from predators, or they're feasting on a cloud of flies – all good reasons why they would group together, but nobody knows how they turn simultaneously, as one mass, like they're telepathically linked.'

'Are you saying you don't know why you do it?'

'All I know is when I look at those birds, they seem happy. Does it matter why something feels good?'

'I suppose not. Is that why you do it? Because it feels good?'

Korn stood, tall and in the shadows of the early evening.

'It doesn't just feel good. That's too cheap. Watching a man die, knowing that I put him there and I orchestrated his death, well, that's beyond words. It's beyond good. It makes me feel like I'm burning with life and power.'

'I know that feeling,' said the Pastor.

'Your little group could get you into a lot of trouble. The FBI are watching right-wing extremists. It's going to be their priority once they deal with the threat of foreign terrorists,' said Korn.

'No one knows I'm involved. No one that I don't trust, anyway. I know you don't share our vision, but our goals are the same.'

'To create fear,' said Korn.

'A white majority county fearful of a small black community is a weapon that can be used. People who are in fear will do almost anything, and they'll listen to those who would save them. It's easier to get a death penalty when a jury is afraid of the defendant.'

Korn nodded, said, 'I could use someone like you. Lomax isn't going to be around forever, and there are certain jobs he is either unwilling or unsuited to perform. I know you have the courage to do whatever needs to be done.'

The Pastor raised his glass in a toast and said, 'Here's to our mutual benefit.'

And so an alliance was formed. It was that alliance that led to the phone call tonight. And the warning. It was in both their interests that Andy Dubois be convicted at trial. Nothing could be allowed to interfere with that process.

For the Pastor, the reckoning was mere days away.

The Pastor turned over the engine and accelerated away from Francis Edward's home. He soon found himself on Main Street. The lights in Cody Warren's office were still burning. He sat in the car, watching and waiting for Betty Maguire to leave.

He didn't have to wait long.

He watched her lock the front door and get into a ten-year-old Volvo that had been parked out front. The engine came to life, and the lights flared, and the Volvo took off. The Pastor followed at a distance. Betty lived alone, just outside of town. He waited until she got onto that lonely stretch of two-lane highway, surrounded by willows that trailed Spanish moss overhead like a soft canopy. The Pastor put on his siren and flashed the red and blue lights built into the dash of his SUV.

Betty pulled over and the Pastor stopped behind her. He took his time before getting out of the car. Letting her wait. Permitting the anxiety to build. Betty didn't trust law enforcement. For good reason.

He took a flashlight from the glove box, approached the driver's side of Betty's car. He stood just a little behind the window. Force of habit. On a traffic stop the officer waits at the rear door, never puts their body in front of the driver's window – less of a target that way and they have a killing angle if the driver pulls a gun.

The Pastor tapped Betty's window. His teeth ground together, his jaw tightening in anticipation as she buzzed her window down. He leaned forward and shone the flashlight into her face.

'What's the problem? I was under the speed limit you—'

Betty's words died in her throat as the heavy Maglite smashed into the side of her head.

CHAPTER SEVENTEEN

EDDIE

Kate and Bloch took the larger room at The Chanterelle. Harry and I took the double bed in the next room and we slept head to toe, but Harry did most of the sleeping. He could damn well sleep anywhere.

I gave it an hour then got up and read the files again. When I take on a case, I must know the evidence and statements like I know my own hand. It has to be imprinted on my mind, otherwise I can't shape it, use it, or know when something comes up during testimony that doesn't fit with the evidence in the case already. It wasn't burned into my brain yet, but I was getting there.

I looked again at Andy's confession.

'My name is Andy Dubois and I give this confession of my own free will and without incentive or coercion. On the night of the fourteenth of May I was working in Hogg's Bar, at the Union Highway Truck Stop. My shift finished at twelve midnight, and I followed a fellow employee, Skylar Edwards, into the lot. I know Skylar. We have worked together for a while. She is pretty and I liked her. I wanted to kiss Skylar, but she pushed me away. I grabbed a hold of her and squeezed. She struggled and I made sure she stayed quiet. I didn't mean to hurt her. She stopped struggling and I squeezed harder. Afterward I felt real bad. There's a stretch of marshland beyond the parking lot, and I took her there and buried her so no one would find her.

That was it. Having spent all of fifteen minutes with Andy, I knew these were not his words. Nobody talks like that, and certainly not a young man. The statement had been typed up, and signed by Andy. The signature was very carefully written, the pen leaning on the page.

To say that the Sheriff's Department and the DA had railroaded this kid into a false confession was an understatement. He'd been beaten, threatened, his mother threatened. Not only that, but the real killer of Skylar Edwards was still out there somewhere.

I spent an hour on the internet doing an image search on rings with five-pointed stars on them. There weren't that many. The markings weren't mentioned at all in the county medical examiner's autopsy report. That made those marks important. The ME is supposed to be impartial, but with a prosecutor like Korn I expected there to be some things added to the report to help his case, or maybe things taken out that weren't so helpful.

I turned off the light, tried to sleep.

Images flashed through my mind. Andy. His mother. A young woman beaten and strangled and stuffed headfirst into a deep, narrow hole in the ground.

I got up, found the plastic bag containing my property, which had been returned to me at the courthouse. There were only two important things. Two necklaces. One was a Saint Christopher's medal that had its own story. The other was a gold chain with a crucifix that belonged to an investigator, Harper. My finger and thumb worked the worn gold of the cross around my neck. She'd died working one of my cases. It was still raw to think about her. That wound would never heal. She died without knowing that I loved her. I should've told her. I should've protected her. I looked over at Harry, his mouth open, his snores filling the room. I thought about him, and Kate and Bloch next door.

They knew the risks, but it didn't make me feel any better. The whole goddamn town hated us. I had put them in danger, but I felt that for now I was able to manage it. If things got hotter I would send Kate and Bloch away with Harry.

I couldn't bear it if something happened to them because of me.

My teeth ground together.

I wasn't going to abandon Andy no matter what happened.

THE THIRD DAY

CHAPTER EIGHTEEN

EDDIE

Kate shook me awake at eight that morning. She was already show-ered and dressed in a suit. Sneakers on her feet and two-inch heels in her hand.

'Priorities today: we file a change of venue motion for Andy, motion to suppress his confession and we get him bail. He's not going to get a fair trial in this town, and the longer he's in that cell the easier it is for the sheriff to lean on him.'

'Agreed. How about breakfast first?'

'Harry told me what happened in the diner yesterday. Maybe we can get breakfast and do a little work there?' she said.

Kate showed me a voice-recording app on her phone, and a wicked smile.

'Kate, you're a good lawyer, but you're spending far too much time with me,' I said.

I looked around, getting my bearings. I was still in a shit hotel room, in a shit town, with a bad case, and about to piss off a whole bunch of people who might want to kill me for it.

I showered, changed into a fresh shirt, fresh suit and felt better. The shampoo in the bathroom smelled of lavender, but that was better than smelling of dried blood. We were out the door early and drove to the diner where Harry and I had been barred the previous morning by the owner, Gus.

We got out of Kate's rental car, and I followed behind. Bloch leading the way. The same faces as yesterday seemed to be around, sitting in the same places, maybe eating the same food.

We followed Bloch to a booth at the window. She wanted to be seen, I guessed.

Kate and Harry sat by glass, Bloch beside Kate, at the outside, ready to step up, and I slipped in beside Harry.

Gus, the same guy in the greasy apron who refused to serve us the day before, came over, his face flushed and shiny with sweat.

'I thought I told you yesterday, we don't serve the likes of you in here. This is a Christian diner. Skylar Edwards used to drink milkshakes right at my counter. I'll be damned if I'm gonna serve you. Now, y'all get out before I call the sheriff.'

Bloch stood up, slowly. The guy was tall, but Bloch met him eye to eye. He folded his arms across his thick chest.

'What happened to Southern hospitality?' said Bloch.

'I'll show you some other things we do in the South, if you don't leave,' said Gus.

Bloch smiled. Cracked her neck.

The guy didn't look as confident all of a sudden.

'You got five seconds, or I'll call the sheriff.'

'Go ahead,' said Bloch.

Gus backed away, unable to compute what was happening. He didn't seem the type of guy who had ever been intimidated by a woman before, and he wasn't totally sure how to handle it. Reaching behind the counter, he picked up a cordless phone, made a call.

Bloch sat back down.

Kate took out her cell phone, activated a voice-recording app and hid the phone under the table.

Harry and I leaned back, looked out the window and waited for the Sheriff's Department cruiser to roll up. It didn't take long. Four minutes at most. Pretty good response time. The two deputies who got out looked first at us, through the window, and then opened up the cruiser and took out their batons. One of them was the moustache I'd punched in the balls the day before – Deputy Leonard. His pal was much bigger, and clean-shaven. He had mean little black eyes that looked too small for his head. Veins stood out on his arms like worms crawling over tan leather.

They came in and went straight to Gus. Two big guys in checkered shirts, ball caps, jeans and a strong sense of civic duty stood up from their half-finished plates and kept their hands loose at their sides. I figured they might try to give law enforcement some back-up kicking our asses onto the street.

The cops came over with the owner.

The big cop beside him had rank. His nametag read 'Shipley, Chief Deputy'.

Shipley stood a ways behind Leonard, watching how his deputy would handle things. Both of them wore black, short-sleeved uniformed shirts. Shipley's was open at the collar and I saw a thick crucifix sitting at his throat. He kept his nightstick low, but I could tell from the white knuckles on that hand he was holding the stick tightly – ready to crack heads at the first excuse.

'Gus here asked you to leave. No one wants you in this town. I'd take the hint, Flynn,' said Leonard. He raised the nightstick, slapped the working end into his palm.

'You should be careful swinging that stick. You might hit yourself in the balls with it,' I said.

'Come on, let's keep this civilized,' said Shipley.

'Why is it we're not welcome?' asked Harry.

'You're acting for that murderer, Andy Dubois. Skylar was a ray of light in this town. We don't want scum like you here. You're not welcome,' said Gus, peeking over Leonard's shoulder.

'But Andy Dubois is innocent until proven guilty. And we intend to make sure it stays that way,' I said.

'He's not innocent,' said Leonard. 'Everyone in this town knows he's as guilty as sin. You folks might want to stay someplace else. Eat someplace else, too. You're not welcome here,' said Leonard.

I glanced at Kate. She was smiling as she said, 'Thank you, Officer.'

Kate took her phone out from below the table. Stopped the recording, played it back to make sure the sound was okay. It was fine.

'That's all we need to file a motion to change the venue for trial. You said it yourself, Officer. Everyone in this town thinks our client is guilty. We'll have to move it someplace else,' said Kate.

Leonard's mouth fell open, but he quickly tried to make up for his mistake by leaning over the table and making a grab for the phone. Kate put it away and his hand took nothing but dead air.

Bloch stood up and both deputies moved back, sticks at the ready. Harry and I followed Kate out of the diner. I stayed at the front door, holding it open for Bloch.

'If I were you, I would get out of town as fast as possible,' said Leonard, pointing the baton at Bloch's smiling face. He took a step forward, fast, drew the baton back over his shoulder, his eyes wide, lips curled into a snarl.

He swung it directly at Bloch's head.

Bloch didn't move. Her eyes locked on him.

The baton froze in mid-air, two inches from the side of Bloch's skull. She was still smiling. She was a statue. No flinching, not even instinctively. If that had been me I would've started to duck at the upswing. Bloch knew he wouldn't hit her. She was psyching him out. Telling the cops they didn't scare her.

Nothing scared Bloch.

Leonard's scowl fell away into surprise. He dropped the baton to his side, looked around to see if anyone was as shocked as he was.

Shipley was a block of ice. He hadn't moved. Hadn't reacted to Leonard's attempt to frighten Bloch. She saw it too. She ignored Leonard, and locked eyes with Shipley. They stood like that for a time, unmoving.

When she was satisfied, Bloch turned away from Shipley and came toward me. I was still holding the door open as she strode past.

'You're such a badass,' I said.

Bloch winked.

Back in the car, with the doors closed, I saw Shipley staring at us as we drove away.

'Leonard is a pussy. A coward, but dangerous with it,' said Bloch. 'Shipley is different. There's a seam of steel running through that guy, and something else.'

'What?' I asked.

'I don't know yet, but it's not just his size. There's something bad inside of that cop. He didn't want to hit me. He wanted to kill me.'

'You do make quite the first impression,' I said.

'It's not me. Did you see Shipley's eyes? They're not just cold. They're dead. Something inside of him is broken. We need to be careful.'

We got back in the car and headed out on the road to find a rest stop, out of town, on Union Highway, where we could take a look at the crime scene once I'd injected coffee into my veins.

CHAPTER NINETEEN

EDDIE

A stack of pancakes with syrup and bacon from a diner on the highway filled me up. I ate it so fast I hardly tasted it. The coffee on the other hand was so bitter and burned that I couldn't drink it. Since I quit drinking alcohol every night, I had to replace it with something. Coffee worked just fine as long as I could get it into my system fast and often. I was beginning to wonder if I'd been subjected to some kind of curse where I was destined never to drink coffee again. I put the coffee aside.

Two Cokes with breakfast eased the caffeine-withdrawal headache.

Kate sat with a laptop in front of her on the table, her dishes already cleared.

'I'm just finishing off the bail motion. Change of venue and motion to suppress the confession is done and waiting. Why don't you three go look at the crime scene. I'll meet you outside when I'm done.'

She had earbuds plugged into her phone, and she was transcribing the statement of Deputy Leonard. This morning's little plan had worked well.

We paid, went outside and Bloch immediately made for Hogg's Bar. The truck stop was really a gas station, post office and diner in a one-story strip mall. A little apart from the strip was a separate low building with a neon pig on the roof, and 'Hogg's Bar' on a faded, painted sign above the door. I pushed the door, but it wasn't open. Too damn early, even for truckers.

All the buildings faced the highway, which was about a hundred meters away. There were huge rigs and semi-trucks parked both in front of the buildings and in the gravel lot behind them. The lot was the size of a football field. I guessed the truck stop and bar were popular. Or at least they were once. The remnants of chicken-wire fence surrounded the area, with trees and wild land beyond. Most of the fence had fallen or rusted away. The body of Skylar Edwards had been found in that area, around twenty feet from the fence. Buried upside down, with her feet exposed.

Bloch went around to the front of the bar; she wanted to trace the steps Skylar might have taken on that night. There was one lamp pole, high and halfway between the bar and the highway. There were no lights in the parking area behind the bar. No security cameras around the bar's entrance. None on the lamp pole. We walked around back.

There was a sign just behind the bar that read 'staff parking'.

'Skylar usually called her father for a ride home,' said Bloch.

'She didn't call her father,' said Harry.

'We need her—'

I was about to say phone, then stopped. I remembered the description of the items found on Skylar or buried with her. The list came back to me, instantly – a purse, some cash, two ATM cards, a library card, gum, make-up . . .

No phone.

'The sheriff doesn't have her phone. It wasn't in her possessions when her body was found. It's missing,' I said.

'Maybe she left her phone at home,' said Harry.

I shook my head. 'She was a young girl, and at that age her phone goes with her everywhere. Plus, there's a statement from her boyfriend's sister, Tori. They talked that night. Tori told her Gary was going to propose.'

'So the cops have her phone?'

'I don't think so. They would've logged it at the scene. Even if they were going to pin this on somebody, they wouldn't have known to get rid of her phone at that time. They would just have logged it, maybe tried to hide it later. Or wiped it accidentally. No, the cops didn't log her phone in her possessions because it wasn't there. The killer took it.'

The rear of the bar had one window, with a neon Miller sign. It wouldn't give much light to this place. Four trucks were parked at the back, probably more on the night of the murder. Bloch strode to the area where Skylar's body had been found. Stopped. Looked back at the bar.

'How far between the rear of the building and where she was found?' I asked.

'Ninety-five yards,' said Bloch. Not ninety. Not one hundred. Ninety-five.

The trucks parked up that morning looked empty, but there could have been guys inside the cabs, getting in their mandatory rest period.

At night, this area would be almost pitch black. Depending on the moon, of course.

Bloch let out a high-pitched scream.

Within ten seconds a guy opened the door of his cab, looked out, asked if everything was okay. Bloch nodded. He went back inside, just as another guy got out to make the same check.

'There could have been music blasting from the bar, but I'd say it would be low volume out here,' I said.

Bloch nodded.

'The injuries to her face indicate that at one stage the attacker only had hold of her with one hand. She had bruising on her arms, two broken fingers. This is the last place she was seen, and she was buried here,' said Harry.

Bloch nodded.

'We know that, but there's a lot we don't know. I think someone might have heard her cry out. Unless she was taken somewhere else, and then her body brought back here,' said Bloch.

'What about her other injuries?' I said. 'We know cause of death was strangulation, but there were ligature marks on her hands and wrists, and she had sunburn over the front of her body. Then she was buried headfirst in a narrow grave. She disappeared the night of the fourteenth of May, going into the fifteenth. Ted Buxton found her the night of the fifteenth. What happened in those twenty-four hours? Was she grabbed in the lot, taken into the brush and murdered? Or was she held somewhere else, maybe outside? And then killed and brought back here to be buried? I don't get it.'

'You're forgetting the marks on her forehead,' said Harry. 'A star-shaped mark from a ring.'

'That was deliberate,' said Bloch.

'What was deliberate?' I asked.

'The bruising on her arms, the broken fingers, all during a struggle, I'd say. He didn't leave marks from the ring anywhere else on her body apart from her head. I think those marks were deliberate,' she said.

We started forward, over the old fence, through the tall grass to an area where the grass had been dug over to retrieve her body. It was about twelve feet across, by ten feet wide. The soil was black and sticky, like clay, but much wetter. Even the boiling sun above us couldn't cut through this humidity. We were all coated in sweat.

'The method of burial is unusual. You could get a shallow grave out of this soil relatively quickly. Why dig down so deep? You'd need to use a hoe, or a pick. It would take way longer,' I said.

'Her feet,' said Bloch.

'What?'

'He wanted her feet exposed.'

'Why?'

'I have no idea,' she said.

Harry took a step back, and I heard a faint splash and the sound of a retired judge swearing, loudly. There was mud from a puddle splashed up the sides of Harry's pants. But he wasn't looking at his pants, and he'd stopped swearing now. Instead, Harry was gazing at the puddle.

The water in the puddle swirled, catching the sun. It was like a star caught in the murky water.

'The soles of her feet weren't sunburned,' said Harry.

'Maybe she was buried after sundown on the fifteenth, maybe only a couple of hours before Ted Buxton found her?'

'It's not just that. Something else would've been shining on her feet,' he said.

He had a strange look on his face. I'd known Harry Ford for a long time. We've been through a lot together. I'd never seen him like this. His eyes were wide, and he looked down, then up at the sky, and then they searched the grass and our faces. His lips trembled and he raised his fingers to them.

'Harry, are you alright? You look . . . scared,' I said.

'The marks on her forehead – the stars. They're a crown. The sunburn, buried upside down – Jesus, it all fits,' he said.

'Fits what?' I asked.

At first, he didn't answer, he closed his eyes, and his lips moved silently, like he was searching for something deep in his memory, trying to get it right. When he spoke again, his tone was low, and his voice trembled with every word.

'And a great sign appeared in heaven: a woman clothed with the sun, with the moon under her feet, and a crown of stars upon her head . . . and there appeared another wonder in heaven: behold a great red dragon, with seven heads, and ten horns, and seven crowns upon its head . . .'

Bloch and I exchanged a look.

'I spent ten years in the back of my father's station wagon as he preached all over this state, reading his Bible to pass the time,' said Harry. 'We're looking for the dragon. That's who did this to her – the great beast of Revelations 12.'

'Like a demon?' I asked.

Harry straightened his back, set his jaw and said, 'No, it's the devil himself.'

CHAPTER TWENTY

EDDIE

Bloch stared at the gas station. Started walking toward it. We followed.

We had been outside for fifteen minutes, no more. The back of my shirt had soaked through, Harry's too. There was a fine sheen of sweat on Bloch's forehead, but she was still wearing her navy blazer and white tee beneath it. She wouldn't even let the sun mess with her. Standing at the gas pumps, in the shade, Bloch looked at the four cameras located in the canopy ceiling.

Harry and I went inside. The air-conditioned Circle K was heaven. Well, almost. Their coffee machine was working, but I was too hot for coffee. I got four sodas, four bottles of water from the fridge and took them to the counter.

The kid behind the counter wore a Metallica tee and a smile that he had learned to wear long ago and couldn't really remember how to replicate.

'Anything else I can get y'all?' he asked.

'Sure, do your cameras cover any of the lot behind the bar?' I asked.

'Uuuhhh,' said the kid.

'We're investigators. You know, the murder that happened in the lot?'

I didn't tell him we were acting for the defendant, nor did I say we were acting for the prosecution.

'Oh, yeah, sure. Terrible thing,' he said.

'Can we take a look at your recordings for that night?' I asked.

'Uuuhhhh,' he said, as if he was both confused and in pain.

'It won't take long,' I said.

'Are you with the Sheriff's Department or something?'

'Something,' I said.

'Uuuuh sure,' he said.

He opened the countertop to let me through. I knocked on the window, alerting Bloch. Harry followed me, but said nothing. There was no mention of security-camera footage in the discovery from the prosecution. There was always a chance of law enforcement overlooking something important, either through incompetence or lack of organization.

I asked the kid his name and he said Damien Green. He was twenty-one years old and his IQ wasn't much higher, but he was being helpful, which was all that mattered.

In the back office was a small safe, stacks of mail-order catalogs on a desk above it and a floor plan of the store on the wall. On the other side of the room was another desk with a computer with two screens, each screen split into four separate views from different cameras. Most of them covering the pumps. There was a camera that showed the entrance lane to the gas station, and another showing the exit. I took a moment to study the views shown by each camera.

'Northwest corner. Screen two, bottom right,' said Bloch, from behind me.

The kid turned and said, 'Do you have any ID?'

'Yes,' said Bloch.

She didn't reach for it. She didn't offer to show it.

'Okay,' said Damien, nodding. He didn't ask again.

I looked back to the second screen. Bottom-left corner. Sure enough. This was the pump closest to the bar, and it showed, in the distance, a side view of the building, which took in the front doors, and back lot for at least the length of the parking lot.

'Do you have the recording for the night of the fourteenth of May?' I asked. 'The night Skylar Edwards was killed?'

'I think so.'

He sat down at the computer, opened a search box and brought up a list of dates and numbers in small type.

'Got it. Do you want to see it?'

'Sure,' I said.

He clicked on one of the list dates. A dialog box popped open. *Cannot Find File.*

Damien tried a couple more times, with the same result. Then he clicked on the file above, May fifteenth, and it could not be found. Both the thirteenth and the sixteenth were available.

'Has someone wiped the file?' I asked.

'Maybe. I don't know. Could be accidental,' said Damien.

'That would be a hell of a coincidence,' said Harry.

'Not really,' said Damien. 'It could've happened when the Sheriff's Department downloaded the footage onto a pen drive.'

CHAPTER TWENTY-ONE

KORN

Tom Wingfield almost took off the door to Korn's office as he came in, his face set in determination and his fist full of paper. Korn rose to his feet, took the pages handed to him and started to read.

'Motions from Flynn. They want bail, Dubois' confession tossed, a change of venue and discovery. Look at the discovery motion. They're saying we held back security footage and now they want it. The judge has set a hearing for three p.m. this afternoon.'

Korn nodded, skim-read the pages. It was almost noon.

His jaw muscle worked up and down, while his eyes flicked side to side.

'Lomax's deputies have given us a problem,' he said. 'Did you see any security-camera footage from the gas station?'

Tom shook his head, said, 'No, I did not.'

'Neither did I. It doesn't read like this kid from the gas station, Damien Green, is lying now, does it?'

'I can't see that he has any skin in the game. Maybe Flynn paid him off or something?'

'I doubt it. Damien doesn't know which deputy took the footage and erased the original – only that they were wearing a uniform. If Flynn was paying for testimony, he'd get the clerk to be more specific.'

'Should I call Lomax?' asked Tom.

'No, I'll handle the sheriff myself. We don't have the footage, so that's the end of it as far the judge is concerned. And there's no point in worrying about Dubois making bail – the family have no money for a bond. There's zero chance of the judge excluding the confession. We don't need to worry about those. No, the major issue is the change of venue motion. Deputy Leonard is on tape practically admitting Dubois can't get a fair trial in Buckstown.'

Tom shuffled his feet, and Korn noticed him playing with a gold ring on his right hand, middle finger. He was fidgeting, twirling it around.

'You were on the force in Buckstown before you transferred here – which one of the deputies took the security footage, and why would they do that?'

'I've no clue,' said Tom.

Grunting, Korn tossed the pages on his desk, turned his back on Tom. Korn leaned over, put his hands on his thighs, hung his head. He squeezed the muscles just above his knee, his lips trembled with the pain.

· He stood up straight, quite suddenly, picked up his cell phone from the desk and dialed the governor's number. His phone was off. He checked his watch.

'I don't have time to drive to Montgomery to see the governor and get back here for three o'clock. Tell the girls outside to keep trying the Governor's Office until someone answers the damn phone.'

'But the governor's not in Montgomery. He's outside of town, at the chemical plant. They're trying to renegotiate their deal with the bank and Patchett is there to try and help them extend their credit,' said Tom.

Whipping his suit jacket from the hanger in the corner, Korn slid his arms through the sleeves and flipped the jacket over his head as he walked out of the office, Tom following.

'Call the plant, tell them I need five minutes with the governor. Then call the TV news channels, the radio stations and the newspapers. Tell them there will be a press conference outside the plant at one o'clock.'

'Any idea what news channels, radio and newspapers you'd like me to contact?'

'All of them,' said Korn. 'Statewide, national if you can get them.'

'What shall I say the press conference is about?'

'Don't say anything yet. Just tell them it's big and it's juicy and they had better be there or I will not forget it.'

Ten minutes later Korn was behind the wheel of his Jaguar on the open road. He'd connected his burner cell phone to the car's Bluetooth, and he was waiting for the sheriff to pick up his own burner. They each had one for emergencies.

'Where's the fire?' said Lomax, answering the call.

'In your department, it seems. Leonard and Shipley had a run-in with Flynn and his team this morning. They've got Leonard on a digital voice recording saying the whole town knows Dubois is guilty. They've filed for a change of venue,' said Korn.

Lomax sighed, said, 'Leonard is dumber than shit. It could've been worse. Shipley has a dark streak. He's on a tight leash, but he can bite if he's provoked.'

'That's not all. Seems a clerk in the gas station on Union Highway has sworn an affidavit to say a deputy from Buckstown took security-camera footage of the forecourt on the night of the murder and the next day, and then deleted the original file. It's the first I've heard of it.'

'Me too. I'll ask around, see if any of the boys remember anything. You worried this might give us another suspect?'

'I don't care if the footage clears Dubois completely. I don't want to know what's on it, I just want to know where it is so I can be sure it doesn't surface and torpedo my case.'

'Like I said, I'll ask around.'

'Be sure to let me know how that goes. Couple of other things. He's applied for bail, but Dubois doesn't have the resources to make the bond. When he goes back to his cell tonight, after the hearing, make sure he knows not to talk to those lawyers. Put someone in the cell with him. Somebody good. I don't want him injured so badly that it delays the trial. It's just a message.'

'And how would you like that message delivered?' asked Lomax.

'Slowly. Maybe just break his fingers. Knuckle by knuckle. His feet too.'

'I'll see to it. Is that all?'

'Oh no, that's just the beginning. Flynn needs to get the message too,' said Korn.

'What do you have in mind?' asked Lomax.

Korn talked some more then finished the call, pulled into the visitor's lot at the chemical plant and made his way to the front of the building. It was a big plant, covered in aluminum siding, which made it cold in the winter and hotter than all hell in the summer. The front entrance was glass, with double doors and a single receptionist behind an old computer.

She saw Korn coming, picked up the phone from her desk.

Korn took shelter from the heat in the air-conditioned waiting area. A black tiled floor that must've been hell to clean, and black leather couches. He remained standing, watching the staircase just beyond the reception desk. After a few minutes he saw hand-made Italian leather shoes descending those stairs. The shoes led to a well-cut suit, blue pinstripe, over a white shirt and a dark, power-red tie the same color as fresh blood. The man in the shirt and tie, suit and shoes, was Chris Patchett, the state governor. He wore his hair a little longer than it should have been, and the thick black mop in a side parting was tinged with gray hairs here and there, at the sides especially. A job like his will do that for you.

'Randal, what's this I hear about a press conference? We don't have an agreement between the company and the bank yet, but I appreciate your confidence in my abilities,' he said.

The two of them shook hands, stepped out of earshot of the receptionist.

'This is not about the chemical plant. I need a favor,' said Korn.

'You know me, I've always got your back. I'm big on justice – it always carries five points in any election. What exactly am I to say to the press?'

Just as Patchett spoke, Korn noticed the first press van arriving. A mobile news van, with the channel's logo on the side and a satellite dish on the roof.

'You're a clever man, Governor. Much smarter than some in the party give you credit for, and you will survive the fallout from this very easily. If anything, I'd say your approval rating will skyrocket with your base. But let's be clear, today I don't want you to be smart. Today I'd like you to say something really stupid.'

CHAPTER TWENTY-TWO

EDDIE

Law is a slow game most of the time. Occasionally, you just have to haul ass.

Harry recorded an affidavit from the gas station clerk, Damien Green. He was honest, and that's a rarer quality these days than it used to be.

Kate worked the paper. She filed emergency motions for bail, change of venue to take the trial out of Buckstown, a motion to suppress Andy's forced confession and a motion for discovery – we wanted that gas station footage.

Harry and I read over the paperwork prepared by Kate, but there was no more to add and nothing to change. She did it better than I could. Kate had a clear, even tone when writing motion briefs. She used the incontrovertible facts as the basis of her arguments, and there's very little anyone can do to counter facts – in a court-room at least.

The motions were emailed to the court, and the prosecutor, and while we were headed back to the hotel in the car, Kate got a call to say the judge would hear all the motions today at three o'clock.

We had time, but very little.

A shower and a change of clothes for me. Kate was still good from that morning. We drove to the courthouse in the SUV.

As we reached the courthouse, I noticed a crowd outside. Men in combat fatigues, thick black vests over their torsos, ball caps and either AR-15s slung on their shoulders or handguns strapped to their belts. A few had American flags, and there were two, maybe three of them holding placards. Around a dozen of them in total, standing at the bottom of the courthouse steps.

'Don't stop outside the court,' I said to Bloch. 'Park around back and we'll see if there's another entrance.'

Bloch sped up, past the crowd and took the long way round, to the lot at the back of the courthouse. We got out of the car, into the sun and the heat rising off the asphalt as if it were hot coals. There was no rear entrance to the building, other than a fire door that hadn't been opened in a long time.

'How did they know about the hearing? You think Korn tipped them off?' asked Harry.

'Maybe he told Skylar's father and he organized this,' I said.

'Are they allowed to carry assault rifles in public?' asked Kate.

'Welcome to the South,' said Harry. 'You can carry a fully loaded machine gun, but you can't carry an open can of beer.'

We walked around front. I led, Bloch at the rear. Harry and Kate in the middle. Single file. It didn't take long for the crowd to spot us.

They recognized me straight away. I saw two in the front pointing at us.

I looked around.

No court security outside.

The leader separated from the group, stood right in our path. No way to get around him and into the court building. He had a grey goatee beard, a combat vest stretched over his American Eagle tee-shirt and a red ball cap with a political slogan, now worn away, covered his bald head. An AR-15 cradled in his hands. His index finger stretched above the trigger. He didn't say anything. He just stood there with his small, bright eyes fixed on mine.

A young man came forward, through the crowd, and stood beside him. He was in his early twenties, blond hair, blue eyes. Good-looking kid, built like a quarterback. He wore blue jeans and a Nike shirt, and unlike the others he wasn't armed.

'Tell him who you are, Gary,' said a voice from the back.

The young man turned at the sound of his name. I guessed this was Gary Stroud, Skylar Edwards's boyfriend.

'Don't let these bastards through,' said Gary to the guy in front of me with the goatee and the rifle.

I turned sideways, trying to slide past him, but he moved to his right, Gary stepping with him, in unison, to block my way. I kept walking. I got right into the man's face, and he used the rifle, held across his stomach, to push me back.

Bloch came around beside me, her right arm bent, fingers open. She had a cannon strapped to her waist. A Magnum 500 that could blow a hole big enough in the guy for me to walk through.

The men behind him moved closer. They were beginning to focus their attention on Harry.

'I'll make you a deal,' I said to the man with the goatee.

I took his wallet out of my pocket, flipped it open and removed his driver's license. I'd dipped the wallet when he bumped into me. It's a force of habit. Easiest way to perform a pocket dip and avoid that contact being noticed is to have physical contact on some other part of the body. It's a distraction, physical and psychological.

'Brian Denvir, of 224 Calabasas Road. Says here you're fifty, but you don't look a day over seventy,' I said.

The realization took a while. These guys didn't look too sharp, and I was sad to say that was probably true. Slowly, he recognized the wallet in my hand.

'Son of a bitch, that's my wallet,' he said, hooking his finger around the trigger of the rifle.

'Pleased to meet you, Brian,' I said, counting the bills in the back of the wallet.

'You've got forty-three dollars and a Pets R Us loyalty card. That's a party. Why don't you go buy a hamster to play with? You could call it David Duke, put a little white dress on it then cram it up your ass.'

His face creased into a snarl.

'Give me my property,' he said, and then he did the last thing I wanted him to do. He took a step back, and he began to extend his left arm, bringing the rifle away from his body, sweeping it up to point right at me.

Before he could get there, Bloch moved in. She put her hand on top of the weapon, there was a metallic clicking sound and when she stood back she had a bullet in one hand and the magazine from the rifle in the other. It all happened in a second, and in one smooth movement. She would've made one hell of a pickpocket. Bloch tossed them both at his feet, then swept her jacket away from her hip to reveal Maggie.

Maggie was Bloch's nickname for her beloved Smyth and Wesson, Magnum 500. One of the few handguns in the world that fired a fifty-caliber round. With five rounds in the chamber, it weighed almost six pounds. Smyth and Wesson had to add an optional muzzle break when selling the weapon as the recoil could snap the wrist of anyone dumb enough to try a one-handed grip.

Brian must've known his guns, because as soon as he saw Maggie he took several more steps backward. His body armor no longer mattered. That thing on Bloch's hip shot a 350-grain round at over two thousand feet per second. It could go through a cinderblock wall like a wet napkin.

'You can all leave now,' said Bloch. 'Or you can reach for your ammo and stay here permanently as a smear on the sidewalk. Think fast, Brian.'

'Your client killed my girlfriend, and he's going to pay, one way or another,' said Gary.

'Are you Gary Stroud?' I asked.

He clenched his jaw, the muscles were working at the sides of his head, his blue eyes focused on me. He blinked once, then nodded.

'Then I'm very sorry for your loss, but you've been misinformed. Andy Dubois didn't kill your girlfriend, and we'll prove it.'

The crowd behind them were growing louder.

Brian's eyes were wide with fear. He knew he'd be the first to catch a bullet.

Bloch winked.

'Okay, boys, that's enough. Put the iron away,' said Brian, backing away, his hands raised.

I put his driver's license back in his wallet and tossed it across the street.

Harry and Kate walked behind me, into the courthouse. Bloch picked up the round from Brian's rifle and the magazine and dumped them in a trash can, then turned her back on the mob and went inside.

At a distance of fifty feet now, with Bloch inside, Brian's balls made an unexpected reappearance. He smiled, and blew a kiss at me.

Maybe getting bail for Andy Dubois would put him in more danger than staying in the Buckstown lock-up. It was a chance I had to take. A bunch of armed, angry idiots I could deal with, but I couldn't help Andy when he was at the mercy of the sheriff and the DA who were trying to put him on death row.

I turned and went into the courthouse. Bloch checked her gun at the security desk and I took off my belt and emptied my pockets for the metal detector.

Harry stood on the other side of the security checkpoint. He shook his head at me, ruefully, and said, 'Come with me to Alabama, Harry. It MIGHT be dangerous.'

I went through security, collected my belongings and sidled up to Harry.

'Listen,' I said. 'If we're pissing these people off, then we've got to be doing something right.'

'We've been in dangerous spots before, but nothing like this. I worry for Kate,' he said.

Kate was gathering the files and motions from the search table. She was a little pale. Bloch came over, took half the files and placed her hand on Kate's shoulder. The two of them exchanged a word. Whatever that word was, it broke the tension.

'Bloch's got our backs,' I said. 'We need to stop just trying to defend Andy. That's not going to be enough.'

'What else can we do?'

'Not us – Bloch. She's going to take down Korn, and the sheriff. That's our best chance of winning this case.'

'And who is going to watch our backs with Bloch out chasing down the DA?'

'We'll look after each other. Now, we've got an hour before the hearing. The Sheriff's Department will bring Andy into court sometime soon. You need to be ready to talk to this kid.'

'Me?' said Harry.

'You and Kate. Get him to trust you. Get the retainer signed. Kate can handle the hearing.'

'Where are you going?'

'I'm going to get him some bail money.'

CHAPTER TWENTY-THREE

KATE

'I'm going to give Eddie a lift. Help him with the bail money,' said Bloch.

Kate nodded, felt a little flutter of nerves in her stomach. She wasn't nervous because of the upcoming hearing – she always felt better when Bloch was around. Walking past that mob outside hadn't helped.

'Hurry back,' said Kate.

Bloch nodded, and left.

Kate and Harry made their way along the hallway of the old courthouse. A door led to the holding cells. Kate could smell the cells before Harry opened the door. It was a combination of decay and stagnant water. The stairs down to the cells were old stone. Each step was bowed in the center from long use. A single strip light above cast more shadow than anything else. It made the depression in the stairs harder to judge and she almost lost her footing more than once.

At the bottom of the stairs was a desk, a set of lockers for lawyers to put their cell phones and a logbook. The single security guard was watching something on his phone and eating a sandwich that smelled almost as bad as the cells.

'Kate Brooks and Harry Ford to see Andy Dubois,' said Kate.

The security guard looked at Kate, then Harry, swallowed the bite of sandwich rolling around in his mouth and put the rest down on the desk. He stood, pulled up his belt and said, 'They ain't here yet.'

'We'll wait,' said Kate.

'You can do whatever you please,' he said, returning to his sandwich.

Kate looked around the small square room. It was airless, with a narrow hallway leading off to the right and, presumably, to the cells. The walls were painted that special, colorless brand of industrial paint – soulless beige. There were some safety notices on the walls about visiting and handling prisoners. The plastic shades on the overhead lights served to dim the bulbs with dust, nicotine stains and a layer of dead bugs. Kate squinted at the wall behind the security guard's desk. On it was a whiteboard with a grid. On the left-hand side it gave a list of cell numbers, and beside each one the name of the occupant and any special notes.

#1 Boyd, Richard – biter. Mouth guard to be applied when moving.

All eight cells appeared to be occupied. Names, cell numbers and notes on each prisoner.

The name on cell four was listed as *murderer*. There was no further information in relation to this occupant.

'I thought you said Andy Dubois wasn't here. He's in cell four.'

'Cell four?' said the guard, turning around to the board. 'What makes you think that's him?'

'His name isn't listed. Your cells are full. He's being brought here by the Sheriff's Department, and the sheriff doesn't want us to speak to him. Would you like me to go on?' asked Kate.

'Let me check,' said the guard.

He took a set of keys from his belt, disappeared around the corner of the narrow hallway. Kate could hear him whispering to someone else. She peeked around the corner, saw the guard talking to a sheriff's deputy. It was Shipley, the big cop with the dark hair and dead eyes.

'I guess Andy just arrived?' asked Kate.

Both of them turned.

'Sure did,' said the guard. 'Follow me.'

Harry shook his head, fell into step behind Kate. As she turned the corner, Kate saw Shipley's wide back as he disappeared through a door at the end of the hall. The guard unlocked a barred door on the left, leading to a wider corridor of cells. Four on each side. Solid steel doors on each.

Kate and Harry followed the guard to cell four. He unlocked the door, ushered them inside. It was an eight-by-eight, tiled room with a wooden bench running around the walls in a U shape. A young man, who looked like he hadn't eaten a full meal in a long time, lay on the bench with his hands over his head. His back to the door.

'Holler or bang the door when you want to come out,' said the guard, before slamming the door shut.

Kate was glad to have Harry with her. The sound of the lock moving, clicking and locking them in was something that never failed to unnerve Kate. She breathed out, slow and steady.

'Andy?' she asked.

The skinny kid turned around.

Kate instantly recognized Andy from the pictures of him online, in the paper and on television. He had a handsome, sweet round face. Large eyes and a small chin.

'My name is Kate Brooks, and this is Harry Ford. We work with Eddie Flynn, the attorney who saw you yesterday in your cell. We're here to help.'

Andy closed his eyes, turned away from her.

'Andy,' said Harry. 'What Kate is trying to say is we're here to see if we can get you out of jail. Today. In around two hours.'

When Andy turned back, he did it quickly. There was surprise on his face, his mouth in an O shape, but this quickly sank. As if he was remembering something – remembering not to believe the promises made by lawyers, perhaps?

'Your mother will be here soon. We think it's best if you are with her, at home, for the trial. What do you think? Would you like to go home?' asked Kate.

Andy sat up, said, 'He told me not to speak to you. He said it would go better for me, and my mother, if I didn't talk to a lawyer.'

'Who told you?' asked Kate.

She was keeping her voice soft and at a low volume, inviting Andy to listen.

'Sheriff Lomax. He's gonna look after me. Look after my mom too when I go to state penn after the trial.'

'And did he tell you what's going to happen after that?' asked Harry.

'He'll give Mom some money. There's no point in fighting this. I just have to accept that this is the way things are gonna be.'

'Andy, the sheriff and the prosecutor want you to be executed. Either by you getting a lethal injection or sitting in the electric chair,' said Harry.

Andy shook his head. 'The sheriff said that wouldn't happen if I co-operated. He made me sign something. I didn't get a chance to read it, but he said it protects me and makes sure my mom is okay.'

Kate opened the file, drew out the court document, filed by the district attorney confirming that he was seeking the death penalty.

She sat down beside him, gently, and gave him the document to read.

'That can't be right,' he said.

'It is right. Look, the court stamped the order.'

He looked at the stamp, put his two fists against his forehead and said, 'I don't understand. This ain't right. I didn't kill nobody.'

Finding the retainer agreement in his papers, Harry gave it to Kate.

'We need you to sign these papers to say, officially, that we act for you and we will do everything we can to save your life, and show the court you didn't kill Skylar Edwards.'

'What about my mom? I don't want anything bad to happen to her. Cody is missing, the sheriff got him. I know it. He'll get you too. He said he was going to put a new guy in my cell tonight. Someone who would teach me not to talk to lawyers.'

Harry and Kate exchanged a look, then Harry knelt down beside Andy, said, 'We're not going to let anything happen to you or your mom. She wants us to help you. And we're going to do just that. You're a smart kid, but you've been tricked and frightened into doing some things that have harmed your case. That stops now. We are here to protect you and fight for you. And there's nothing the sheriff can do to us. We're a team, and we're pretty tough. If you want to live, for your mom, pick up that pen and sign that paper. We need to get you out of here today.'

Andy thought about it for a while. Maybe too long. Then he took the pen, wrote his signature. He leaned so heavily on the page the nib was scraping the wooden bench.

'Great, now that's out of the way, I have some questions,' said Kate.

'What kind of questions?' asked Andy.

'The important kind. Let's start with this one. There's a witness, Ryan Hogg, says you were arguing with Skylar when you left work that night. Is that true?'

'Skylar and I never had a cross word between us. We were friends.'

'Did you see anyone else with Skylar that night, after work?'

'No, she was thinking about meeting her boyfriend at a party, but I don't know if she ever got there. I walked home.'

'Okay, good. This one is a little more difficult. The police say you had a scratch on your back. Your skin and DNA was found under Skylar's fingernails. Can you explain how that might have happened?'

TWENTY-FOUR

KATE

Kate had appeared in front of several judges in her short career so far. She could tell by the look on Judge Chandler's face this wasn't going to be an easy afternoon.

One of Eddie's tips. Know the judges. Some are fair. Some are biased in favor of men, or cops, or business, and mountains are to be moved in an effort to avoid having them try your case. In law school they don't teach you that even the best case can be lost in front of a bad judge. You have to learn that for yourself. Where Eddie hardly made any notes on his files, Kate made copious notes on everything. She had a notebook on judges. A dossier on each one she encountered or heard stories about. There were stories about Chandler. Some of them online, from the disaffected families of defendants that had been sent to jail by Chandler, or worse, to death row. They said he was too close to the prosecutor. That he hated defense attorneys and their clients.

She could believe it all.

The prosecutor, Korn, hadn't even spoken to her. He was skulking behind his desk, like a great spider. Harry sat at the defense table beside Andy, whispering softly to him, keeping him calm and explaining to him what was going on in court.

'Yesterday, Andy Dubois had representation on the scale of minus one. Now it seems he has a whole team of fancy New York counsel. Tell me, Miss Brooks, has your client won the lottery?' asked Judge Chandler.

'No, Your Honor. The disappearance of Cody Warren is still a concern to my client, and myself, as I'm sure it is to you,' said Kate.

Judge Chandler remained still for a moment, then his eyebrows flicked upwards, like antennae, detecting an attorney who was of considerable talent.

'I read your motions, Miss Brooks. Bail? Really? In a capital murder case?'

'Yes, Your Honor. My client has no passport, he does have family and strong links to this community. He has never been so much as arrested before this charge, and he is a vulnerable young man—'

'Who says he's vulnerable?' interrupted Chandler.

'In my view, given his age and inexperience of the judicial system, Andy Dubois is vulnerable.'

'Will a psychologist be appearing in court to testify at trial?'

'If need be, yes, Your Honor,' said Kate, more confidently than she liked.

'Until they do, keep your opinions to yourself, *dear*,' said the judge. 'I don't care what you think, or what you believe. You're not giving opinion evidence, you're a lawyer. Don't ever make such a statement in my court again.'

She could feel Harry's gaze on her. Harry had kind eyes. He was a gentle man, who could, when it suited him, summon a lion's courage. She knew, without even looking, Harry was telling her to stay calm with those big, brown eyes of his.

In her one-inch heels, Kate wiggled her toes. Fiercely. Another one of Eddie's tricks. No one can see you do it, and it takes away your nerves and anxiety. Kate found it worked on quelling anger too. Her jaw flexed, once, her toes went crazy and she returned to the business at hand. Best way to make the judge pay was to do a good job for her client.

'As I was saying, Your Honor, my client—'

'Is granted bail,' said Chandler, leaning back in his chair with a smug look on his face. 'For a cash surety of five hundred thousand dollars. The full amount to be lodged with the court before he sets foot out this door. That is the lowest amount I can conceive of on such a serious charge.'

It may as well be a million, or ten. Andy didn't have five dollars. Kate nodded at Harry, who took out his phone and began typing.

'Your motion to suppress is denied. He will say the sheriff scared him, or lied to him or whatever else he can think of to retract his confession. I'm not interested. Make those arguments in front of a jury, Miss Brooks.'

Two motions down. One granted, but without hope of getting the money. Kate swallowed, straightened her back; she was on much stronger ground with the change of venue motion and discovery. Particularly, the discovery motion, there was just no way she could lose that one.

'I've read your motion on change of venue. Mr. Korn, what have you to say on this matter?' asked Judge Chandler.

'I think the motion is redundant, Your Honor. May I enter into evidence this video clip?' he said, and gestured to his assistant DA. 'Mr. Wingfield recorded the statement made today by Governor Patchett. Perhaps we could play it for the court?'

Wingfield produced a laptop, opened it, clicked and prodded at it until the screen displayed a still video, ready to play. Another assistant produced a high table, which sat in the well of the court so the judge and Kate could see. Wingfield hit play then took his seat again.

The video looked as though it was paused, midway through a press briefing outside some kind of factory.

'And while I'm here today I just want to reassure the people of Buckstown, and all the good people of Sunville County, that your district attorney will not rest until there is justice for Skylar Edwards. She was a popular young woman in this town, a valedictorian and prom queen. She was taken from us while enjoying her first year of college. Andy Dubois will pay for his crimes. I know there are a lot of concerned citizens out there, justifiably horrified and angry at the viciousness of this heinous murder. All I can say is, one way or another, justice will be served . . .'

Kate couldn't quite believe what she had heard. The governor just said Andy Dubois was guilty, on live TV. And she knew every paper, local news and radio station would carry that soundbite for at least a day or two. The entire jury pool had just been poisoned. She glanced at Korn, saw that strange attempt at a smile on his face.

She guessed he may have had a hand in the governor making that statement. It was smart, ruthless and in this court, he could get away with it.

'Miss Brooks, I don't condone the governor's statement, but I'm sure a direction from me to a jury to ignore any press statements will suffice. It looks as though any argument you have that the jury pool in Buckstown is compromised now applies to the entire state. We're not moving this case to New York, young lady. The motion to change venue is denied,' said the judge.

'Your Honor, I wonder at the timing of that press conference. It appears to be most convenient to the district attorney. I would ask the court to issue a censure on the governor and the district attorney and move this trial from the victim's hometown, at least?'

'Denied. Now, your motion for discovery is a different matter.'

Kate felt the tingling sensation in her stomach.

There was sound evidence for this motion. One that the DA couldn't brush off, even if Judge Chandler was in his pocket. Whatever was on that security footage could prove Andy innocent, and if the judge could be persuaded the DA withheld this evidence, the judge would have no choice but to throw out the entire case against Andy. This was a big moment. Kate felt that pressure and welcomed it. She'd trained for moments like this.

'This motion can be dealt with quickly,' said Judge Chandler, turning his attention to Korn.

'Mr. Korn, does your office, or the Sheriff's Department, hold any security camera footage for the night of fourteenth and fifteenth of May, in this case?'

Korn, stood, looked at Kate as he said, 'No, Your Honor.'

'Well, then, Miss Brooks, there is your answer. Your motion is—'

'Wait, Your Honor,' said Kate, loudly, asserting some authority. 'I have a sworn affidavit from a Mr. Damien Green, a store clerk at the gas station, who states that the Sheriff's Department obtained security footage from that night and removed it from the premises on a pen drive. He further alleges that they went on to delete the footage from this server once they had copied it. We believe the district attorney has exculpatory evidence that he is withholding from the defense. We want that evidence, or, in the alternative, this court to dismiss the charges against our client and sanction the prosecution. Mr. Damien Green is an independent witness and his affidavit carries significant weight in any court.'

Korn looked around the room. Sitting in the back of the gallery he caught sight of Patricia Dubois, Andy's mother. Kate had spoken to her only briefly, telling her she would do her best but not to get her hopes up about Andy coming home. Korn hollered for a deputy, causing Patricia to jump in her seat.

The doors at the rear of the courtroom opened and Sheriff Lomax came in. Kate imagined he might be listening to the proceedings outside. Awaiting the call from Korn, like a Rottweiler poised to attack on command. Behind Lomax was a deputy and a prisoner. A young man in a ripped tee-shirt. His right eye was bright purple and almost swollen shut. He was handcuffed to the front. The deputy pulled him along by the cuffs, then gestured for him to take a seat in the gallery.

'Your Honor, this is your next case. It might be useful to illustrate it briefly. This is Mr. Damien Green, the same man Miss Brooks refers to as having provided an affidavit regarding video evidence. Mr. Green is charged with possession and supply of illegal drugs – methamphetamine, Your Honor. I understand he will be pleading guilty to those offenses.'

Kate had seen some dirty moves pulled by her opposition. Nothing like this. They must've busted Green straight away – soon as they saw his name on the affidavit. Korn had torpedoed her motion. It was hard to tell from here, but Green had good skin, he was well fed, clean, apart from the ripped tee-shirt, and he had worked in the gas station for the last three years. He wasn't making a fortune as a clerk in a Circle K, and most drug dealers and users don't hold down employment too well. He appeared to Kate, from her little dealings with him, like a straight-up working Joe, nine-to-nine shifts, pulling his weight and making an honest buck. He was also timid. The sheriff must've hit him hard to do that to his eye. If she had to guess, she would say the drugs might have gotten into Green's possession from the trunk of the sheriff's car.

'Hardly a credible witness now, Miss Brooks?' said the judge.

'Your Honor, may I have a short continuance to speak to Mr. Green?'

'No! I don't want to talk to her. She made stuff up and that man behind her told me I had to sign it,' yelled Green, from the benches. He was looking at Harry.

'I'll ignore that last statement. But it looks like he doesn't want to talk to you, Miss Brooks,' said Judge Chandler.

All of Kate's nerves had gone. The pressure too. The only thing keeping her on her feet was the fist she held behind her back. Tight as a ball, her fingernails buried in her skin. Korn gazed over at her, a smug grin on those worm-thin lips.

'Things change pretty fast around here,' said Kate.

'Your motion for discovery is denied. Jury selection begins in the morning, and as is my practice in this court, we expect that to take a day, maximum. I'll be looking forward to it. Oh, and do let me know if your client posts the five-hundred-thousand-dollar bail. The bail office closes in fifteen minutes. And remember, it's the full bond, cash only. Case adjourned.'

'Wait with Andy in the cells. Tell them you need a consultation. Buy us some time. I'll call Eddie,' said Harry, the phone already in his hand.

Kate took Andy's arm to make sure she was not separated from him by the court bailiff. She had already decided she wasn't going to leave him alone with these men. Damien Green came forward, his one good eye was full of fear as his case was called. He had been hurt and framed because he'd helped them. This was a rotten town, and Kate was prepared to burn it to the ground to save Andy.

'What's happening?' asked Andy.

'It's okay,' said Kate. 'I won't leave you. We're going back to the cells to talk. That's all. It's going to be alright. I won't let them take you.'

Lomax drew his nightstick from his belt and approached Andy.

'Let's get you back to lock-up,' said the sheriff.

CHAPTER TWENTY-FIVE

EDDIE

Bloch parked up outside the Buckstown branch of the National Bank, turned up the air conditioning and closed her eyes.

'Are you tired?' I asked.

She raised a hand, spread her fingers and tilted her palm, back and forth: *so so*.

'I'm really tired,' I said. 'Harry snores.'

Ignoring me, Bloch settled her head into the seat back. Ex-cops had an uncanny ability to get shut-eye whenever they needed it.

My phone buzzed. Text message from Harry.

Half a mil. Cash. If we don't get him out now the sheriff might kill him. They're sending another prisoner into his cell tonight.

Shit. I dialed a number and it was picked up fast.

'Eddie, how's it going?' said Berlin.

'Not so good. No sign of Cody Warren. Two quick things. I need you to put out a cell phone search on the victim's phone. It wasn't in her possessions when they found the body.'

'Warren already asked me. As far as cell site geography goes, her phone was either switched off or destroyed at the scene. It hasn't showed up on any cell phone masts since the night of the murder. What's the second thing?'

'The sheriff has Andy in the county lock-up and he's working the kid. Andy is going to plead guilty to a crime he didn't commit if we don't get him out of there. He's scared, and I can't win this case with him in there. I've got to get him out, talk to him. Get him to tell the truth. If we don't get him out he could be beaten to death anytime.'

'How much?'

'You always have a way of cutting to the chase. Half a mil. Cash.'

'For bail? Jesus, couldn't you have gotten it down some? Andy won't earn half a million dollars in his lifetime.'

'I can't save this kid's life if he's murdered in his cell. If he turns up for trial, which he will, then you get it all back. We're on a clock here. I'm parked outside Buckstown National. I need you to transfer it, right now.'

'I need a little more notice than that.'

'Right now. This kid may not make it through the night. Beating Andy to death or hanging him in his cell is not beyond these folks.'

'Alright, goddamn it, but just make sure he doesn't skip bail. He's your responsibility. If he ships out, you owe me five hundred grand.'

'Agreed.'

'Alright. Go into the bank, check on an account in the name of Forbes. I'll authorize you. We've got accounts for operatives, US treasury will take twenty-four hours to notice, by that time I'll have moved some money around to cover it. Just get him out.'

He hung up.

Bloch opened her eyes.

'We're in business,' I said.

Buckstown National was a marble and glass affair, with two tellers and a heavy security. Bloch brought an empty leather bag from the car; she'd stowed the contents in the trunk – a shotgun, bulletproof vest and ammo.

The bag reeked of gunpowder.

The teller checked the computer, took a copy of my ID and checked with the manager. Then she came back and said, 'Mr. Flynn, you're fully authorized for a withdrawal of five hundred thousand. We can have that for you next week.'

'Next week? No, I need that now.'

'I'm sorry, we don't have that in the vault. We can give you one hundred twenty-five thousand today, in cash, but that's all we've got.'

'Is there another branch nearby with additional funds?'

'Closest bank to us is in Mobile. Ninety minutes in this traffic.'

My phone rang in my pocket – Harry.

'Eddie, we need that money, right now. The bail office is closing in fifteen minutes. I'll try and stall the clerk, but you've got to get here asap. I don't know if I can persuade her to stay open much later.'

'Does it have to be cash? Did he specify cash?' I asked.

'Yep. The court won't take a banker's check or bond. Cash only. Do you have it?'

'The most I can get is one-twenty-five.'

Harry sighed, 'Lomax is already swinging that nightstick. Kate is staying with Andy in the cells until we post bail, but if we don't get him out he's going to get the beating of his life for talking to us. He may not be breathing come the morning.'

What the hell was I gonna do? I was three hundred and seventy-five thousand short.

'Harry, do they have a counting machine in the courthouse office?'

'You're in Buckstown, Alabama,' said Harry. 'The counting machine is a sixty-one-year-old divorcee named Agatha who is the clerk and has the hots for me.'

'Bloch, did you ever see the Harlem Globetrotters?' I asked.

Bloch's right eyebrow reached for the ceiling.

'It'll be fine,' I said. 'You'll get the hang of it.'

I put the phone to my ear, 'Harry, you ever see the Harlem Globetrotters?'

'Twice. Are we abandoning the trial to play ball?'

'No, I've already got a player. I just need you to whistle.'

CHAPTER TWENTY-SIX

EDDIE

Harry Ford is one of the most charming men on the planet. I think it's that deep voice of his. Like honey rolling around in a barrel. He's good-looking for a senior citizen, funny too, without being crass. He's irresistible to certain women, of a certain age. Although, the fact that there were now three ex-Mrs. Fords spoke to the fact that his charms didn't last forever. By the time Bloch and I arrived at the bail office, the bail clerk, Agatha, was well on her way to becoming the fourth Mrs. Ford.

Agatha was recently divorced, with a generous head of neatly combed gray hair, a button-down sweater over a neatly pressed white blouse, and grey slacks. She was sitting at her desk in the small bail office, upstairs, laughing at one of Harry's jokes. Harry was sitting on the desk, and Agatha was gazing into those brown eyes of his like they were made of candy.

'Agatha, these are my colleagues, Mr. Flynn and Miss Bloch,' said Harry, rising from the desk with Agatha as we came in.

Bloch didn't like titles. She was Bloch. Not Miss Bloch. Not Ms. Bloch. Just Bloch. Harry knew it too, but he was more concerned with keeping Agatha under his spell. Harry mouthed *sorry* to Bloch, and in return she gave Harry a quick, sour look before turning it into a full smile for Agatha.

Agatha pointed at the bag handcuffed to Bloch's wrist and said, 'Is that the bail money?'

'Sure is,' I said. 'Five hundred thousand. Cash.'

'Then come on into the office, sweetie, I'll need to count it. Set it over here, if you wouldn't mind,' said Agatha.

'No problem,' I said. 'But Bloch here will be with the cash until we've handed it over. Security procedures, you understand.'

'Of course,' she said.

Harry leaned over, whispered something in her ear and Agatha let out a peel of wicked laughter.

Bloch set the bag on the desk. Opened it. Took out a stack of bills held together with a rubber band and placed it to the right of the bag, on the desk, in front of Agatha. I stood on Agatha's right. Harry walked around behind us.

Undoing the rubber bands, Agatha began to peel at the corner of the stack of bills, her lips moving in a low whisper as she counted. The stack was made up of five hundred one-hundred-dollar bills. Agatha's fingers worked quickly as she moved through the roll of cash in under two minutes.

'Fifty thousand,' she said. Putting the rubber bands around the stack, and placing it to her right, in front of me, as Bloch handed her another stack.

Harry began whistling.

'I know that tune,' said Agatha, as she counted. '"Sweet Georgia Brown". Wasn't that what that basketball team used to play to?'

'The Harlem Globetrotters?' said Harry.

'That's it. I love that song,' she said.

Agatha counted like an experienced cash handler. She was accurate and fast. One time, her fingers peeled two notes at once, and she licked her thumb, and went straight back to the start of the pile.

By the time she finished there were ten stacks of bills on the counter. Each stack was just over two inches high.

'Five hundred thousand, on the nose,' said Agatha.

'Can I get a receipt?' I asked.

'Why sure,' she said.

Bloch undid the handcuffs on the bag, dropped them inside and resealed it with the zip.

Agatha made a call, asking for Dubois to be brought up to the bail office. She prepared a receipt for half a million dollars, signed it, stamped it from the office of the Sunville County Court, and gave it to me.

'Thank you,' I said, putting the receipt in my wallet.

Agatha had counted the money correctly. And she had counted out five hundred thousand dollars. Ten stacks of fifty thousand.

Five hundred one-hundred-dollar bills in every stack she counted.

Yet I knew there was only one hundred and ten thousand on the table.

The problem for Agatha was that she had been counting the same stacks.

Every dollar bill, of every denomination, weighs exactly one gram. A C-note and a buck weigh the same. Every bill issued in the United States is the same size – 6.14 inches long by 2.61 inches wide. With a few fifties on the top and bottom of each stack of one-dollar bills, the stacks could not be told apart.

When Agatha had finished counting the first stack of fifty thousand, Bloch handed her the second stack, again with fifty thousand dollars in it, precisely. While Agatha put her nose and her rubber thimble to work, leaning over the desk, Bloch took a stack of ones and tens with fifties on top from the bag, reached behind her back, and gave it to me, behind Agatha's back. I retrieved it with my right hand, behind my back, and switched it with the real stack. The real bundle of fifty grand went behind my back, and behind Agatha's back, straight back to Bloch. She put it in the bag with her left hand so she could take it out and give it to Agatha when she was ready for a fresh bundle to count, not knowing she'd already counted this bundle. If Harry stopped whistling, it meant Agatha had stopped counting and might notice me switching the stacks. As long as he was whistling, we were good. Bloch and I passed those stacks behind our backs, between Agatha, like Hallie Bryant and Willie Gardner of the Globetrotters, while Harry played their song. Agatha placed the ten stacks in the safe, closed it and locked it.

'We're all set. Good luck, Harry. Maybe I'll see you around?' asked Agatha.

'Of course, I'll see you for that dinner when all this is taken care of,' said Harry.

We left Agatha in her office and went downstairs with the bail order.

'Eddie, if I end up getting married again, you're gonna owe *me* five hundred grand,' said Harry.

'Don't worry,' I said. 'I'm good for it.'

CHAPTER TWENTY-SEVEN

EDDIE

The sight of Andy Dubois, stumbling up the stairs from the cells, put a brick of pure rage in my stomach. He was so thin, and weak, Bloch had to almost carry him up. There were sores on his ankles, elbows and hands, from rubbing against the concrete floor.

When Patricia saw him up close, it was all too much for her. The combination of joy at having her son in her arms, and realizing the emaciated, sick young man he had become sent her wailing in pain and relief.

'How'd you get so damn skinny? Did they feed you in there?' she asked.

'I didn't like none of the food. There was something sharp in my mash potatoes. It cut my tongue, made me bleed from my behind,' he said.

Her eyes narrowed, unsure of what this meant. I knew exactly what it meant, but I would never tell her. The Sunville County deputies had been putting crushed glass in Andy's food. Any wonder he wasn't eating.

She held him close, and half carried him toward the front door. Harry was in the car, waiting to take them home. I didn't see Kate with him.

He rolled down the window as I approached.

'Where's Kate?'

'She's gone to pick something up for me from the hotel.'

It had taken a bit of time to get Andy's bail processed. The forms completed and his property returned. As I opened the door to the SUV, I saw Kate, turning the corner, with a brown paper package in her hands. The Chanterelle was only a ten-minute walk from the courthouse. She gave the package to Harry, who thanked her and put it in the glove box. Kate got into the SUV. Bloch and I would walk back down the street, get into my rented Prius and meet them at Patricia's house.

Patricia had to lift Andy into the back seat. He'd only walked the guts of five hundred yards and he was covered in sweat. Not from the sun, though. Andy was used to the sun. This was from sheer physical exertion of moving a body with no fuel in the tank.

Bloch drove the Prius, following Harry along the back streets, then out onto the highway and then the dirt back roads with ghost communities surrounding Buckstown.

We arrived at Patricia's house just as the sun began to dip behind the tall trees that surrounded her property. There was no welcome party from the cops or any white nationalist thugs. For now, Andy could get some food and some rest.

Andy and Patricia went inside with Bloch. I got out and approached Harry and Kate. Kate was outside the SUV, getting some air. Harry remained in the driver's seat, the window open.

'What's in the brown paper package?' I asked.

'You don't want to know,' said Kate.

'Well now I need to know. How come you had to pick it up?'

'Because Harry isn't registered at the hotel. He needed a name that was checked-in to the hotel before the courier would agree to accept it.'

'Harry, what's going on?' I asked.

He leaned over to the glove box, took out the package and unwrapped it. Inside was a rosewood box. Handmade, about the size of a folded *New York Times*. He opened the lid to reveal a Colt 1911 and a magazine, held in place with a foam inlay.

'I called Denise this morning. Asked her to get this couriered to me urgently,' said Harry.

'You called her after we inspected the site where they found Skylar's body, didn't you?'

Harry didn't reply. He had that look again. The same one he'd had this morning.

'That really rattled you, didn't it.'

'This is my service weapon,' said Harry. 'It's older than you, but more reliable. I feel better having it on me. This pistol and I have been through some rough jungle.'

He closed his eyes, lifted the gun clear from the box, loaded it and pulled back the slide, chambering a round. Soon as he heard that slide licking a bullet into the firing chamber, his shoulders dropped, he breathed out and slowly opened his eyes.

'How long since you've used that thing?' I asked.

'It's been a long time. And yet, not long enough.'

'Harry, maybe you should go back to New York. Sit this one out,' I said.

'Do you think I'm too old?'

'No, I know you're too old, but that's not the problem. This is not a criticism, not in any way, but there are some cases that get under the skin and they stay there. You know this better than I do. I can see how much this one is getting to you and—'

'You've got it wrong. I'm not upset by this case. I'm scared. And you should be too. All of you. The man who killed Skylar Edwards was sending a message.'

'What message?' asked Kate.

As he spoke, Harry's eyes were far away, and sweat beaded on his face, running onto his lips. 'In Revelations 12, the woman survives her encounter with the devil, who is cast out, and war erupts in heaven. In Revelations 15, God ends the war by unleashing seven angels, with seven plagues, upon the earth. Skylar Edwards's death isn't the end of something. It's just the beginning.'

For a moment, neither Kate nor I spoke. Her fingers beat out a nervous rhythm on the hood of the SUV, then she reached inside the car and placed a hand on Harry's shoulder.

'This is just some nutjob, Harry. We're going to find who killed Skylar and make sure they're put away.'

'Sure we are,' he said. 'In the meantime, I'm going to keep my gun close and pray I don't have to use it. I'll stay out here in the car. I'll move up the dirt road a little, make sure I can see the main highway. You go inside,' said Harry.

'I was going to ask Bloch to watch the place,' I said.

'Bloch needs to start looking into Korn and chasing down any leads on Cody Warren,' said Harry.

'Fair enough,' I said. 'I'll—'

'You stay here,' said Kate. 'I'll stay at the hotel with Bloch and I can handle jury selection. You need to talk to our client. There's a lot of questions we still don't have answers for.'

'When you were in the cells with him, did you get a chance to ask him about the scratches on his back, and the fact that his blood was found under the victim's fingernails?'

'I did,' said Kate, her head pointing to the ground.

'What did he say? Did he have a plausible explanation?'

'He didn't have any kind of explanation. He just shook his head, said he didn't know.'

'This case gets better by the minute,' said Harry.

Kate and Bloch left in the Prius. Harry moved the SUV along the single lane dirt road that led to Patricia's house. I hung around the living room watching Patricia and Andy look at old photographs and cling to one another.

There were so many questions I needed to ask, but right then I couldn't. Andy looked so tired, and so frail, and it was just good watching him be with his mother. He'd been locked in a cell for months, beaten, abused, and I thought it would be better for him to feel more like himself before we started talking about the nightmare he'd just woken from.

Andy ate half a peanut butter and jelly sandwich with a glass of milk and went straight to his room. He was soon sleeping soundly in his own bed. I ate the other half of his sandwich, and Patricia fussed about making me some chicken, which I refused. There was a lightness in her step. Her ankle was still badly swollen, but she wasn't letting the pain slow her down, nor was she letting the thought of the upcoming trial ruin her evening. Tonight, she had her son home, and nothing was going to stop her smiling.

Still, I had a job to do. And I needed to know one thing now, because without an answer we were just going through the motions of putting up a defense. I couldn't ask Andy, but it wouldn't hurt to ask Patricia.

'Andy told Kate he didn't know how he got those scratches on his back. He also said he didn't know how his DNA could've been found underneath Skylar's fingernails. I don't want to bring you down. Getting him home is a miracle. But I want to make sure he stays home. Do you have any ideas? Anything that might help?'

'I'll talk to him, but you should know my Andy don't lie. If he don't know, then he don't know. He always tells the truth.'

I thanked her, and she told me she was going to bed and there was no need for me to stay. They would be safe.

'I'd like to stay tonight. Just for my own peace of mind. If it's okay with you. I don't want to impose. I can sleep in the car with Harry,' I said.

'The couch would be more comfortable. I'll fetch you some blankets. Oh, Mr. Flynn . . .'

'Eddie, please.'

'Eddie,' she said, trying the name on for size. 'Thank you for bringing home my son.'

'My pleasure,' I said.

Getting Andy out of jail wasn't easy. Keeping him off death row was a whole other ball game. One that I was increasingly convinced I was destined to lose.

She fixed up the couch, then went to her room.

I was tired, but too damn hot to sleep. Instead I made tea, and went outside onto the small porch to take in the night. The thick, dense trees were alive with sound and the faint odor of decay came to me with the soft, warm wind. I took off my tie, unbuttoned my shirt and scanned the trees. It was almost one am. I knew I should go out and relieve Harry soon, but somehow it felt wrong leaving Patricia and Andy alone in the house.

The pull of New York City felt strongest when I was in places like this. I'd grown up in Brooklyn, amid the traffic, and the street kids, and the crime, and the music, and the long afternoons of laughter leaking out of barbershops and corner bars. Put me in a dark alley with three tough guys and I had no fear. Not like now. I didn't like being away from the city lights, in the dark, with the animals, the snakes, the spiders and insects and Christ knows what else out there, slithering and scuttling around – making too much damn noise.

I slumped into Patricia's rocking chair on the porch, sipped my tea.

When I opened my eyes again, the ice had melted in my tea. I must've dosed off.

It was so dark I couldn't see more than a few feet beyond the thick set of trees that surrounded the property. The SUV was parked way up the dirt track. I didn't know if I would be able to see it even if it had lights on.

I put down the glass, got to my feet and stretched.

That's when I heard something. A noise that was unmistakable.

A car door slamming.

I took out my phone, called Harry's cell. Maybe he was just going for a leak in the woods, and had stepped out of the SUV for a minute. Maybe not. The phone rang and rang.

Harry didn't pick up.

Whatever dark reason there was behind the murder of Skylar Edwards, I had been pretty sure today that none of it could really have been part of some biblical plague theory. Harry was a lot older than me and, if I was honest, a lot smarter, but he was raised with the church and part of that had never left him.

I told myself he was fine. Maybe I'd imagined the car door slamming. He was probably asleep. That man could sleep through damn near anything.

He was fine. I was sure.

Pretty sure.

I tried him again. No answer.

I vaulted the porch rail and set off sprinting toward the dirt road.

CHAPTER TWENTY-EIGHT

THE PASTOR

'Did you grow up around here?' asked the Pastor.

Francis Edwards gazed out of the passenger window of the Ford pick-up at the trees blurring by on the side of the road, somehow ghostly in the moonlight.

'I was raised in Gold River,' said Francis, flatly.

'I know that town. Not far from here. Pretty good high school football team, if I recall,' said the Pastor. 'Did you play?'

'Me? Of course. I was big and fast back then. That's all there was to do in Gold River. Play football and chase girls.'

His chin dropped at that last word.

'Tell me about Skylar,' said the Pastor. 'It's good to talk things out now and again. And it's just you and me. I won't breathe a word to anyone.'

'I know you won't. I trust you that way, given your job and all.'

The Pastor nodded, kept his eyes on the road ahead. There were no streetlights, just the blacktop cutting through old steamy forest. He could only see as far as the headlights could throw and so he deliberately kept the speed down. This wasn't his car, and that made him careful, but he was mindful of what he had in the car with him. The Pastor could not afford to have this car searched if there was an accident.

While he was a patient man, the Pastor was just about done with Francis avoiding his questions, no matter how difficult they were, or how they tugged at his grief.

'Pain is a real thing, Francis. I think of it like a gas. If you let it fill up your gut, and you don't let it out, eventually you're gonna blow and it's not going to be pretty.'

Nodding, smiling, Francis said, 'I get it. Skylar . . . she was my whole world. Everything I did in my life, from the day she was born, was for her and Esther. I knew I was never going to be a good enough player to turn pro. I guessed that early. But I wasn't exactly good at schooling either. It was going to be the chemical plant or driving a tractor like my daddy. And let me tell you, when you grow up on a farm, the very last thing you want to do for a living is be a farmer.'

The Pastor nodded. The farm he'd grown up on grew cotton and pain. He had the scars on his back to prove it.

'No, sir, no way I was cut out for farming. I liked driving, so I got a job hauling. It's not a bad life. The open road. Radio, CDs. All the bad food you could ever want. I enjoyed driving my truck, but looking back these past few months, I regret it now.'

'You regret being a truck driver?'

'More than anything,' said Francis. 'It took me away from my family. For two weeks sometimes, at a stretch. I'd give anything to change that. To go back, and get that time again. One minute Skylar was chewing on my finger, cutting her teeth, the next she was graduating first in her class. The prom queen, can you believe it?'

'You must have been very proud?' said the Pastor.

Francis started to speak, then slapped his fingers over his mouth. Swallowed something down. Something big and hard, and then he blinked rapidly. He didn't want to cry in front of the Pastor. Men like Francis do cry, of course. But the very last thing they ever want to do is cry in front of another man. That would be wrong. Shameful.

'I was so proud of Skylar, but tell you the truth, I . . . I didn't know her. There's an age where they just stop talking to you. And I wasn't there long enough to notice. She was a good kid, smart and kind. She was good to that boy, Andy. God help me I wish he was dead right now, and he'd never met my little girl.'

The Pastor watched closely, taking his eyes from the road, and didn't avert his gaze from Francis's face until he saw the first tear fall. Then he looked back at the road. That straight dark road that only led them deeper into the forest and swamps of Alabama as the lanes narrowed and the trees grew taller and deeper all around.

'I'm sorry,' said Francis, wiping his nose on his wrist, and taking a big sniff.

'Don't you worry about a thing. It takes a real man to cry. Never forget that. You know why?'

'No, I surely don't.'

'Because it takes a real man to love that deeply. Because that's what makes us cry, Francis. Love. Don't ever be ashamed of it.'

'I never thought of it that way.'

The Pastor nodded, said, 'I'm going to turn off just up here. Head into the scrub, if you don't mind. It'll be a little bumpy, but don't worry about it. It'll just make sure we're awake,' said the Pastor.

'I know you said you wanted to take a drive and maybe talk, but are we going somewhere in particular?'

'You'll see in a minute or two.'

Neither of them spoke for a time. The pick-up sported an elevated chassis and off-road tires so the ride along the grassland wasn't as bumpy as the Pastor had anticipated. He'd bought the pick-up online, and the pink slip was made out to a fake ID, making the plates and the vehicle virtually untraceable.

As they neared a thick tree line, the Pastor killed the lights. For a few moments, they were blinded as they rolled slowly along, and then the Pastor's eyes adjusted to the moonlight. He slowed, and stopped the vehicle. Turned off the engine.

'Nice driving gloves,' said Francis, nodding to the Pastor's hands as they sat atop the steering wheel.

'They're not driving gloves. I want you to get out, close the door quietly and come with me.'

They got out, and both took care to close the doors with the least noise possible. The Pastor headed off to the trees, which were only twenty feet away, and beckoned for Francis to follow.

'Where are we—' began Francis, but the Pastor cut him off by holding his finger to his lips. They moved slowly through the trees. The ground was soft and wet with summer moss. Each footfall sent an odor of sweet decay to the Pastor, who breathed deeply. That smell was part of his childhood. Maybe once a month he would take off from the farm, during the night, into the nearby forest. His plan had been to build a tree house and live there. He always got caught the following evening, as his father was, among other things, a skilled tracker. No matter how hard the Pastor had tried to cover his trail, no matter where in the forest he tried to hide, he would always hear his father's voice as he crunched through the leaves and twigs on the forest bed. And then he would hear him quoting scripture. That was the worst part. Lying in a hollow log with centipedes, spiders and bugs, listening to his father talking about damnation, or fathers from the Old Testament who were willing to sacrifice their sons to appease God's will. And waiting. Just waiting for the inevitable moment when he would feel his father's huge hand take hold of his ankle and haul him out of his hiding place, his safe space. The wet, dark hole was always safer than home.

The Pastor stopped, turned and held out a hand to Francis, telling him to come forward and take a look. The ground fell away in front of them, to rocks and dead trees and track below. A steep drop, maybe thirty feet.

'See that house in the distance?' said the Pastor.

Francis nodded.

'That's Andy Dubois' house. He's in there now, sound asleep. You know he got bail today, right?'

'I heard,' said Francis.

'How does that make you feel? The boy who killed your little girl is at home right now, in bed with a bellyful of chicken and cornbread. You tell me, is that right?'

'No, of course not. He should get the needle or, better still, the chair. I wish they would just let me have ten minutes with him, in a locked room.'

The Pastor nodded in agreement, asked, 'And what would you do to him? Tell me.'

'I'd make him suffer,' said Francis.

'Well now, look at the house again. See the beginnings of a track. Follow it to the right and there, you see that SUV?'

'I see it, barely. It doesn't have any lights on.'

'In that Chevrolet is one of the lawyers who represents Andy Dubois. Think about that. They want to put him back on the street. I can't let that happen.'

'What can you do?' asked Francis.

'Come along and watch,' he said.

The Pastor moved to his left, where the drop wasn't so steep, and moved quietly down toward the SUV. Francis followed him, but at a distance. The Pastor came out of the trees behind the vehicle and waited for Francis to catch up. He beckoned to Francis to wait there, just on the side of the track, about thirty feet from the car. The next few minutes would be crucial. This was a turning point. Once he took the next step, there was no going back. He had an idea how Francis would react. He hoped he was right. If he had guessed wrong, and Francis reacted badly, then he might have to kill him. And that would be disappointing.

The Pastor turned his attention back to the SUV. A single occupant. A male in the driver's seat. The only thing visible was the back of his head – a crop of gray hair. His chin was resting on his chest, as if he had fallen asleep.

It was almost too easy.

He took a knife from his back pocket, flipped it open. The ivory handle always felt a little too slippery in his grip, especially when wearing gloves. This was not a knife that should be used to cut. It had a very different and singular purpose behind its design. The point was incredibly sharp and hard, toughened steel. A slight curve in the blade didn't alter its strength. This was a knife made for stabbing. And many years go, when it was an early prototype of the switchblade, it had been used for that exact purpose. A flower had been embossed onto the base of the handle.

A white camellia. It had belonged to one of the founding members of the group, and as soon as the Pastor saw it, he knew he had to have it. The weapon was said to have been used to murder a man in the Louisiana legislature who was anti-slavery. The blade had been put though his eye. It had cost several thousand dollars through a discreet dealer who also traded in Nazi and KKK memorabilia. Like all such artifacts, the provenance was difficult to verify. The Pastor knew it was the real thing as soon as he held it in his hands. Somehow, he had sensed the blood that had licked over this blade.

The Pastor knelt at the driver's door of the SUV, listening. Making sure there was no one else around. Then, he reached for the door handle, took it in his grip, ready to pop it open at any second.

Francis was watching. His fists clenched, lips drawn back over his teeth. Eyes narrowed.

The Pastor smiled. The rage inside of Francis was pure. The anger that only a bereaved parent can muster.

He would need to be quick now. In one fluid movement, he yanked open the driver's door of the SUV, pushed up from his knees and twisted his torso. Years of working the land as a young man had made him strong. Time in the gym had added immense power. And he used all of it in one explosive movement, swinging his arm, using his shoulders and core. A quick burst of torsion in the muscles. Like a prizefighter coming up out of a duck, straight into a right cross. A snap to the movement. There was less than half a second between the door being flung open and the thrust.

The knife found the spot on the old man's neck. The blade disappeared through the flesh and bone, all the way to the hilt.

He saw the look in Francis's eyes then. There was no time to waste.

The Pastor beckoned him over.

They stood for a few seconds, looking at the old man dead in the driver's seat. The knife jutting from the side of his head.

'We become brothers tonight, Francis. There's no going back. We will fight to the death for you, and we expect the same in return. Tell me you'll swear to that.'

Sweat covered his face, and he was breathing hard with the adrenaline pumping through his system like hot motor oil. He held out a hand to the Pastor, said, 'I swear.'

'Good. Very good. Now give me a hand with something from the pick-up,' said the Pastor as he pushed the driver's door shut.

CHAPTER TWENTY-NINE

EDDIE

Running at full speed in a hundred and ten-degree heat, with eighty-nine percent humidity, is a lot like swimming through hot soup. The air doesn't feel the same. It's too warm and wet. I pumped my legs as I turned onto the dirt track. Patricia's home lay in the well of an incline. The single lane mud road was all uphill and steep as hell. Not so bad for a car, but in leather-soled shoes it was slippery.

I could see the outline of the SUV up ahead. It was a darker, harder shape against the dull grey black of the dirt road. I looked for the back of Harry's head in the driver's seat, and at first I couldn't quite make out what I was seeing.

Then I saw that his head had slumped to the side. Maybe he was sleeping.

Maybe not.

A thought came unbidden. Two words that repeated in my mind.

Not again.

Not again.

And instantly, while my body struggled desperately up a muddy track in the middle of swampy Alabama, my mind was in a hospital corridor and I was still in high school. My dad was dying. I'd held his hand for eleven hours that day. My mom had told me to take a break I don't know how many times, but I wouldn't. I didn't want to leave him. I didn't want him to die without me being there – holding his hand. For most of that day he'd slept. The rare cancer had almost finished him. He had woken just for twenty minutes that day. Too weak to talk, he watched some *Starsky and Hutch* on the portable TV in the room. He'd always loved that show – the car in particular. It was a 1976 Ford Gran Torino, in bright red, with a white vector stripe and a Windsor V8 engine rolling on black-walled tires with five-slot mag wheels.

When the show was over, and the credits started, my mom asked me to get her a soda from the machine in the hallway. I let go of his hand, took the change from her purse and left the room. As the can of grape soda crashed to the dispenser drawer, I felt a hand on my shoulder. It was Mom. I was about to ask her what she was doing – that she shouldn't have left Dad all alone. But I didn't say anything. I knew by the look on her face he was gone. And he had died hard in those last few moments. She saw it coming – sent me away on an errand. She didn't want me to see that. I know that now, but back then I felt like I had let him down. I had not been there when he died, and it haunted me for a long time. In the hallway that night she gave me my father's Saint Christopher's medal.

I could feel that same medal bouncing around my chest as I pounded up the hill toward the SUV. I just knew that night, in the hallway of the hospital, that my father was dead. That same feeling hit me now, in the center of my chest. It had happened again. Harry was dead – I had not been there for him.

As I got closer, panting now, the moonlight slashed across the rear window, touching the Chevrolet badge on the rear door, and then it was gone as a cloud claimed the light. The further uphill I got, the wetter the track became, and each step sent an ever-increasing amount of mud onto my pants. I didn't care about that, but I didn't want to fall, so I cut right onto the grass and moved along the tree line. It was tougher in the grass, but I could at least move without losing my balance.

From this angle I could see a little of the interior with another brief pool of moonlight. I almost fell when I saw that ethereal light hit something silvery and white. As I approached, at speed, I couldn't tell what it was.

I reached the SUV, put my hand on the driver's door to fling it open and that's when I froze.

The hilt of a knife protruded from a bloody mass of gray hair. I fell back, hands covering my mouth. I had no air with which to scream. All I could do was stagger backwards as I felt a hard ball growing in my chest. It felt like I was being strangled from the inside. Panic, shock, and terrible pain hit me all at once and I fell to my knees.

I could smell the bleach from the hospital. My mother's slender hand on my shoulder. The metallic taste in my mouth. It was all happening again, as if it was real.

Then I heard something that had no place in my dark memory.

I could hear a whine. It grew louder. At first, I thought I was the one making the sound, and then the pitch changed as it grew louder still. The sound of a big engine, revving high. I glanced to my right, toward the highway, and I saw the headlights tearing through the trees, straight down the lane toward me. The car was going way too fast.

If killing Harry was meant to be a trap to lure me into a dark wood to be murdered too, then I was damn sure I was going to take that bait. Only I wasn't the one who would end up dead. My fists balled and the pressure in my chest eased. I got up, roared, and charged down the lane, tears stinging my eyes. The car kept coming. It accelerated around the same time the beam of its head-lights fell across my face.

'COME ON YOU MOTHERFU—' I couldn't even finish the shout. Not enough in my lungs.

The car slowed. Stopped. I heard a door opening.

I was only forty feet from it.

I was not stopping. Even if they had guns. They had killed my friend. The best friend I ever had. Harry had been a mentor, a father, a brother . . . he was everything to me.

I couldn't see past the lights. No point in squinting to try to make out a face. A figure stepped in front of the beam. Only a silhouette to me.

The torso, the legs and the arms. And the gun in their hand.

Thirty feet away, and I saw them raise their right arm. The gun hand. Leveling the barrel center mass.

There was no way I was going to get close enough to do any damage before I lost a vital organ.

The silhouette's arm straightened.

My left foot slid out from under me. My hands flew out to the sides as I tried to regain my balance and stay on my feet. It was no good. I went down face first into the dirt.

Scrambling around, trying to get my feet beneath me I heard footsteps coming closer, squelching through the mud. The ground was so slippery, and the shock of seeing Harry dead, the run up the track in the heat – I couldn't stand. One last effort got one foot under me, and then I slipped and went down hard.

The footsteps stopped.

I heard the *click* of a pistol hammer being pulled back.

And then the man with the gun spoke.

'Eddie, what the hell are you doing?' said Harry.

CHAPTER THIRTY

EDDIE

'Eddie . . .' said Harry.

I didn't hear what he said next. I was on my feet. My arms wrapped tightly around him. My head on his shoulder.

'I thought that was you in that driver's seat,' I said.

'That car is grey. The SUV behind me is blue. It was so hot I couldn't stand being in the car without the air conditioning on. The battery started to run down so I took it for a quick run. Thought I'd drive up and down the highway to check for cars coming this way. I'm sorry. I was only gone for fifteen minutes.'

I relaxed my grip, stepped back and held his shoulders.

'I don't care, I'm just so glad you're alive.'

'Of course, I'm al— What did you say?'

'There's a dead guy in that car down the lane.'

Harry looked beyond me to the SUV. Then his fingers moved to his shirt and he swore.

I'd managed to get most of the mud from my shirt onto his, and his suit pants.

We approached the vehicle slowly.

'Watch where you step. There are tracks,' said Harry. He took his keys from his pants pocket and activated a small key ring torch.

'Get up on the grass at the side,' he said.

I did what I was told. Harry went right, I went left, and we trudged along the side of the lane until we got back to the SUV. My hands were shaking, and I wasn't taking anything in. Slowly, the adrenaline was giving way, but I wasn't quite there yet.

Harry shone his torch inside while I bent over, gripped my knees, tried to get my breathing under control.

'When you said there was a dead guy in this car, I think you meant dead *people*,' said Harry.

'What?'

'There are *two* bodies in this SUV. Jesus, it's Betty Maguire. And the man beside her . . .'

'It's Cody Warren,' I said.

THE FOURTH DAY

CHAPTER THIRTY-ONE

LOMAX

'Is that you?' came a thin voice from upstairs.

It was just after midnight when Lomax kicked off his muddied boots in the hallway, and hollered, 'Who else do you think it might be?'

'Just checking it's you. And not some crazed killer roaming these parts,' said Lucy, lightly, the smile evident in her tone.

The joke bounced off Lomax, heavily. He shook his head, trying to clear the latest image from the front of his mind. Cops get good at this, given time. Most police officers will, at some stage in their career, see or experience something traumatic. It's part of the job. For some, it happens once in their career. For others, it's once a week. The trick was to compartmentalize – to leave that shit at the door, like a pair of mud-covered boots.

Korn had wanted a warning sent. Lomax had placed Cody Warren's body in the lawyer's SUV and driven it off road to Andy Dubois' house, and left it there, as instructed. Korn had arranged to take care of the rest. It stood as a clear warning to Flynn and his people.

It wasn't like this was something Lomax hadn't done before. He'd killed people in the past. During his tour in Desert Storm. It had never bothered him much. He was doing it for his country. That's what he told himself, but really he knew it was for a paycheck. The first time he'd shot someone on US soil was much different, but it paid better. Lucy didn't know half of what he had done. Shit, she didn't know any of it.

He should have been home hours ago. He'd called Lucy. She said she felt better today. She could think. She'd almost finished knitting her cushion. Not much vomiting today. The pain was tolerable. She would wait up for him. He could bring some cocoa to bed when he got in.

Since she had stopped taking her meds, Lucy had regained much of her old personality. She smiled easily, watched her soaps and read her magazines.

'There's warm cocoa on the stove,' she said, from upstairs.

Lomax toed his slippers on, went to the kitchen. There, on a low heat, a pot of cocoa blowing steam around the kitchen. He used a kitchen towel to take the pot off the heat, and poured two cups of cocoa and took them, carefully, upstairs on a tray with some cookies. Lucy was in bed already, reading a paperback Janet Evanovich novel. She loved the Stephanie Plum books.

He put her cocoa down on the nightstand, offered her a cookie.

'No thank you. I'll be sick if I eat at this time. So tell me, how was your day? Did you do some good?'

She used to ask him that question a lot when he first joined the force – *Did you do some good today?*

In the beginning, he was usually able to find something to say without much difficulty. Then the answers started becoming thin on the ground. Eventually, she stopped asking. She must have sensed that the question shamed him so. The only thing he could remember today was how difficult it had been to move Cody Warren's body from the chest freezer to the car. The beating he'd given the gas station clerk was almost completely forgotten.

'One of those days, huh?' she said.

He didn't answer. Instead, he undressed, brushed his teeth and washed his face and hands. Looking at his shirt on the bathroom floor he saw specks of blood: back spatter, either from Warren's body or, more likely, the gas station clerk. He took his uniform downstairs with the rest of the clothes he'd worn that day, put them in the washing machine and got the thing going. One consequence of Lucy's illness that had been useful was that he now knew how to do laundry, how to work the tumble dryer, wash dishes and all the rest of the chores she had performed. It was hard work. But Lucy told him he would be glad he learned now, when she was here to give him instructions. It would be no good him trying to learn it all after she'd gone.

He went back upstairs, put on his pajamas and got into bed. The cocoa had cooled. He couldn't bring himself to drink it, and the thought of the cookie made him feel nauseous.

'Don't fret,' she said.

'I'm fine. I had a long day is all,' he said.

'Did you see Korn today?' she asked.

'I did,' he said, with a knowing sigh.

'I don't like that man. I don't like the thought of you being around him. I told you that time he came for dinner, there's something missing in there. He's just a big hollow tube of meat, if you ask me.'

Lomax said nothing.

'No heart. No soul. Be careful with him, Colt. That's all I'm saying.'

'I know,' said Lomax.

'I curse the day he came to this town,' she said.

'We've put a lot of bad people away, you know. The place is a lot safer since he became district attorney.'

'He doesn't care who he puts away. Sometimes I figure he just wants to watch some folks suffer. I think he gets a kick out of it, you know that?'

He rolled over, put an arm around Lucy, who was still sitting up in bed.

'You told me that a hundred times. I'll keep an eye on him. Make sure he doesn't do anything wrong.'

He felt her hand on his arm, squeezing. It was reassuring in a way that little else was in his world. Lucy still had strength.

'You're a good man, Colt Lomax,' she said, and kissed him lightly on the forehead. He still had hold of her when he fell asleep.

Lomax woke with a bad taste in his mouth. He was still holding Lucy. He opened his eyes, looked up. She must've read all night. She was still sitting up in bed, but now her head had slumped forward, and her eyes had closed. Her arm had fallen on the bed covers, but the book remained open in front of her.

'Hey, you should lie down. You'll get a crick in your neck,' he said.

Lucy didn't answer. He looked up into her face once more. This time he was alert, that tiny seed of panic in his chest.

'Hey, lie down I said.'

She didn't answer. He touched her cheek, brushing hair away from her face, and then leapt backwards out of bed.

Lucy was cold to the touch. She'd died in the night, in his arms, quite peacefully, it seemed. The cup of cocoa was still on the nightstand. Untouched. Lomax grabbed at his face and hair, and a sound escaped his chest. It was the same kind of noise made by people the world over. It sounds the same no matter what language is spoken.

It was a wail. A cry and a scream from a throat strangled by a crushing wave of sudden grief.

Lomax went outside, to the porch. Sun was coming up. He sat in his rocking chair and he rocked and cried and held himself and cried some more as the hot red sun rose over a dark land.

She was gone. And the pain couldn't touch her now. Not the cancer, nor the pain of finding out what he had really become. She would be spared that, at least.

Despite his grief, he smiled with bitter relief. Lucy died believing him to be a good man. She would never know the kind of man Korn had helped him become. For that, he was thankful. Thankful that she had died before she found out.

Her last words played through this mind on an endless, bitter loop.

You're a good man, Colt Lomax.

CHAPTER THIRTY-TWO

EDDIE

Neither Harry nor I were trained investigators, and we didn't want to go any closer without a professional.

It didn't take Bloch long to get out to the Dubois place. She took a torch from the car, then held it in her mouth as she wrapped plastic bags over her shoes and put on a pair of latex gloves. A terrible smell was coming from Cody's SUV, but Bloch didn't seem to mind. She approached the vehicle slowly, took pictures with her phone from all sides, and especially of the footprints, and then opened the doors of the car and had a good look at the bodies and the interior. There was a pink slip in the glove box confirming the car belonged to Cody Warren, but there were no files in the trunk.

And no photos of Farnesworth's autopsy.

Cody Warren looked wet, like there was a thin layer of slime on his cheeks. He wore a business suit that clung to his body – it too looked wet but there was no blood on him anywhere. A knife protruded from the side of his neck. It looked as though someone could have stabbed him through the rolled-down window. Bloch took a long time examining the knife and especially the hilt. Betty's dress and body were dry except for her face and neck, which were covered in blood. She slumped down in the front passenger seat, beside Cody.

Bloch asked, 'Did either of you touch anything?'

'Not a thing,' I said.

She nodded, said, 'I need to take pictures of your shoes.'

Harry and I turned our backs, lifted our heels so Block could get a good picture of the treads.

'What does this look like to you?' I asked.

'It's strange,' said Bloch.

'What do you mean?' I asked.

'It's half-assed. And there's a mistake,' said Bloch.

Harry and I exchanged puzzled glances. Sometimes Bloch spoke under the pretension that we were all on her wavelength. The truth is she was often way ahead of all of us.

She sighed, said, 'Betty has been beaten, and shot in the head and chest with a .22. There's some blood on the passenger door from the chest shot, judging by height, but I don't see any from the head shot. Cody Warren didn't die from the knife wound. There's a bullet hole behind his ear. Small caliber again. There's a gun in the foot well under the brake pedal.'

Bloch paused, waiting for us to catch up. I was a little clearer, but not all the way there yet.

'The gun in the foot well,' I said, 'is it a .22?'

Bloch nodded.

'So you think it looks like Cody Warren beat Betty, then shot her twice and killed himself?'

'That's what it's made to look like, apart from the knife.'

I nodded, said, 'Just so I'm clear, you're sure it didn't happen that way?'

'Impossible,' said Bloch. 'Cody's been dead a lot longer than Betty. Can't tell how long because he was frozen.'

'Frozen?' said Harry.

Bloch nodded, said, 'He hasn't thawed properly yet. His eyelids are still frozen shut.'

'Richard Kuklinski, a serial killer and hit man for the mob, used to do the same thing. Stick a body in the freezer, sometimes for months, and then thaw it out and there's no way of telling when that person was killed,' I said.

'Was that the mistake?' asked Harry.

'No, there are a lot of mistakes,' said Bloch. She beckoned us closer and pointed to the ground.

There were a few different tracks on the driver's side. As if a couple of different people had walked over the ground. One was Bloch, one was me, and there were at least two others.

'Someone drove the SUV here. Parked it. Moved Cody's body into the driver's seat. On the passenger side there are two different footprints, both in the same line, as if they were following each other's steps precisely. They double back on themselves,' said Bloch.

Harry and I stayed clear of those footprints as we crossed the track to look at the passenger side.

Bloch continued, 'The footsteps on the passenger side are close together as if—'

'As if two people were carrying something heavy between them,' I said.

Bloch nodded, pointed into the cab of the vehicle and shone her torch at Betty's dress. The bottom of the dress had ridden up, and was bunched around her waist.

'Two men carried her body here and put her in this car,' said Bloch. 'No woman sits in a car with her dress ridden up like that. It's not perfect, but it's enough to make the Sunville County sheriff declare it a murder suicide. I know small-town sheriffs, and this is how they'll write it up.'

'What about the knife?'

'That doesn't fit with making it look like a suicide. They can leave Cody's body long enough to thaw out before calling the medical examiner. Won't take long in this heat. Maybe none of that matters if the sheriff and the medical examiner are on Korn's payroll or under his control. They could file a report saying these people drowned if they wanted to.'

'The knife is a message for us,' said Harry. 'Someone killed Cody Warren and Betty Maguire, and dumped their bodies a half mile from Andy Dubois' house. The knife confirms it.'

I could tell even Bloch didn't follow this completely.

'How is the knife a message?' I asked.

'The flower on the hilt. It's a white camellia. The Klan weren't the only group of murderers and racists in the South. There were the Knights of the White Camelia out of Louisiana, though they had chapters in other states. The Klan were mostly poor white folks. The White Camelia were much more dangerous, although there were never very many of them. A group of wealthy men. Powerful men.

A lot of ex-Confederate officers founded the group, and they were joined by newspaper editors, doctors, lawyers, landowners, lawmen, and even judges. The cream of upper-class Southern society. They lobbied, used their wealth and influence to try to advocate for the supremacy of the white race. They murdered, harassed and destroyed whole black communities.'

'I'd never heard of them,' I said.

'They died out in the 1870s, supposedly. Although with the nature of underground movements like this, you can never tell for sure. Look at the hilt of that knife. That's mother of pearl, and old silver and steel. I've seen pictures of knives just like that, buried in the bodies of white folks who were against the White Camelia. Most of them were Republicans, I should add. Lincoln's party was the one crying for tolerance in the South for a long time.'

'Things change,' I said.

Harry nodded, said, 'This is a warning. If we continue with this case, we're in serious danger. All of us.'

Bloch stepped forward and stared into the SUV. Her jaw muscle moved as she clenched her teeth. I knew she was burning those images into her memory. Two innocent people, dead.

We didn't have much choice but to call the law. The Sheriff's Department sent two deputies I didn't recognize. They took a statement from me and called in forensics. I left them to it and went back to Patricia's house. As I set foot on the porch, I heard a noise coming from inside the house. I opened the door and saw Patricia and Andy sitting on the couch.

They were sitting together. Patricia had her arm around Andy, her palm gripping his right shoulder. With his left hand, he gently patted the top of her hand, and rocked back and forth as Patricia whispered to him, telling him it was alright.

When I'd first seen Andy in that cell, he was doing the exact same thing. Patting his shoulder, rocking back and forth. Trying to comfort himself. It looked like they did this a lot, mother and son, comforting one another in their own way.

'Andy had a nightmare. Happens a lot. It's okay, he'll come around. What was all that business with the sheriff?' she asked.

She'd obviously seen the police lights on their cruiser when it arrived.

I didn't want to tell her. Not now. Not yet. Everything is worse at nighttime. Some things should only be said in the daylight.

'I'll tell you tomorrow. It's okay. Is Andy alright?'

'He just needs some time. I'll see if I can get some meds tomorrow. We're all out.'

'What kind of medication?' I asked. I wasn't aware of Andy being on any kind of meds.

'They're for his anxiety. They don't come under Medicaid, and I can't always afford them. If my ankle is good for a couple of weeks, I can stock up. But it's been bad, these past months.'

Only in the greatest country in the world would a working mother have to weigh up buying medication for herself or her son. She would go without, and endure the pain if it brought Andy some ease. I knew she would.

'Is this a recent thing, the anxiety?'

'No,' said Andy. 'I've had it from a teenager. Can't sleep, can't eat. And I get panic attacks. Stress makes it worse sometimes.'

'Did you get access to meds in the jail?'

'No, they wouldn't give me anything.'

There was nothing in the files about Andy being on any kind of medication or having been diagnosed with any kind of anxiety disorder.

'Do you mind me asking if anything brought on this anxiety? There doesn't have to have been anything in particular, of course. Sometimes people just get ill. But if there was something, maybe some kind of trauma, I'd like to know about it. I don't want any surprises in court.'

Patricia and Andy rocked together on the couch, and I could see it calming him. His chest didn't heave so much, and the shaking in his legs had stopped.

'There wasn't one incident,' said Patricia. 'People don't understand what it's like being a young black person in America. I'm fifty-seven years old, Eddie. I thought life would've been easier for my kids. I don't think things are better for black folks, if anything they're worse. Is it any wonder a young black man is on anxiety pills in this country?'

'I think you might be right. Lot of people out there feel they can speak their mind now, no matter how repulsive. This stain has always been on America. It's just that we're able to see it a lot clearer these days. Things will get better, in time,' I said.

'Do you believe that?' she asked.

'I think there's a new generation who are not going to stand for this shit. Andy's part of that. Young men like him will save us all.'

Patricia gazed at her son as I spoke, and I could see the hope straining tears from her eyes.

'You said you had a nightmare, Andy. What was it? Talking about it can make it better.'

He looked at me then, and in all my time on this earth, I never saw someone so scared.

'I've had the same dream every night for the past while,' he said. 'I was tied to a big chair, but the chair was on fire and I couldn't get out of it. Mr. Korn was there. Laughing at me – watching me burn.'

CHAPTER THIRTY-THREE

TAYLOR AVERY

Taylor Avery turned off the hot water faucet. Listened carefully.

There it was.

Soft knocking at his front door.

He grabbed a dish towel, dried his hands. Before he left the kitchen, he reached up on top of the refrigerator for his pistol. He removed the locking mechanism with the key from his keychain, held the gun low, by his side, as he made his way toward his front door. Taylor was a man of average height, with light brown hair. He was a dairy farmer, and work was long and hard, which built lean strength over his frame.

The Avery farm was at least a mile from their closest neighbor, who was also a dairy farmer. It was after midnight. His wife and teenage boy were asleep upstairs. Whoever was at the door was not on a social call. He didn't have a peephole in the door or any kind of security system. He was holding his security system in his right hand. He opened the front door to find a tall man standing on his porch. He wore a suit and was gazing out over the land, unconcerned about who would answer the door. The porch light gave a yellow hue to his pale skin.

'Mr. Avery?' said the man.

Taylor squinted in the darkness. The man was not armed. His hands were clasped in front of him, as if he were in church. It took a moment, but Taylor soon recognized the man at his front door.

'Mr. Korn? Is that you?'

'The very same. You mind stepping out for a few minutes so we can talk?'

Taylor didn't need the gun, even though he still felt fearful at the sight of the district attorney at his front door. He locked the pistol, placed it on the hall table, and went outside. He gestured to one of the chairs and watched Korn fold his long frame into it. It was not an awkward maneuver, but it looked as though chairs were somehow alien to Korn. As if his height and shape were not made to fit most things. Once he'd sat down, he held out an open hand to the chair next to it.

Taylor took a seat, and as he did so, he caught a strange scent on the air – decay. On the table beside the chair was a paperback of *To Kill A Mockingbird*. Avery's favorite novel. He liked to read it every year, in the summer. He could remember sitting on this very porch, after helping his father in the fields that day, a cool glass of lemonade beside him and the light of an oil lamp illuminating Scout's world. Which was, at that time at least, not so very different from his own.

'My apologies for the call at this hour. I've been somewhat busy preparing for a trial. You may have heard about it. I'm prosecuting the Dubois boy. The one who killed Skylar Edwards.'

Taylor nodded, 'Sure, it's all over the town. The papers too. Poor girl.'

And then, Taylor stopped talking. He knew why Korn was here. He swallowed, and told himself to be more careful with his words.

'I am aware that you have received a summons for jury service, Mr. Avery. Given how far you live outside of town, and the fact that you have not read any articles on the murder, nor watched any news reports, it's likely you will be selected to serve on the jury for that case.'

Taylor had read a lot of articles. Watched a lot of news reports. He'd pretty much said so not two seconds ago. He simply nodded, keeping his tongue in check.

'This farm has been in your family for a long time. Five generations, so I'm told,' said Korn.

'That's right. We've been lucky. Running a farm is no easy business. Never has been, and it's only getting harder,' said Taylor, who decided farming was a safer subject than murder trials.

'As you know, I have responsibility for the law in this county. But I am aware of all that goes on, administratively. There's talk of a casino looking to buy some land out of town. Build a mall, movie theater, all that jazz. You heard about this?'

Taylor nodded. He'd had offers to buy his land from two separate law firms on behalf of large companies looking to develop just such a venture. He'd declined them both. Even though the offer was good and would have set him and his family up for another two or three generations. In truth he didn't even consider it.

This was Avery land. They had several rye fields, which kept the cattle fed, and they had enough left over to sell on the side along with the milk. They were largely self-sustaining. His father had worked the land all his life, just as his father had before him, and Taylor was set upon doing the same.

'See, if there's a commercial development which is in the county's best interest, there are certain laws they can use to purchase land. They can get court orders, and you and your family would have to move. Those orders usually mean you don't get full market price for your property. Maybe twenty cents on the dollar. Maybe less.'

Taylor suddenly felt cold, even though it was a warm evening.

'I am not without influence, you know,' said Korn.

'I guess,' said Taylor.

'No need to guess. Take my word for it. I can make those orders go away. I can make the casinos go away. Or I can help fast-track that process and get you kicked off this farm by winter. Maybe you can remember that when you're deliberating on your verdict in the Dubois case. You're a respected man around these parts. Fair, I've always said. And your fellow jurors will no doubt follow your lead. Don't you think?'

'It's possible,' said Avery.

'I think they will. You persuade your fellow jurors to find Andy guilty and your grandson will be milking cattle in that shed over there when he's your age. If you were to question my judgment, well, that would be a bad thing. Your tenure on this land is in my gift. For now, I give you that gift. But gifts can be taken away if nothing is received in return.'

Korn leaned forward, and Taylor caught the smell again. It reminded him of the time he found a dead turtle underneath the house.

'It would be a travesty of justice if that Dubois boy was set free by a jury,' said Korn.

It was clear to Taylor what was expected from him. He didn't know anything about the case other than what was in the news. Forensic evidence linking Andy Dubois to the murder, so they said. Still, he knew Korn shouldn't be here, and he didn't appreciate being threatened. Some rural folk have an extremely keen mind, sharper than any street hustler. An innate wisdom, perhaps.

Taylor nodded. Said nothing.

'I believe we have an understanding, Mr. Avery,' said Korn, extending a long, pale hand.

Taylor took the handshake, surprised by how cold Korn's skin felt, as if it had been in an ice bath.

'Goodnight,' said Korn.

Taylor watched him leave, get into his car and drive away quietly. He didn't know Andy Dubois, Skylar Edwards or her family. When the jury summons arrived he had silently prayed that he would not be called as a juror, because it would mean hiring someone else to help with the farm while he was at court. If he was selected, he would do his duty according to the law and his oath on the Bible. Taylor took these things seriously. Church every Sunday, with the family, without fail. He didn't like Korn, even before he had threatened him. There was something odd about the man. A strange light in his eyes that Taylor only ever saw fleetingly, but which sent a chill down his back, nonetheless.

One thing that was as important as his land was his name.

The Averys were part of the land. Their blood and sweat had sewn those crops for decades, and their cattle had grazed their fields through their own generations. The Averys paid their debts and gave what they could to the poor. Now a man of the law was asking Taylor to betray his oath, and his name, if called upon.

He shivered on the porch. It wasn't the temperature – it was the physical relief of being free of Korn's presence. He couldn't wait to be free of his stink. Protecting Avery land was his life's work. He wondered what he would be prepared to do to keep it.

He sat down in the chair, picked up the copy of *To Kill A Mockingbird* and placed it on his lap. Absently thumbing the pages, he wondered now at the choice before him. Soon he might have to choose between his good name and his farm. There didn't seem to be much of a choice to be made. His son, of fourteen years, lay sleeping in Taylor's old room upstairs. This land was his son's birthright, and he told himself he would have to do whatever it took to protect it.

CHAPTER THIRTY-FOUR

EDDIE

It was hard on Andy, bringing him back to court the day after he got out. I wanted more time for him to settle, so we could talk more easily, but the court had made its demands. At least this time Andy was in a decent set of clothes. New ones. Well, almost new. Using her savings, Patricia had bought Andy a suit from a second-hand store. It would have fitted him once, before he was arrested. Now it looked like two Andy's could live in that suit. The shirt wasn't much better. It looked like Andy's neck was a brush pole sticking out from the collar.

'Now, don't you look fine,' said Patricia.

Andy sat nervously in front of her, at the defense table. He turned around, gave her the thumbs up. He knew she had spent her last dime on this get-up, and he wasn't about to taint that for her. It was Patricia's way of helping. She made sure Andy looked well for court. Like the decent young man he really was.

Patricia sat in the front row of the gallery. There weren't too many people in the courtroom that day. Some reporters, some interested citizens in white tees and beige chinos including Brian Denvir, this time without his AR-15. The father of the victim was in court. Kate pointed him out to me, discreetly. He wore a blue button-down shirt and black pants, and his face told a story of great pain that no one would want to bear. He caught my eye, stared.

I nodded, but didn't smile.

The pain that boiled behind his eyes turned into something else and aimed it in my direction. Now there's a man who would stand on my throat given half a chance. It was hard to blame him. He'd been told by law enforcement that Andy Dubois killed his little girl, and no matter what happened in the courtroom, that thought might never change.

At the defense table I had Harry on my left, Kate on my right. Andy sat beside Harry, who was taking great care with the kid. Harry never had children, but the affection he showed for this young man made me think Harry might have regretted it.

Kate was ready with a folder full of notes on potential jurors. I'd flicked through it that morning, after a sleepless night. It was good work. Better than I could do.

Korn was already at the prosecution table, a few assistants beside him. I looked around the court, but I didn't see the sheriff. The judge, Chandler, entered the court and we stood to attention. The judge announced that this was the *voir dire* hearing for jury selection in the case of Sunville County v Dubois.

'There are over one hundred prospective jurors waiting in the wings, counselors. I expect you both to work fast. In my court, I make the ruling on death qualification, and I don't need you to spend more than five minutes with a juror before I make up my mind. Is that clear, Mr. Flynn?' said the judge.

I nodded.

This was my first death-penalty case, but I knew the pitfalls already. In this town, it didn't much matter who was sitting on that jury. None were likely to be open to the prospect that Andy might be innocent until proven guilty. And there was another problem – jury selection in a death-penalty case was different to any other jury selection process in the criminal justice system.

In a capital-murder case, the jury has to be 'death-qualified'. They have to be willing to impose the death penalty if the defendant is convicted. The questions jurors are asked in these cases tend to be about whether they would impose the death penalty, or whether they would never impose such a sentence even if the defendant was guilty. This skews the case in favor of the prosecution right away. Most women, minority groups, Catholics, and liberal-minded people are opposed to the death penalty and would never bring home such a sentence, even if they were to find someone guilty. This means they don't get to serve on juries in capital-murder cases. The consequence is most death-qualified juries have little racial diversity, and it's a majority of white, Protestant, male Old-Testament dudes who would just as soon take the defendant out into their backyard and shoot them in the head before a word is spoken in court.

The fact is a death-qualified jury is more likely to convict. Period.

And considering the question they are most asked at the start is whether they would pass a death sentence, this sends a message to even unbiased jurors that eventually they are gonna have to consider imposing that sentence. So the jury is not thinking about whether the prosecution has proven its case, all they're thinking about is if can they kill the defendant. The effect is a cloud of guilt that haunts the defendant from jury selection to verdict.

Andy had the worst case stacked against him, on all fronts. And there didn't seem to be too much we could do about it.

'Remember,' said Kate, pointing to a list of names she'd written down, 'we've got to bump these jurors no matter what.'

Kate had been through the answers to the jury questionnaires that had been completed in advance. She had picked out twenty-five jurors that we had to avoid, based on their answers.

The judge called in fifteen potential jurors and gave them an introduction to the process. To cut through the 'bull', as Judge Chandler put it, he asked if any of them felt so strongly against the death penalty that they would never impose it. Four reasonable citizens of Sunville County raised their hands, and they were summarily dismissed.

He began probing the remaining eleven more closely on the question, and another five were jettisoned.

'We may as well not be here at all,' said Harry as Chandler dismissed another juror.

I was surprised that he'd gotten rid of so many jurors already. Historically, the death penalty was favored by the country as a whole. The population of the United States has been polled about the death penalty every year since the late 1930s. The very first year that a majority of Americans said they were against the death penalty was in the 2019 poll. For ninety or so years, most Americans thought executing their fellow citizens was a good idea.

*

Four p.m., and ten jurors were on the stand. Two more were required. We had used all of our ten pre-emptory challenges, which allowed us to kick jurors without any reason being stated. We could still challenge for cause, but that was going to be tough in front of Chandler. Kate was on her feet, questioning a dairy farmer called Taylor Avery.

'You have read news articles on this case?' asked Kate.

'That's correct, ma'am.'

'You have watched news reports on the case?'

'Yes, ma'am.'

'Having watched those news reports, and read those articles, how can you distinguish between what was reported, and what the facts are in this case?'

'I don't believe everything I read in the papers, and I mostly don't believe what I see on TV, ma'am.'

Good answer. I was beginning to like Mr. Avery. I could tell Kate was warming to him too.

'How do you decide what you believe to be the truth, Mr. Avery?' asked Kate.

'Well, with the news, if it came out of Washington it's most likely not true. Or it's just someone's truth. My pappy always taught me there are two sides to a story.'

'What do you do in your spare time, Mr. Avery, when you're not working the farm?'

Judge Chandler rolled his eyes. He wasn't going to tolerate too much of this.

'I read,' said Avery.

'What do you read?'

'Fiction, mostly the classics.'

Kate took her time, focusing on Avery. He had no reason to lie. She leaned over to me.

'I think he's not bad. What do you think?'

'If he's being truthful about reading then I say we take him. Readers have empathy. Anyway, there's no challenge for cause here. Let's take him.'

Kate said, 'Your Honor, we accept Mr. Avery as the eleventh juror.'

Judge Chandler directed Avery to a seat.

Eleven jurors sat in the box. Seven white guys. Two African American men and two white women. That's what happens in death-qualified jury cases.

One place left to fill.

A young African American woman came forward and took her seat on the stand. Her name was Imelda Falls. She rated high on Kate's wish list of jurors. Korn had one pre-emptory challenge left, and he used it.

Kate was waiting for him.

'Your Honor, Batson challenge,' said Kate.

Under Supreme Court law, a pre-emptory challenge cannot be used for any discriminatory reason. You can't dump a juror just because of their skin color, religion or sex.

'Very well, Mr. Korn, you are required to state your reasons for this challenge,' said the judge, with a heavy sigh.

Korn rose to his feet, buttoned his jacket and cleared his throat. Giving himself time to think.

'Your Honor, I believe it improper for the defense counsel to question whether my judgment is biased. However, I will state the reason. Miss Falls is not a juror the prosecution believes could deliver a fair verdict, based on her answers to the questionnaire.'

'Which answers, specifically?' asked Kate.

'Young lady,' said the judge, 'you do not ask questions of the district attorney. He has given his answer. It is Batson compliant. I see nothing prejudicial. The juror is dismissed.'

Just like that.

I whispered to Kate, 'Don't sweat it. Chandler may as well take a seat at the prosecution table.'

She nodded. I could see the blood rising to her cheeks. Kate wanted to rip Chandler a new asshole, and I didn't blame her. In fact, if she could get away with it, I would hold her jacket.

'Next juror,' said Chandler.

Another young woman took the stand. Younger than Imelda, and white. I glanced at Kate's jury list. I knew her first name already

– Sandy. She used to work at Gus's Diner, and her non-VW death-trap of a car was parked outside The Chanterelle.

It was Korn's turn to ask questions.

'Do you know any of the parties or witnesses in this case?' he asked.

Sandy Boyette wore a white blouse, black pants and a red ribbon in her dark hair. She took a moment to think, showing she understood the question. She glanced at me. Fast. Half a second at most. Then said, 'No.'

Korn went through the motions, but she was bulletproof. She said she had no moral objection to the death penalty, and it would be something she would consider if the defendant was convicted.

I whispered to Kate, 'Let's take her. No questions. No objections.'

'I'm not sure about her,' said Kate. 'She's not much older than the victim, they lived in the same town. I don't think they could have avoided each other. She probably knew her, or knew of her, and she would identify strongly with the victim. That makes our job harder.'

'Trust me,' I said.

Kate nodded reluctantly and when it was time, we accepted Sandy as the last juror.

Two alternates were tacked onto the end in double-quick time, then the judge said, 'We've spent more than enough time assembling this jury. We begin the trial day after tomorrow. Mr. Korn, Miss Brooks and Mr. Flynn, be ready.'

We left the court, and I had one question in mind.

Why did Sandy lie to the prosecutor by saying she didn't know me?

CHAPTER THIRTY-FIVE

EDDIE

The room at The Chanterelle was beginning to feel smaller every time I walked in. It was past eight in the evening, and we had been hitting the case files all day. Bloch had been on the phone most of the day and Harry and I were reading and thinking. Kate was filling the room with notes and more paper than I knew what to do with. The case seemed to be expanding but we were no further on.

'Any luck getting a hold of the pathologist, Farnesworth?' I asked.

Bloch shook her head.

'Okay, leave him to me. You get on Korn and stay on him until you get something we can use.'

Bloch nodded.

'We need to discuss strategy for the prosecution witnesses,' said Kate.

'I know, but I can't think straight right now.'

Harry got up out of the armchair, took a piece of paper and pinned it to the wall with a tack. He lifted a sharpie and began to make a list of prosecution witnesses.

'Who have we got? The prosecution have Skylar's father, Francis Edwards. He'll testify either at the beginning or the end of the case. Something to get the jury's blood up. Then the DA's friendly medical examiner, Miss Price, to give the jury the gory details. Next, we've got the DA's forensics expert, Cheryl Banbury. She confirms Andy's blood was present beneath Skylar's fingernails. We still don't have a plan of attack on any of this. The owner of Hogg's Bar is gonna tell us he saw Andy and Skylar arguing that night, and that'll be all she wrote. Korn won't need the jailhouse snitch, Lawson, or Sheriff Lomax to go through the signed confession from our client in order to get a conviction.'

'On top of that, we have a poor jury,' said Kate. 'Even if we did have a counter-argument for the forensics, and the bar owner, we're stuck getting Andy out of a confession. I just don't see us winning this one, Eddie. I'm sorry, I think Andy is innocent, but I can't see a way out of this.'

I nodded. 'That pattern mark on Skylar's head is important. The state's medical examiner left it out of the report. That means it doesn't suit the DA's case, and I can't figure out why. Why get that mark omitted from the report? It's not as if it was missed, and it's not because Andy wasn't arrested with a ring like that one; I'm sure Korn could have found one just like it and planted it on Andy. No, there's something else. Something we're not seeing.'

'We're not seeing the security footage from the gas station on the night of the murder, that's for damn sure,' said Harry.

'Korn is so careful to cover his tracks,' I said. 'He breaks the rules, hides evidence that helps the defense, and I think he had something to do with Cody and Betty's murders. Just look at the guy – he's like a walking corpse. And he's obsessed with the death penalty. No, if we're going to take this guy down and save Andy, we have to play the game smarter, and dirtier, than Korn.'

I took out my cell phone, selected a contact and hit dial.

He answered fast. No hello, no pleasantries, he didn't have time for it.

'I heard about Cody and his office manager. You okay?' said Berlin.

'We're fine. We don't scare easy. Look, this guy Korn has Andy's prosecution sewn up tight. He's hidden or destroyed security-camera footage, which might have shown us the real murderer and exonerated Andy. And our medical examiner won't talk to us. I think he's gotten to him too. Cody and Betty's murder sends a message.'

'You think he had a part in that?' asked Berlin.

'I can't prove it, but I think so.'

'What can I do?'

'I need some more money.'

'I checked the account, there's still three-hundred and seventy-five thousand dollars available. Is that not enough?' asked Berlin.

'Nope. I need that for something else. About another hundred grand should do it,' I said.

'What is that extra hundred grand for?'

'I don't think you want to know.'

'Eddie, I think it's best if I know precisely what it's for.'

'Fair enough. I want to bribe a juror . . .'

THE FIFTH DAY

CHAPTER THIRTY-SIX

EDDIE

I had one day before trial. I rose early, headed off in the Prius by my-self before first light. Sunville County was the smallest in the state, but it was close to the second most populous county and the seat of that county – the city of Mobile. It was pronounced *Mohbeel*, which I guessed was some kind of French or creole hangover. In compari-son to the tiny Buckstown, it was way more relaxed. I guessed that probably only half the people on the street were armed. This was as laidback as you could get in Alabama.

I parked on a hilly street, just after nine in the morning, got out of the car and approached a large, detached property in a white-picket-fence suburb. It was the kind of place that had rules about how high your lawn could grow before someone else would mow it for you and then hand you a bill. I opened the gate, walked up to the porch and rang the doorbell. Like every home on the street, the house was in great shape and looked as though it had been freshly painted.

The door was answered by a man in a dressing gown. He was sixty or so, with a ribbon of white hair surrounding his bald dome. The gown looked expensive – red silk. Thin, so it could be worn in the summer. I saw a revolver-shaped bulge in the right hip pocket. The man looked wary of callers, even in the daylight.

'Doctor Farnesworth?' I asked.

'Who are you?' he asked, his hand disappearing into the hot pocket.

'My name is Eddie Flynn. I'm an attorney. I represent Andy Dubois,' I said, stepping forward, jamming my foot in the door.

He tried to close the door, turn away, but the door hit my shoe and wouldn't budge.

'You're trespassing,' he said.

'I'm talking to a professional witness who isn't holding up his end of the contract.'

'I'm retired,' he said.

'So is Cody Warren. Permanently. His office manager, Betty, too.'

'Betty's dead?'

'They were found last night. Both bodies dumped in a car on the Dubois property. Doctor, I know you're scared, but I need to talk to you.'

He paused, and I could see his mind running calculations, his eyes darting left and right. I got the feeling he had figured Cody was dead. But Betty surprised him. The murders had not been in the papers or on TV. The Sheriff's Department were going quiet on this one, which was more than suspicious.

He let go of the door, stepped outside and checked both sides of the street. No pedestrians, and except for the Prius, there were no cars. Everyone in this neighborhood had a driveway. Only visitors, or folks keeping an eye on things, would park on the street.

'Is that your car?' he asked, pointing to the Prius.

'It's a rental, but yeah. Can we talk inside?'

He ushered me indoors, fast. Closed the door and showed me into a room to the left of the hallway. It was an oak-paneled study, with bookshelves lining one wall. The curtains were pulled in this room, and the only light came from a banker's lamp on his desk. He didn't sit down, didn't offer me a seat on the couch.

'What do you want? I already told you, I'm retired.'

He was out of breath, but it was panic and fear rather than exertion on his part.

'Cody Warren hired you to perform an autopsy on Skylar Edwards. You found marks on her temple, made with a ring. Those marks are not in the medical examiner's report. I think that's important. Either the ME missed them, which I don't think is likely, or she was told to omit them from her report. Why do you think that is?'

'Isn't it obvious? The suspect Korn found for the murder didn't have that ring. The ring could be used for reasonable doubt. Let me tell you something, Mr. Flynn, there are very few unsolved murders in Sunville County. Many suspect that the few unsolved cases that they do have were probably committed by the DA himself, or those close to him.'

'You think the DA is a killer?'

He shook his head. 'If you have not arrived at that conclusion on your own then I can't help you. He lives to watch the executions he has orchestrated. Either in the chair or with the needle, or . . . by other means.'

'All the more reason to help me save Andy Dubois.'

As I spoke that name, Farnesworth's face changed. He turned away, unable to meet my eyes, his gaze fell and his features too. The name of Andy Dubois was a sliver of shame that pricked at this skin.

'I can't help you. I told you I'm retired,' he said again, his voice low.

'You were retired when you took the job from Cody. What's changed?'

'Everything. I did the autopsy, wrote my report and discussed it with Cody. At some stage he had to share it with the prosecutor through discovery. Day after my report was served on the District Attorney's Office, I got a phone call to say it would not be in my interests to testify if I wanted to keep breathing.'

'Did you tell the sheriff about this?'

'The phone call came from the Sheriff's Office.'

'Lomax?'

'Yeah, Lomax was a good man before he met Korn. I don't know how to explain it to you properly, maybe I don't have to, but Korn has a way of getting to people. Climbing inside them with his filth. Infecting them. Not long after he became DA, the capital-murder cases in the county went through the roof, and Lomax bought a new car. Then soon after, a new house, his wife started shopping at all the expensive stores in town. Look, do you need me to draw you a picture? Korn put Lomax on the take. And once you make a little compromise, you're finished. Then it's a one-way street. Taking a bribe becomes turning a blind eye to some evidence tampering, then actively evidence tampering, then destroying evidence, then destroying people like Cody and Betty. Sooner or later, you realize that street has taken you someplace you never expected to be.'

I knew the story only too well. I'd seen it before in cops. It doesn't happen overnight. It's a slow accretion; little by little they become more corrupt until it consumes them. It's a frog in cold water, which slowly comes to the boil.

'Why would Lomax pull the trigger for Korn? That's a big step. Is he being blackmailed?'

'I don't know. Korn has a way of making people do whatever he wants. And if he can't control someone, they won't be around for much longer. That's why I can't help you. I don't want to meet the business end of a shotgun on my way to the mailbox one morning.'

I didn't want to pressure Farnesworth. He looked like a scared old man. But the thought of Andy sitting in an electric chair was by far the greater evil.

'Look, you took photos when you examined the body. Betty told me they were in the trunk of Cody's car with the case files – but they're missing. I need those photos, and I need you to testify about the marks on the victim's head. If you do this, I'll protect you.'

'You going to move in with me, son? No disrespect, but you're going to have a tough enough time staying alive yourself.'

'Story of my life,' I said. 'Look, there has to be a way of me using the photographs and keeping you out of it. None of the other reports or photos show that marking on the victim.'

'I'm sorry about your client. Truly, I am. But I'm not willing to die for him.'

'I've got friends in New York. I can have a full protection team on a plane, on their way here in under an hour. Please—'

'There's no way I'm taking that chance.'

'So Cody and Betty died for nothing, Skylar's killer walks free and Korn gets to fry an innocent kid in the electric chair? Is that what you're telling me?'

He took a step back, his bottom lip trembled as he sucked in air.

'You used to be a doctor. Isn't it a doctor's first duty to preserve life?'

He hung his head. I could see the question was eating him up inside. Not the rhetorical question I'd asked him. No, the big question. The question we all ask ourselves at one time or another. It is the question implied in Martin Niemöller's confession speech in 1946. His words were given poetic form and now adorn several holocaust museums. Martin said that when they came for the socialists, he did not speak because he was not a socialist. Then they came for the communists, the trade unionists, then the Jews, and he was not a communist, a trade unionist, nor a Jew, and he did not speak. The last line haunts the heart.

Then they came for me – and there was no one left to speak for me.

At what point do you take a stand? When will you speak?

That's the question in Farnesworth's mind. I could tell by the coats on the rack in the hallway, and the way the place was decorated, Farnesworth had a wife – one he probably cared for very much. He was weighing up the risk of harm coming to her, against the dark shame that would come from refusing me.

'I can't,' he said.

I'd asked myself the question a long time ago. And I'd spoken. I stand in court for those who need me, no matter what. It had cost me everything. My marriage, my relationship with my daughter. And more recently, a woman I had grown to love very much. Doing the right thing has consequences, same as doing nothing. And it can be just as hard to look at yourself in the mirror.

I nodded. I understood Farnesworth's fear. He was right to be afraid.

'Okay, but now you've got two choices. I know you've got the photos, and I need them. You can give them to me, or I can take them. There are no halfway houses here, Doc.'

'I'll give you the damn photos, but I will not set foot in a courtroom. That means you can't use them in the trial, right?'

'Just give me the photos,' I said.

He moved to the desk, unlocked it and fingered through some files before withdrawing an envelope and handing it over. It was open, and I reached inside and withdrew the photo book.

'I think whatever was in those photos got Cody and Betty killed,' said Farnesworth. 'I'll have to live with that.'

I found the close-ups of the wounds on her head.

'The star-shaped impact pattern wraps around the front of the skull. Like she was imprinted,' he said.

The photos got closer and closer on the wounds, showing a zoom progression. The final picture, probably taken with the camera lens almost touching the skin, was the one that had gotten Cody killed. I was sure of it. I didn't know what it meant, but I knew it was trouble.

'Are those symbols on her skin above the star?' I asked.

'I didn't see them initially. My eyes are not what they were. Cody saw something in the photographs I'd taken and got them enlarged. Then he came to see me to talk it over. When he walked out my front door that's the last anyone saw of him.'

'What are those marks? Are they burns?'

'No, they're bruise patterns. The skin wraps around an object that comes into contact with it at speed and with force. The impact site can appear white with discoloration around it, making the shape clearer. The symbols were on the ring. They are repeated, very faintly, with each blow, but that was the wound with the best visual of the imprint. That's the photograph that Cody thought was important.'

I saw what looked like a crescent shape and two horizontal dashes connected by a vertical line. The symbols were small, maybe only a quarter of an inch. I knew the symbol on her skin was a mirror image of the symbol on the ring.

It was two letters. Sitting just above the star.

F C

CHAPTER THIRTY-SEVEN

BLOCH

Bloch stood on the corner of 15th Street and Main, scanning the parking lot on the opposite side of the street. A parking lot behind a wire fence that could take maybe fifty cars. On either side of the lot was a post office that looked like it had been there for a while, and a bagel shop that looked like it had been there five minutes. On Bloch's side of the street was a warehouse, and a candy store that faced the lot.

It was 10.01 in the a.m., and the person she was supposed to meet was technically one minute late. She caught herself grinding her teeth, stopped it. Popped a piece of Juicy Fruit in her mouth and sighed.

If Bloch said she would be somewhere at a certain time, she was there, at the exact spot, where she was supposed to be, at the exact time or earlier. She could not abide being late, or anyone else who wasn't on time. Things were supposed to be done in a certain way. She still struggled with those who were not on her program.

A Lincoln Navigator entered the parking lot across the street. The tires crunching over the layer of gravel at the entrance, and then rolling onto the smooth concrete. The Lincoln reversed into a space, and a lady in a beige top, flannel pants and hemp shoes got out of the car. She had brown hair, tied up, and a necklace of fine gold with a lump of what looked like jade on the end of it. Bloch crossed the street and met the lady as she was exiting the lot.

'Jane?' asked Bloch.

'Yes, you must be Bloch,' said the lady. She smelled of fine oils. Sweet and rich. Bloch imagined Jane spending her evenings eating vegan food, while listening to classical jazz and catching up on this week's *New Yorker*. Jane had money. Enough that she didn't need a real job and was content to devote her time to a number of charities. One of which was a charity campaigning for convicts on death row. Jane was the vice-chair.

Bloch nodded in greeting.

'Well, this is where it happened,' said Jane. 'Like I said, there's not much to see. The car dealership closed after Mr. Sequentes was murdered. It lay vacant for a long time, then as the businesses came to this side of town, they needed more parking and this lot opened up. It's quite cheap, for the area. Four dollars an hour.'

Bloch wasn't interested in how much it cost to park.

'Did you bring the file?' asked Bloch.

Jane folded her arms, shifted her weight onto one hip, angled her head.

'Can you tell me your interest in all of this? I didn't see your name mentioned anywhere in the file.'

'I work for a law firm,' said Bloch.

Jane didn't move. Didn't ask anything else. She was trying to let Bloch know this wasn't enough. Not even close.

'We represent Andy Dubois,' said Bloch.

'Oh, I heard about that case. That starts tomorrow, right? So why are you asking me about Darius Robinson?'

'I'm not interested in Darius Robinson. I'm interested in the district attorney.'

'Look, don't waste your time. Randal Korn is well protected. There's nothing on him that we could use in Darius's case. He covers his tracks. Darius had a shit lawyer for his trial, but a damn good one on appeal, and Cody Warren couldn't find anything to use against Korn. Sorry,' said Jane.

She let her arms fall to her sides, took a step back. She was going to leave.

'Cody Warren is dead,' said Bloch.

'Dead?'

'His office manager too. Executed and left in Cody's car outside Andy Dubois' house.'

'Oh my God, that's . . . just awful. Those poor people. Oh my God, do you think the district attorney had something to do with it?'

Bloch raised a single eyebrow.

Jane was dumbstruck for a time, and Bloch didn't have that kind of time to waste.

'Let me look at the file, please.'

'What's the point? If there was something there, Cody would have seen it.'

Bloch sighed. She didn't like to talk. Conversation wasn't her thing. But she needed to get a look at that file.

'If there's nothing in that file that's useful to me, you haven't lost anything. Just the half hour it will take me to read it. If I find something, you can apply to have Darius Robinson pardoned, posthumously.'

Jane stopped. Looked Bloch up and down. Said, 'And what makes you think you can spot something that one of the best attorneys in this state missed?'

Bloch toed the gravel with her boot, said, 'It's what I do.'

Jane fell quiet then said, 'Oh my God, how are you going to read the file in half an hour? There's like two boxes filled with documents in my trunk.'

There goes Bloch's eyebrow again.

'Come on then,' said Jane.

It had taken Bloch a few days to look through the last twenty death penalty cases prosecuted by Korn. Maybe two of them would have been taken as capital-murder cases by other district attorneys, but Korn had prosecuted them all to the fullest extent the law allowed, seeking the death penalty each time. Of those twenty, ten of the defendants were evidently guilty. Not that they deserved to die, thought Bloch, but they wouldn't gain a lot of public sympathy if she managed to find wrongdoing on the part of Korn. Of the other ten cases, nine were young men who were either intellectually or psychologically challenged. They had workable defenses, but nothing that caught Bloch's attention.

Until she came across the case of Darius Robinson. He was convicted under the state party laws, which say that if you participate in a crime, you are liable for the entirety of the crime, even if you only played a minor part. Darius was convicted of robbery-homicide. He was the getaway driver for an ex-felon named Porter who took some money from a used car lot and shot the owner in the process. Darius maintained he didn't know Porter had a gun, and he was just giving him a lift to pick up a car he'd bought. And when Porter came back to the car, running, with a gun in his hand and a bag of cash, he threatened to shoot Darius if he didn't drive them away.

Porter was later shot and killed by police, and Darius was tracked down because two people saw his license plate.

That was what aroused Bloch's attention.

If you're going to commit an armed robbery, it's a bad idea to use your own car. In fact, you have to be pretty stupid to do that. And Darius Robinson didn't seem the stupid type.

Jane opened the trunk of the Lincoln, Bloch grabbed a box, took it to the rear passenger seat, got in and started flicking through the papers. She was done with one box in ten minutes. Jane handed her the second box.

Nineteen minutes later, Bloch took a single page from the second box, said, 'I'm done. Come with me.'

They left the car, and Jane followed Bloch out of the lot and across the street to the candy store.

'We spoke to the owner, Dorothy Majors. She just confirmed what she told the police. She didn't hear or see anything. She's quite deaf,' said Jane.

When the door to the candy store opened, the top of the frame rung a bell.

Almost instantly, a woman appeared behind the counter from a back room, wearing a blue apron over a white blouse. She had icing sugar on her cheek, and more on her hands and apron. When she moved, there was a small white cloud of sweet-smelling dust. Her hair was white, and it was difficult to tell how much of the stuff was in there too.

'Good morning,' said the lady.

'Good morning,' said Bloch. 'I'm from the district attorney's office. I want to talk to Dorothy Majors about the Darius Robinson case.'

'Oh, well I'm Dorothy. I thought that was all over and done with. He's . . . wasn't he . . .'

'He was executed last year,' said Bloch. 'We're just tidying a few details before we close our files, I hope you don't mind.'

Dorothy waved a hand and said, 'No, not at all. What do you need from me?'

Bloch handed her the statement. It was the only statement from Dorothy on the file, and it was one prepared by the attorney who handled Robinson's appeal.

'You made a statement to these attorneys that you didn't hear anything that day.'

She took the document, glanced at it. There were only a few lines, confirmed who Dorothy was, her address, and that she didn't hear the shot because she was hard of hearing, and she didn't see anything either.

'Yeah, I remember signing this. I didn't hear the shot, so I had no reason to go out and look at what was happening,' she said, but she could not resist a glance, over Bloch's shoulder, at the doorbell.

Dorothy had heard the bell when Bloch and Jane came in.

'Good,' said Bloch. 'So you didn't tell them that you really *did* hear the shot, and that you went outside, and you *did* see what happened.'

Dorothy smiled, less sweetly than before, and said, 'Remind me where you're from?'

'The district attorney's office. It's okay, ma'am, you can speak freely.'

Dorothy was silent for a time. She used a cloth to wipe down the counter as she thought about the question.

'Who told you I heard the shot?' she asked.

'Stands to reason, ma'am. Your little bell above the front door rings at around forty decibels. A jet engine burning one gallon of fuel per second is one hundred forty decibels. Porter used a nine-millimeter Beretta to fire a parabellum, hollow-point round. He did this outside, one hundred and five feet from you. The resulting sonic boom would break the sound barrier at *one hundred sixty* decibels. You heard that tiny bell just now. So you heard the shot.'

'I went out, like I told the sheriff, after I heard it and I saw the guy with the bag. He was standing on the street, pointing the gun at the driver of the car, yelling that if he didn't unlock the door, he was going to kill him. That's what I told Sheriff Lomax. He said I should keep that to myself. He didn't get me to sign nothing. Is that still alright?'

'That's fine, ma'am. Did you have a similar conversation with the district attorney?'

'No, I only spoke to the sheriff. Did I do something wrong?'

'Don't worry, thank you for your co-operation. If we need anything else, we'll be in touch.'

Bloch walked out of the store, the bell tinkling above her, and Jane following behind with her mouth open.

'Oh my God,' said Jane.

Jane seemed to say that a lot. Bloch took her phone out of her jacket and stopped the audio recording. Saved it as a file and emailed it to Kate.

'No one picked up on this before. Like, how did you *do* that?' asked Jane.

'I told you. It's what I do,' said Bloch.

CHAPTER THIRTY-EIGHT

KATE

Bloch had taken the SUV, Eddie had the Prius, which left Kate and Harry with the non-VW deathtrap. Harry drove it to the truck stop and parked behind the bar. It was noon. Opening time. Kate was on the phone to Bloch.

'I listened to the recording from the candy store lady. Great work, but it doesn't get us Korn,' said Kate.

'We can use it to get to him. Dorothy Majors implicates Lomax in perjury and perverting the course of justice. We can use it to flip him.'

'So we make Lomax cut a deal with Berlin in exchange for his testimony against Korn.'

'Exactly.'

'Okay, I'll talk to Eddie,' said Kate, and hung up.

'You think Lomax will flip on the district attorney?' asked Harry.

'He has no choice. I doubt he'd go to jail for him. I heard Lomax has a sick wife. He won't want to be parted from her. This is how we get Korn, I can feel it.'

Harry nodded, glanced through the windshield at Hogg's Bar.

They got out of the car, into the hot sun, and quickly made their way to the front entrance. Inside, the bar was dark. The contrast to the blazing sun was too much for Kate. She had to stop, blink a few times, before she could adjust to the low light. The windows were covered up with thick plastic sheeting, and the light from the neon signs behind the long bar that faced the door, the videogames and digital jukebox, were all that she had to navigate.

There half a dozen small round tables and stools scattered between the door and the bar, and a set of booths on the left. Maybe six of them, with a light over each table, but the lights weren't on yet. Two beams rose from the corners of the bar, to the ceiling. Each beam was studded with horseshoes.

A man stood behind the bar, wiping a beer glass with a white dish cloth. There was no one else in the place, but from the smell out of the kitchen they were getting ready for a busy lunch service. The man put the glass down, wiped the back of his neck with the cloth then tossed it into a sink. He wore a red and black checkered shirt, blue jeans and black tee. Either he hadn't shaved for a week or he was supposed to look that way. Kate couldn't decide.

'Can I get you folks something?' he said.

'Sure,' said Harry, pulling up a stool at the bar. 'The coffee smells good. I'll have two bourbons on the rocks, a water and a cup of coffee.'

The bar man nodded. He poured two glasses of iced water, put one in front of Harry and one facing the stool next to him. In places like this it paid to keep the customers hydrated. Less chance of them dying from heatstroke before they paid the check.

'Kate, do you want anything?' asked Harry.

Kate took a seat next to him, took a sip of the water. 'This is fine, thank you.'

The barman came back with Harry's drinks and a cup of joe.

'Two bourbons *and* coffee?' she asked.

'Oh, don't worry, the coffee isn't for me,' said Harry. He took out his cell phone snapped a picture of the coffee. 'Eddie hasn't had a decent cup of coffee since we left New York. This picture will drive him nuts.'

'Why didn't you just get a double bourbon on the rocks?'

'Because bartenders will always give a more generous pour to a single. Am I right?'

The barman nodded at Harry. 'You've been around,' said the barman.

'I have. Mostly bars,' said Harry. 'Say, are you Ryan Hogg?'

The barman was leaning over the bar to clean it when Harry asked the question. His cloth stopped when Harry stopped speaking.

'Who wants to know?' asked the barman.

'We're lawyers for Andy Dubois,' said Kate.

He sighed, then continued wiping down the bar, this time more vigorously.

'I already told the sheriff what I saw,' he said.

'So you're Ryan,' said Kate. 'Andy seems like a good kid.'

'I thought so too, but you never can tell,' said Ryan.

Kate exchanged a glance with Harry. Ryan had a lingering soft spot for Andy. She could tell. Harry saw it too.

'The DA says Andy murdered Skylar Edwards. We don't believe that. What do you think?' asked Kate.

Ryan put the cloth down, came over to them and leaned on the bar, both hands spread wide.

'I cried the night they found Skylar. She was special. Smart, pretty, a heart of gold. She had time for everyone. Lot of people in this town were proud of her. She looked after Andy when he was working here. Kept him straight. Made sure his work was up to scratch, most of the time. I don't know why they argued that night. But I saw it with my own eyes. They were standing right at that front door.'

'Can you describe how Andy was behaving toward Skylar?' asked Kate.

'He was hollering at her. Skylar was no flowerchild – she was giving it right back at him.'

'Did Andy seem angry?' asked Harry.

Ryan looked at the doors, as if recalling the detail in his mind and letting it play out in that space.

'He raised his voice. I guess so.'

'What do you think they were arguing about?' asked Harry.

'I got no idea, but he was real mad.'

They paused, Kate shot Harry another glance, and he nodded. Time to pop the sixty-four-thousand-dollar question.

'Ryan, do you think Andy killed Skylar?'

He shook his head. 'I'm just trying to run my bar. I already told the sheriff I'm just gonna tell it straight. This is what I saw. That's all. I don't need Randal Korn sneaking up my ass.'

Harry sighed.

Kate understood Ryan's fear. No one would want Korn as an enemy. But that didn't explain why Ryan was lying. Not really. Andy said he didn't have an argument with Skylar that night. They never argued, and she believed Andy. She glanced down at Ryan's hands, spread out on the bar.

'Thank you. Is it okay if I use your bathroom?' asked Kate.

'Sure, round the corner,' said Ryan.

She got off the stool went around the bar to a set of doors marked bathrooms, and pushed through, her heart beating fast now. She took out her cell phone, sent Harry a text message.

Beyond the door was a short, narrow hallway. A fire exit dead ahead. A wall on the right painted white, but now covered in graffiti. On the left were two doors. With 'Hogs' and 'Sows' written on each respective door. She waited, listening at the door she'd just come through, waiting to hear the . . . and there it was. The alert signal from Harry's phone to announce he got a text. Kate went through the door for 'sows' and wondered why on earth any woman would ever set foot in this goddamn place. She splashed water on her neck, washed her hands, dried them and then returned to the bar.

Harry met her eyes immediately.

Kate took her stool as Harry swallowed the last mouthful of booze in front of him, and put the glass slowly back on the table.

'Say, Ryan, do you mind if I get that coffee to go?'

'No problem,' said Ryan, grabbing a go-cup from the shelf above the coffee machine. He picked up Harry's coffee, carefully poured it into the cup.

As he did so, Kate angled her phone at Ryan, and snapped a few shots. He gave the cup to Harry and apologized that they had run out of lids. Harry settled the tab, and they got up to leave the bar.

'Thank you for your help,' said Kate, as earnestly as possible.

For the first time since meeting him, Ryan Hogg eyed Kate suspiciously.

Kate said nothing to Harry as they left. Not a word in the parking lot. They didn't speak until they got into the car.

Kate thought she might know why Ryan was lying.

'Did you get the shot?' asked Harry.

She flicked through her phone, found one of the pictures she'd just taken and spread her thumb and forefinger across the screen to enlarge a section. It was a picture of Ryan Hogg as he poured Harry's coffee into the go-cup. On his right hand sat a large gold ring.

With a five-pointed star in the center.

CHAPTER THIRTY-NINE

LOMAX

The last of the mourners put their empty plates in the sink, told Lomax again how sorry they were and then left. The funeral was going to be in two days' time. He had another forty-eight hours of this shit to go through. He didn't want another cake in the house, he didn't want to make more coffee or see or speak to anyone else for a long time.

The people who came to pay their respects were friends of Lucy's – neighbors, townsfolk, shopkeepers, nurses, the usual. It had been a long illness, but her passing was so sudden in the end that people were quite unprepared for it. She had fought the disease and had never let it take her dignity or her strength. Perhaps for that reason it was still a surprise for some.

Lomax left the dirty plates, glasses and mugs where they lay, went upstairs, and thought Lucy would have ragged on his ass for not clearing up. He couldn't face it now. He just wanted to lay down. In the bedroom, he toed his boots off, lay down on Lucy's side of the bed. Inhaling, he caught the scent of her perfume. It was still on the sheets. For a while, he cried, and then slept. When he woke, he looked at the clock on the nightstand and saw it was past five in the evening. He was hungry, but he didn't want to eat.

Rolling over, he examined the figurine of a policeman standing at a lamp pole. It had been Lucy's, given to her by a friend when Lomax got elected sheriff for the first time. It was twenty-five years' old, that porcelain figurine. Lucy stared at it, every night, and the figure, in its way, stared back at her.

Lomax had strayed from the light. Korn had drawn him into the dark. He pulled open the drawer on Lucy's nightstand, hoping to find her perfume. This was Lucy's private space. He never normally went near her drawers or her closet. She liked her things just so and this was off limits to Lomax. He had his own closet, after all. He looked inside the nightstand drawer and saw the bottle of perfume.

Beside the bottle of French perfume was a white envelope. Letter sized. He sat up, drew it out and read the name, written on the envelope in that familiar hand.

For Colt. For after.

He turned the envelope over, and carefully prized it open. He didn't want to tear it. Lucy's writing was on the other side, and she had written his name, and that was precious. Something to cherish.

Inside was a handwritten letter.

Dear Colt,

My love, I know you won't find this until after I'm gone. Please don't feel so bad. I have loved you all my life. I love you still. Make sure to eat. I know how you get.

I love how you've taken care of me during this illness. How you've rubbed my feet, bathed me, washed my hair, even crushed up my pills and put them in yoghurt when I couldn't swallow them. You can be so thoughtful.

I love the house you made for us. It has been a special joy to me these last few years. And don't think I am ignorant of the cost. You've been carrying a weight around your neck. I've seen it. It started not long after Randal Korn came into our lives, and there's not a day goes by I don't regret you ever clapping eyes on that man. He's rotten inside. And he's trying to make you just like him.

You are not like Randal Korn. You're a good man. I know it. I knowed it the day I married you. Something has beaten it down. But that good is still in you, Colt Lomax. I see it when you put on my slippers for me, when you help me to the bathroom, when you make cocoa late at night.

He's made you do bad things. Things you wouldn't a done before. This life is so short, and so sweet. I couldn't talk to you about this before. You know I couldn't. I tried, but you wouldn't listen. Whatever you have done has hurt you, deep down. And I don't want you hurtin' no more.

Do some good every day. Like you used to. You've got your lucky rabbit's foot. Nothing bad is going to happen to you when you've got it on your keys. It will keep you safe. But don't delay, my love, cut this man out of your life for good.

For me.

Please.

Do this and I'll be waiting for you.

Your loving wife,

Lucy x

Lomax stared at the letter, unable to speak. Unable to move.

He jolted when a teardrop appeared on the page, smudging the ink. Carefully, he placed the letter on the nightstand and wept for his wife.

And for himself.

After a while, he got up and opened the wardrobe. There was a shoebox beside the lockbox for his personal weapon. He took down the shoebox and opened it up. Inside was a pen drive containing the security footage that covered the gas station for the forty-eight hours covering the disappearance and murder of Skylar Edwards. This was the only copy of that footage. He'd deleted the original from the server in the gas station.

Once the medical examiner's report threw up some inconsistencies, he had continued his investigation into Skylar's murder. A couple of days after Dubois was charged, he'd found the gas-station footage. He still couldn't believe what he'd seen. Skylar got into a car. That same car came back the next evening, just after dark. By zooming in, he had seen the driver take something heavy out of the trunk of the vehicle and make his way to the grassland beyond the lot.

He knew the driver. The real killer. More importantly, on the night she went missing, Andy Dubois could clearly be seen leaving the area, and he never returned.

It was time to make his confession, and to stop Randal Korn before he put another innocent man in the execution chamber.

CHAPTER FORTY

EDDIE

I met Kate and Harry in a chop house fifteen miles from Buckstown. It was a side-of-the-road kind of place, with blue and white checkered tablecloths and food that came on plates with dividers. Three different sections. One for meat, one for hushpuppies or onion rings and one for greens. Harry and I ordered barbeque pork. Kate opted for a chargrilled chicken salad.

'So, what's got you so excited?' I asked.

Kate's right heel had been bouncing on the hardwood floor beneath the table since she sat down.

'I saw the ring that caused the wounds on Skylar Edwards,' she said.

I leaned forward.

'We were looking for a large ring with a five-pointed star,' she said. 'Ryan Hogg has the exact same ring,' she said, and produced a photo.

I could see Harry's forearm in the picture, so I presumed she'd taken this photo today. The next picture she showed me was a close-up of the ring. An ostentatious gold ring, with a white jewel star in the center.

'Can you zoom in any closer?' I asked.

Kate adjusted the picture, but it wasn't good enough quality to see the smaller details on the ring.

'I talked to Farnesworth. There's good news and bad news,' I said. 'Good news is he is pretty specific about the markings on Skylar's body from the ring. There are actually two letters above the star, an "F" and a "C" but I can't tell if there's lettering above Hogg's ring.'

'We could always go back and get a closer look,' said Kate.

'I don't know how wise that would be right now. You haven't asked me the bad news yet.'

Harry closed his eyes. He was way ahead of me. Kate hung her head. They'd both clocked the problem.

'Farnesworth won't testify,' said Kate.

'Right. He's beyond scared. And with good reason. The lawyer who instructed him is dead, along with his office manager. He's taking the warning seriously. It doesn't matter if we find the real killer and the matching ring; without Farnesworth we have no way of introducing the marks on her skin into evidence for the jury. It won't be part of the case at all.'

'And we can't get another medical examiner to testify because Skylar's body was cremated,' said Harry.

'What about we hit Farnesworth with a subpoena?' asked Kate.

'That's possible, but it's professional suicide. Even if he answered the subpoena and came to court, he wouldn't co-operate on the witness stand. We'd have to treat our own expert witness as hostile and that is a recipe for disaster in a death-penalty case. It's Andy's life on the line, here. We can't afford any mistakes,' I said.

The food sat untouched on the table. We fell into silence. Harry broke it when he picked up his fork and started eating.

'When I was in Vietnam we ate when we could. You never knew when you would get another hot meal. Eat something, both of you. We'll figure it out,' said Harry.

'What is there to figure out? We're dead in the water. We've got no defense. Eddie, we should pull this case. Get a continuance and let's take some time to regroup.'

'No, putting the case off for a month or two isn't an option. For a start, you think Judge Chandler would give us a continuance? Not a chance in hell. Not that it matters, because we're going to be in the same shit situation a month from now. This case isn't getting any better.'

'We're going to lose,' said Kate.

'It looks like it,' I said. 'All the evidence points to Andy Dubois, and the jury probably won't listen to us anyway. I've had tough cases before, but nothing like this. Korn has rigged a favorable jury, he's scared away our witnesses . . . he's got forensic evidence of Andy's blood under the victim's fingernails, two confessions, a witness that establishes Andy as the last person to be with her before she disappeared – there's no end to how many ways we're going to lose this case.'

Kate shook her head, said, 'We don't have a way to win, but I didn't get into the law to start bribing jurors either,' said Kate.

A couple of days in the sun had brought out more of the freckles across her nose and on her cheeks. Strands of hair clung to her forehead, laminated there in sweat. She wore a black tee under her grey suit, the jacket hanging from the chair. The heat and the case were getting to her more than I had anticipated.

'Look, you have nothing to worry about. I'll never ask you to break the rules or bend the law. We're partners, remember?'

'That's what I am worried about. If you get caught, they'll say I must have known about it because I'm your partner. I'll be screwed too.'

'No, you won't,' I said.

'How?'

'Look, Korn is playing this one as dirty as it comes. It's personal for him. This is war. Lawyers have died, for God's sake. Professional witnesses won't testify because they're afraid he will kill them. Playing by the rules isn't going to be enough to save Andy. I think I can save him, but I've gotta get down in the dirt with Korn to do it. There's no other way.'

'There has to be a way to win without breaking the law.'

Harry started laughing.

'Did I say something funny?' asked Kate.

'We're dealing with a prosecutor who thinks he's above the law. I used to think like you, too. Then I realized, well, actually Eddie taught me, that justice and the law can be very different things,' said Harry.

'I just don't like it.'

'You think Bloch has never stepped outside of the rules?' I asked.

She picked up her fork, started to pick at her food.

'Bloch does her own thing. I'm not saying she's above the law either, she's just, you know, Bloch, she's—'

'*Different,*' said Harry and I, at the same time.

'Yeah,' said Kate, nodding.

'She wouldn't fit in around us if she was normal, whatever the hell that is,' I said.

The mood lightened with Kate's smile. Harry gave her a very gentle nudge with his elbow. She nudged him back, harder, in the ribs, and he let out one of his trademark rolling laughs that infects everyone within hearing distance. Harry never had a daughter. We used to work with an investigator named Harper. She and Harry didn't quite have a father/daughter relationship, but it would've grown into that if we hadn't lost her the year before. Her death hit us both like a dump truck.

I still dreamed about her. Most nights. When she died, I knew this was a wound that would never heal. I would carry it around the rest of my life. Only two possibilities. Either I would learn how to live with it, or it would kill me. I had a daughter, and I couldn't let her down. Even though, sometimes, I didn't want to be in the world without Harper.

I took peace from the little things. Like now, watching Kate and Harry smiling and laughing together. Kate looked up to him, and he admired her strength and intelligence. Soon he would be complaining she didn't eat enough and she would be moaning that he hadn't taken his pills. A father and daughter-type relationship was on the cards. Kate's father was very much alive, but you can have many parents. And everyone needs a mentor. I was damn sure there was nothing I could teach her.

Right then I was glad I was at the table with them. It was a passing moment of levity, and it broke, just for a second, the crushing weight of representing a man who would be put to death if we lost.

Those are the stakes. And they don't come higher.

We enjoyed our food, and for the time it took us to demolish the plates, that burden lifted.

'Have you heard from Bloch?' I asked.

Kate filled me in. She had something on Lomax. Enough to put him away, potentially.

'So is she gonna brace him? See if he folds?' I asked.

'She said she was going to talk to him first. In private.'

'Shouldn't someone go with her? Who knows how he'll react? It could get violent,' said Harry.

'Bloch told me she'd make it clear there were other copies of the recording of Dorothy Majors. Lomax is smart enough to know hurting Bloch won't solve the problem. Plus, this is Bloch we're talking about. It's Lomax who should be scared. If Bloch gets Lomax to agree to talk to Berlin and testify against Korn, then this could stall Andy's case, maybe give us a chance to get the case before a new district attorney. They won't want to touch any ongoing case of Korn's,' said Kate.

I nodded, said, 'Let's see what Lomax has to say first. Ask Bloch if she wants me to tag along. Just for company.'

'Why don't you call her now?'

'I can't right now. If she wants me to go with her, tell her I'll be by the hotel a little later. You two head back now, start thinking about ways to attack the forensics. Did you move Andy and his mom into the hotel?'

'It took some chicanery to sneak past the receptionist, but we managed it,' said Harry.

I didn't want Andy and Patricia out in the middle of nowhere. It was easier to protect them at the hotel, and they had agreed to move for the duration of the trial.

'Great, make sure they order whatever they want on room service. I'll get the check here,' I said.

Harry wiped his lips on a napkin, scrunched it, put it on his empty plate and said, 'You gonna stay for coffee?'

'I sure am. I have to meet someone.'

'Who are you meeting?' asked Kate.

'Better if you don't know.'

They left shortly after. Harry was reluctant. Kate agreed it was best if she didn't know what I was up to. Plausible deniability was always best when it came to my practices. The waitress came over to clear the table.

'Can I get you anything else?' she asked.

'Yes, I would love a cup of coffee. In fact, make it two, please, ma'am.'

She smiled and brought me two mugs of steaming black coffee. I put sugar and creamer into them both and finished the first cup fast. Just as I started the second, a young woman came into the restaurant. Sandy Boyette wore a leather biker jacket, with a red tee underneath and blue jeans. She had lost her job in Gus's Diner a few days ago, sold us her shit heap of a car, and now she was juror twelve in the Dubois case.

I checked my watch.

Dead on time.

There was no reception desk in the restaurant, and no sign to tell customers to wait until they were seated. In this place you put your ass in the first spot you found and were grateful for it.

She looked around the restaurant. It was getting full. Maybe sixty people. Families, couples, even a few guys in business suits. Barbeque cuts across all social classes in the South. And good barbeque, like this, is the closest a Southerner will get to communism.

I raised a hand, held it there for a few seconds until she saw me.

Nervously, she looked around at the other diners as she made her way over to the table. Then sat down.

'How did you find me?'

'I have a pretty good investigator.'

'I shouldn't be talking to you,' she said.

'Nice to see you too, Sandy,' I said.

'You know what I mean,' she said.

'It's okay. I don't imagine you would get many people from Buckstown going this far for barbeque when there's a smokehouse on every street corner.'

She nodded, said, 'Still, it's probably a good idea to keep this short. This place is out of the way, but it's not like it's private either.'

'This won't take long. I thought we should talk,' I said.

'What about?' she asked.

'Couple of things that are bothering me. First, when you were asked by the prosecutor if you knew any of the parties in the case you said "no" and I want to know why.'

'It's real simple. I don't know any of them. I don't know you. I sold you a car, in like five minutes. That's it. It's not like we hang out. No offense,' she said.

'None taken. But you do know me, no matter how brief our meeting. Why did you lie to the judge?'

'Was it a lie? It just didn't seem important. It's not like now, where I'm a juror and you're a lawyer in the case. That means we should not be meeting or talking,' she said.

There was a question hanging between us, like the light that hung from the ceiling shining a halo in the center of the table. I let that question sway in the wind for a time while I leaned back in my seat and decided if I wanted to ask it.

She was smart enough to know the question. She had invited it. I could tell the question was swinging toward her. She could ask it just the same as me. And right then it seemed she would. I could see it there, skirting the smile at the corner of her red lips.

I decided it would be more polite if I took the initiative.

'Sandy, do you want to make some money?'

Her lips pursed, her eyes clicked toward me, locked on, like the reels on a slot machine.

'I am in a unique position to alter the outcome of this trial,' she said.

'In Alabama, a conviction and death penalty can be imposed with a majority verdict of ten jurors. One not-guilty vote isn't enough.'

'One is a start,' she said.

'Sure is. How much would something like that cost?'

She thought for a moment. She didn't want to price it too high, nor did she want to sell herself too low. This was a crime. A felony. It would carry serious prison time if she were found out and convicted. That risk necessitated a rich reward.

'Twenty thousand dollars,' she said.

'Oh, I think we can do better than that. Tell me, do you like Disney characters?'

CHAPTER FORTY-ONE

BLOCH

Bloch pulled up across the street from the Sheriff's Department. A line of cruisers outside, polished and idle in the streetlight.

Before she made a move, she thought things over.

Her next step had a number of possible outcomes. Confronting the sheriff with evidence of obstruction of justice, perjury and more could go a few different ways – most of them south. A man this deep in the well will climb over a pile of dead bodies for a glimpse of the sun. The other possibility was he put his hands up, played it smart, and agreed to testify as a witness against Korn. That was her hope. That there was some smoking ember of goodness left in him that she could fan into a flame to burn Korn's house down. It was best if she did this alone. Bloch had been a cop once, and she knew how to talk to police.

She got out of the car, crossed the street to see two patrolmen leave the building and make their way to one of the cruisers. She didn't recognize them. Night shift. There was something about them that appeared different, but at first she couldn't quite put her finger on it.

Then she saw it. Both patrolmen wore black armbands on their right biceps.

As she passed them on her way to the station she said, 'Evening, why the black armbands?'

One of the patrolmen said, 'It's a mark of respect. The sheriff's wife has been sick for a long time. Cancer. She died last night.'

'Oh God, I didn't know. I'm in town and thought I'd swing by and see him. Is the sheriff inside? We used to work together, long time ago,' said Bloch.

Both patrolmen stood still and cast their eyes on Bloch. They looked at how she stood. Back straight, thumb in her belt, head high and with an ease around them both.

'Where did you two serve together?' asked the patrolman.

'I was in the 2nd Precinct, Mobile. A bail jumper pulled an armed robbery as he passed through my beat and ended up here. Lomax wanted him found before his bankroll ran out and he got the idea to start robbing people here. We got him, in the end. Well, Lomax got him.'

They had listened close to all she had said. There were over four hundred cops in Mobile, and nobody knew them all. Bloch sure sounded like a cop. She didn't tell them she was an ex-cop gearing up to take a bite clean out of Lomax.

'That sounds like Colt. Anyways, he's not here. He's probably at home.'

'I'd like to pay my respects,' said Bloch.

'We can pass on a message. I'm sure . . .'

'In person. It would be rude not to,' said Bloch.

The patrolmen looked at each other, shrugged and one of them started giving directions. Bloch thanked them. They had bought her routine, and even if they had some doubts about Bloch, they thought even if they were wrong, the sheriff could easily handle himself against a woman.

Bloch guessed they were that stupid.

Back in the car, Bloch typed the address into the satellite navigation. Got nothing but a general area north of the town. She took off and told herself she would find it. The property sat a few hundred yards south of Devil's Creek – a narrow, fast river that fed into the Luxahatchee River.

As she got closer to the red pin on her navigation system, the road turned from a two-lane to a single lane, and then on the left she saw a gap in the trees. A dirt road with a mailbox to the right of it. She stopped the car. Reversed back. The mailbox had a name written on it in white paint.

Lomax.

She reversed a further ten feet, then swung the car onto the track.

Her headlights were already on full beam, but they couldn't penetrate the trees. The track swung left and right, around great oaks, which meant her field of vision extended only as far as the next corner – usually no more than fifty feet or so. Then, without warning, the dirt road straightened and there in front of her was what looked like an old colonial house. Yet it was too pristine to be anything other than a new house built in the old style. It was white, with a wrap-around porch. Bloch pulled in and parked beside the sheriff's cruiser.

When she got out of the car she was hit with the sound of the crickets and cicadas singing their midnight love songs.

The ground had been torn up. A lot of cars had been through recently. Glancing around, she saw tire marks all over the grass, some even leading behind the house. The lights were on inside. On the first floor at least. Kitchen and lounge, probably. Bloch found herself stomping up the steps, her boots thumping the porch boards, making sure her presence didn't come as a surprise. That would not be wise in this town, in a house that stood alone. Especially not at night. Especially not when the owner was armed. Especially not when the owner only needed a small excuse to unload a shotgun in your face.

She took a step toward the front door. The top half of the door had frosted glass. There were curtains behind the door, held back in a bow with pelmets.

One floorboard creaked so loudly it was almost a scream. One more step and she was right at the door. She raised her arm, closed her fist, pulled it back.

Knock.

The second knock coincided with another noise.

The sound of a .45 handgun firing a single shot.

CHAPTER FORTY-TWO

LOMAX

He woke sometime later in his bed. It was dark outside, and there was a noise downstairs. Footsteps, and something else. Lomax took his Sig Sauer .45 ACP from the lockbox on the top shelf of the wardrobe, checked the load, cocked it and stepped lightly into the hallway.

The lights were on downstairs. He descended slowly, the muzzle of the weapon sweeping back and forth until he saw a man in his home, carrying dishes.

In the kitchen, Randal Korn wiped his hands on a towel and then pressed the start button on the dishwasher before closing it. The dirty dishes left by the mourners had been cleared.

'You can put the gun down,' said Korn, without looking up at Lomax on the stairs. 'I thought you could use a hand to clean up. It seems the least I could do.'

Lomax didn't answer. He just came down the stairs, casually, but he didn't put the gun down. Instead, he held it by his side and watched Korn move around the kitchen, filling the coffee machine with water, then coffee grounds, and then setting it to brew.

'Lucy wouldn't have approved,' said Lomax.

Korn buttoned his suit jacket, leaned against the counter and folded his arms. He said nothing for a time. The coffee maker gurgled and the smell of freshly brewing grounds mingled with the faint odor of rotten flesh that followed Korn around.

'She wouldn't have wanted you in her kitchen,' said Lomax.

'It's not her kitchen anymore. It's yours. I am sorry for your loss. Truly, I am.'

'What do you want?' asked Lomax.

233

'To pay my respects. Of course.'

'You've paid them.'

Korn looked at the coffee machine as it began to spurt black liquid into the bun flask, before returning to Lomax.

'Thought we could have a cup of joe. Talk.'

'There's nothing to talk about.'

'Oh, but there is. There's so much we need to discuss. The trial begins tomorrow. I realize you have your priorities, but I will need you at court after the funeral. Your testimony is key. That is your duty, and I know you will hold to it. You're a good man. I always said so.'

Lomax knew Korn was no physical threat. And any fear he had of the man himself had been drowned by his grief and the flood of anger that came with Lucy's letter. Anger at himself, and the man who stood now in his kitchen, infecting the air around him with his filth. Lomax put the gun down on the marble counter top, beside a padded manila envelope he'd addressed a few hours before, ready to be mailed in the morning. Briefly, Korn's gaze fell across the envelope, and his eyes flared for a second. Then he turned away. Lomax walked through the kitchen to the lounge, sat down heavily on the couch, put his head in his hands.

He breathed in and out, fiercely, fighting down the emotion coursing through him.

'I used to be a good man. But that hasn't been true for a long time,' said Lomax.

Korn limped in after him, placed a mug of hot coffee on the table in front of Lomax. The armchair in the corner had a small table beside it. Korn sat there, put his coffee down and leaned forward. His knees were spread wide apart, his fingers steepled together, his hands hanging between his legs. It could have looked like a contemplative pose, but with Korn's body it looked unnatural. Almost insect-like.

'I know this is hitting you hard. I have done all that I could for both of you. I'm glad you had the funds to do everything that could be done for Lucy,' he said.

Funds was a strange way to put it. Korn gave him money. Some from busts, some of his own personal wealth as well. He was rich, alright. In all the time he'd known him, Lomax hadn't seen Korn wear the same suit twice in a month.

'I just want you to know that I am here in your time of need, Colt,' said Korn.

He had never used the sheriff's first name before. Not that Lomax could remember. He must be concerned if he's sinking so low.

'I am not in any need. I've lost my wife, and there's nothing I can do about it. I just wish I'd listened to her, talked to her more when she was here. Lucy sure didn't like you,' said Lomax.

'She saw the good work we were doing, together, and perhaps because of that she feared for you. You know, you can't put away that many murderers without someone trying to take you down. That's what they do. They try to attack you. You must always be ready to crush your enemies. Before they do it to you. You were protecting Lucy by working with me, and I was protecting you both. Maybe she didn't understand, not fully.'

'It wasn't that,' said Lomax. 'She didn't want me to do anything that could compromise my integrity. I did more than compromise it. I threw it in the trash. That's what I did. That's what you made me do.'

'You're a free man. Are you telling me that the money I gave you was not accepted in friendship, as partners?'

'I should never have taken a dime.'

'Then Lucy would not have had this house. She loved this house, didn't she?'

'She did, but she loved me more,' said Lomax.

'What are you telling me?'

'I'm done. That's what I'm saying.'

Korn leaned back in the chair, put a finger to his lips as if to quieten his reaction. Dull it down. Until it could be tempered into honey.

'You are too fine an officer for me to lose. What will it take to make you stay? There's the funeral to pay for, of course. And if this house has too many painful memories, you could move. I can give you a couple of hundred thousand right now. Tonight. And there's more if you want it?'

'There's no amount of money. I want free of it. I want it all out in the open. What we did. The people we've hurt. The men we've killed, and the lawyer I shot in the head—'

'It was all a just cause. God's cause, Colt. Cody Warren and that bitch had one purpose. To set murderers free. We don't let the guilty go free. We burn them. That's our calling.'

'*Your* calling, maybe. Look at Andy Dubois. I got him to confess when it suited us to wrap up the case, fast. We let the real killer go free. You suspect as much. I know that. It was plain the moment we saw those photos from the medical examiner.'

'But don't you realize we had to stick with Dubois to get a conviction. The ME's photos give Dubois reasonable doubt, and Dubois' confession gives the real killer reasonable doubt, *if* Dubois was innocent. The only thing we can do to give Skylar's family some peace is get a conviction. You think he's innocent? His kind are all the same. If it wasn't for Skylar's case, I would be prosecuting him for something else down the line. If anything, we're probably saving lives putting Dubois down.'

That was how he saw it. That twisted logic had once fooled Lomax, but no longer. He thought that maybe he had allowed himself to be swept up in this bullshit in the past. That thought was no salve for his conscience. Lomax knew that Korn just wanted to take another soul with the chair. Didn't matter who it was or whether they were guilty or innocent. He lived to kill. It had taken Lomax some time to see it, but now it was clear. He knew what he had to do.

'I can't do this no more. Dubois didn't kill that girl,' said Lomax.

Korn remained very still, listening to every word. His jaw opened, lips parted to speak, but he hesitated, as if a thought remained unformed, then burst into life as he said, 'It was you, wasn't it? You took the security-camera footage from the gas station.'

'I needed an insurance policy. The footage changes everything. I'm going to release it. This trial must stop, and you've got to let Andy Dubois go. The real killer is on that video.'

'I'm not going to lose this trial, and I'm not going to lose you, Colt. We're friends. I was there for you when Lucy got sick.'

Lomax wiped something from his eyes, said, 'When she was first diagnosed I just thought it was bad luck, you know? It was right after we got the house, we had some money behind us and we didn't need to worry about anything. *Right* then. She got sick. And I think I did that. I made her sick. The things I've done, that shit comes around, you know?'

'No, I don't know,' said Korn.

Lomax fixed Korn in his red-eyed gaze and said, 'You will. You can't put that many people to death and it not come around to bite you in the ass someday.'

'That's where you're wrong. My father had money, and he passed it to me. People think wealth bestows power, but my father knew better. Real power comes from holding life and death in your hands.'

'You're full of shit. You talk about killing someone, but you've never liked getting your hands dirty. You don't have the balls to do it yourself – that's why you like putting all those boys on Yellow Mama, watching them squirm and roast. You're sick, and you're a coward.'

And with that, he hung his head, nodding slightly, to himself. He had made up his mind. This had to stop. Korn had to be stopped. For him.

For Lucy.

He heard Korn get up out of the chair with a sigh. Heard his footsteps on the wooden floor, coming closer. They stopped right in front of Lomax. He saw those polished, patent leather shoes reflecting his broken face.

'I'm sorry I got you into this,' said Korn.

'I am too. I just can't be a part of this no more,' said Lomax.

As Lomax stared at the floor, and the polish on Korn's leather shoes, he thought he heard something. That creaky board out on the porch.

'And I am sorry for Lucy, and your loss. You *are* right about a couple of things, though,' said Korn.

'Yeah?' asked Lomax, as he raised his head.

His eyes flared wide as he saw the barrel of the Sig Sauer he had left on the counter, now in Korn's hand, and pointed at his head.

In his other hand was the envelope containing the pen drive. He must've lifted them from the counter when Lomax turned his back.

'First, I don't like getting my hands dirty, but sometimes I don't have a choice. Second, you *really* can't be a part of this no more,' said Korn.

CHAPTER FORTY-THREE

BLOCH

Soon as she heard the shot, a couple of things happened almost instantly.

First, she stepped to one side, fell into a crouch and swiveled on her right foot at the same time, so that she turned and dropped and her back found the wall of the house beside the door.

Cover.

Second, Maggie was in her right hand, muzzle up at the sky, ready.

There had been no conscious thought process. These movements happened almost independently. A mix of instinct and training. She moved to her left, pushed up from her knees and stole a glance through the window. She saw a modern kitchen, again rendered in the old style of country kitchens, but with a black marble worktop and cream cupboards. No one in sight. She tried the next window and saw a lounge. Lomax was on the couch, his head thrown back over the upright cushion, so she couldn't see his face.

She didn't need to. The bright red patch on the couch said it all. Lomax had taken a round to the head.

Dropping back into a crouch, Bloch moved toward the front door again, staying low. As she reached it, she heard the low murmur of an engine coming to life. It was coming from behind the house. Edging along the wall, she heard the pitch of the engine change as the revs grew higher, and yet the sound grew fainter as the vehicle drew further away.

Bloch peered around the house and saw another track. A back road. And on this road she saw tail lights, two hundred yards distant, moving swiftly away. Instantly, her gun came up. Bloch had to develop a vice grip on the gun, so most of the pressure

239

on the weapon came from her right index finger pad, and her left thumb pad, using her forearms to squeeze those pressure points together. Her feet were shoulder-width apart, knees slightly bent, and leaning forward a touch. Arms bent. When she first shot Maggie she'd used a standard pistol grip, right arm locked, left arm bent, and almost broke her wrist and her shoulder. The Magnum was going to kick, no matter what. The only thing Bloch could do was manage that recoil by using her forearm and shoulder muscles as shock absorbers.

She exhaled, found the center sight with her dominant right eye.

Hitting the car from this distance was not a problem for Bloch. Not even with a weapon that wasn't designed for long-distance accuracy. The only question was what part of the car she would hit. At this distance, Bloch was reasonably certain she could still punch a hole through the engine block and stop the car. The round would go through the trunk, the back seat, front seat, dash and into the target. But a gust of wind, or too much tension in her trigger finger could mean the difference between that shot, and the round going through the trunk, back seat, front seat, *the driver*, the dash and the engine. She didn't know who was driving. It didn't seem fair to put a hole the size of a basketball in someone without being introduced first.

She let Maggie drop by her side.

Narrowed her eyes. The shape of tail lights were quite distinctive. She'd seen those same lights recently.

On Randal Korn's Jaguar.

Bloch swore as the car disappeared into the trees, then returned to the house.

Before doing anything else, Bloch fished in her pocket and drew out a pair of latex gloves. She put these on and wiped at the spot on the door where she had knocked. Next, she tried the front door. It was open. If anyone else was in the house then they weren't going to be friendly. The Magnum slipped out of its holster on her waist, and she held it low as she checked first the lounge, the kitchen, and then every room in the house.

Clear.

She didn't touch anything, moved slow and silent. The rooms were neat and tidy, nothing out of place. Except the master bedroom. A letter lay on the pillow. She read it and then returned it to the bed. A letter from Lomax's deceased wife, Lucy. Something like that is bound to hit a grieving spouse in the gut with a steel girder. She didn't know Lucy or Lomax, and Lomax was pretty low in her estimations, yet Bloch felt herself moved by the letter.

When she returned downstairs she stood in the doorway of the lounge, taking her time. She would hear any cars approaching. This was worth the risk.

Lomax had been sitting on the couch when he died. A gun lay beside his right hand on the couch. The grip just a few inches from his fingers. As if he had simply opened his hand and let it fall on the cushion beside him. Bloch leaned over the gun, took a sharp sniff of air at the muzzle. It had recently been fired.

Standing over Lomax, she looked down behind him, at the couch. There was blood and matter not just on the wall behind him, but on the couch. In fact, most of the spatter was at the base of Lomax's neck. There was an entry wound in the center of his forehead.

To anyone coming to this scene it was a suicide. He'd just lost his wife and he'd found a letter from her. It was not a good letter. A cop would put two and two together and wrap up the case as suicide. A lot of cops ended up eating a bullet from their own gun. This was just another one of those stories. That's what it looked like.

Even if Bloch didn't know that there had probably been someone else in the house when the shot was fired, and that someone had driven away fast, she still would've found the scene bogus.

The bullet entered the body at the forehead and came out at the base of the neck. Intercranial ballistics is not rocket science. Bullets generally take a certain path unless deviated by something very hard and tough.

Bloch took hold of Lomax by the shoulders, slowly drew his body forward. Among dark matter on the couch was also a hole, which was parallel to the exit wound at the back of the neck.

If Lomax blew his own brains out, then he had leaned back in the seat, tilted his head to look at the ceiling, put the gun to this forehead and then pulled the trigger.

No.

Didn't happen that way. Lomax was looking up at the gun pointed down at him when someone else pulled the trigger. If it had been Korn who pulled the trigger, then he was intimately familiar with the work of the local crime lab and he would've wiped the weapon clean before tossing it onto the couch beside Lomax.

Bloch returned the body to the couch, stepped back and made her way to the door.

She stopped at the front door, her grip on the handle.

The letter upstairs. She thought it might be useful. She turned and went upstairs to take a picture of it on her phone.

When she came back down, she closed the front door carefully, then turned her attention to the outbuildings. A large one, like a work shed, and a smaller one. She chose the larger of the two to start with.

Her search didn't take long. Even though the work shed was padlocked shut, there was a small window. Using her flashlight she picked out what looked at first glance like a coffin in the corner, with the lid up. Of course, it wasn't a coffin. It was a chest freezer. And the layer of ice on the lid had a patch of red staining.

This is where Cody Warren had been hidden. Probably his SUV would've been hidden in here too.

Any sympathy Bloch felt for Lomax slipped away quickly as she got into the car, fired the engine and drove away fast.

CHAPTER FORTY-FOUR

KORN

Korn gently rested the needle on the record. The familiar burst of ticks and scratches came from the speakers, and then Korn's favorite piece of music – Beethoven's Sonata in C minor, opus III, performed by Jorg Demus on Beethoven's own Graf piano. The piece was recorded live, in Bonn, in 1970, to mark the 200th anniversary of Beethoven's birth.

When he first heard the piece, as a young boy of eleven, he had hated it.

The piano sounded tinny, and strange. It wasn't until a year or so later, when he learned the piano was made by Conrad Graf especially for Beethoven, that he began to listen more carefully to the piece. Beethoven was almost totally deaf at this stage of his life, and Graf made every effort to intensify the sound from the piano, including adding an extra string to the upper register. Parts of the piece require the keys to be struck with incredible force and speed. Korn liked to think of Beethoven hammering those same keys, desperately trying to hear the same sound that Korn heard on the record, knowing that the composer had been cruelly robbed from experiencing his own gift.

And that was when Korn fell in love with it. In the same music that caused others so much joy, Korn heard only Beethoven's anguish and pain. And he reveled in it.

That's when he knew he was different. It wasn't entirely his father's influence. And in some ways he was lucky, in that he knew himself at an early age. Nothing gave him more pleasure than suffering.

He didn't own a TV. Occasionally he listened to the radio in the car, but not often. He sometimes felt that he was a man born in the wrong time. He read his books, listened to Beethoven, Mahler and Wagner, and that was mostly enough for him.

Korn went upstairs, into his bedroom. A single lamp burned in the dim room, barely penetrating the darkness. He took off his suit jacket, hung it carefully in his closet. Then his tie. He placed his shirt in the laundry along with his socks. He took off his shoes and polished them with a brush and a cloth for five minutes, then placed them in their spot in his huge closet.

He sat on the bed. Took deep breaths. Lay back on the sheets, his legs dangling off the edge as he worked himself up to the job.

He unbuttoned his pants, slid them down to the top of his thighs then stopped. He sat up, and then, very carefully, he pulled his pants down to the floor and shuffled his feet out of them.

The smell hit him immediately.

Even with the tight, clear plastic wrap on his right thigh, the odor came through. He sometimes thought that others could smell it. Not that Korn cared what others thought of him personally.

He found the end of the wrapping and pulled it. There was a flash of pain as he yanked it free.

No, it would be way too painful to take it off in this manner. He found scissors on the bedside table and cut away the plastic wrapping to reveal the bandage. Now the smell was powerful. He cut away the bandages, wet with blood.

The leather garter, right around his thigh, would need to be soaked in bleach again. It was almost ruined. He had a new one in his safe, but he didn't feel like using it. Not yet. Not until he could rid himself of the infection. He reached under the belt, undid the clasp and peeled away the garter from the back of his thigh, slowly. This had to be done inch by inch.

Because of the pins.

The belt had left an indentation on the skin because it was on so tightly. The five steel pins on the underside of the belt had clotted in the puncture wounds they'd left on the front of his thigh. He had to yank each one out.

The five pin holes in his flesh were red, angry and clearly infected. The smell from his leg was almost making him gag, and it didn't look much better. He took the iodine from the bedside cabinet and applied it to the wounds, sucking on his lips, gasping with each dab from a cotton bud.

When he was done, he took a shower, used more disinfectant on the leg and then took his daily dose of antibiotics. He wondered whether they were having any effect. He had been taking them for so long now it was possible he was immune. Perhaps he needed to up the dose or change the meds again.

Korn lived alone. Always had, from the day he moved out of his father's penthouse apartment in the Upper West Side. Pain was the only companion he needed. And it had served him well. Driving him, giving him that little electric boost every few minutes to remind him that he was alive.

He thought about the events of the evening. When he had visited Lomax he did not expect that he would have to kill him. In the past he had wondered about the man. It had taken little to corrupt him. Money. Something so simple. Something that Korn had in abundance and so many others did not. It had started small, and of course Korn had poured poison into Lomax's ears constantly – reminding him of their mission. Justice and retribution for those hurt and killed by the evil in this world. Lomax had bought it at first. He thought he was on a mission to tip the system in their favor. The system that benefitted rapists and murderers, giving them a court-appointed lawyer and presuming that they are innocent.

They're all guilty.

Korn knew it. And it didn't take a whole lot to persuade Lomax.

That damned wife of his never liked Korn, that was true enough. Still, he had been able to wear Lomax down. Slowly increasing the seriousness of the actions Lomax had to take in order to secure a conviction. Taking drug money for himself, or losing evidence vital to the defense, soon turned into Lomax ignoring witnesses who could exonerate defendants, even quietening them. It didn't take long for Lomax to become beholden to Korn. Korn's own corruption infected Lomax, and there was no amount of iodine and penicillin to clean that wound.

He thought about killing Lomax that night and found it curious that he didn't feel any thrill when he had shot him in the head. Korn thought about his old man – Nicholas Korn. Korn Equity and Investments started trading in the sixties, and by the eighties his father had become obscenely rich. He was smart, and knew how to play the market, but the secret of his success was his ruthless streak. He was prepared to do what even the worst of the Wall Street wolves would not.

You can't become a billionaire without hurting people. Not in the world of finance. And Nicholas had a lot of enemies. Korn remembered sitting in his father's study, on Christmas Day, when he was sixteen and having his first glass of Scotch with the old man. His father had been in an unusually good mood that day. He hated Christmas, wouldn't allow decorations in the house. The holiday season was never a joyous one in that home, not since Korn's mother passed away when he was ten. So that evening was special. Korn remembered the fire in his throat from the liquor, the smell of his father's cigar as he sat the young man down and told him why he was in such great spirits. It was little to do with the holidays.

His father's greatest rival had been put out of business one month before. The man had crossed Korn senior and he had never forgotten it. Korn's father had an opportunity to buy a company in which his rival had invested a huge portion of his wealth. A good company. Retail. Thriving in the booming early eighties. Korn senior bought up their suppliers, one by one, then cut off the retail chain. Its stock plummeted, and Korn bought the company, with a promise to rescue it. He closed the business down the next day. It had cost him close to a hundred million dollars, but that was money he could easily afford to lose.

The rival was destroyed. The rest of the rival's investments suddenly didn't look so good, and his fellow investors saw that the man had a Korn-shaped target on his back.

'So where is this man now?' asked Randal. 'Plotting his revenge?'

'Not likely,' said his father. 'He lost his house last week. Same day his wife left him, taking the kids with her. I heard this morning he had thrown himself off the top of his old building. The one I bought last month. He's a stain on the sidewalk, son.'

Randal didn't know what to say, but he felt something then. A little spark in his stomach. Excitement.

'You see, son, any stupid motherfucker can pull a trigger. If you want to kill your enemy you have to use your brain. Your cunning. There is nothing like the feeling of utterly destroying a man. Watching him disintegrate. Watching his wealth, his dignity, his humanity being stripped away, piece by piece. That's power, son. That's *true* power. This is why I want you to work for me. Someday, you could take over. Run the company for me. You've got it in you, you know. There's a killer in that little heart of yours.'

Randal remembered that conversation perfectly. He had clinked glasses, and watched his father laughing about his rival committing suicide on Christmas Eve, but that was not what gave Korn fond memories. It wasn't the unusual closeness with his father. They never had a bond, and never would. No, it was something else.

Korn realized at that young age what he wanted to do with the rest of his life. He wasn't interested in money, and finance bored him. He didn't want to answer to fellow shareholders, or investors, or God forbid have any clients to deal with.

No, he wanted power. Plain and simple.

The power that was in his father's eyes that night.

The power of life and death.

It had taken some time to come to terms with that desire, but it had felt natural to him. He stopped fighting it when he went to law school. He knew then that he would be a prosecutor and then a district attorney. But he would need to move – there was no death-penalty work in New York.

He would find a little county, and he would work his way up to district attorney, and he would have that power. That was what Korn lived for. That chemical, emotional, even sexual high that came with watching a man jitter on the electric chair and knowing that he had put him there. And kept him there, and that he had the power and skills to do it again. And again. And again . . .

Korn then opened his laptop, inserted the pen drive, and watched the footage. When he closed it again, he felt a thrill. Dubois was innocent. The thought of getting him convicted and watching his execution became that much sweeter. If the footage on the pen drive ever got out, it would ruin Korn, and set Dubois free. He couldn't allow that to happen. He could go downstairs, get a hammer from his toolbox, and smash the thing to pieces.

But he knew the smarter play would be to hang onto it. Now he knew who had killed Skylar Edwards, and that gave him leverage. The Pastor was an ally, of sorts. Now, he could become Korn's weapon, if he played it right.

Korn turned off the bedroom lamp and lay down on this bed. He hadn't eaten and had no desire for food. He wanted sleep. The Dubois trial would begin in the morning.

He was just beginning to doze off when his cell phone rang. He picked up.

'Tom, it's late. What's up?' asked Korn. It was his assistant DA, Wingfield. Maybe calling with news of Lomax's suicide.

'I've been keeping an eye on Flynn, like you asked. And, well, there's been a development.'

'What's that?'

'I followed him into the chop house, kept my head down, and then something incredible happened. A juror came in. She sat down with Flynn and they were talking.'

'A juror on the Dubois case?' asked Korn, sitting up now.

'You bet. Sandy Boyette. I tailed her to her apartment after the meeting, made sure it was her.'

'You think he was trying to bribe her? Did you see anything exchanged? Any bags? Packages?'

'No, they just talked.'

'This is important, Tom. I need you to think very carefully. How did he meet her in the chop house? Did they arrive around the same time?'

'He was already there, having dinner with that old judge and his co-counsel, Brooks. They left, Flynn stayed. Then the juror came in and went straight over to his table.'

'Did he beckon her over?'

'Not that I saw.'

'She just came and sat down opposite him?'

'Yeah, but they were talking straight away. It looked like he was expecting her.'

'What did they talk about?'

'I couldn't get close enough to hear any of it. But they talked for like twenty minutes. Then he left.'

'It's not enough,' said Korn. 'At the moment all we have is Flynn talking to a juror in a public restaurant, which of course he shouldn't be doing, but it's not enough for jury tampering. We need more. A lot more.'

'Are you going to tell the judge about this? You could get the juror thrown off the trial and Flynn reprimanded by the bar?'

'No. That's not nearly enough. We could put Flynn behind bars for a long time, along with the juror, but we need evidence of money changing hands. Did you get a picture of them together at least?'

'Sure did. If it's a bribe, which it looks like, I can get a warrant to monitor her bank accounts.'

Korn said, 'Flynn is too smart for that. It will be cash. Nothing that could be traced back to him. If we had the cash, then that might be enough because there would be no way for Sandy to explain where she got it. Yes, that might be enough. You'll need to keep on Flynn. Watch him. He will have to get the money to her . . .'

He paused.

After thirty seconds Tom said, 'You still there?'

'I'm still here. I'm thinking. It takes two jurors to vote *not guilty* for Flynn to get a mistrial. We can ride this out a little; there's no immediate risk to the trial if he just has one juror. But there's no guarantee when he will actually pay her off. He might wait until he gets the verdict, maybe even a few months, and then pay her. That would be the smart way to handle it.'

Korn neglected to add that this is exactly how he would've handled it.

'Would she wait that long? Could she trust him?'

'It's safer for both of them. And I suppose if he didn't pay her, she could always go to the police and rat him out. I remember her juror profile – she has a lot less to lose than Flynn.'

'So, what are we gonna do?'

'You stay on Flynn. Leave the rest to me. In forty-eight hours Flynn will be back in county lock-up and he won't ever leave. Lot of bad people in there. Detainees stab each other all the time . . .'

CHAPTER FORTY-FIVE

THE PASTOR

The Pastor tapped his ring on the steering wheel as he watched Professor Gruber leading Francis Edwards from his home. Gruber unlocked his car parked outside the house, and both of them got in and Gruber drove away. They were going to meet some like-minded men. One in particular, named Brian Denvir. The Pastor would not ordinarily associate with men like Denvir, but they had their uses. They were simple men, really, with weak minds and an unusual amount of fear. Brian had organized a protest outside the court building yesterday, at the Pastor's suggestion. As well as highly suggestible, Brian was friends with Gary Stroud, a similarly basic young man, who had been dating Skylar Edwards. Brian's fear of change, and primarily his fear of the black community, and fear of immigrants, had led him to an unhealthy interest in firearms.

Racism armed Americans better than the NRA could ever have hoped.

The Pastor feared nothing, and he sometimes laughed to himself when he thought of men like Brian, who couldn't go out and buy a donut without a handgun or sometimes a rifle hanging off their shoulder.

Little men. Simple men. Men who could be fed enough hate and fear to pull a trigger. To his disappointment, Francis was not proving to be quite as easy to mold as the Pastor had envisaged. They had spoken that morning. Francis called him in a panic.

'I've been vomiting all morning,' he said.

'Was it something you ate?' asked the Pastor.

'You know damn well it wasn't. I can't stop thinking about it. You *killed* that lawyer, and we carried that woman to the car. The woman you killed—'

The Pastor cut him off. 'You mean the corrupt lawyer and his employee who were working to free the man who murdered your daughter?'

Francis was quiet for a time, and the Pastor listened as he caught his breath.

'That doesn't mean I should—'

'Yes, it does. Have you learned nothing these past few months? This is a war, Francis. You have to pick a side. This isn't about law and order when the system is rigged against us. We've got to fight it all. Make our stand. Your daughter was a casualty, and if that doesn't get your ass fighting then I don't know what will. But really, you don't have a choice. The minute you watched me kill that lawyer, and grabbed Betty Maguire's feet and helped me move her into that car – that's the minute that you signed up. You became a soldier. It's not a crime if it's right. We're building something better here . . .'

The Pastor talked to him for an hour. Calmed him down, but also let him know, in no uncertain terms, that he was now an accomplice. If he talked to the authorities, he would go to jail, and who would look after Esther if he was behind bars? After the conversation, the Pastor didn't believe that Francis would talk to anyone about that night.

But he was also quite sure that without some major pressure, Francis would not be able to fulfill his ultimate objective.

It was only two days until the reckoning.

That's why the Pastor was outside Francis's home. He knew the one person who could bring Francis around, who could urge him to fully grasp his destiny, was his wife, Esther. The Pastor gazed from his vehicle at Francis's house. A light burned in the window of the lounge. He would wait another few minutes before going inside. He didn't want to appear as if he was maneuvering Francis out of the house so he could speak to her privately. That would arouse suspicion with Esther. And he wasn't on good terms with her. He knew that she sensed something dark in him. Some people had that gift.

He picked up his messenger bag, got out of the car and slung the strap over his shoulder as he approached the house. The doorbell sent a chime ringing inside the house, and he saw the drapes in the lounge twitch. The front door opened, just a few inches, and Esther peered out. She wore a pink toweling night robe and rose-colored carpet slippers.

'He's not here,' she said.

'Oh, I thought I was picking him up,' said the Pastor.

'No, your friend already did that.'

The Pastor smacked the heel of his palm off his forehead, smiled, said, 'It's been such a busy day. I'm sorry to have disturbed you. Tell me, how are you?'

'My daughter's murderer goes on trial in the morning. How do you think I'm feeling?'

The Pastor dropped the warm smile, reset his features into a somber expression, and said, 'Yes, I know. I can't imagine what you are going through right now. I talked to the DA this afternoon about the trial.'

That last statement caused Esther to take a step back as she looked the Pastor up and down again. She knew he would probably have a close relationship with the DA, given his job. It was obvious. And yet it was something that seemingly had not occurred to her.

'I can give you an update now, if you like? Sometimes trials aren't as intimidating if you know the process and what's going to happen from day to day. I can catch up with Francis in a little while. I don't mind,' he said.

The door opened wider, but Esther said nothing. She was still thinking. The trial was the most important thing in her life at that moment. It was the last thing that could be done for her daughter, and she wanted the man who killed her to pay. She wanted to know everything about it. Esther's thoughts were the same as any grieving mother's would be, and the Pastor knew this.

'Okay, if you tell me what the DA said, that would be a kindness. Do you want to come in for a minute?'

'Sure,' said the Pastor.

Esther led him inside, through to the little kitchen. She stood with her back to the counter, folded her arms across her chest and avoided the Pastor's gaze.

'Well, what's gonna happen tomorrow? Is he gonna change his plea? I read about that in some news articles on similar cases. To avoid the death penalty, they take a plea and there's no need for a trial. I would like that. I just don't know how much more we can take.'

'That can happen. I've had no word that this is what Dubois plans to do, but I wouldn't bet on it. Mr. Korn wants the death penalty. And he tends to get it. How would that make you feel? If Dubois was put to death, I mean.'

She shrugged her shoulders, shook her head, said, 'I don't know. At first, I wanted him to die. I know that. But I don't know what his death would achieve. I don't know how I feel about it. Maybe he deserves to die, but I don't know if I want to go through all of that.'

'I know it's tough. The trial will move quite quickly. Mr. Korn is one of those lawyers who likes to get things over and done with. For the families, you understand. Some lawyers stretch these trials out for weeks. He'll be working much faster; this isn't a complex case.'

'I'm glad of that.'

Taking hold of the back of a chair at the dining table, the Pastor asked, 'Do you mind?'

She shook her head, he pulled out the seat and sat down.

'I've been wanting to talk with you, Esther. I know you don't agree with some of my views, but I can assure you I meant no offense. I've seen too much suffering in this county. It's folks like Francis that need to stand up. Make a statement that this kind of violence won't be tolerated.'

Her expression changed. She shook her head and looked around the kitchen until she found a pack of Camel's behind a sugar bowl. Taking a match from the pack by the stove, she lit a cigarette, blew a cloud of smoke at the ceiling but said nothing.

'Francis is a good man. Hell, you're good people. I've seen this so many times. White folks who won't protect themselves from those who would do them harm.'

A derisory laugh turned into a cough, and Esther covered her mouth while she cleared her throat. Then said, 'You mean black folks are a threat? I don't buy your racist bullshit. Francis is hurting, real bad. He's not thinking straight, and I don't want you or your pals filling up his head with hate. Hasn't he been through enough?'

'You both have—'

'Wait, wait a minute. Is that what this is? Did you come here to talk to me? Use my daughter's murder trial as an excuse to try and talk me round to your way of thinking?'

'This isn't about you. We need Francis. That's the truth. Men like him are important for us. But now that you mention it, yes. I did come here to see you. We need you to help Francis see that he has to stand with us and be part of this cause.'

'You shouldn't have brought your sorry ass here. You will never persuade me that your bullshit is any good for my family.'

The Pastor stood up.

Esther took another drag on her cigarette, lifted her head, extended her neck, and blew smoke out of the side of her mouth.

'I came here because we need you to help Francis get to where we want him to be. I never said anything about trying to persuade you. I know you can't be persuaded. Francis just needs a nudge. Something to tip him over the edge. Your help will be invaluable . . .'

The Pastor's right fist shot out, and up, and rammed into the left side of Esther's neck, causing a loud *slap* as it hit home. Her mouth opened, her fingers clawed at her neck as her knees gave way. The blow wasn't hard enough to crush her windpipe, but her throat had spasmed and she began to cough and panic and scramble around on her knees trying desperately to draw air into her body.

From his messenger bag, the Pastor took a pair of leather gloves, slipped them on quickly, and then took a length of rope from the bag. One end was already tied in a noose. He moved around behind Esther, slipped the noose over her head and cinched it tight around her throat.

He placed his left knee between her shoulder blades, forcing her down flat on the ground, and pulled on the rope. Her throat closed completely. He watched her neck turn bright red. She began to make a sound. It was the sound of a human being trying to gasp air when none could enter their windpipe. The noise sounded somewhere between a choke and a deep swallow.

Her fingers clawed at her throat, and the Pastor gritted his teeth as he pulled. He wanted those sounds to stop. He found them uncomfortable to hear. To drown out the sound he recited the Lord's Prayer. It remained a comfort to him. He had said it thousands of times. As a boy, in the dark, hot box in the back yard. Sweating, and losing consciousness in the heat. The words of that prayer always made him feel better.

By the time he'd finished, Esther had stopped struggling. The sound ceased, and her body went limp. The Pastor relaxed his grip on the rope as he felt something wet on his left knee, which was on the floor. He stood up, a wet patch on that knee, and saw that Esther's bladder had released.

Moving around the body, he picked her up at the waist, turning her on her side. He grabbed one arm. Kneeling, he hauled her body onto his shoulder and stepped carefully into the hallway. Setting her down at the foot of the stairs, he took one end of the rope and walked up to the first floor. Looping the rope over the rail of the banister, and then through one of the posts, he began to take up the slack.

Then, he pulled. This was a test of his strength, and one that he met easily. The rope sawed into the wooden rail as he hauled it up, hand over hand, until Esther was suspended three feet from the ground. At which point he tied off the rope and descended the stairs.

The rail above him creaked as Esther's body swayed gently from side to side. Her neck was horribly distended, and her face and eyes were filled with blood. The Pastor retrieved his messenger bag from the kitchen and left the house quickly.

Gruber had been informed he should stick around after he dropped Francis home. He would need to be there when the police came, to comfort Francis, and make sure he didn't do anything stupid like put a gun in his mouth.

The sight of his wife, having hung herself, would be exactly what Francis needed. The last of his inhibitions would be thrown off. He would be a man with nothing to live for. A man whose only option was to join his family in their graves.

Perfect, thought the Pastor.

CHAPTER FORTY-SIX

EDDIE

I sat on the bed in The Chanterelle, listening to Bloch. She talked a little while she messed with the police scanner, which she'd brought out from her travel case. Kate was listening and looking at the photos I'd gotten from Farnesworth. Harry lay down on the bed, his eyes closed.

'What was the name of the lady you met from the Darius Robinson innocence campaign?' I asked.

'Jane? No. She hasn't told anyone about the conversation in the candy store. I called her and checked,' said Bloch.

'Then it was the candy-store lady, Dorothy Majors,' said Harry, from the bed.

'No, I checked with her too,' said Bloch.

'Well, somebody tipped off Korn that we had the juice to flip Lomax. It wasn't anyone in this room, so it had to be Dorothy or Jane,' I said.

'I think it was the letter,' said Kate.

Bloch nodded.

Kate had bought a printer in the electrical store on Main Street and hooked it up to her laptop, which allowed Bloch to print the photos of the letter to Lomax from his deceased wife.

'I think that kind of a letter changes someone,' said Kate. 'Think about it. Lomax loved his wife, she finally succumbs to the cancer, he's been nursing her for years and years and then she drops a bomb on him from beyond the grave. It fits.'

'It might,' I said, as I skim-read the letter again. There was something about this letter I knew was important, but I didn't know what quite yet.

'Okay, so let's say he has a change of heart. He tells Korn he's going to rat him out? Confess to everything and bring Korn down with him? Why would he tell him?'

'I think Lomax underestimated the lengths that the DA is willing to go,' said Kate.

We talked it over some more, and then fell into quiet as Bloch found the Sunville County Sheriff's Department radio frequency. She hadn't called in Lomax's death, seeing as how she'd trespassed on his property and looked over the crime scene. It was too risky to alert the police, but she felt bad about not letting officials know. She was sure someone in the department would call out and see him, even just to pay their respects, and she wanted to know the instant that happened.

I sat on the bed beside Harry, with my fist on my chin, squinting at Kate's picture of Ryan Hogg's ring. Harry snored beside me while Kate paced the room.

As well as listening to the scanner, Bloch was trying to listen to Kate and I muttering about the picture of the ring on Hogg's hand.

'It could have lettering above the stars; I mean, I think there's something there but I just can't make it out,' I said.

Kate took the phone from me, adjusted the angle, said, 'We're going to need a better picture. Let me see the photos you got from Farnesworth.'

'I haven't seen those yet,' said Bloch.

Kate nodded at her, said she would let her see them in a moment. For now, Kate held Farnesworth's autopsy photos, and her phone, side by side.

'I can't tell,' said Kate.

'Let me take a look,' said Bloch.

Bloch first examined the picture of Hogg's ring, then the autopsy photos. Soon as she looked at them, I saw the skin tightening on her forehead.

'What is it?' I said.

'You got it wrong, Eddie,' said Bloch. 'The lettering indentations on Skylar Edward's forehead are not "F" and "C". The "C" is only a partial indentation. The letters are "F" "O" and "P" above the star.'

Kate's mouth fell open.

'How do you know that?' I asked.

'Because now I know the exact ring that the killer wore. We all got it wrong. The five-pointed star has nothing to do with the occult. The star symbolizes law enforcement. The star is a shield. The FOP don't use membership cards. Instead, their members wear rings.'

'What is FOP?' asked Kate.

'It's the Fraternal Order of Police,' I said. 'A lobbying group and membership organization that represents police officers across the country. The man who killed Skylar Edwards is a cop.'

'Or used to be a cop,' said Bloch. 'And it gives us a different problem. The ring is not unique. There could be thousands in circulation.'

No one said anything. We had been hoping the ring would lead us to the killer. But now it only gave us suspects. Lots of them. No one spoke as we took it all in. The silence was quickly filled by the hurried, anxious voice of the dispatcher on Bloch's police scanner.

'*All available units, assistance required at a probable suicide . . .*'

Bloch nodded as she listened. This was the call coming in about Lomax. Bloch wanted to know how they were going to call it, and whether there would be any suspicion over the death.

'*. . . address is 491 Peachtree Avenue . . .*'

Bloch's eyebrows knotted together, she said, 'That's not Lomax's address. It's—'

'Skylar Edwards' address,' said Kate.

Bloch was halfway out the door when I said, 'Wait up. I'm coming too.'

For forty-five minutes Bloch and I watched Francis Edwards weeping in the back of a Sunville County Sheriff's cruiser. The dispatcher had said the call was a probable suicide. It didn't take much to surmise Francis's wife had been the one to take her own life. There was a rotund man in a tweed jacket in the seat beside him, his hand around Francis's shoulders, whispering to him in an attempt to calm him down. Francis was a big man, and the car shook with his sobbing.

The medical examiner was just leaving as a Jaguar pulled up outside the place. Korn got out of the car, approached the ME and they had a conversation on the front lawn.

'That's our cue,' I said.

We got out of the SUV and approached Korn and the ME, Miss Price.

'Mind if we take a look inside?' I asked.

Korn turned his large frame toward me. Fine lines from little sleep at the corner of his eyes.

'What do you want, Flynn?' asked Korn. 'This is a separate case. It has nothing to do with your client.'

'That's where you're wrong. Dubois didn't kill Skylar Edwards. Someone else did. It's suspicious her mother commits suicide on the eve of Dubois' trial. Maybe Esther Edwards couldn't deal with the guilt of killing her own daughter and then framing an innocent man,' I said.

Korn took a step back, those fine lines around his eyes deepened in anger.

'You're not suggesting Esther Edwards murdered her own daughter?' he asked.

'That's the defense theory,' I said. 'Now, you better let us in the house so we can gather evidence to make that case. If you don't, I'll need to wake up the judge and get a court order so I can go in and take a look.'

'This is outrag—' but Korn didn't finish expressing his indignation. I could tell by his expression, something had clicked in his mind. The anger lines disappeared, and he pursed his lips, pressing them tightly together, yet the corners of his mouth drew into the smile he was desperately trying not to show.

'No need to wake the judge,' he said. 'You two go right ahead. I'll let the officers know you can view the scene.'

'Thank you,' I said, and I walked away, toward the front door. I heard Korn holler to the deputy at the front door to let us in so we could look around, but make sure we were accompanied.

When we were out of Korn's earshot, Bloch said, 'Are you really going to run that as a defense?'

'Accusing the victim's mother of her murder is just about the worst thing we could do. Especially if it looks like she took her own life because she couldn't deal with the loss of her child. That would alienate the jury. In fact, the jury would hate us forever for making that suggestion. It's a terrible idea. Korn knows this. That's why he's letting us take a look. He wouldn't otherwise. First rule of trial law is you let your opponents make their own mistakes, and then you expose them. Korn thinks he's playing it smart by letting us run all the way with that theory.'

Bloch said, 'You're pretty smart, for a lawyer.'

The deputy on guard outside the house stood aside as we approached, signaled to one of his colleagues he should follow us around inside. Make sure we didn't mess with the scene.

Soon as you stepped through the front door, the horror was there to be seen. No wonder Francis Edwards was losing his mind in the back of a squad car.

Esther hung facing the front door. A crime scene photographer was still snapping pictures, which explained why they hadn't cut her down yet. Judging by her face, cause of death was consistent with strangulation. Her eyes were black eight balls, and her tongue had swollen and hung, distended, from her open mouth. She wore a pink robe, which had fallen open. Beneath the robe she had on a silk pair of pajamas, also pink. A dark patch covered her groin and stomach. As we got closer, I picked up the smell. Her bladder had emptied.

There were no other marks or signs of violence. A classic suicide. Except, of course, it wasn't.

Bloch gave me a look. She was good at that. Lucky for her, because she didn't like to talk, and at times, like now with a cop behind us and a crime photographer in front, it was wise not to speak openly. But I read her look.

She had spotted it too. When someone dies, the bladder and bowels will void at some point shortly after as the muscles relax. There was a wet patch of urine on Esther's crotch and stomach, instead of a dark trail down her legs. The carpet beneath her suspended body was quite dry. She'd wet herself lying on her front.

I watched Bloch wander past Esther, through to the lounge. I went upstairs, careful not to touch the rail.

At the top of the stairs I turned right and examined the rope. A thick knot, looped and doubled and knotted again around the banister and posts that ran along the first-floor hallway for the length of the stairs.

I got up, looked at the rail. A notch had been sawed into it, by the rope. I looked at the six inches of rope that descended from the rail to the thick knot. There were flakes of white paint in the fiber. I snapped a picture of the notch in the rail, the paint flakes and the carpet.

I'd seen enough. I went downstairs, Bloch looked up at me as I came down. She gave me another look. This time, with a slight nod.

We went outside, without a word.

Korn had left the scene by this stage. We got into the car, turned on the engine and drove away before either of us said anything.

'There's a wet cigarette on the kitchen floor with a strong smell of urine coming from it,' said Bloch.

'I thought you might find something like that. The carpet below her was dry. Upstairs, there's a notch on the rail where the rope has burned through it and paint flakes on the rope leading to the knot.'

Bloch nodded.

'Who killed her?' I asked.

'The same person who killed her daughter.'

'What makes you say that?'

'It would take a strong individual to haul her up those stairs, and stronger still to keep her there with one hand while he tied the knot. That's consistent with the strength used in Skylar's murder. The big question is, why did he kill Esther? And why tonight?'

THE SIXTH DAY

CHAPTER FORTY-SEVEN

EDDIE

It was two-thirty in the morning and I was still awake, my mind racing, and Harry snored loudly in the bed beside me.

A lot of times I don't sleep on the eve of a trial. I don't sleep much anyway, but the thought of going into that courtroom in the morning with so little ammunition, a jury and a whole town stacked against Andy filled me with a dread that sat on my chest. I got up, dressed, and went down one floor to Patricia and Andy's room. I listened outside the door and heard voices, so I knew they were awake before I knocked.

Patricia let me in, then resumed her seat on the side of the bed beside Andy. A single lamp burned in the corner.

Patricia put her arms around her son. In their trademark embrace, he rocked back and forward, patting her hand that seemed rooted to his shoulder.

I sat down in the chair opposite.

'Nightmares?' I asked.

Patricia spoke softly, 'He's afraid, and I keep telling him there's nothing to be afraid of. He didn't do it, and God will make them see that.'

I didn't tell her that God doesn't usually make an appearance in Alabama, and hardly ever in their criminal courts.

'I've been thinking about the case. There's so much we don't know. Tell me more about Skylar,' I said to Andy.

'She was real nice to me. When I started working in the bar I didn't really know what I was doing. I didn't know how the ordering system worked, how to load the dishwasher, or work the register . . . she helped me. Ryan didn't want to know me, not really. It was Skylar who taught me the job. She was always talking about what she was going to do when she finished college. Had her eye on a job in Seattle with a company that did research. No matter how she was feeling she always had a smile.'

'Was she unhappy sometimes?'

'Rarely. She used to fight with her boyfriend, Gary. I could always tell they were fighting because she typed on her phone with both thumbs when she was mad.'

'What kind of phone did Skylar have? It wasn't with her belongings when she was found.'

'An iPhone, I think. It was pink with little gems on the back spelling her initials.'

'Did they fight a lot?'

'Just arguments. He wasn't violent or nothing. Mostly they argued about politics. Gary was a big supporter of the president, you see.'

'And Skylar wasn't?'

'You could say that. She saw him for what he was, and she got mad that Gary was taken in by it all. He didn't like me. Gary, I mean. Sometimes I would walk Skylar a little, until her ride showed. If it was Gary picking her up, he would always give me the meanest looks.'

'Does Gary wear a ring?'

He thought for a moment, said, 'I don't think so, no.'

'Who do you think might have killed Skylar?'

'Tell you the truth, I'm still in shock. I don't know anyone who could've done that to her. She was the sweetest person, I just don't get it.'

'Andy, I know it's scary. I will need you to be brave. At some stage you might have to tell the jury that you didn't kill Skylar, and that you were forced to sign this confession.'

I opened the file to the page containing Andy's confession.

'They said everything would be alright if I signed it. If I didn't, my mom would get hurt. And they'd hurt me even more. I was still groggy, I guess. Lomax was hitting me with the baton, cracked one over my head and I must've blacked out. When I woke up, they were hammering me for the confession and I . . . I just wasn't thinking straight. I didn't want to sign it. I knew I shouldn't, but I was scared.'

Andy spoke softly. His tone even and full of conviction. He had large eyes that bloomed in the half-light of the room. Those eyes were full of fear.

I wanted to tell Andy that everything was going to be alright. That Harry, Kate and I were going to win this case for him. That this nightmare would soon be over and he could go back to his books, go to college, meet a girl, study hard and make his mother proud, and have the rich and rewarding life he deserved.

But I couldn't. There is always hope. But right then, eight hours before his trial began, there was no comfort I could give him. This wasn't to do with the system, which was stacked against him anyway – it was the cops, and the DA, and the biased judge, and the biased jury. I can get past one or two of those problems.

But not them all.

Not this time.

CHAPTER FORTY-EIGHT

EDDIE

We arrived at the courthouse before 8.30 a.m. There were no protestors outside. I guessed the boys with AR-15s and Confederate flags didn't get up until past noon. Andy, Patricia, Harry and Kate filed into the courtroom to take their seats.

I waited outside in the hallway, hands in my pockets, walking the floor.

Korn was going to open the case to the jury, and I would then give a responding statement. I had made some rough notes the day before, but they weren't good. I walked the empty hallway, up and down, my feet echoing on the stone floor tiles. Moving around sometimes helped me think.

It wasn't working this morning.

I was relying on Bloch finding some missing diamonds. The security footage from the gas station was still in the wind, or so I hoped. Bloch didn't dismiss the idea. She just nodded and said she would go and see if she could find it.

I didn't ask where she was gonna look.

One thing was for sure, she wasn't going to find anything in time to give me a decent point to make in my opening speech to the jury.

To get a conviction, Korn would need ten of the twelve jurors to bring in a guilty verdict. In New York, you need a unanimous verdict. I only ever needed one juror to be on my side, in my entire career. Now I needed two, and if I messed up, my client would die an excruciating death.

Normally, I have an idea. A theory in a case, which I can tell the jury about at the beginning of the trial. An opening statement shouldn't contain an argument, just an indication of what the evidence will show the jury. I didn't have a theory for this case yet. Not a full one. Not by a long shot. Strolling up and down outside the courtroom, I had very little I could tell the jury.

Someone else killed Skylar Edwards, but we didn't know who.

Ignore the forensic evidence proving Andy's skin was under the victim's nails, and the corresponding scrape on his back. Ignore the eyewitness testimony that Skylar and Andy were arguing the night she disappeared. Ignore the confession Andy made to the sheriff, and the second confession to his cellmate.

That was a lot to ask a jury to ignore.

No way. It would be hard enough to make a dent in any of this evidence even with an open-minded and impartial jury.

I needed something else. Something big to shake the twelve souls on that jury stand.

While I'd been walking back and forth, a steady crowd had beaten its way into the courtroom behind me. Now it was quiet in the hallway. I checked my watch.

Almost time.

The case was giving me nothing.

I decided the best thing to do was focus on something else instead of the damning evidence against Andy.

I was going to shout 'fire' in a crowded theatre.

Sometimes the best way to deal with incriminating evidence is not to deal with it at all.

With the jury settled in their seats, and the crowded gallery behind us quieting down, Korn stood to make his opening statement. The defense table was crowded, but it needed to be. Harry and Kate flanked Andy. I sat beside Kate. Patricia was in the first row of the gallery, right behind Andy. She could just about lean over and touch him. Before this trial was through, he would need her hand on his shoulder.

Korn had risen slowly to his feet and waited while the chatter of the crowd fell from rippling whispers into a respectful silence.

It was a good performance. Commanding. This was his house. We were trespassers.

'Ladies and gentlemen of the jury, first I want to thank you for your service to this county, and to the family of Skylar Edwards. Look, there, in the front row behind my assistant district attorney, Mr. Wingfield,' he said, sweeping his hand toward the seats behind the prosecution table, in the gallery. A man in his fifties with red hair and a puffy face already wet with tears. Francis Edwards. There were no spare seats in the courtroom, apart from the front row behind the defense table, where Patricia sat. And in one other spot. There was an empty space beside Francis.

'Skylar Edwards was brutally murdered by the defendant, Mr. Dubois. Her boyfriend was going to propose to her the night she was killed. Instead, she was cruelly taken from her loved ones by the defendant, Andy Dubois. Skylar's father, Francis, is here to watch justice served on the man who beat and strangled his daughter to death, and then buried her body. Nothing that happens in this courtroom can assuage his grief. He will carry it with him for the rest of the rest of his life. You will notice Skylar's mother is not here. She could not bear the loss of her child, and sadly took her own life not twenty-four hours ago.'

Some of the jurors nodded. They must've heard already. This is a small town after all. Others let out an audible gasp.

'Francis is here today for his wife, and his daughter. You, the jury, can give him the dignity and nobility to carry this grief by convicting Andy Dubois of Skylar's murder. That's justice. It's a shield to help families bear their burden. That shield is not in my gift to give him. I can't give Francis justice. Trust me, I would do anything to give him one moment's peace. But I cannot. I do not hold that power.'

He paused, let his eyes linger on the grief-torn face of Francis Edwards. The jury followed his eyes to that man. He kept his gaze on him, and theirs. He made Francis the focus for the entire room. He wanted the jury to feel that pain. For his grief to make the jury uncomfortable. It was human nature – people have an innate willingness to help those in need. He was tapping into our better instincts, twisting them around for his own purposes.

It wasn't a theatrical performance by any means. I believed every word Korn had spoken, if I took him at face value. Knowing what

I know, I could see underneath that mask. There was nothing so low as a man who would use a parent's suffering for his own ends. He didn't care about Francis or his late wife. Didn't care about Skylar, probably. He wanted to win. If he had to flay those people alive to do it, he would.

'Only you, ladies and gentlemen of the jury, have the power to help this man. To do that, you must listen to the evidence in this case.'

Finally, he was through with his emotional hook. Now he turned to the evidence.

'The defendant, Andy Dubois, confessed to this crime. Twice. Once to his cell mate, John Lawson. And once to law enforcement. That's right, he fully admitted his guilt to the Sunville County Sheriff's Department. You will read that confession. Now, it seems he has changed his mind. He wants to suppress that confession, and his motion was denied by the judge. You will get to read it and decide if he was telling the truth when he confessed. His fancy legal team, from New York City, will try to tell you that the confession was coerced from Dubois. It's up to you to decide for yourselves if that is true.

'Now, apart from a full confession to murder, what other evidence points to this defendant as the perpetrator of this heinous crime? There's plenty. He was the last person to be seen with Skylar Edwards on the night she died. His blood was found beneath the fingernails of the victim. There's a scratch on his back, consistent with the victim scraping at his flesh, in a desperate attempt to be free of his clutches.'

One of the jurors, a woman in a beige cardigan, over a beige blouse, curled her lip in disgust and confusion and pointed her beige face in my direction. She couldn't really understand why we were having a trial at all. Surely this was all a foregone conclusion – the guy confessed, for Christ's sake.

She wasn't alone on the jury stand in giving me some curious and unwelcome looks. A big man in a plaid shirt gave me the eye. It was the same disappointed expression he would use on cold callers and insurance salesmen. We were all just wasting his time.

'I want you to listen to the prosecution case, and keep in mind all that I have said. But more importantly, keep Skylar's father in mind. Do not allow yourself to be distracted by the baseless defense arguments. Mr. Flynn and those in his big-time New York law firm will argue that it's possible Esther Edwards killed her own child, and then took her own life last night because she couldn't live with the guilt. He's *actually* going to put the blame on the victim's dead mother, before the poor woman has even been buried. And he'll do that in front of the lady's grieving husband. Treat this argument with the *disgust* it deserves.'

The whole jury was looking at us. Every single one.

Harry leaned over, whispered, 'The jury want to send us to death row along with Andy.'

'Ladies and gentlemen,' continued Korn, 'justice is in your hands. It's up to you to give it to Francis Edwards. You do that by sending the defendant to the execution chamber. You do that by listening to the evidence, instead of listening to the defendant's *fancy* lawyer.'

He took another beat, let his eyes roam over the jury. They were small slits of black below his eyebrows, and yet I was sure those eyes would take in every face. When he'd let the silence build long enough, he turned to the judge, nodded and limped back to his seat.

Judge Chandler's face contorted from a look of respect and admiration for Korn, into surprised dismay when he fixed his gaze on me. Like I was something nasty he'd discovered on the sole of his shoe.

'Mr. Flynn, do you wish to make an opening statement at this time?'

It sounded more like a threat than an invitation.

I stood and said, 'I do, Your Honor, can I get a five-minute comfort break?'

'Make it quick,' he said.

We adjourned for a few minutes. I went straight to the men's bathroom, got in the stall and locked it. I unbuttoned my suit jacket, grabbed a hold of the breast pocket of my shirt and yanked it until it tore at one side, exposing an inch of flesh beneath. I closed my jacket, opened the top button of my shirt and loosened my tie.

I was ready.

CHAPTER FORTY-NINE

EDDIE

'Members of the jury, my name is Eddie Flynn, and I'm an attorney from New York. That part of Mr. Korn's opening statement is true. A lot of what he told you is *not* true. Here's one lie, just by way of example – we are *not* claiming, and *never* have claimed that Esther Edwards murdered her own daughter. He knows we've never made that case. There's not one court filing, not one piece of paper ever lodged with this court that even hints we would make that argument. And if I'm lying about that, the judge will tell you.'

I took a beat, swung around and looked at the judge. What I said was correct. Some defendants hint at their case through discovery or other motions. Judge Chandler's jaw flexed as he ground his teeth. He wanted to contradict me, but of course he couldn't. I'd used the judge to force a wedge between the prosecutor and the truth.

I turned back to the jury.

'You see? For Mr. Korn to tell you we were making that case is nothing more than an appalling lie, and he should apologize to Francis Edwards for using his wife's suicide to try to score points with this jury.'

I made sure to turn away from the jury and the judge, right then, and give Korn a wink.

He'd fallen for the trap I'd laid last night. His face, normally a brighter shade of corpse, turned just a little red. That one really burned him. Now the jury at least has the idea in their head that Korn might be misleading them. If they don't trust Korn, then maybe Andy has a chance.

I wasn't done with Korn yet, and I turned my attention back to the jury.

'I *am* a lawyer from New York City. That part is true. However, I'm anything but *fancy*. I grew up in Brooklyn, my father never worked a steady job and my mother waited tables all her life. What Mr. Korn left out of his speech is that he's from New York too, only he grew up in a thirty-million-dollar apartment on the Upper West Side. His father was a Wall Street powerbroker. He got his law degree in a private college – I got mine from night school. Look at Mr. Korn. That's a nice suit. Hand-cut Italian cloth, and that's a gorgeous silk shirt beneath it. My suits are Italian too. I get two of 'em every winter from Big Momo's Warehouse in Jersey. Not the same quality, though,' I said, and opened my jacket letting the jury see the small tear on the breast pocket of my shirt.

'There's only one fancy New York attorney in this room, and it ain't me.'

I was surprised when I heard a few laughs from the gallery, and even saw one or two jurors smile.

It was going well. I'd made the jury think about Korn, instead of Andy.

Things were about to go disastrously wrong.

I was counting on it.

'But this case is not about me. It's not even about Skylar Edwards. And it's certainly not about Andy Dubois. This case is about the district attorney for Sunville County, Mr. Randal Korn—'

I was expecting it, but I was still surprised at the speed at which Korn got to his full height and called out *objection*.

'Objection sustained. Mr. Flynn, you are not permitted to use this court to launch a personal attack on the district attorney for this county, is that clear?' said Judge Chandler, his nose wrinkled, and his lips drew back over yellowed teeth. He flicked his gaze to the jury before settling his ire on me. He wanted the jury on his side. The judge is supposed to guide the jury to making their own fair and impartial decision.

He was trying to shut me down. I'd expected it and now I was going to lean into it, by spelling it out, straight and true to the judge, and making sure the jury would hear every last word.

'I am permitted to frame the context for the evidence that will be presented in this case, Your Honor. It's highly irregular for the prosecutor to object to the defense's opening statement. That's not the only irregularity in Mr. Korn's career, by the way. In this case, we will show Andy Dubois was framed for this murder by the district attorney and the late Sheriff Colt Lomax. We will show that Mr. Korn has the highest death-penalty conviction rate in modern history and that he will use the administration of justice as a weapon to kill whomever he pleases, for his own personal enjoyment. He is an evil in this county, and he is asking the jury to be complicit in his crimes. I think the jury needs to hear this, and if you are trying to stop me from alleging police and prosecutorial corruption in a death-penalty defense then *you* are part of the problem too. Go ahead, tell me I can't make that argument and I'll have you and your decision roasted, slowly, by an appellate judge before you've got time to take your head out of the district attorney's ass.'

The cells below the courthouse were spotlessly clean. Certainly better than the county lock-up. They were brighter too, and didn't have the stench of human waste running through them. It's always the same. Courthouse cells are the cleanest because eventually the stench travels and all it takes is one judge to catch a whiff of piss and there will be a cleaning crew working up a cloud of soap suds within the hour.

My sneaky speech to the jury hadn't gone down too well with Judge Chandler. He whispered to the court security officer and I was arrested right at the defense table and taken away.

I thought I had pushed the envelope too far by swearing in court, and as a rule I never do it, but on this occasion my blood was up. I'd been down here for the best part of two hours and that was enough to cool my head.

As defenses go, this wasn't a bad start.

I'd had worse.

There's not a lot to do in a jail cell but think. And I had a lot on my mind. One thing that kept occupying me was Lomax. I'd read the letter from his wife and I was more and more convinced that Lomax had had a change of heart. I imagined his conscience getting the better of him, and instead of keeping his mouth shut, he vented at Korn. And that would have been the end of him. Any redemption he could have sought had been taken from him. People change. The road can have unexpected turns before you get to the end. Alexander Berlin had taken that turn, sending me here to save Andy Dubois. Korn, on the other hand, was too sick to make that change. He was the exception. The two percent. One of the people who had been built wrong, or became twisted early in life and can't even see the turn coming, never mind feel the need to take it.

I heard a key in the lock of the blue steel door.

Kate came in, sat down on the painted concrete bench and waited for the door to close behind her before she started speaking.

The door slammed with a clang that shook the fillings in my teeth.

'Well?' I said.

She held a finger to her lips, waited. After a few seconds we heard the faint sound of boot heels disappearing out of earshot. The guard, returning to his station, disappointed that he couldn't hear our conversation. There were no cameras or mics in this cell. Nowhere to hide them.

'It's bad. There will be a hearing after the trial finishes for the day so Chandler can decide what to do with you. He shouldn't be hearing the case at all, but I didn't want to push it too far. Unlike you,' she said.

'I know, sorry. I was just worried I wouldn't get the reaction from Judge Chandler that we needed. I guess I overdid it.'

'Just a little,' said Kate.

'So, apart from that, are we good?'

'We're good. I take over for today.'

'You got your speech ready?'

'Good to go.'

We had shouted fire in a crowded theatre. And there was a real fire. There's no doubt of that. It was a simple deception. It doesn't matter what Korn says, or what evidence he calls to the stage for the crowd. If we can convince them the building is on fire they're not going to listen to a goddamn word of the play.

'How are you feeling about taking on the medical examiner, Miss Price?'

She looked to the ceiling, blew out her cheeks and said, 'I'm feeling the pressure on this one.'

We couldn't use Farnesworth's autopsy report because he wouldn't testify. Kate and I had a plan to bring it in through a back door. It was risky, and the likelihood was it wouldn't work. If it failed, Andy was sure to be convicted. This might give us a chance, but it was all falling on Kate.

'We could ask for a recess until tomorrow, you know,' I said. 'If you don't want to do this, I understand. It's asking a lot—'

'I can do it,' she said.

'I know you can. You've just got to put it out of your mind that this is a death-penalty case. I think that responsibility messes with some lawyer's heads. Don't let it get to yours. Just take it nice and easy.'

'I'm from New Jersey, I don't do nice and easy,' she said.

'Okay, then how do you want to handle Miss Price?'

Her finger rested on her lips for a moment while she thought about it, then Kate said, 'I think I'll put her skinny ass through the fuckin' wall.'

CHAPTER FIFTY

KATE

Kate waited until the courtroom had settled down, but she didn't need to wait for long. She felt that familiar tumbling sensation in her stomach right before she spoke in court for the first time in a case. That was okay. That was normal. She would be worried if she felt calm. She needed that nervous energy. She used it, made it into fire in her belly that she spewed at her opponents.

She stood, ready.

The jury had spent the best part of an hour in their room, talking over what they'd just heard and seen while Kate and Korn had argued with the judge over Eddie's fate. The time the jury had alone was useful. Eddie had told them the DA and the judge were corrupt, and then he got arrested for saying it. They weren't thinking about the DNA evidence, they weren't thinking about the scratches on Andy's back or the witness who saw Andy and Skylar together just before she disappeared.

They were talking about Eddie. And Korn, and the judge. And Kate knew she had to keep them on that subject.

'Ladies and gentlemen of the jury, I will be brief. It is the defendant's case that he is being framed for this crime. That the evidence against him has been fabricated. He was an easy target for law enforcement who just wanted to make a quick arrest. He was an easy target for a district attorney to secure a conviction. We hope that you will not think of him as an easy target for execution. We will show that there are major problems with the evidence the district attorney seeks to use. All we ask you to do is keep your minds open. Mr. Korn stands before you today as a record holder. He has sent more men to death row than any other prosecutor in the history of the United States.'

Kate took a moment to pause and take the jury's temperature. Some were disinterested, already with their arms folded, the shutters firmly closed. A few looked to Korn, and then back at Kate.

'I don't believe that Sunville County is more dangerous than any other place in America. I don't think you believe that either. So why is it that this county sends more people to death row than any other? The statistics show us this was not the case before Mr. Korn became district attorney. Ask yourself, are you happy to be the death-penalty capital of the United States? Because today Andy Dubois is fighting for his life. And Mr. Korn wants you to take that life. There is more to this case than the murder of Skylar Edwards. Our case is that Skylar's murderer is still out there, and an innocent man sits before you. One murder will not avenge another.'

One of the jurors sat up straighter, shifted his gaze to Korn and kept it there. He looked uncomfortable, as if a hot fire had just been lit beneath his seat. Kate remembered his name instantly – Taylor Avery.

She had more to say, but she saw that some of the jurors were at least beginning to think about this. And that was enough, for now. She thanked the jury and sat down.

'Mr. Korn, would you like to call your first witness?' said Judge Chandler.

'Yes, Your Honor, the People call the county medical examiner, Miss Fiona Price.'

A tall woman rose from the gallery, made her way through the swing gate, past the prosecution and defense tables, and then stood at the entrance to the witness box. Everything about her was sharp, thought Kate. She wore a long black coat of fine material over a black, silk suit. Her dark red lips were like two uncut rubies encased in the alabaster cliff of her face. Either she wore very pale foundation, or her skin was completely without color, like virgin snow. Her hair was curly, short, and each lick bounced with the movement of her head. Kate didn't like the look in her large, round eyes. There was little color in them, pale gray, with small hints of blue. Corpse eyes, with bright red veins snaking through them. Kate was almost surprised to see those eyes move. It was as if something dead had been reanimated.

A cold woman, who does cold work with the dead. Kate could think of nothing worse than dying and having Miss Price be your final guardian.

The clerk administered the oath.

Miss Price handed the Bible back to the clerk as if it was a hot coal. The displeasure of holding the book was clear, in the narrowing at the corner of her eyes and the pursing of her bloody lips, which now looked more like slices of liver.

Kate shuddered and wrote down Price's name on her legal pad. She was taking this witness.

Korn quickly confirmed Price was the medical examiner for Sunville County, and that she had performed an autopsy and examination of the victim's body.

She affirmed these questions with a simple, but authoritative, 'Yes.'

The crowd was silent. Korn popped out routine questions and Price answered them with her loud, 'yes,' which increasing sounded like ice cracking. Kate felt gooseflesh on her arms. She put down her pen and rubbed at them. Even being around Miss Price made her flesh cold.

Harry leaned over, whispered to Kate, 'For your first question, ask Miss Price what she knows about one hundred and one missing Dalmatians.'

Kate hid a smile behind her fingers.

When she looked back at Price, she didn't feel quite so intimidated. Her confidence was returning. Sometimes monsters lost their power when they were made ridiculous. Harry nodded at her. He had given her exactly what she needed.

She looked at the witness stand as Korn's assistant, Wingfield, set about erecting a life-sized photograph of the victim, lying in the dirt beside a large hole in the ground. There was blood on her face, bright red beneath flecks of dark earth. The blood luminous, almost matching her red nail polish. It was a huge photograph, almost to scale. Kate watched Wingfield set up the stand and noticed a large gold ring on his finger. He was too far away for Kate to see what the pattern was on the ring – there was definitely something there. He was a large man. Very strong, and it might have been a championship ring, or some other kind of commemorative ring.

Harry tapped her on the back of her hand, pointed at his finger and then gestured toward Wingfield. He'd spotted it too. He got up, moved across the aisle and asked Wingfield if he'd like a hand. The assistant DA declined. When Harry got back to his seat, he made a note on his legal pad.

It's an FOP ring. Wingfield must be an ex-cop.

The FOP were like the Freemasons, but for cops. And Kate wasn't surprised there were at least two people she'd seen with those rings. There were probably more, but she hadn't noticed. She would be on the lookout now.

Once Wingfield set up the picture, and got it stood securely against the frame, Price got permission from the judge to approach the photograph. From her coat pocket she produced a telescopic pointer, which she flicked open with practiced skill. She pointed at the victim's arms and began.

'I'll go through the injuries as I found them, Mr. Korn. You can see the bruising on her forearms. Here, here and here,' she said, and pointed them out with her retractable stick.

'This is indicative of the deceased fending off blows with her arms. She fought back. If you look at her left hand, you will see the little finger and middle finger are swollen and misshapen. The little finger was dislocated at the proximal interphalangeal joint, with a fracture of the neck of the proximal phalanges. The middle finger is dislocated at the metacarpophalangeal joint, and there is fracturing of the distal and intermediate phalanges. There is some bruising and laceration to her head and face. None of these injuries were fatal.'

Kate finished writing the answer given by Price and looked up to see Harry in deep thought. He looked like he had something to say, but whatever it was, he kept it to himself for now.

'And what was the cause of death?' asked Korn.

'Strangulation. This is evident by petechial hemorrhaging in the eyeballs and around the face, the bruising pattern around the throat and the fractured hyoid bone at the front of the throat.'

'Miss Price, can you sum up, from the injuries you've seen, how they occurred?'

Kate wanted to stand and object, but she let this one go. She would need some leeway with Judge Chandler, who looked her way, expecting an objection. She shook her head. Chandler raised an eyebrow, his lips curled into a brief smile at the corner of his mouth, then he turned his attention back to the witness.

'This young woman was attacked, beaten severely and then strangled to death. She attempted to fend off her attacker. She fought back, but the attacker was too strong, and eventually overpowered her.'

'Thank you,' said Korn. 'No further questions.'

Kate stood up fast, before Korn had time to limp to his seat, making sure to blast her first question across the courtroom, and across the district attorney.

'Miss Price, as medical examiner you are involved in every homicide and suspicious death in the county, correct?'

'Correct.'

Korn reached the prosecution table, but he didn't sit down. Instead, he bent over, and extended his index finger to touch the wood, as if he was going to use it to spring back up with an objection.

'You examined the bodies of Cody Warren and Elizabeth "Betty" Maguire, two days ago. What was the cause of death in each case?'

Korn's back straightened like a flick knife swishing open, locking in place. He briefly caught Price's gaze, then addressed the judge.

'Objection, Your Honor, irrelevant!'

Kate wanted to get to this question fast, before Korn had time to settle behind his desk, clear his thoughts. He had gotten his objection across, but he'd used clumsy phrasing, giving Kate the opportunity she was after.

Before Chandler ruled, Kate got straight in with a hard jab at the prosecution.

'Your Honor, the murder of a much-respected attorney who practiced in this court demands some basic courtesy from the district attorney. Cody Warren and Betty Maguire were members of this community. Mr. Korn should not let his animosity towards those victims rob him of respect for members of the profession.'

Judge Chandler held out his palms to calm the situation before anything else was said. Kate could not have elicited any testimony that Korn hated Cody Warren. There was no witness who could say that and no way to get that statement in front of the jury. Except, she just did.

'Your Honor, I meant nothing by my objection towards the . . . I mean I bear no ill will—' began Korn, but Judge Chandler cut him off.

'I think tensions are running high. The court accepts you meant no disrespect.'

Kate ignored the judge, focused on the jury. The farmer, Taylor Avery, and a few others were not looking at the judge – they were staring at Korn and it wasn't with anything that Kate thought could be admiration. There were questions in those looks.

Kate threw a lifeline, a compromise, into the barrel.

'Your Honor, I understand the basis of the objection, but I can deal with this matter in two questions, and then move on.'

'I think that sounds reasonable, but I must ask, with respect to the late Mr. Warren and Miss Maguire, what is the relevance to this case?'

'That will be clear to the jury before long,' said Kate. 'This is a capital-murder trial; I would request some leeway.'

Chandler leaned back in his leather chair. Lifted his chin toward the ceiling and swung the seat side to side, weighing his decision. Kate swallowed, and stood still, her fingers locked together in front of her. She needed this one to go her way. There are moments in a case where the whole thing stands on the edge of a thin blade. This was one such moment.

'I'll allow the two questions, but then you will need to move on,' said Chandler.

Kate nodded, turned to the witness.

'What was the cause of death established for Cody Warren and Betty Maguire?'

'They were both shot in the head with a low-caliber pistol.'

'Last question on this matter. At the time of Mr. Warren's death, and Miss Maguire's, they were representing the defendant in this case, Andy Dubois, correct?'

'Correct,' said Miss Price.

'Thank you for your honesty; just a moment, please.'

Kate nodded, turned and began to shuffle through some papers on the defense table. She had her next line of questions written out, edited, practiced in front of the mirror in the hotel, and memorized. She didn't need to look at her notes. She was buying time. Time for the jury to think about the last answer given by Price. For the jury to establish, in their own minds, the link between Korn hating Cody Warren, and Warren and Betty's murder, and their involvement in representing Andy Dubois. Some jurors wouldn't make the leap, but some would at least begin to wonder. She held on as long as she could, turning pages over on the desk for what felt like minutes. It was under thirty seconds, but it was enough. When Kate turned back, Taylor Avery was rubbing his chin, his eyes a thousand miles away. He was thinking.

'Miss Price, in your autopsy report on Skylar Edwards, there are no mentions of bruising and lacerations to the victim's head and face, correct?'

'It seemed to me to be irrelevant. I did mention that generally some lacerations and bruising were found,' said Price.

'So, you noticed lacerations and bruising but didn't detail their location and appearance in your report?'

'Yes. They were obviously not material to the cause of death.'

Kate's throat went dry. Her mouth too. She licked her lips and thought about asking the next question. She didn't know what Price would say, which was always dangerous. But she pressed ahead.

'Did the lacerations on her forehead form any pattern which might give you an indication as to what might have caused them?'

It was out there now. And Price considered it for a moment. Kate had no idea what was going to happen next. She didn't have any contrary evidence to put to Price, so she was at the mercy of this answer, whatever it might be. While she waited, she took a few steps back from the witness stand, so the prosecution table was in her eye line. She saw Wingfield wiggle that gold ring from his finger and put it in his pocket.

Price's eyebrows knotted together and her gaze landed, uncomfortably, on Harry. Kate stepped forward to the defense table. Harry had a handful of documents in his hand. He was holding them up, for Kate. She took them from Harry, who then picked up the bundle of photographs taken by Doc Farnesworth of the bruising to Skylar Edward's forehead and gave them to Kate too. Kate didn't attempt to hide the photos – she let Price see that she was holding those photos in her hand, then whispered a *thank you* to Harry.

'Your Honor, maybe the witness would like a brief comfort break,' said Korn.

'I only have a couple more questions. As long as Miss Price is forthcoming with her answers, we'll be able to release her in a few minutes,' said Kate.

Kate had no doubt Korn had told Price to omit the bruising from her report, and then told her not to mention it on the stand as the defense's expert would not be testifying. He'd put Price in a hard position. And now, standing in front of a defense attorney who was asking about those lacerations with their expert's report in their hand – that rattled the hell out of Price.

Kate cracked a smile at the corner of her mouth. Price's eyes widened. Kate was letting her know that she held a Royal Flush. And if Price was going to try and bluff, she would lose her house.

'Miss Price? You seem to be having difficulty. Tell me, did the district attorney's office prep you for your testimony here today?' asked Kate, and she took a moment to glance down at the photos, and then back to the witness.

A fine layer of sweat broke over Price's top lip. She looked to the prosecution table and said, 'I discussed the contents of my report with the district attorney and his assistant, Tom Wingfield.'

'Then you should have no problem recalling the autopsy findings. There was a pattern to the bruising, correct?'

'From memory, there might have been a pattern,' said Price.

'You mean there *was* a pattern to the bruising?' asked Kate.

Price hesitated, swallowed, and nodded.

'For the record, we need you to say *yes*,' said Kate.

Price looked at Korn and found his eyes boring into hers. Kate caught that look, wondered if it was disappointment or a restrained hatred. Price was in no man's land. She didn't want to get caught out as a liar, but she didn't like where Kate was leading. Price averted her eyes from Korn, looked at the jury and said, 'Yes.'

'Skin has a certain elasticity, correct?'

'Correct.'

'And if certain parts of the skin are struck with force, that can leave an impression of the area that contacted the skin?'

'That's possible, but again, not relevant to cause of death in this case,' said Price, now trying to keep her head above water.

Kate ignored the attempt, pressed on.

'There are a number of star-shaped bruises on the victim's fore-head. They are in a row, uneven, and each is under an inch long, is that correct?' asked Kate as she separated a page from the bundle in front of her, as if she was about to use it.

'I don't know if it was exactly that shape, but it was similar.'

'Could this pattern have appeared on the victim's head from a punch if the attacker had been wearing a ring?'

'That's possible.'

Kate strode forward, handed a page to the judge, and then another to the prosecution.

'Your Honor, as the witness has now acknowledged the pattern of bruising, I would like to enter the following as a defense exhibit. It's a printout of a webpage that offers certain types of rings for sale. I'd like to ask the expert's opinion on this ring.'

Chandler looked at the webpage printout, but not in great detail. He seemed bored and hadn't appreciated where this was going.

Kate and Eddie had already discussed this strategy. Korn wouldn't object. He didn't want to draw any attention to what his expert had left out of the autopsy report. The expert had said it was irrelevant to cause of death, and the more Korn fought it, and made a fuss over it, the more importance the jury might attach to it. No, he would sit on his ass and say nothing. And that's what he did.

The judge admitted the exhibit.

'Miss Price, the ring offered for sale from this website has a star in the center. From the dimensions listed, it would appear to corre-spond exactly to the size and shape of the marks on the victim's forehead, isn't that correct?'

Kate gave Price the printout so she could take a closer look.

'I can't really say for certain.'

'But they look identical, their shape, and they are the same size, wouldn't you say?'

'I don't know, I would need to examine the ring,' said Price.

Without knowing it, Price had left a window open and Kate decided to throw her case through it.

'They are Fraternal Order of Police rings, very commonly worn by current and former law enforcement officers. You mean to say you've never seen a ring like this before?'

'No, I haven't.'

'Strange, I thought you would've seen it on the hand of assistant district attorney Wingfield when you two discussed your autopsy report?'

Price drew breath to respond, and it froze in her chest. The courtroom fell silent.

'I don't believe I saw him with that ring,' said Price.

'Maybe he took it off and put it in his pocket, like he did a few minutes ago?'

Wingfield leaned back in his seat, wiped the sweat from his face through his hair.

Judge Chandler intervened; he'd had enough of this. He spoke to the prosecutor like he wanted his help to settle an argument with a child. It was derogatory, offhand and he had no idea he'd just handed the defense the first round.

'Mr. Wingfield, the defendant's attorney seems to think you have a ring in your pocket? Could you disabuse her of that notion?'

Wingfield's left hand shook, visibly, as he stood. Lying to a judge is like playing Russian roulette with three bullets in the chamber. It can only go one of two ways. Safest bet is not to lie. You can always explain away anything else.

'No, Your Honor, I could not,' said Wingfield.

'I beg your pardon,' said the judge. 'You *could not* what?'

'I could not disabuse her of that notion,' said Wingfield. 'I've got my FOP ring in my pocket, Your Honor.'

Chandler's skin turned almost as pale as Korn's. He threw a hand at the district attorney, as an apology.

'Miss Price,' said Kate, capitalizing on her momentum, 'I suggest that you left the bruising on the victim's forehead out of your report because it did not suit the district attorney's case. The bruising was probably caused by a ring like this one, and the defendant does not possess such a ring, unlike the assistant prosecutor and the majority of law enforcement in this county. Is that about right?'

'No, that is not correct.'

'No further questions,' said Kate.

She sat down beside Harry, and Andy leaned over to her and whispered, 'Thank you, Miss Brooks. Thank you for fighting for me.'

Kate looked at the jury, who for the first time appeared unsettled.

That was a good sign. Because it wasn't going to get anywhere near as good as that again.

CHAPTER FIFTY-ONE

BLOCH

At the back of the court, sitting at the edge of the last row of seats, Bloch listened as Kate tore apart the county medical examiner.

Bloch had been listening to the ME's testimony. A few things that had been bothering her now seemed much more important. The injuries that Skylar sustained were unusual. Hearing them spoken out loud, and elaborated on, made them much more prevalent in Bloch's mind. As Price stood down and made her way back to the gallery, whispers began among the crowd. It was a natural, brief lull in the proceedings, and as the judge and the attorneys were quiet, the crowd was allowed some hushed chat. Bloch scanned the crowd.

Then she saw it.

First, Francis Edwards got up out of the front row, made his way to the aisle. His teeth gritted in barely checked fury. Kate's cross-examination of Price would've been hard for Francis, particularly after he had listened, in detail, to the injuries inflicted on his baby girl.

A short, fat man got up out of his seat when he saw Francis heading toward the doors. It was the same guy, in the same tweed jacket, who had comforted Francis the night before in the back of the sheriff's cruiser.

Without saying a word to Francis, the man put an arm around him, and led him out of the courtroom.

As they passed Bloch, on their way out, she turned and asked the lady next to her for the time. It was past four.

Bloch waited until the doors closed behind the two men, counted to five then got up and left.

In the hallway, Bloch caught a glimpse of them as they exited the front door and turned left toward the parking lot. Bloch followed, keeping her distance. She lingered at the exit, listening. The sound of car doors closing, then a throaty rasp from a V8 was her signal. Bloch turned left out of the courthouse toward the lot and saw the two men in the front cab of a red pick-up. It was new and looked expensive.

She got to the SUV, fired it up, but the pick-up had not moved. Bloch made a call on her cell. It was not so long ago that she was a cop, and an even shorter length of time since she had done some consulting work for law enforcement. Officer development, mostly. Non-lethal self-defense training, and advanced driving. Her call was answered, and she said her name, and called out the license plate of the pick-up, asked for any sheets, then ended the call.

Less than a minute later, her cell rang and a female voice said, 'Xavier Gruber, sheets will take a while, but there are no priors . . .' and then gave his address and hung up. It was simpler and safer for both of them to avoid pleasantries. Just the facts.

Bloch typed the name into a search engine on her phone and found an image of the man she had just seen. He was Professor Xavier Gruber – listed among University of Alabama faculty as Head of Chemistry. Bloch flicked through the rest of the results on her search and found a press release, which stated that Gruber was currently on long-term suspension, pending a disciplinary hearing. It seems he'd made a speech at a political rally that contained overtones of white supremacy.

After a few minutes, another pick-up, this one blue and much older, drove into the lot and parked parallel with Gruber's truck. The driver of the blue pick-up leaned out of the window and had a conversation with Gruber. Then he drove out of the lot, and Gruber followed, with Francis in the passenger seat.

Bloch waited until both vehicles had exited the lot before she began her pursuit. She wasn't concerned about losing them. The Confederate flag fluttered on an aerial pole, five feet over the bed of the blue truck. She was in no danger of losing this one. They didn't drive far, and soon parked up on the street, in town. They got out of the cars and approached a door beside a business called Buckstown Insurance Services. The business looked like it had been closed a long time. Bloch guessed the door was a separate entrance for the floor above the insurance brokers, maybe an apartment. She got a good look at the driver of the blue truck and recognized him from a few days ago. Brian Denvir it had said on his driver's license. He wasn't wearing a bulletproof vest, nor did he have a rifle slung on his shoulder, but Bloch eyed the Glock strapped to his waist. Gruber brought a bulky black suitcase with him, and together they all disappeared inside.

In under a minute Bloch saw a light shine from the dormer window. There were no nearby vantage points to get a look inside that floor, so she had no choice but to sit tight. While she watched the front door, she made another call. She was still waiting for her contact to come back with any sheets on Gruber, meaning any police files or paperwork law enforcement held on him. They had already told her Gruber had no prior convictions, but there was paperwork there, somewhere, and they were having difficulty accessing it. Growing increasingly impatient, she was about to call her contact again when they called Bloch.

'There's paper, but I don't have the clearance,' said the voice, and hung up.

Judging by Gruber's suspension from the university for suspected white supremacist views, and given the company he was keeping with Brian Denvir, Bloch suspected Gruber was on a watch list somewhere. It was a strange time to be an American, she thought. After September eleventh, the single largest threat came from overseas terrorists. That had changed. The FBI, the Department of Homeland Security and other intelligence and law-enforcement agencies recognized the single greatest threat to the country now came from white supremacist domestic terror groups. They were increasingly well organized and funded.

Bloch thought about the blade found in Cody Warren's neck. And the emblem upon it – the White Camelia. With that thought came a tickling in her throat, and a knot in her stomach. Bloch didn't like feeling emotional. In her mind, feelings didn't make good bedfellows with cold rationality and facts. The tools of her trade. Sometimes, no matter how hard she fought it, her feelings choked her thoughts. From a young age, Bloch was wary of emotions. She didn't understand them, for the most part. They were difficult, hard to control and never seemed to be of use. While she showed affection to her family, to her best friend Kate, and occasionally to the women she dated, Bloch preferred to keep her distance from others. Erecting barriers, both physical and psychological. She didn't shake hands, certainly didn't hug others, and didn't say much.

But now and again, all her practices, her barriers, her critical mindset, everything was overwhelmed. It was happening more frequently since she'd reconnected with Kate and joined the law firm as an investigator. She liked Eddie and Harry. And letting them into her life had caused more frequent bouts of deep-felt emotion.

The light snapped off in the window, and within a minute Gruber, Denvir and Edwards were back on the street. Bloch heard a creaking sound and looked at the steering wheel. It was bent under her grip. Her first reaction to a group of racists was always revulsion, and then anger. Her jaw began to ache, and she realized she was biting down on her teeth. She blew out a few quick breaths, rolled her shoulders and cracked her neck. The hatred bleeding through her brain prevented her from thinking, and she could not allow that.

As soon as the analytical part of her brain, the dominant part, kicked in, she noticed Gruber didn't have the case with him any longer. Francis Edwards had the case, and he put it in the footwell of Gruber's vehicle as he got in. Gruber drove them both away. Denvir waited a short while, then he left, the exhaust from his pick-up firing from the turbo as he screeched away.

Bloch got out of the car and approached the front door they had exited from not moments before. There were two locks on the door, including a dead bolt. She could get through it, but she didn't want anyone to know she'd been inside. Instead, she walked up to the end of the block, counting the premises as she went, then turned left and found the alleyway that ran behind the buildings. She counted as she walked. Stopped at steel double doors that were as old as the building itself. The lock on the doors had rusted out. The handles on the doors were ten inches from one another and secured together with a steel chain and a padlock. This was meant to be a fire door, and chaining it from the outside was illegal, but probably the only way to secure the rear of the property now that the door lock had seized.

The padlock looked as new as the steel chain it secured. There were any number of ways to bust the lock or the chain, but she didn't need to. All she needed to open the lock were the scissors from her keychain multitool, a soda can and some spit.

Bloch found a Dr Pepper can in a nearby dumpster, cut a strip from the can four inches by one inch, then cut a 'U' shape in the center of the strip. She folded up either end of the aluminum strip to make a shim, which she threaded through the bar of the padlock and pulled tight. A little spit on the base of the lock bar, and then she slid the U-shaped section down the bar, into the lock housing and between the bar and the lock notch. The bar popped open. She unthreaded the chain, went through the door to a covered alleyway that led to a set of iron stairs, painted black – the fire escape for the first floor. At the top of those stairs she found a window, closed but not locked, and after she put on a pair of latex gloves she pushed it open from the outside.

The space inside was not an apartment. It had once been an office, but it was clear that now it had another purpose. A flag, framed above a bank of filing cabinets, bore the same flower she had seen on the hilt of the blade found in Cody Warren. Bloch began pulling open the cabinet drawers. The first cabinet was empty, the second was stuffed with flyers. The same flower symbol was on the background of the printed slogans.

SAVE THE SECOND AMENDMENT.
SAVE YOUR CHILDREN.
SAVE THE WHITE RACE.
JOIN THE WHITE CAMELIA MARCH ON
MONTGOMERY.

The next drawer was filled with batteries and electrical wires and in the one below that was a box filled with cell phones and charging cables. In the last cabinet were files, stacked in neat rows on sleeves.

She pulled out the first one, opened it and found it contained a single memo on a civil rights organization based out of Mobile. It listed the employees, their home addresses, social media handles, telephone numbers and the names and addresses of their family members. The next file was on a law firm in Montgomery, again listing employees and all their personal information. Bloch flicked through the row of files and came across the names of local companies, members of the legislature, police officers, judges, Democrat party politicians, and then, a file that sent a shiver across Bloch's skin. The file had a simple title on the cover – Jews. Inside were memos on ordinary men and women, postal workers, officer workers, small business owners, and all of their personal information, sometimes even photographs.

There were files with titles like Blacks, Hispanics, Gay . . .

The last file had no label. When Bloch opened it she saw that it contained a list of local churches, and behind the list, print-outs of news articles. They were all the same story. The failed attempts at detonating a bomb in predominantly African American Gospel churches.

Block slammed the cabinet shut so hard it rocked on its base. She was panting, her fists balled, eyes wide.

There was one final drawer. No files in this one. Just one large roll of heavy-duty paper. Bloch lifted it clear and unrolled it. She found herself looking at a schematic for a large and very old house with four columns over the entrance. The house was part residence and part office space. There were line drawings and annotations on the plans, in small handwriting with words like *Finley Ave, exit 3, choke point 2* and *holding area.*

She typed the street names into the maps app on her phone and got an aerial view of Montgomery, Alabama. The rally point had close access to the interstate. The building in the schematic must be close by, and after a few minutes of checking the landmarks in the area, she found it.

Bloch climbed out the window and left the building the same way she had come in, careful to lock up after her. She got in the car and drove back to the court at speed, running the lights, and flooring the accelerator.

She needed to get Eddie out of the cells, and make sure she was with Andy and his mother at all times. This group were organized, connected and they had a plan.

Bloch's best guess: they were planning an all-out assault. With what aim she didn't know. It could be an assassination, or kidnap, or both. The building in the plans was the seat of power in the state. The governor's mansion.

CHAPTER FIFTY-TWO

EDDIE

When the bailiff brought me back up to the courtroom it had cleared. There was just Harry, Kate and Judge Chandler. Korn had already left, along with his assistant, Wingfield. My handcuffs were undone, and I stood beside Kate, for the second time, with her as my attorney. I couldn't wait any longer – I needed to know how we'd done that day.

'How did it go with Price?'

'Good, we got the ring in play,' said Harry.

Kate leaned over, whispered, 'I'm going to have to start charging you, Eddie.'

'Don't worry, this is the last time.'

Chandler cleared his throat, and Kate began to talk. He waved her words away into silence then said, 'The disrespect you have shown this court requires a levy. There will be a fine of a thousand dollars, or ten days' incarceration. Can you pay that, Flynn?'

'Cash or card, Your Honor?' I said.

'I think you like those cells,' said Harry.

'I'm getting a lot of thinking done,' I said, putting on my jacket as we went outside to the parking lot. 'I'm not sure, but I have a working theory on the DA's forensic evidence. Where's Andy and Patricia?'

'Bloch came and took Andy and Patricia back to the hotel. She tailed someone from the court, and she needs you to call her right now so she can explain. She says we are in way over our heads and she wants you to call in the cavalry,' said Kate.

'Last time I checked we don't have a cavalry,' I said as Harry handed me back my cell phone. Soon as it switched back on, I saw the text message from Bloch.

CALL ME. RIGHT NOW.

As we drove back to the hotel I spoke to Bloch on the phone. She filled me in on the details of who she had followed, and what she had found. We had already parked outside the hotel, and I was on my way up the stairs to Andy's room while she was still talking.

'There's an imminent threat. We have to bring in the FBI,' she said.

'We're outside the room, come into the hallway and we'll talk.'

The door opened and Bloch came out, closed it behind her and we stood there, in a hallway so hot and humid the condensation was running down the walls as if the building was sweating. We kept our voices as low as the pale wall lamps whose light didn't reach the floor.

'You need to call the feds,' said Bloch.

'I'm going to call Alexander Berlin. If he wants to bring in the FBI, great. We can only fight so many battles here. Andy is our priority. We get him off, we've got a chance at taking down Korn. I didn't come here to take on the Nazis,' I said.

'White supremacists,' said Bloch.

'Same thing. I don't want anyone to get hurt, and certainly not by these assholes, but if their immediate target is the governor, at least it takes some of the heat off Andy. All we have to do is keep him and his mom safe until we get through this. After that, the FBI, Homeland Security, ATF, Delta Force and the goddamn Avengers can level that building for all I care. We don't want to fight too many battles. They may have killed Cody and Betty, and you can bet I want them to pay, but we can't take them on now. Francis Edwards lost his daughter and his wife and he's hurting. It's easy to see why he's involved with those guys, and I bet he's right on the edge of losing it. Denvir, the guy from the protest the other day, he's just looking for an excuse to shoot somebody. I don't know this other guy Gruber, the university profess—'

Something hit me. I could almost hear the *click* in my head as I made the connection.

'You said Gruber was the head of the Chemistry Department in the University of—'

'Alabama . . .' said Bloch, and I saw her expression change, the skin on her forehead tightened and her eyes shimmered, as if she had just caught a glimpse of a lodestar in the distance.

'Skylar Edwards was a Chemistry major . . .' she said.

'He probably knew her,' said Harry.

'But he knows her father, too,' said Kate. 'Could be he knew Francis Edwards for years through this hate group, long before Skylar even went to college.'

'Not likely,' said Harry. 'Andy didn't have a bad word to say about Skylar's father, and Francis would occasionally give Andy a ride home. I don't think anyone involved in one of those groups would let their daughter have a friend like Andy. That just doesn't happen.'

'So you think Francis got involved in this group after Skylar's murder?' I asked.

Nodding, Harry rubbed his chin, said, 'Makes sense. A man in that much pain, unable to deal with the loss of his child. I'd say he sounds exactly like the kind of angry, lost soul to get recruited by a hate group. They probably reached out to him.'

'Then what happened to his wife?' asked Kate. 'You said it looked like homicide. You think he killed her?'

'I don't think so,' I said. 'I watched him in the back of that sheriff's cruiser. He was totally lost in grief. Crying uncontrollably, his sobs shook the whole car. To me, that didn't look like a performance. He didn't kill his wife.'

'Then who did? Why was she killed? Why was Skylar murdered?' asked Kate.

Harry and I shook our heads. It was possible Skylar was murdered simply because she was a beautiful young woman who fell under the red gaze of a monster. It happens, and there's no motive, no reason. There is evil in men and women. Some people disagree. There are any number of reasons that a human being might kill another – revenge, drugs, alcohol, mental illness, even money. Sometimes, it is beyond all of those things. Sometimes people kill because they enjoy it. And if that is not evil, then I don't know what is.

Bloch stared at the wall opposite her. Her mind a thousand miles away. She was close to something. The piece that they were missing, which explained this whole terrible mess, was close. That star in the night sky was almost within sight.

'I'll stay up and watch the hotel entrance,' said Bloch.

'I'll come get you in a few hours,' said Harry.

'I want everyone to get some sleep tonight,' I said. 'We've done well to get this far, but tomorrow Korn holds all the aces. The two most compelling pieces of evidence in any criminal trial are DNA evidence, and a confession from the defendant. Either one is enough for Korn to get a conviction. I've got an idea how to attack the DNA evidence; I'm still working on the confession. Don't think we've won this case. Not for a second. We could get our asses kicked tomorrow and if that happens, Andy dies. Bloch, I need you to run an errand early tomorrow morning. If it plays out like I think it will, we've got a shot.'

Kate was going to work a little more, then get some sleep. I went downstairs, stood outside the hotel and watched Bloch take up a seat in the lobby. Her mind still working. I took a breath of hot, sweet air and called Berlin.

He sounded pissed.

'When were you going to tell me that Esther Edwards died?' he asked.

'I'm running a defense in a capital-murder trial. I've been busy. How did you know about Esther?'

'I work for several US intelligence agencies, Eddie.'

'Do you know that Bloch found a white supremacist terror cell this afternoon?'

He fell silent, said, 'Tell me everything.'

CHAPTER FIFTY-THREE

KORN

It was close to midnight when Randal Korn pulled up outside the grocery store on Duke Street, behind the Sheriff's Department cruiser. He got out of the car, popped the trunk and removed a bulging, brown leather gym bag. On his way past the cruiser, he knocked the side window. The deputy, Leonard, nodded.

Korn approached the door next to the grocery store. There were three buzzers. He pressed the one for apartment two, and waited. Glancing around the street, he saw no one on the sidewalk. A few cars parked a couple of hundred yards away, but no activity. He pressed the buzzer again. This time, a voice came over the intercom.

'Hello?'

'It's the Sheriff's Department, open up,' said Korn.

The buzzer sounded, Korn pushed the door open. In front of him was a small, narrow hallway leading to a set of stairs. He climbed the stairs, found another hallway and three doors. Two on the right, which were the apartments over the grocery store, and one on the left. He went left and knocked on the door for apartment two.

Sandy Boyette opened the door, just a crack, the security chain in place, and looked out at Korn.

'The police are outside. Look out your window, then come back and open this door. You're in a lot of trouble, Miss Boyette,' said Korn.

She didn't close the door, but left it open a crack. The chain still on. Korn listened to the sound of Sandy padding across her apartment floor, the rattle of the blinds clattering closed. He heard more rustling, bare feet moving hurriedly. As if she were quickly tidying up. She came back, the security chain snicked free and the door opened.

'What do you want?' asked Sandy.

Korn made his way inside and said, 'I'm here to see if I can help you stay out of prison, Sandy.'

She was dressed in Minnie Mouse PJs, her hair messed up from bed. A single lamp in the corner of the apartment gave out a weak light. It was a single room, with a bed in one corner, a sink and a camp cooker in the other. There was one door leading off the studio space to what Korn supposed was a closet converted into a bathroom and shower. One low table and two armchairs on opposite sides of it, one leather and ripped at the bottom, the other green fabric with the armrests and cushion faded from use.

'You'd better sit down,' said Korn, taking the leather armchair.

Sandy stood, folded her arms and said, 'What the hell is this about? I've done nothing wrong.'

Korn put the leather gym bag on the table, opened the zip and spread the bag open to reveal tight stacks of fifty-dollar bills.

'It's late, and you're due in court in the morning. Let's cut the bullshit, Sandy. I know you've been talking to Eddie Flynn, and he has offered to buy your vote on the Dubois jury. I can't let that happen. I know everything, apart from how he's paying you. I figure he doesn't want to arouse suspicion, so he'll send you the money what . . . six months after the verdict?'

Sandy said nothing, but Korn watched a vein grow in her neck, the skin around it blushing.

'That's the smart way to do it. And Flynn is smart. Your guarantee is that you can expose him if he doesn't pay you, and of course he has more to lose. That's how he sold it to you, I'm guessing?'

'That's not true,' she said, and was about to say more but thought better of it.

Tilting her head to the side, Sandy pressed her lips together tightly. Korn guessed she was waiting for the other shoe to drop.

'I can't wait that long to expose Flynn. Here's your way out of this – you will vote *guilty* at the end of the trial. Don't think you can hide your vote; I can have the jury polled after the verdict. Your vote is recorded. Once I have my conviction in the Dubois case, I will have Flynn arrested. You will give a deposition that he bribed you with this money,' said Korn, pointing at the gym bag.

'Fifty thousand dollars. More than enough to buy your vote. You are a witness co-operating with the district attorney's office and in return you will face no criminal charges. You get to walk away, Sandy. If you refuse, I will have you arrested right now. You'll serve fifteen, maybe twenty years. I won't give you long to make your decision because there is only one choice. My offer walks out the door with me in five seconds. Then the officers will come up and place you under arrest. Make the right choice.'

He began counting, silently. Sandy let out a nervous breath, ran her hands through her hair once, then used them to cover her face.

'That's three,' said Korn.

Sandy hugged her arms, nodded and said, 'You're going to arrest me for something I didn't do. I talked to Flynn. I sold him my car about a week ago. He wanted to know why I didn't tell the judge I'd met him before. That's all.'

'Twenty years, Sandy. Think about it. This is your last chance. You agree to give that deposition. State for the record Flynn bribed you or your life is over.'

Sandy hung her head, nodded, said, 'I don't want to go to jail, I'll do it.'

Korn's lips parted in what passed for a smile.

'Clever girl. Don't let me down. Now, Deputy Leonard is going to come in here and take a photo of this money. Just to prove you've got it. Call it insurance. And don't think about telling Flynn. If I can't put him away, I'll have to settle for you.'

CHAPTER FIFTY-FOUR

THE PASTOR

'Is everyone there already?' asked Gruber.

'Everyone, except for Francis,' said the Pastor.

'This heat is killing me,' said Gruber as he wiped at his brow with a handkerchief before stepping carefully over a fallen tree trunk. A small torch in Gruber's other hand didn't give him much light. He was trying to follow Denvir's trail through the woods. The big man was up ahead, leading the way. The Pastor was last in line, behind Gruber.

'Why are we meeting all the way out here?' asked Gruber.

'Because tomorrow is the seventh day. The reckoning is almost upon us. All the preparations are made, and I don't want to take any chances of being seen together. No one comes out here at this time of night. No hunters, no fishermen. We need to go over everything. Make sure we're ready,' said the Pastor.

There was a clearing up ahead, and as they came through the trees the terrain began to climb, leading up to what appeared to be a steep bank.

'The Luxahatchee used to run right through this part of the forest,' said the Pastor.

Gruber said nothing. He was not interested in the land. Something that the Pastor never understood. Gruber was a man of science. He liked numbers, chemicals, reactions, which were predictable based on evidence. His personal reading had led him to apply that scientific mind to some of the fouler social theories. Eugenics. Population control. And inevitably into what Gruber called 'radical race theory', but of course there was nothing radical about it. Not to the Pastor. To him, it was clear and had been for two thousand years. The white race was clearly superior, and the dominant race. It should not be diluted with the blood of others. The Bible said as much. To the Pastor, the day the United States abolished slavery was a mistake. The Bible didn't outlaw slavery – didn't say it was a sin. It was the natural way of things.

'Look there,' said the Pastor, shining his torch on a patch of the bank.

A small cluster of flowers grew in the thick grass, trying desperately to reach higher than the blades of green that surrounded them.

'White camelias,' said the Pastor. 'You see how the grass tries to choke them? We can't allow that to happen to us, gentlemen. We have to be strong, and reach for the sunlight.'

'Is it much further? I don't see the others anywhere,' said Gruber.

'They're on the other side,' said Denvir, standing at the top of the bank, shining his torch over the top, to the channel below.

'We'll all be together very soon,' said the Pastor.

There were seven in the White Camelia, including the Pastor.

Brian Denvir, a bigot and fanatic who believed there were aliens in Roswell; a massive government conspiracy by the Democrats where the deep state operated a pedophile ring out of the back of a pizza parlor; and that the Nazis had at least gotten some things right – they'd just gone about it the wrong way. After Brian came Gruber and then three others. Richard Barnes was a wealthy peanut farmer who loved his guns, the Confederate flag, and had never employed an African American in all his years. Next were the brothers. One a doctor, the other a lawyer. The Reed brothers had been raised in Mobile and never wanted for anything. Hard work had taken their father through the ranks of the Mobile Police Department to a senior position, all despite his open and apparent racism. The brothers were cut from the same cloth. Wealthy and influential, they had funded the cause in secret.

The Pastor looked on as Gruber reached the top of the bank and gazed over the ridge.

'Oh my God,' said Gruber. 'What happened?'

The Pastor looked down into the channel at the dead bodies of Richard Barnes, Cole Reed and Seth Reed. They'd all been shot through the chest and head.

Gruber was intelligent. Of that, there was no doubt. He could spin a lie, he could build a compelling argument around his views and he even knew how to construct a detonator, but he was never quick on the uptake.

It wasn't until Denvir drew his Desert Eagle that he realized what had happened to the other members of the White Camelia once their usefulness had been exhausted. He held up his hands in surrender, and fell to his knees, but before he could plead for his life, the gun bucked in Denvir's hand.

Denvir kicked Gruber's body over the bank, then aimed and fired two more shots. Still with the gun hot in his grip, he stared at the bodies below and said, 'And when you don't need me anymore, are you gonna kill me like the others?'

The Pastor shook his head, found the pickaxe he'd left at the side of the bank.

'You don't have anything to worry about, Brian. They weren't like you and I. We know what has to be done, and we have the stomach for it. Gruber could fashion a bomb, but he didn't have the heart to set it off. Ever wonder why those devices didn't explode in those churches?'

'You mean he messed them up on purpose?'

'That's exactly what I mean. He understood the need for bloodshed, and he encouraged and facilitated it, but he wouldn't get his hands dirty.'

'But what about the case he gave to Francis?'

'That's fine. I checked it myself. It will work. He had no problem building something for someone else to use. In his mind it absolved him of responsibility, you see. Like I said, we're the only *real* knights. We understand a revolution is born in blood. The others were weak. And there can be no weakness in our ranks. Now grab that shovel over there and give me a hand,' said the Pastor.

Denvir nodded, holstered the gun. The Pastor threw the broad, flat end of his pickaxe into some loose dirt at the top of the bank, levered the handle down and tipped a load of soil onto the bodies below. Denvir bent down to grab the shovel, then stopped, moved around and bent over again, this time keeping the Pastor in sight.

'I told you not to worry, Brian. Now, is everything in place for tomorrow?' said the Pastor, continuing to lever dirt over the side of the bank.

'Everything is ready,' said Brian.

'And you know what you have to do?'

'I'm clear. I've got some of the guys ready too. They're locked and loaded. All they're waiting for is my signal.'

'I've dreamed of this for a long time. The reckoning. Tomorrow we unleash hell. And then we'll take back our country.'

THE SEVENTH DAY

CHAPTER FIFTY-FIVE

BLOCH

Bloch pulled the SUV into the lot of a strip mall on the edge of town just after nine in the morning. It was an unusual cluster of stores. A laundromat, diner and video-rental store. Bloch couldn't remember the last time she'd seen a video store, but wasn't surprised to find one in Buckstown. This place was still in the 1980s. Some folks in Buckstown thought it was the 1880s.

She was on an errand for Eddie. He had a hunch. A theory, really. And Bloch thought he might be onto something. This would be the litmus test.

Across from the strip mall was County Hall. The seat of legislature in the county. Bloch crossed the street, kept her head down as she passed the security cameras at the entrance to the county hall parking lot. She didn't want her plates showing up on those cameras. Nothing that could tip off Korn.

There were a few dozen cars in the lot. Every bureaucracy needed people to keep the machine moving. The entrance to County Hall was via lacquered pine double doors. One was held open, the other shut. Inside, Bloch found a list of internal fiefdoms printed on a plastic board and affixed to the wall. Little placards on the board gave directions to various floors and offices. The office she wanted was on the first floor, room 5.02. She followed the signs to the room. It was small, with a six-seat waiting area and two counter windows. No one was waiting, so she approached the first counter. There were no staff behind the counters, but through the Plexiglas she could see someone sitting at a desk by the window. Bloch coughed, hoping to catch the woman's attention. It didn't work. A sign told her to ring the bell for attention. Bloch looked around but couldn't see a bell. Then, on the next counter, she saw it, slapped it and waited.

A lady with a high, tight weave in her hair and a hand-knitted cardigan over a white silk blouse tutted behind her desk, then got up and slowly came forward. The flesh on her feet spilled over the top of her tight, one-inch heels, and her glasses hung around her neck on a gold chain. As she reached the counter Bloch caught the scent of old sweat beneath the lady's perfume.

'Can I help you?' said the lady, in a way that made Bloch feel like the last thing this woman wanted to do was help anybody. She had the air of someone who liked to poke cats with sharp sticks and blame it on the neighborhood kids.

'Yes, I would like to see the death certificate for Colt Lomax, please,' said Bloch, smiling politely.

The lady behind the counter put her glasses on, and gave Bloch the once over, then pushed the glasses down to the end of her nose as if she didn't like what she saw.

'And you are?' she asked.

'A customer,' said Bloch.

'Are you a relative of the deceased?'

'As far as I know in this county you don't have to be a relative to view a death certificate. The only information that is required is the date of birth and the name of the deceased.'

The woman's bright red lips pinched into a small red ball, sucking in her cheeks. She pushed a form through the slot in the window and said, 'It's twelve ninety-five for a copy.'

Bloch put thirteen bucks on the counter, slid it through with the form completed.

The woman read the completed form, said, 'Is that your real name?'

'Far as I know you're not entitled to ask me for ID.'

She sucked on her lips some more then disappeared in back. A few minutes later she reappeared, with change and a document in her hand. She slid the document through the window slot with the change on top.

'Will that be all, Miss *Mouse*?'

'No, just a second,' said Bloch. She read the death certificate. Cause of death was recorded as self-inflicted gunshot. Death by suicide. Bloch checked the column on spouses, and it read *Lucy Anne Lomax (Deceased)*, but no date of birth.

'I'd like the marriage license for Colt and Lucy Anne Lomax. And, please, call me Minnie,' said Bloch.

The lady almost sucked the rouge right off her lips as she bent over, retrieved another form and slid it to Bloch.

'That'll be another twelve ninety-five.'

Bloch filled in the form, handed over the cash. The lady disappeared, came back five minutes later with a copy of the marriage license. Scanning it, Bloch found Lucy Lomax's date of birth. Bloch asked for a death certificate form for Lucy Anne Lomax, filled out the form, paid the fee, watched the lady behind the counter roll her eyes, suck her cheeks and go get the certificate.

When she came back, she said, 'Will *that* be all?'

Bloch read the death certificate, smiled and said, 'Yes, this is all I need.'

CHAPTER FIFTY-SIX

KORN

Breakfast at the Blue Turtle Tavern at the invitation of Acting Sheriff Shipley was not to be dismissed lightly, even if Korn was in the middle of a murder trial. He was to meet him at seven-thirty, but didn't arrive until almost eight. That way he could grab a quick coffee, and then get to court with an hour to spare before the trial recommenced.

As the maître d' showed him to the table he saw that this would not be a quiet meal. The table was circular, and almost full. Seated beside Shipley was Governor Patchett. Next to him was Deputy Leonard, and then Ryan Hogg and Korn's assistant DA Tom Wingfield. Korn took a seat with Wingfield on his right, and Shipley on his left. All of them were enjoying bacon and eggs with the Blue Turtle's famous grits on the side. A plate of biscuits, with only a few left, sat in the center of the table. The men said their good mornings to Korn.

He sat down slowly, taking his time to stretch out his right leg. He needed the pain that day and had tightened the garter by a notch. The leg had bled badly that morning, and he wrapped it in additional bandages and gauze to stem the bleeding. Even so, just on the drive over he spotted a stain on the leg of his dark gray pants. Most wouldn't notice it, and he didn't have time to go home and change.

Those around the table certainly didn't notice. They had already resumed their conversation, apart from Shipley and Patchett.

'Nice to see you, Governor, but I thought you would've gone straight back to Montgomery after the meeting at the chemical plant,' said Korn.

'I was, then I got a call from our new sheriff here. He's quite the officer,' said Patchett.

Shipley cleared his throat, turned to Korn and said, 'We got word of a viable threat. An extremist group has apparently been planning a full-scale assault on the governor's mansion. The aim is to take the governor hostage and kill everyone else in the building.'

'How reliable is your information?' asked Korn.

'It's one hundred percent accurate,' said Shipley.

'He's right,' said Patchett. 'Four hours after Shipley called me, my security advisor got a call from the FBI to say they'd heard about it through their channels. It's real, alright.'

Korn wondered, just for a second, how an acting sheriff might hear about a planned terror attack on a high-profile public figure before the Federal Bureau of Investigations. 'My God, and do you know who is behind it?'

Shipley was about to speak, but the governor cut him off, said, 'Of course, it's the radical left. It's probably some kind of paramilitary cell within Antifa. This country is under threat, you know. We have to be willing to meet this enemy.'

'Rest assured, Governor, that's exactly what we'll do,' said Shipley.

Korn noticed, not for the first time, that Shipley's irises were so deeply brown that they looked black. The flame from the tealight on the table became trapped in those eyes, as if their darkness reached out to capture the flame – and drown it in pitch.

'I figure I'm as safe here as anywhere else. Maybe more so, with our new sheriff here,' said Patchett. 'This is my home county. And besides, there's this trial, and of course a funeral for our sheriff coming up in a few days. It makes sense that I stay here, for now.'

'Well, I'm just glad you can enjoy our hospitality a while longer. These are dangerous times,' said Korn.

'You're telling me,' said Patchett. 'Do you know the president suspects the Democrats are going to try and steal the election next year?'

Many years ago Korn's father had dealings with the now president. Thought he was a chump, like the rest of New York.

'The president says a lot of things. But I'm not concerned about him. It's you we need to worry about—' But Korn didn't get to finish the sentence.

'Not anymore,' said Shipley. 'My men will make sure the governor is safe, with all means at our disposal.'

That phrase – *All means at our disposal* – struck Korn as slightly ominous. He wondered if Shipley might welcome an attack on the governor as an excuse to use his more draconian methods.

'So how is the trial shaping up?' asked Patchett.

'It's early days but I know we've got the jury on our side in this one,' said Korn.

'Fuckin' A,' said Wingfield. 'Mr. Korn is on fire. And we've got all the big guns coming today. Mr. Hogg, here, is testifying. That's why he's with us today. And we have two witnesses who say Dubois confessed – his cell buddy, Lawson, and then Deputy Leonard will testify to the confession Dubois signed with Sheriff Lomax, God rest his soul. Today is a game changer – Dubois is done.'

While Wingfield believed he was being helpful, Korn couldn't help but wince at that phrase he'd used – game changer. He knew Patchett would grab a hold of that one.

'A game changer? So it hasn't been going so well up to now?' asked Patchett.

'It has proved more of a fight than I'd first thought. That's fine. I enjoy a challenge,' said Korn.

'The jury will hear the confessions today, and that'll be all she wrote,' said Leonard.

'That's right,' said Shipley. 'A jury can never understand why someone would confess to a crime they didn't commit. There's just no getting past that with a jury, and he confessed not once, but twice.'

Pouring himself a coffee, Korn regarded Shipley closely. The veins standing out on his forearms against the muscle, the fat gold ring on his finger and the reptilian intelligence that burned behind his narrow eyes.

'When do I testify?' asked Hogg.

'Later today probably, but don't worry. You're testimony will be short and sweet,' said Wingfield.

'I just want this over with. I should've known better than to hire Dubois,' said Hogg.

'Lot of people make the same mistake,' said Shipley. 'Sooner or later you realize their kind is all the same.'

Leonard nodded, but no one else said a word. Korn had an unusual distaste for human life in general. He told himself it didn't really matter what color his victims were. They all screamed and died the same. Yet, the underlying racism of authority in the South was ever present. He'd seen it his whole career. But this was the first time he'd heard it spoken aloud in a more public conversation. This wasn't a whispered discussion among two conspirators. It was out in the open now. The silence which followed the statement was not uncomfortable. If anything, it felt natural for it to come out in the open now, in these times.

'Just nail this son of a bitch, won't you, Randal?' said Patchett, breaking the silence.

'Rest assured, we'll be strapping him into Yellow Mama someday soon,' said Korn.

He took another few minutes to finish his coffee and left Wingfield, Hogg, Shipley, Leonard and Patchett to finish their breakfast. As the hostess brought him his briefcase, he thought how easily the Pastor hid in plain sight these days. No one would suspect one of the men at this table was a multiple murderer.

He had the security footage, which gave him leverage over the Pastor. Such a man could be extremely useful. A time would come when he would become more of a threat than an asset, and when that happened Korn would kill him, just as he had killed Lomax.

CHAPTER FIFTY-SEVEN

EDDIE

Bloch met us at the courthouse with the death certificates. I didn't need to read them to know that we'd had the first piece of luck in this trial. My theory was right. But that didn't mean there wasn't a hundred miles of hard road ahead of us. We didn't have a knockout punch – we had a shot. That's all.

And sometimes they miss.

Bloch looked up at the front row of seats and waved at Patricia. 'How are they holding up?' asked Bloch.

'Nervous as all hell. They haven't slept in days.'

Together we walked up to the defense table. Patricia, bent over, had her arm through the uprights of the front row, holding Andy's hand. He was at least eating better at the hotel, but that suit shirt still looked like it could accommodate at least three Andys. Patricia had worn her best dress again. It was midnight blue, with small white and yellow flecks running through the fabric. Her hair was tied up, and she wore what she called her Sunday gloves. A pair of old leather gloves that her mother had given to her to wear to church. They must've been a gift she received in her youth, because the gloves now stretched tightly over her hands.

'Today's going to be tough,' said Andy.

Bloch simply smiled at him. It was the first time I'd seen her holding back. She wanted to say something encouraging – something hopeful, but she knew today we had a mountain to climb and only one thin rope. Instead, she bit her lip, and patted Patricia on the shoulder. I saw Kate watching her and taking a small moment of pleasure from the exchange. She knew Bloch better than any of us, and we all knew the only time Bloch had physical contact with

316

someone was when she was breaking an important limb. Bloch's hand on Patricia's shoulder was a big deal. A small miracle in a cold courthouse where miracles were few and far between.

God knows we needed one right now.

Glancing at the seats behind the prosecution, Bloch said, 'Francis isn't in court today?'

'No,' said Harry. 'Haven't seen him. You want to take a drive, see if you can spot him?'

Bloch nodded and left just as the judge came into court. Then the jury. And then we were off, for what I knew would be one of the hardest days I'd ever had in a courtroom.

'The State calls John Lawson,' said Korn.

These were the first words spoken in court that morning. Korn stood a little straighter, a little taller. His shoulders were no longer hunched, his expression focused on the jury. Maybe he'd settled down into the rhythm of trial. The first day of any trial is always fraught, no matter who you are and how many trials you've done. It takes some time to find your feet, see where you are with the jury, with the evidence, and find a path.

Korn had found his. His assistant DA, Wingfield, looked pensive, hunched over the prosecution table.

From the back of the court a man in a brown, tight-fitting suit came forward. He wore a thin, sharp beard that snaked along his jawline and split over his upper lip. If I didn't know it was real, I would swear someone had drawn it on his face with a magic marker. A scar sliced his left eyebrow in two, like it was a fashion statement. The suit looked expensive, but I could tell he hadn't worn it in a long time. The arms bulged, the material spread tight across his chest and thighs. As if it had shrunk, or, more likely, Lawson had grown. He hadn't worn the suit in a while because he'd been inside, and there's nothing much to do there except lift weights and read.

And figure out how to get the hell out of there.

He took the Bible in his left hand, kissed the cover of the book like it was a holy relic, then held it aloft and repeated the oath. The judge gave him permission to sit.

'Mr. Lawson, what is your current address?' asked Korn.

'I'm at the state penn right now,' he said. Lawson spoke in a strange accent. It was southern, but not the slow drawl. He spoke real fast, and his lips barely moved so it came out as a mumble, and sounded like '*Imma-at-state-pen-rightnaw.*' The court stenographer stopped typing, turned and whispered to the clerk, who in turn spoke to the judge.

'Could you talk a little slower, and more clearly, please, Mr. Lawson. The court stenographer is having a little trouble with your accent,' said Judge Chandler.

The stenographer mouthed a *thank you* to the judge.

I looked at the stenographer, her fingers moving swiftly across the keys, and it gave me an idea.

'You mean you are currently serving a jail sentence?' asked Korn.

'That's right,' said Lawson, this time more slowly. Taking care to pronounce his words more effectively for the stenographer and the court.

'Have you served all of your sentence in the penitentiary?'

'Nah, for a while I was in county. I shared a cell with the defendant, right there,' he said, pointing to Andy.

'How long were you sharing a cell with the defendant?'

'Couple of weeks, maybe, I don't know.'

'Did you become acquainted with the defendant?'

'Yeah, we were cellies, you know? You don't got a lot of room, sharing bunks. We were locked up twenty-three seven. You got to get along with the guy you're bunkin' with. Otherwise you go crazy.'

'Would it be fair to say you became friends with the defendant?'

Lawson wiped his mouth with his hand, then drew his index finger and thumb along the lines of his moustache, tracing his beard line down the sides of his mouth to his chin.

'Not friends, exactly. Not after he told me he killed that girl.'

'Take your time, Mr. Lawson, tell the jury exactly what the defendant told you.'

He sighed, closed his eyes, then said, 'We were in the cell, late at night, and I heard him crying. He was on the bottom bunk, you know – I was top dog. I heard him crying below, he ain't never been inside before. I told him to hush, that there ain't no use in crying. He just gotta get through it. He said he deserved to be here. That he should never have killed that girl.'

When he finished that answer, he looked around the court. First at the jury, then at Korn.

'Did you ask him what girl he was referring to?'

'I knew it was that girl got killed at the truck stop.'

'Did you say anything in response to this statement from the defendant?'

'I just told him there was nothing he could do now 'cept confess. Tell the cops everything. He said he couldn't do that because they would fry his ass.'

The stenographer let out a sigh that was more of a bellow of frustration. He was still talking too fast for her.

'Thank you, Mr. Lawson. Just one last thing, have you been promised anything by anyone in my office in return for your testimony in court today?'

'Nah, man. I'm just here to tell it like it is, you know?'

'Thank you.'

Judge Chandler looked at me, raised his eyebrows as if to ask if I dared to question the witness. Kate whispered something to Harry, and both of them turned and began speaking softly to Andy. He was shaking his head, more agitated than I'd seen him for a while. It's hard sitting quietly while someone stands in a courtroom and lies about you.

I stood up and moved around the defense table, taking my place in the well of the court. Lawson cocked his head to one side and met my gaze. He looked smug. Like there was nothing I could do to shake him.

'Mr. Lawson, how long is it since you last put on that suit?' I asked.

His eyebrows knotted together, his lips pursed and curled down at the corners and his head shot back on his shoulders. He looked confused, like I'd just asked him to name the capital city of Peru.

'Ah, I don't know? Six years maybe?'

'The last time you would've worn that suit was probably at your sentencing. Am I right?'

'Right.'

'So, you've served six years. What were you sentenced for?'

'Distribution of narcotics,' said Lawson.

'You were dealing drugs?'

'Yeah, but I never killed nobody,' he said.

'I didn't say that you had. How long do you have left on your sentence?'

'A little under eight years.'

'And you served six years in the state penn, and then, for some reason, you were transferred to the county lock-up for two weeks, is that right?'

'S'right,' he said. He was getting a little agitated, and his answers were speeding up.

'Transferred straight into the cell with Andy Dubois?'

'Yeah.'

'And you were there for two weeks?'

'Somethin' like that.'

'You testified the defendant confessed to murder. When did you tell law enforcement about the confession?'

'I told the guard I wanted to speak to the sheriff.'

'*When* did you tell the guard?'

'I don't know, the next mornin', maybe?'

'And when did you speak to the sheriff?'

'That day.'

'And when were you transferred back to the state penn?'

'Couple days later.'

'Why?'

'I dunno, I just go where they tell me.'

'And you didn't make any kind of deal in exchange for your testimony here today?'

Lawson leaned forward, spoke directly into the mic, 'No.' Loud and clear.

'You didn't agree anything verbally with the DA for time off in exchange for your testimony?'

'No.'

'And you didn't sign any agreement that says you will get time off your sentence in exchange for your testimony?'

'No.'

It's an old story. A jailhouse snitch will say anything to make a deal and get time off of their sentence, but the last thing the prosecutor wants is for a jury to think the snitch is lying. The DA wants the jury to believe the testimony has not been bought or bribed from the witness – that this is the unvarnished truth and nothing else.

There's only one problem with that.

It's bullshit.

There are no honest jailhouse snitches, and there never will be.

'Just so the jury understands, you're saying you did *not* make *any* kind of deal to shorten your sentence in exchange for your testimony today?'

'No, I did not,' he said, almost triumphantly.

'Why not?' I asked.

'Huh?'

'Why didn't you make a deal?'

He looked around the room, exchanging a glance with Korn. He didn't know what to say.

'I just didn't,' he said, eventually.

'There's nothing wrong with making a deal. It happens all the time. An inmate comes into possession of information that could help the authorities, he displays his willingness to co-operate and the district attorney cuts him a deal with the parole board. The parole board wants inmates to be fully rehabilitated before they're released. Working with the authorities to help resolve other crimes is good evidence of the inmate starting down a path to becoming a reformed citizen. So I ask again, why didn't you make a deal?'

'I told you, I don't know. I just wanted to tell the truth, that's all. The girl had been killed, I wanted to help the cops catch this guy,' said Lawson, talking real quickly now. The stenographer grimaced and hammered at the keys on her machine.

I took a small step toward the witness. He was unsettled and had forgotten to keep his answers slow and steady. I needed to push a little harder.

'I'm not asking you to reveal anything sensitive or confidential if you don't want to, but I'd be interested to know what your lawyer said when you told him you didn't make a deal?'

Another step toward Lawson. I wanted him to feel like I was closing in on him. Giving him no room.

'I ain't spoken to my lawyer about it,' he said.

I was about to take another step, then stopped. Shook my head, confused.

'Wait a second, I know it looks better for the prosecution if you haven't made a deal. An informer doesn't carry much credibility with a jury if they're only testifying to help themselves get out of jail. Sometimes the prosecutor doesn't want the jury to know there is a deal. It makes their testimony more credible. You understand that's how these things generally work, right?'

Lawson swallowed, said, 'I understand.'

'You see that lady over there typing as I talk?'

His jaw flexed as he looked over, then said, 'Yeah.'

'She is the court stenographer. She types out every word said in this court. If there is a dispute about anything that is said in this room, the record decides it. Your testimony is on the record. You understand that?'

'I do.'

'Well, what happens if you go before the parole board in six months, and they say they know nothing about a deal with the DA? You're on the record, under oath, telling this judge and this jury that there *is* no deal. Your lawyer knows nothing about a deal, and there's no paperwork. What if Mr. Korn says there's no deal? Do you think the parole board will believe you over Mr. Korn?'

The room was cool under the ceiling fans, but it didn't stop the fat pimples of sweat breaking out on Lawson's forehead, and rolling down into his eyes, his cheek, and into his beard. His eyes were narrow and locked on Korn.

'I'm a defense lawyer, Mr. Lawson, I know what it's like to come up against the district attorney, and so for your benefit, and your benefit alone, I'm going to ask you again, did the district attorney offer you a deal in exchange for your testimony today?'

Two jurors leaned forward, anticipating the answer.

Lawson wet his lips. Wiped the sweat from his face.

'For *the record*, Mr. Lawson, please answer the question,' I said.

'He said he would put in a good word with the parole board.'

The jurors who had leaned forward, Avery and another juror, swung their gaze at Korn. I followed their line of sight. Korn smiled, shook his head.

'So, he did make you a deal?'

'Yeah, that's right.'

'I see, so when you testified that there was no deal, you were lying?'

'Nah, I just misspoke.'

'Just to be clear, you lied to this jury about a deal with the district attorney, but you weren't lying when you said Andy Dubois confessed to the murder of Skylar Edwards?'

'Somethin' like that.'

'When you were arrested on the narcotics charge which put you in jail, did you plead guilty or not guilty?'

'Not guilty.'

'And you were convicted?'

'Yeah.'

'You lied to the jury in your original trial, you lied to this jury today about not making a deal with the prosecutor, but you expect this jury to believe you when you tell them Andy Dubois confessed to murder?'

'This is bullshit, man. Do I still get my recommendation to the parole board for early release?' he asked, looking around the room.

I turned to the jury, held up my hands, and said, 'I have nothing further to ask this witness.'

Korn stood, ready to re-examine, and repair some of the damage.

'Mr. Lawson, I just want to make something clear for the jury, and for the record, we did not make a deal for your early release in exchange for your testimony, correct?'

Lawson leaned forward, his finger pointing at Korn, his lips drawn back in a snarl. He was about to go at it with the prosecutor when the judge butted in.

'I don't think this witness carries credibility. If he is implying that the district attorney misled the court by eliciting false testimony, then we can ignore this witness.'

Korn saw Chandler throwing him a lifeline. He took it and Judge Chandler ordered Lawson from the stand. It didn't shut him up, though.

'We had a deal,' he said as he was escorted from the witness stand by two corrections officers.

The judge had saved Korn, but I got the impression he wasn't happy about it. For the first time, Korn got the kind of look Judge Chandler previously reserved for me alone. Either he didn't like Korn being sloppy, or Chandler had a moral line that the DA was stretching over.

Korn's case was shattering around him. He sat down, looked at his notes on the table. I saw that he was gripping his right thigh tightly. A red stain emerged on his pants, just at the top of the area where he pinched his flesh.

He let go, said, 'The prosecution calls Mr. Buxton.'

Buxton was the truck driver who'd found Skylar's body. He was not an essential witness, and I wondered if Korn would even call him.

Kate leaned over, whispered, 'Korn is on the rails. He's calling an easy witness. Buxton doesn't say anything controversial. This is Korn getting his rhythm back. We have to pull the trigger on Buxton.'

'No,' I said. 'We plant the questions with Buxton. Then we answer them later. If Korn is struggling, we need to make sure he stays that way. Give him something else to worry about.'

Kate nodded, said, 'I'll take Buxton.'

CHAPTER FIFTY-EIGHT

KATE

Kate watched Ted Buxton take the stand. He wore a white shirt, blue tie and tan pants. A large man in his late forties, with brown hair, free from any gray, worn in a side parting. He was clean shaven, with a scent of soap and shoe polish catching Kate's nose as he walked past. Buxton had put on his Sunday best for his court appearance.

He was sworn in and Korn rose awkwardly to his feet to address the witness. Before he did so, he placed a fat volume of statutes in front of him on the table in an effort to hide the bloodstain from the jury when he stood. Kate had noticed it too and wondered how he had hurt himself. It didn't look like he had anything in his hands when his leg started bleeding, so she assumed it was an old injury, but it had looked like he had coaxed it into bleeding, as if he was punishing himself.

Some powerful men were like that. Through acting for various women in sexual harassment lawsuits, Kate had heard all kinds of stories from the victims. Mostly, they were the same story – a man who didn't know how to speak or behave appropriately. That's it. That's the story. The rest were just details. But some of those details kept reappearing in different stories. Powerful men often fantasized about being hurt, or helpless.

Kate thought that the prosecutor may have hurt himself, on purpose.

'Mr. Buxton, what is your profession?'

'I'm a truck driver.'

'And where were you on the night of the fourteenth of May, of this year?'

'I was taking a rest break at a truck stop on Union Highway.'

'What does that involve?'

'I was taking some shut-eye in my cab. I'd driven my fill that day, and I needed to take my rest. I figured I'd save the hotel bill and sleep in the cab.'

Kate liked Buxton. There was no bullshit. He looked like a man who was simply there to tell the truth, and nothing else.

'Did anything occur on that night?'

'Not a thing.'

'What did you do the next day?'

'I had delivered my load to the chemical plant already. I live here in town and my street is too narrow for the rig, so I left it in the truck stop, walked home, spent the day with the kids and then my wife dropped me off at the truck stop that evening so I could refuel the rig and go take another load.'

Hesitating, Buxton swallowed, cleared his throat of either nerves or the emotional memory, and then spoke again, his voice wavering, his eyes suddenly wet.

'I was at the truck when I saw something rustling in the tall grass beyond the lot. I went to take a look and that's . . .'

'Please go on, Mr. Buxton.'

'That's when I saw the turtles. They were gathered around in a circle. I couldn't tell what it was they were a chewing at. Not at first. I looked closer, that's when I saw it was a pair of feet. The soles were facing up toward me. They looked blue in the moonlight.'

'And what did you do then?'

'I called the sheriff,' said Buxton. 'I'd heard the Edwards' girl was missing, so I didn't hesitate.'

'Thank you,' said Korn, and resumed his seat.

The jury liked Ted Buxton. Attacking him would be a mistake. Kate knew she would do better by making Buxton a defense witness.

'Mr. Buxton, what time did you arrive at the truck stop?' asked Kate.

'Around ten-thirty that night. Something like that.'

'And did you stay in your truck the whole time?'

'Pretty much, yeah, I had my lunchbox in the cab. Oh, I used the washroom in the gas station once, maybe. When I got there. That's it.'

'Did you hear music from Hogg's Bar in your cab?'

'Sure did. After I ate, I put my head down. The music kept me awake for a while.'

'Are you a light sleeper?'

'Not especially.'

'But the music was enough to keep you awake?'

'Yeah.'

Kate glanced at the jury, then returned her attention to the witness. It was the subtle body language moves that she was becoming more adept at using. She was, in her own way, telling the jury – *that was important. Remember it. Now watch this.*

'You didn't hear a young woman screaming or calling for help at any time that night?'

He shook his head. 'No, no way. If I'd heard that I would've come a runnin'. I have a daughter around that age.'

'And you didn't see the victim earlier that night, before you found her?'

'No.'

'And at any time that night did you see the defendant?'

'No, not that I recall.'

'Mr. Buxton, the prosecution's case is that Skylar Edwards left Hogg's Bar around midnight, with the defendant, and that they were arguing. Their case is the defendant beat the victim, striking her to the face multiple times, that the victim managed to scrape the defendant's back with her nails on her right hand, and that in the struggle two of the victim's fingers on her left hand were dislocated and broken. Then she was strangled to death and at some stage either that night, or the day after, she was buried where you found her. You understand that is the prosecution's case?'

'I guess,' said Buxton.

'But you didn't hear any screaming, or any sound that would've been made in that struggle, did you, Mr. Buxton?'

'I did not.'

'Thank you, Mr. Buxton. Nothing further.'

Korn had no re-direct, and let Buxton leave the stand. Judge Chandler watched Buxton walk down the aisle, and out of the doors at the back of the court. He called a break, and Kate thought she saw something in his expression as he got up off his seat. There was concern, and doubt. And all of it pointed toward the prosecutor. Kate didn't want to get her hopes up, but it looked like Chandler was coming around to the notion that Andy Dubois might be innocent. She pushed the thought away for now in case it distracted her, and made a note of the witnesses yet to testify for the prosecution.

The DNA expert Cheryl Banbury who tied Andy's DNA to the material under Skylar Edward's fingernails. Deputy Leonard, who would prove the confession and testify to the scratches on Andy's back. Ryan Hogg, owner of Hogg's Bar, and finally Skylar's father – Francis Edwards, who would pull on the hearts of the jury.

No guarantee of the order of the witnesses but Kate guessed Korn would leave Francis until last. He wasn't even in the courtroom after all.

'Who's the next witness?' asked Kate.

Eddie shook his head, said, 'I have no idea. Korn is scrambling. He could do anything. We haven't had our last surprise in this case.'

CHAPTER FIFTY-NINE

EDDIE

We were close to saving Andy's life, and I knew Korn was at his most dangerous when he was cornered. Those kind of men always are. He got off on the power of the job. When you hold life and death in your hands, with no checks and balances, and no one to answer to, it's easy to become a monster. Korn had money, a first-class education and should be representing small countries from behind a marble desk in a twenty-five-thousand square-foot office in Manhattan. Instead, he was in a shitkicker town in Alabama bringing home a hundred grand a year. This wasn't failure for him. He had sought this job out. He was already a monster when he took the job. It was the power that attracted him.

During the short break Korn had changed his suit. He now wore a thick, navy pinstripe. Something to hide the bleed from his thigh. Either it was a wound that wouldn't heal, or it was a wound he wouldn't allow to heal. Some men don't just get their kicks from causing suffering; he enjoyed pain itself. If I coldcocked him with a straight right hand, he might not enjoy that so much. Certainly not as much as I would.

The judge and jury filed in, and Korn threw the ball into the air.

'Call Doctor Cheryl Banbury,' he said.

A lady in a lemon jacket and black pants came forward. She looked to be in her late fifties, maybe early sixties. Her dark brown hair had thinned, and it was pulled back from her face in a ponytail. There was a pinched look to her features, as if there was a clamp on the back of her head pulling the skin in her face tight across the surface of her skull. Only the pale glaze over her green eyes and the liver spots on her hands gave away her age.

She took the oath, looked sweetly at Korn, and gave him her qualifications as an expert witness when he asked. It looked like a well-practiced routine. They'd had this dance before, many times. The familiarity made me wonder how many men the good doctor had helped Korn execute.

The thought made me shiver.

The sweat on my back was drying, making me cold. I was glad of it. I needed to be super sharp with this witness. She'd been in the wars. Doc Banbury would be a formidable opponent.

'You were presented with two exhibits to examine and compare, is that correct?' asked Korn.

'Yes, as I detailed in my report. Fingernail clippings, and a DNA swab.'

'Now, I know there's a lot of scientific detail in your report, but could you explain to the jury, in layman's terms, the result of your findings?'

'Of course. I first examined the substances on the underside of the fingernails and took a sample. Some of it was blood and skin. Minute particles. I examined these particles and was able to extract the DNA pattern.'

'And what is a DNA pattern?'

'It is like a genetic code, for a human being. Everyone is different. Everyone has their own code.'

'What did you do with the DNA swab from the defendant?'

'I extracted the DNA from the swab and identified the markers – the patterns of DNA which help us establish the code. Then I compared the DNA markers from the blood and skin found under the fingernails and the DNA swab from the defendant.'

Doc Banbury left the answer hanging there, pausing, while she took a sip of water. Building anticipation in the jury. She was good.

'My comparison found that the DNA was a scientific match.'

'A match.'

'A scientific match, yes.'

'Just so the jury is clear, the blood and skin found under the victim's fingernails came from the defendant?'

'As far as science can tell us, yes.'

'And what is the probability that this is a match?'

'We are more than ninety-nine percent certain.'

'Thank you,' said Korn, sitting down with some satisfaction on his sharp face. I knew why he looked a lot happier. The jury were eating every word from Banbury. It was strong testimony. Science was telling them that the victim and Andy were engaged in a struggle, and she scraped his back, leaving his DNA under her nails.

Game over.

I felt a hand on my arm. Harry, pulling me into a whisper.

'She's good, make sure you pin her to the ground before you pull the trigger. Any wriggle room and Andy is a dead man.'

He was right. It came down to this moment. If we didn't turn this witness around, it was all over. Before I got up to cross-examine, I took a final look at Andy and his mom. Her arm snaked through the rail separating the gallery from the defense table. Andy had turned his chair, so the judge wouldn't see, and had taken her hand.

Patricia knew her boy. No matter what evidence Korn said he had – she knew her son wasn't a killer. None of that mattered for much if we couldn't save him.

I'd had time to think about this, and I thought I had a narrow window of attack. The key had been Andy. He'd told me that the cops had beaten him until he was unconscious. And I believed him. The evidence we'd found over the past few days had built up a picture in my mind. Fragments slowly connecting.

Now it was time to put them all together.

I took a breath and hammered down the first pin.

'Doctor Banbury, am I right in saying you were provided with two samples for analysis by the Sheriff's Department?'

'Yes. Two exhibits. Fingernail clippings and a DNA swab from the defendant.'

'How were these exhibits provided to you?'

'The sheriff, God rest his soul, dropped them off at the county lab, where I signed a receipt when I took them into my custody.'

'How long have you been a DNA expert for the county?'

'Fifteen years, now.'

'You had a good working relationship with law enforcement, established over a long period?'

'You could say that, yes.'

'Which exhibit did you examine first?'

'The fingernail clippings from the victim.'

'You were examining the material beneath the nails, is that right?'

'That's correct. I was made aware that the defendant had some scrapes on his back that could be fingernail marks, and I was testing to see if any of his skin, blood or DNA was in the material beneath the victim's nails.'

'I see. There was some other material found on those nails, apart from genetic material?'

'Yes, some chemical compounds. I became aware that the victim was studying Chemistry at undergrad level at the University of Alabama. I guess she may have come into contact with all kinds of substances.'

'Could you read out the list of materials that you found on the nail clippings that wasn't genetic material?'

Banbury looked to the judge, said, 'May I refer to my report?'

'You may. This is testimony, not a memory exam,' said Judge Chandler.

From the pocket of her yellow jacket, Banbury drew out a pair of fine wire reading glasses, perched them on her nose and turned to her report, which she held in a plastic folder. She flicked through a couple of pages, and then found the paragraph and began to read.

'I examined the fingernail clippings provided in a sealed evidence bag marked CL12, and found the following:

'Blood, skin, general detritus, powder residue.

'The powder residue tested as particles of Anticholinergic (four parts), Sertraline (one part), Morphine Sulphate (four parts), Phenothiazine (most likely prochlorperazine) (one part).'

'Sertraline is a drug, isn't it, Doctor? It's an anti-anxiety drug, commonly referred to as Zoloft?'

'Yes, that's correct.'

'The three other compounds that you found, let's look at each one. Anticholinergic is also a drug, isn't it? It's used in Benadryl, a muscle relaxant that helps with stomach cramps?'

'Yes.'

'Morphine sulphate can be taken in tablet form to ease pain?'

'Yes.'

'And the last substance, prochlorperazine, is an anti-emetic. It can help control nausea?'

'I guess, I'm not a pharmacist.'

'Neither was the victim. She was studying Chemistry, not pharmacology. That's an unusual combination of substances to find beneath someone's fingernails, wouldn't you say?'

'In my experience, you find a lot of unusual things under fingernails,' said Banbury.

I had to be tighter. More pins.

'Let me rephrase, have you ever found that combination of substances beneath any other fingernail clippings that you have examined?'

Doc Banbury nodded, very slightly. She knew we were in a battle of words, and this was one point to me. Although she had no idea where I was going with it. No one did. Apart from Kate, Harry and Bloch.

'No,' said Banbury, 'I don't believe I have found that combination of substances from fingernail clippings, but then again, all samples have their own individual characteristics.'

The doc thought she was parrying another blow. That's what I wanted her to think.

'And the substances found beneath those nail clippings can give us vital evidence, correct?'

She was more wary now, but she had no choice but to confirm.

'Yes, they can tell a story. Like who scratched someone on the back.'

The doc was getting her shots in any way she could. I had to ignore that one for now. I was working on the bigger picture, but I made a mental note of her answer. I was going to ball it up and throw it right back at her.

'Just to be clear, you were testing the substances found on the nails, not the nails themselves?'

'Correct, there was no need to examine the DNA of the nails themselves. Their origin was clear and already established by the chain of evidence from the sheriff. Plus, DNA extraction from a human fingernail is a much more difficult process.'

Time to tighten my finger on the trigger.

'The defendant in this case, who denies any kind of altercation with the victim, has no memory of being scratched. He doesn't know how the scratches got on his skin.'

'Well, he would say that, wouldn't he? To my mind, it's clear.'

'Doctor, I'd like to show you a photograph of the victim. It's the prosecution's photograph number two.'

The clerk reached behind her desk and lifted clear a blown-up photograph of the victim, lying on the dirt floor behind Hogg's car.

'First, I'd like to thank the prosecution for enlarging this photo. It's helpful to the defense. Doctor Banbury, look at the victim's fingernails, please.'

Banbury took off her reading glasses, turned and stared at the picture.

'The victim is wearing bright red nail polish. Doctor, in your examination of the victim's fingernail clippings, you don't mention nail polish as one of the compounds found besides genetic material.'

Banbury swallowed, said, 'Yes.'

'Where are the nail clippings now?'

'They are in my lab.'

'Doctor, think very carefully before you answer, but to the best of your knowledge, the nail clippings you examined did not have traces of nail polish upon them, isn't that right?'

She hesitated, looked at the photograph. She was studying it, narrowing her eyes to focus on the nails.

'The polish may have chipped off when the nails were cut,' she said.

'Wait a second, let's back up. So you are confirming that the fingernail clippings you examined did not have nail polish on them?'

'Correct, but like I said, it may have chipped off.'

'I suppose that's possible, but all of it? Without leaving any trace?'

'It's possible,' she said.

I reached down to the defense table, picked up three copies of a document, gave one to the prosecution, one to the judge.

'Your Honor, in light of the answer provided by this witness we would like to enter this document into evidence, at this time,' I said.

'This is irrelevant,' said Korn.

'Your Honor, the relevance will be demonstrated by this witness.'

Judge Chandler looked over the document, and took his time, reading every word on the page.

'I don't see the relevance, and it may prove that the jury doesn't see the relevance either, but I'll allow the question. This is a capital-murder case,' said Judge Chandler. He had tried to minimize the relevance of the document, let the jury think it was unimportant, and maybe they wouldn't pay too much attention.

I gave a copy of the document to the witness and asked her to read it. She read it. At first, she was confused about why I was showing her this document, then, when she reached the bottom of the page, her expression changed. Her eyes flared open, her lips parted, and she looked immediately to Korn. There was nothing he could do about this.

'Doctor, when you mentioned Sheriff Lomax earlier, you made a comment – *God rest his soul*. I take it you were good friends with the late sheriff?'

'We were acquainted through our respective positions. I suppose we built up a rapport over time.'

I was trying to tease it out. Not making it too obvious. She wasn't playing ball, so I had to ask it straight.

'In your experience was he an honest man?'

'Yes, he was a good man.'

Bingo.

'His wife thought so too,' I said, and I reached out a hand. Kate placed three copies of a photograph in it. I handed them to the judge, Korn and the witness.

'I wish this photograph to be entered into evidence.'

'Your Honor, is Mr. Flynn seriously asking this court to allow this photograph into evidence?' asked Korn.

Judge Chandler looked at the photograph, then seemed to weigh it in his hand. He looked at the ceiling, then at Korn, then the photo. The judge had been in office for many years. Longer than

Korn. Longer than the sheriff. I could've been wrong, but I detected a shift in the judge. He'd known Lomax for a long time. He'd known him before Korn came to town, and there was something stirring in the judge.

'Is this photograph genuine?' asked the judge.

'It is, Your Honor. If there is any doubt, I'm sure the original is in possession of the Sheriff's Department. It can be produced if there is any dispute over its authenticity,' I said.

'I'll admit this evidence,' said the judge.

'Your Honor, this is outrageous—' began Korn, but he didn't get to finish.

'No, Mr. Korn. It is not. I have made my ruling, and you should respect it,' said the judge, right into Korn's incredulous face.

I turned to look at Kate and Harry. They looked like the judge had just pulled a live rabbit out of his robes. There had been a change in the room. In the temperature. A goddamn battleship like Chandler doesn't turn around on a dime like he just did. I guessed he saw something in that photograph that struck him personally. A bell had been rung in the judge. One that I didn't even know he had.

I gave the witness a copy of the photograph.

'This is a photograph of a letter. It was written by Lucy Lomax, the late wife of Sheriff Colt Lomax. It was probably the last thing he read. He was found shortly afterward, and it is believed by the authorities that he committed suicide. I'll give you a moment to read the letter, but it's clear his wife thought he was a good man, but that he had been led down the wrong path.'

Banbury read the letter.

'Well, I had a good opinion of the sheriff,' she said.

'You were aware that the sheriff's wife, Lucy Lomax, had been suffering from cancer for a long time before her death, just a few days ago.'

'I was aware.'

'The document in your hand is the death certificate for Lucy Lomax. At the bottom of that document, as is the custom and practice in the county, is a list of her known medical conditions at the date of death and a list of her prescribed medication. Do you see that?'

'I do.'

'At the time of her death, just this week, Lucy Lomax was prescribed Benadryl, Zoloft, morphine sulphate and prochlorperazine. The exact combination of substances found underneath the fingernail clippings you examined, correct?'

Banbury nodded.

'For the record, we need an audible *yes* or *no* for that answer.'

'Yes, that's correct.'

'You'll also see in the letter she left behind for her husband, that she thanked him for looking after her. I quote, *I love how you've taken care of me during this illness. How you've rubbed my feet, bathed me, washed my hair, even crushed up my pills and put them in yoghurt when I couldn't swallow them.* The fingernail clippings you examined didn't come from the victim, did they, Doctor? You examined Sheriff Lomax's fingernail clippings. He ran his fingers through the skin of the defendant after he'd been beaten unconscious in his cell. That's the logical conclusion, isn't it?'

Her face blushed as she said, 'I can only testify as to the tests I undertook. I did not obtain the samples.'

'Earlier you said the substances beneath fingernails can tell a story, like who scratched someone on the back. It's clear who did the scratching in this case, and it wasn't the victim, was it?'

Doc Banbury looked at the floor, then threw back her hair, shaking it off her shoulders like she was shaking off a conclusion she didn't want to face.

'I examined the samples given to me, and reached my conclusion based on the information given to me by the sheriff.'

'It was too late for Sheriff Lomax. It might not be too late for you, Doctor Banbury. I'll ask you again, do you now believe that the fingernail clippings you analyzed came from the victim? Or could they have come from the sheriff himself?'

Banbury looked at Judge Chandler. He was staring at her, hard, over the rims of his glasses. His fist underneath his chin.

'In light of what I've heard today, it's possible they came from the sheriff instead of the victim,' said Banbury.

Noise is important in a courtroom. It's never silent, even though it's supposed to be. Everyone whispers, coughs, mutters and tuts.

All the damn time. Right then, the only noise in the room came from the jury. Some of them looked around at their fellow jurors. Others gasped, some swore under their breaths. This was the reaction I was looking for. Hoping for. Maybe half of the two tons of weight that had sat on my shoulders shifted, just a little. I felt my lungs fill properly for the first time since Berlin came into my office and told me about Andy Dubois.

Lomax died because he went looking for redemption. I was sure of that. The judge had seen it too. He probably remembered that young sheriff – the one described in Lucy's letter to her husband. The young man who wanted to do good, who carried a lucky charm, who wanted to make a difference. Maybe Judge Chandler recognized something of himself in that letter too.

Women have a way of cutting through bullshit like a hot steel knife through a cherry pie.

I told the judge I had no more questions for the witness. I didn't want to mess it up. I had gotten much more than I'd hoped for and it could only go downhill from here.

I had a mind to ask the judge to direct the jury to dismiss the case due to police and prosecutorial misconduct. But I knew it wasn't enough. It hadn't been proven. I decided I would save it for the speech to the jury.

'Your Honor, we would request a recess to prepare our final witnesses for tomorrow,' said Korn.

The court adjourned for the day. The look I got from Korn as he packed away his papers gave me the chills. He had been given a series of gut punches and he was ready to fight back. His gaze shifted to Andy, and it was then that smile played at his lips.

Something was coming.

Something bad.

Korn had some kind of ace. Some sort of insurance policy and he was about ready to cash in.

CHAPTER SIXTY

BLOCH

Sitting in the SUV with the AC off and the window cracked open an inch, Bloch watched for cars stopping outside the first-floor property she had broken into the day before.

She had driven around town and its outskirts for a couple of hours and hadn't spotted Francis Edwards anywhere. His car wasn't in the driveway, and she hadn't seen it that day. After chasing her tail, she decided to wait outside the office where the White Camelia had their meetings.

Forty-five minutes she'd sat there, sweating in the sun, and watching the street. None of the vehicles she had seen yesterday were parked close by – no pick-ups with Confederate flags, and no vehicles on the street outside the property. The town was quiet in the noon sun. Almost peaceful. And yet, something lurked in the dank air. A feeling of malevolence that Bloch couldn't shake. There was another side to small American towns like this. A dark side, soaked in bloody history and hate.

She popped the cap on a cold bottle of water she'd bought in the gas station and drank half of it. While she replaced it in the cup holder she saw something in her peripheral vision. Something she might have missed five seconds ago.

The door to the office opened. A man exited, closed the door behind him. He wore a panama hat, light-gray suit with a messenger bag slung over one shoulder. The hat kept his face hidden in shadow. This wasn't Denvir, Francis Edwards or Gruber. She had not seen this man in the building before.

He didn't stay on the street for long. A black SUV pulled up by the curb and he got into the front passenger seat. Bloch turned the key in the ignition and pulled out behind the SUV, keeping her distance. Tinted windows made it difficult to see inside, but she thought there was only the driver, the panama hat and no one else in the back.

The vehicle swung through the town, then headed into the more densely populated areas – the mostly white suburbs. Bloch had been all around Buckstown and the scars left by the Jim Crow laws were still clear. African Americans, Hispanic and the few Asian families she had seen were all on the other side of town in poor housing. There were very few in the bigger, more modern houses west of Main Street.

A tingle of electricity made the hairs on the back of her neck stand up as the SUV turned left into Peachtree Avenue, then slowed and stopped up ahead, outside 491.

Francis Edwards' house.

Bloch took her camera from the glove box, focused on the SUV and snapped a picture of the license plate. She would check it out soon as she had time. Bloch adjusted the zoom on the camera to get a good look at whoever got out of the passenger seat.

CHAPTER SIXTY-ONE

THE PASTOR

The Pastor unbuttoned his suit jacket, took off his hat and placed it on top of one of the filing cabinets. There was no ventilation in the office, and he didn't want to open the windows. He didn't want to attract any attention from the street. He selected the files he wanted from the cabinet, closed it and then found the schematic for the governor's mansion, put that in his bag along with the files.

He took a moment to look around.

His vision had been born in this room. The great things to come all started with conversations in this place. Secret conversations. And there were two men who would now bring his dreams to life. Everything he had worked for came down to the events that would unfold on this day.

He slung the bag over his shoulder, retrieved his hat and put it back on. A vicious heat threatened to crack the sidewalks today. It reminded him of those days in the box. The sun a burning God – peeling the black paint from the timbers of the box, cooking him in the darkness within as he begged his father to let him out.

'Pray, boy. Pray for forgiveness and it shall set you free,' was all his father ever said in response to his pleas for help.

And so the Pastor prayed. He prayed his father would die just like his mother, and give him some peace.

The Pastor's father did die eventually. It was a hard death. The Pastor was home, visiting after his first summer of college. The full scholarship freed him of debt, but he didn't have much to live on. There had been offers made on the farm, and the Pastor's father had refused to sell – saying that he would die on the property, soon as let it go to a stranger.

When the police found the Pastor's father he was out back, at the chopping block, which was nothing more than a wide, flat stump of an oak tree. The base of the stump was scarred where the axe had been buried after each session of chopping wood. The Pastor's father was laying down beside the block, his left foot partially severed. The sheriff thought it clear that the man must've slipped, hit his ankle with the axe and bled out quite quickly.

The Pastor knew that wasn't true. It had taken several hours for his father to die after he had hit him in the leg with the axe. He could've ended the suffering much sooner. One blow to the neck or head with the axe is all it would take. Instead, the Pastor had wrapped some fine wire around his father's injured leg, and nailed the other end of the wire down to the stump. His father could crawl away, try to get to the phone in the house, or maybe even get to the front porch and cry for help there, but he would be doing that minus his foot.

Instead, he called out for help, and cried and begged his son to release him.

'Please, let me go!' cried his father.

'Pray, father. Pray for forgiveness,' was the Pastor's response as he watched the man die.

It was hot that day. Just like today – the Seventh Day.

The day his angels would release their fire on the land, and call men to arms in the first battle of what he believed would be a holy war. Prayers didn't save anyone. Only action.

As the Pastor hit the sundrenched sidewalk he looked around, shielding his eyes beneath the brim of his hat. He saw a dark SUV in the distance. Too far away to tell if anyone was inside. He checked his watch and waited some more. Then a black SUV pulled up and he got inside. Denvir accelerated away as the Pastor buckled his seat belt, checking the side mirror as he did so.

The dark SUV pulled into the street behind him.

'Is that a tail?' asked Denvir.

'Maybe,' said the Pastor.

'You want me to lose 'em?'

'No, that won't be necessary. I think we should let them follow. It might be useful,' said the Pastor.

They drove through the town. Into the white, middle-class suburbs. Turned onto Peachtree Avenue and came to stop outside Francis Edwards' address.

'You know what to do later tonight, after I give the signal?' asked the Pastor, handing the files he'd taken from the office to Denvir.

'I think so. My boys are ready. I've got them on high alert. They're already in their tactical armor, their dicks in their hands and their guns loaded into their trucks. All I need to do is give the word.'

'Good. Go through the files again. Just to make sure there are no mistakes. Start with the Jews, then work your way down.'

And with that, the Pastor swung the strap of his bag over his head, adjusted his hat, and got out of the car. He walked up the path, opened Francis's front door with his keys, went inside and shut it, firmly, behind him and snapped on a pair of gloves.

He took a laptop from his bag, set it on the coffee table in the lounge, opened it up and powered it on. Then he took the schematic of the governor's mansion from his bag, as well as a plastic folder, and placed these items on the couch.

Making his way to the back door, he glanced once at the kitchen floor. He could still hear the noise Esther had made as she choked to death. There was a key sitting in the lock of the door. He turned it, but before he opened the door he saw a figure vault the fence at the back of the yard and quickly disappear from view as they dropped into the tall grass.

Quickly, he crouched down on the floor, then got onto his back and drew his gun. He aimed the Glock at the window at the top half of the door.

Soon as a head appeared in the window, he would put a bullet through it.

CHAPTER SIXTY-TWO

BLOCH

She had zoomed in, taken a few shots, but the hat kept his face in shadow. Soon as the figure went inside she threw the wheel around, turned the car and drove to the end of the block. Her cell phone in her hand, Bloch dialed her contact, read out the license plate, asked for a quick turnaround by text message and hung up.

A helicopter flew overhead. That was the second chopper she'd seen today.

The houses backed onto a line of trees that ran between this development and the next one over. Bloch made her way through the trees until she found the fence at the rear of the Edwards property. It was five feet high and sturdy. She took a run up, vaulted the fence into the yard. The lawn had not been cut in a while. There were a few benches here and there, a tool shed and a paved area at the back door with patio furniture. She kept low and quiet as she approached the back door, which she guessed led into the kitchen. No sign of anyone through the lounge window.

She reached the back door in a crouch.

Maggie in her right hand.

Her left extended above her head, reaching for the door handle.

She stopped. Wondered if she should chance a look through the glass pane that made up the top half of the door.

Otherwise, she wouldn't know what she was walking into. Maybe the man in the panama hat was armed. She would be quick. One glance.

Standard no-knock entry procedure for police. If you could get a quick look through a window, gather some intel on the layout of people inside – that's gold.

Her heartbeat had kicked up the tempo. Her breathing wasn't labored but the charge of adrenaline that was coursing through her body was pumping her lungs harder. Training and perfecting her grip prevented the gun from shaking in her hand. She took a moment. Closed her eyes for a second and took control of her breath.

She was afraid. And this was completely normal. Every cop got scared before they went through a door. Every single one. The fear kept them sharp, but it also led to mistakes. There was no way to stop that fear, the only thing to do was control it. Bloch had been shot on the job. Her vest had taken the rounds, but she never forgot it. That's why she carried a cannon and knew how to use it. Her training and instinct gave her a drop of maybe a second on anyone else, in any house. That was enough to fire a single round from Maggie. And she never wanted to be in a position where one round was not enough. Never again.

Especially not today, when her Kevlar vest was safely in her luggage in The Chanterelle.

Before she looked, she gently pulled the handle on the back door. It moved. It was unlocked. She didn't have to break the glass or kick down the door. She could slide in, which might give her another couple of seconds before the man in the house realized she was there. And every second counted.

Bloch got her feet beneath her, pushed up from her knees to look inside.

CHAPTER SIXTY-THREE

THE PASTOR

He watched the handle on the back door twitch.

There was someone outside that door. Right now.

No time to wait for them to pop their head above the window.

He fired two shots just to the right of the door handle. A small crack appeared in the window pane just above the handle. He listened, heard the sound of a body hitting the decking outside the door, a groan and then silence. The Pastor got to his feet and then ran for the front of the house. He barreled through the front door, slamming it shut behind him, got into the SUV and before he could tell Denvir to floor it, the tires were already smoking.

'What happened?' asked Denvir.

'There was someone out back. I put them down. We're so close now, I can't let anything stop us.'

The Pastor checked his watch.

'It will take time for them to find the body. If they're still alive, should take ten minutes for the paramedics and the Sheriff's Department to respond. Another half hour to put out an APB on Francis. They're too late. He's already on the road.'

'Jesus, we're cutting this fine,' said Denvir.

'Look, there's too much heat. We can't take the chance of anyone cracking. Not at this stage. I know we were going go let Ryan Hogg testify but the DA is going to have to do without him. After you drop me off, go finish Ryan. Text him on his burner, tell him to meet you at the bar. It's already closed today because he was supposed to testify. Tell him to keep the place closed until you get there . . .'

'Then do it as we planned?'

'Yes, shoot the place up a little. Take whatever's in the cash register and make it look like a robbery.'

'Got it.'

The Pastor took off his hat, flung it in the back seat.

It was a baseball hat.

CHAPTER SIXTY-FOUR

BLOCH

She moved her back away from the side of the house, pivoted on the balls of her feet so that she was now directly in front of the door. Maximum view inside and she would be ready to dive low and fire from the floor if she saw someone immediately.

She reached for the handle again, stopped.

From this angle, directly facing the door, she noticed two bullet holes in the wood. The window was cracked just above the bullet holes. There had been no damage to the back door when she was in the house checking out the kitchen after Esther Edwards was murdered. This was recent. Glancing at the decking, she saw splinters.

This was recent. Maybe hours ago. Maybe minutes ago.

A text message came through on her phone.

The license plate you asked about belongs to Homeland Security.

Bloch opened the door and the man in the kitchen took off his panama hat and said, 'I was wondering when you were going to come in.'

Bloch kept Maggie pointed at the guy as she stepped further inside.

Then she recognized him, and the relief blew out of her body in one big exhalation, her shoulders sagged, and she lowered the gun.

'Mr. Berlin,' said Bloch. 'I didn't recognize you without the—'

'Coat? Yes, it's become something of a costume these days.'

'Eddie said you were going to update the FBI. We weren't expecting you.'

'It has gotten to the stage where my involvement has become unavoidable, Miss Bloch. I take it you tailed me from that office the White Camelia were using?'

'Yeah, I—'

'I've been watching this house. I saw a man in a baseball hat enter through the front door, and I went around back. He took two shots at me from the kitchen floor. One I caught in the vest, and the other damn near took my head off. He ran out through the front door. I checked the property, and then I went back to their office. Come on over here, take a look at this.'

Bloch joined Berlin in the living room, saw a laptop open and the plans of the governor's mansion sitting on the coffee table. The front door opened and Bloch reached for her weapon, but Berlin held up a hand, telling her to relax. A blond-haired man walked in wearing a black suit, white shirt and black tie. He wore sunglasses and no expression.

'This is Mr. Anderson,' said Berlin. 'From Homeland Security. He's my driver.'

Anderson nodded.

Bloch nodded back, then turned her attention to the plans.

'Did you take those plans from their office?' she asked.

'No, the man in the baseball hat left them here. That's why I went back to the office and checked. They've cleaned that place out. The plans have been left here. And this laptop. Look . . .'

He ran a finger over the touchpad, bringing the laptop to life. Bloch leaned over and saw a chat forum open. She skim-read the title of the forum and a couple of comments. It was a radical-left chat room, discussing planned protests, attacks on hard-right action groups and what Antifa could do to help.

'What is this?' she asked.

'This has been planted here, Miss Bloch, to make it look as if Francis Edwards has been radicalized by communist radicals.'

'Radicalized? Why?'

No sooner had she asked the question, than the answer came to her. She took out her cell phone, called Eddie.

'Eddie, I'm at Francis Edwards's house with Berlin,' she said, and then told him what happened to Berlin, and what he had found. Eddie was always quick on the take. She didn't need to spell it out.

'We've been asking ourselves the wrong question about this case,' he said. 'We've been wondering why anyone would target Skylar

Edwards. Jesus, Skylar wasn't the target. The target was Francis. But why? Why him?'

'Because of his job,' said Bloch.

'A truck driver?' asked Eddie.

'No,' said Bloch. 'He's not a freelance driver, and he doesn't work for a haulage firm. He works for Solant Chemicals.'

There was silence on the phone.

Berlin gestured to Bloch, asking to speak to Eddie.

'It's me,' said Berlin. 'I've contacted Solant Chemicals. Francis showed up for work today, for the first time in months, and went out with a load. I asked them where the truck was right now, and they said he'd disabled the tracking device. I don't want to put out an APB because I don't know who in local law enforcement I can trust. Not yet. I've contacted the Governor's Office and they're already on high alert. I've got FBI and Homeland Security in helicopters looking for the truck.'

Eddie said something, but Bloch couldn't hear it. She didn't need to. It was the same question she would've asked.

What's on the truck?

'Propylene,' said Berlin.

Bloch swore, closed her eyes. If a tank full of propylene erupted it would cause a BLEVE – boiling liquid expanding vapor explosion. There was one every few years around the world. Most people wouldn't know about them, and they rarely made the news, but chemistry professors, like Gruber, would know. A BLEVE explosion of a propylene tank could wipe out a city block.

In Manhattan.

Berlin held the phone to his ear, but he was looking at Bloch as he spoke, as if he were addressing both of them.

'Edwards has been radicalized, but not by the far left. He's been taken in by the White Camelia. They've targeted him, indoctrinated him, and then destroyed his life systematically. A man who has a grudge, a cause and nothing to live for is highly dangerous. Francis is going to blow himself up. I have no doubt of that. The only question is who is he going to take with him.'

CHAPTER SIXTY-FIVE

HARRY

Harry Ford put down his empty glass of bourbon on the bar and called for a refill. Eddie had gone out to try and get some sandwiches and bottled water. Either he was taking his time or the good folk of Buckstown were being their usual helpful selves. The bartender at The Chanterelle was a young man who probably wasn't old enough to buy himself a drink and appeared happy about it. As he poured another bourbon for Harry, he gave him a look that was usually worn on the faces of those parishioners who were in the front row for eight o'clock mass on Sunday morning and knew in their hearts they were simply better people than the rest of the congregation behind them.

'The next one will make it six bourbons in a row,' said the bartender.

Harry studied the boy, said, 'How old are you?'

'Old enough to pour you a drink,' said the bartender.

'Fair enough. As long as you keep pouring, you and I will get on famously.'

'How many are you planning to have?'

'As many as it takes, kid. Why?'

'No reason, it's not good to get so drunk, you know?'

Harry leaned back in his bar stool, as if getting further away from the bartender might improve the situation.

'You would be the first bartender I've ever met who doesn't believe in getting people drunk. I hate to break it to you, kid, but you might not be cut out for this business.'

The bartender poured the bourbon, slid the glass to Harry and went about polishing a beer glass with his cloth.

The small bar in The Chanterelle had one round table, behind Harry, and then a set of double doors leading to the reception. A glass pane was set in the wall beside the double doors so the bartender always had a view of the receptionist. To Harry's left the wall was covered in photographs of old Hollywood stars – Frank Sinatra, Dean Martin, Brigitte Bardot, Audrey Hepburn, and more. Harry noticed there were no pictures of Sammy Davis Jnr. To his right a window looked onto the street.

It was this window that Harry kept an eye on. It was open, and anyone coming into the hotel, or pulling up outside, Harry would hear. There was no TV or music in the bar. It was like an airport lounge, only with less atmosphere.

A semi-truck pulled up outside, rather suddenly. The engine was revving too high when it pulled in, and the airbrakes screamed. He craned his neck, got a look at the driver.

It was dark out, but in the light from the dash Harry made out a familiar face.

Francis Edwards.

The skin on his face was redder than usual, sweat had stuck his hair down flat and he was breathing hard. He had a cell phone in his hand. The screen lit up. He tapped at the screen, looked at the hotel, looked back at the screen then tapped some more. Then he held the phone to his ear.

Harry heard a phone ringing. He swiveled the bar stool around and took a sip of his bourbon. The ringing died when the receptionist picked up the phone. Harry couldn't make her out, but he assumed she was giving the normal telephone greeting for the hotel, in the same dead-man's tone she seemed to do everything else.

Her expression changed. She looked out toward the front door.

The receptionist had a deeper tan than anyone Harry had ever met before. She had a face like a walnut, and just as hard, but right then Harry swore he saw her become paler. She slammed down the phone, looked left and right, her hands outstretched, palm up. She was talking to herself.

Checking the window, Harry saw Francis put the phone down and lean toward the wheel for a better look at the front of the hotel.

'What the hell is she doing?' said the bartender.

He had stopped polishing glasses and was now staring over Harry's shoulder through the glass pane at reception. Following his incredulous look, Harry saw the receptionist waving at the bartender, her arms beckoning him to her, and then flailing in the air, like she was desperately trying to land an airplane.

'Excuse me,' said the bartender. He threw up the counter top, walked out of the bar. The receptionist took hold of him and marched him right out the front door.

Francis watched them go, then blew out his cheeks, and let his head hit the rest behind him. Then he had another phone in his hand. Different from the smartphone he held before. This was old model. A Nokia maybe, with a small display.

Harry's cell phone rang. It was Eddie.

'Get Kate, Andy and Patricia and get out of the hotel right now. I'm only a few blocks away.'

'What's happening?' asked Harry.

'It's Francis Edwards. He was the target of this whole plan. They killed his daughter and his wife to break him. Then they gave him an enemy. He's in a truck with enough propylene to blow up half the town. I don't want to give him a target, so we've got to—'

'He's out front. In the truck. Right now,' said Harry.

'What? Get Kate, the clients, and get the hell out!'

'You need to call Kate,' said Harry. 'She's in her room.'

'Harry, whatever you're thinking of doing, just put it out of your mind. Get Kate and—'

Harry ended the call.

He hung his head for a moment, thought about his jacket, draped over the seat behind him, and the Colt 1911 in the inside pocket of that jacket.

Life certainly has its moments. In some ways a life can be defined by the decisions taken in a single heartbeat. Harry had already had his fair share. At fifteen years old, he lied about his age on an application form for the US Army. Heeding the advice from his night school tutor who suggested he take a law degree at college, which the Army paid for. And the moment he invited a young con artist for lunch after watching him argue his way out of liability for a car accident.

Harry drained his glass, got up off his seat and went behind the bar. He helped himself to the bottle of bourbon and nipped two glasses with the fingers of that same hand and came back around.

He left the jacket where it was, the gun still in the pocket, walked out of the lounge, through the empty reception and onto the street. Francis didn't seem to notice Harry; he was too busy staring at the little black phone. Harry opened the passenger door of the truck and got inside without saying a word.

'The hell you think you're doing?' said Francis.

There were tears mingling with the sweat on his face. His eyes were red and wet. On the little phone Harry saw a number displayed. It was the type of handset with a keypad, and a green phone symbol to make a call, and a red one to hang up. Francis had his thumb resting on the call button. Harry knew there was another burner phone somewhere on the truck, which would act as a triggering mechanism as soon as it received a call. It would make a circuit and cause an explosion big enough to rupture the tank and ignite the contents.

Harry closed the door, dropped one glass into his lap and began pouring the bourbon into the other. It was a double, at least. He put the half-filled glass on the dashboard, poured out another. This one he put in the middle of the dash.

'Will you join me?' asked Harry.

'You're one of those goddamn New York lawyers, here to set free the man who killed my daughter. I don't drink with the likes of you.'

'Suit yourself,' said Harry, swallowing the shot in one.

'You have no idea what's happening,' said Francis. 'Maybe it's good that you're in here with me.'

'I know this whole truck is now a bomb,' said Harry. He glanced down and in the space between his feet and Francis's was a large briefcase. Probably packed with explosive, not enough to cause major damage on its own, but enough to rupture the tank and ignite its contents, which would do more damage than Harry wanted to imagine.

'I know you can trigger the device at our feet by pushing that call button. I know I left a gun in the bar, in my jacket. A Colt 1911. My old service weapon. I made a choice tonight. I knew what you were doing, and I could've put a round through your eye from the lounge of the hotel. But I didn't. I came here with a bottle, and I don't intend to drink it all on my own.'

From the look on his face, Francis didn't know quite what to say.

Harry poured another, said, 'You know, I can see that you're hurting real bad. I'm very deeply sorry about what happened to your daughter and your wife. From what I've read about your daughter, she strikes me as a special person. A good person. That doesn't come from nowhere. I think you're a good man, and your wife was a good woman too. Pain, grief, injustice – it can change people.'

Breathing hard, Francis said, 'The whole system is stacked against us. Us whites. I was too blind to see it before.'

'You know that's not true. The people who put this idea in your head. The people who gave you this case, that phone – they don't care about you. They live off hate. It's all they've got. I can't believe there was hate in your house when Skylar was growing up. People don't start off hating one another. It has to be taught. It's learned. You didn't teach this shit to your daughter. She was friends with Andy, and his color didn't matter to her. It shouldn't matter to you.'

'What matters is he killed her, and you're helping him,' he said.

Harry poured another drink, said, 'You were in court the other day and I'm sure the DA, the newspapers and TV news have been keeping you up to date. Now you know there are a lot of questions about the night of Skylar's murder, which the prosecutor can't answer. Skylar didn't die in that lot; someone would've heard the struggle. And Lomax scratched Andy's back. His nail clippings that were analyzed for Andy's blood, not Skylar's—'

Cutting off Harry, Francis said, 'Lomax knew Dubois was guilty. Lomax was just making sure he didn't get off.'

Harry lowered his head, 'Lomax saw an easy arrest. He didn't care about getting the right person for Skylar's murder, just the one he could convict. Lomax had his own troubles, too. His wife, and a poisonous man whispering in his ear every day. He had his own pain. You know, people who are in pain do one of two things. They either want to make sure no one else goes through the kind of pain they are dealing with, or they want everyone to hurt like they do. You know only one of those options has a future. If you cause others pain, you will forever be its prisoner. You know that. That's why you haven't gotten out of this truck. You could walk away, detonate that device from a mile away. But you're here. You want it all to end. Don't you want to know the truth about what happened to Skylar?'

For a few seconds, Francis stared at the glass of bourbon on the dash. Then he looked at the phone in his hand.

'Why should I believe you?' he asked, fresh tears in his eyes, his thumb touching the call button.

'I think you'll know the truth when you hear it. A lot about that night doesn't make sense. It doesn't fit with the prosecution's case. The marks on Skylar's face, those came from a cop's ring. That's not a fancy lawyer argument, the marks are there. On her skin.'

Francis's breathing quickened even more, he shut his eyes tight and punched the steering wheel.

'This is all bullshit, you're lying to me,' he said, taking the phone in two hands.

'Maybe I am, maybe I'm not. That's up to you. I wouldn't be here if I didn't think you were worth saving. I would've just shot you in the head from the bar window. Now, either you pick up that glass and have a drink with me, and I'll tell you what really happened to your daughter, or you push that button. It's up to you.'

CHAPTER SIXTY-SIX

EDDIE

Soon as Harry hung up on me, I called Kate, told her to grab Andy, Patricia, and Harry if she could, and get the hell out of the hotel. Then I called Bloch, put the phone away and ran.

My feet pounded along the street. I was five minutes from the hotel. I'd dropped the sandwiches and the drinks soon as I got the call from Bloch, and just sprinted back in the direction of The Chanterelle.

A large SUV pulled alongside me and the rear passenger window buzzed open. It was Bloch.

'Get in,' she said.

The vehicle stopped, I ran around to the other side and got in. Berlin was in the passenger seat up front and a guy I didn't recognize was driving.

'Harry's going to try to talk this guy down. I know it,' I said.

'Why would he do that?' asked Berlin.

'Because he's old and stupid and he believes in people.'

I held onto the backseat as the SUV turned off Main Street, tires protesting at the speed and angle of the turn, the car leaning to the left, forcing my right shoulder into Bloch, my head turning quickly, looking for the truck.

I didn't need to look too hard.

'Up ahead,' said Berlin, from the front seat. 'Slow down, drive past it so we can take a look.'

The man behind the wheel put pressure on the brakes, slowing the car, and we cruised past the truck. Harry was in the cab with Francis, and he was pouring himself a drink.

'Stop the car,' said Bloch.

Berlin waved at the driver to keep moving.

'Stop! Edwards is still in the cab. Harry's with him,' she said, pulling at the door release. The door didn't open. All doors were locked and controlled by the driver's console.

'Let me out,' said Bloch.

I grabbed the door release, pulled on it. Nothing happened.

'Wait. Anderson, turn this thing around. Go back and then swing the car so I can see what's going on in the cab of that truck,' said Berlin.

The guy I guessed was called Anderson spun the wheel, and we drove past the truck, maybe another hundred yards and then he put the SUV across the street, blocking any traffic from getting near the truck.

Anderson pulled a pistol from a black suit jacket.

'There's no shot,' said Berlin. 'You might rupture the tank.'

'Flank him, to the side. Let me out,' said Bloch.

She was agitated, her voice well above normal volume. This was Bloch in a panic.

'Calm down, Bloch,' said Berlin. 'There's no shot. Even if you flank this guy and put two in his head the round could ricochet. You could hit Harry, or the round could bounce off the inside of Edwards' skull and tear a hole through the cab and the tank.'

'Let me out. I'll take Edwards out of the cab before I put him down,' she said.

I got a good look inside the cab. Harry had a glass of bourbon in his hand. Edwards was holding a mobile phone. Harry's lips were moving, Edwards was listening.

'Harry's trying to talk him down. We have to give him a chance,' I said.

'Let me out of this car and I'll take down Edwards. We're losing too much time,' said Bloch.

Berlin's voice cut through the car. 'You can't! He'll see you coming and blow the whole town.'

Bloch let out a roar, punched the back of the seat.

Berlin was right. There was nothing we could do. Not now. If we spooked Edwards in any way, then it was all over.

I could taste bile in my mouth, I wanted to be sick. I couldn't look, but at the same time I couldn't take my eyes off the cab. Harry was still talking. He looked relaxed. A bottle of bourbon appeared and Harry refilled his glass, then took a sip. There was another glass on the dash between Harry and Edwards. The glass had bourbon in it, but it sat untouched.

I swallowed, listened to my heart kicking at my chest.

'I should never have left him,' said Bloch.

Francis Edwards was holding a phone. An old one. A burner. Disposable, and probably a detonator. His eyes were wild. He was rocking back and forth in the cab, gently. Holding the phone in his hand, wiping away tears and then staring hard at that phone.

Harry continued to talk.

Edwards threw his head back, his mouth wide open. I heard a faint scream. A cry, from his throat. I tried to speak, but I couldn't make a sound. I had no breath. I grunted, forced the words out.

'We've got to do something! He's going to trigger the detonator.'

CHAPTER SIXTY-SEVEN

KATE

Kate woke suddenly. She was slumped over the dresser, her head resting on her forearm, a sea of paper in front of her. Still in her suit.

Her phone was ringing.

She picked it up. It was Eddie.

'Hello?' said Kate, her voice still thick from sleep.

'There's a truck outside the hotel with a bomb inside. Get Andy, get Patricia and get the hell out the back, right now and get clear of the building. Don't come out the front door! If you see Harry, grab him, if not just get out!'

He hung up before Kate could process the information, never mind speak. Kate looked around the room. Her case files and notes were spread out all over the beds and the desk. She needed them. Andy's case depended on it. She got up, telling herself to keep it together. She tried to take a deep breath, but it didn't work. Her chest was closing up, her stomach cramping. Panic was taking hold.

She left the paper where it was, ran down a floor and started hammering on Andy and Patricia's door. Andy answered straight away. He'd been watching TV with his mom.

Kate stumbled over the words at first, put her hand on the doorframe to steady herself, and then said, 'We've got to get out of here right now. It isn't safe,' said Kate.

Andy went back into the room, Kate holding the door open, and he started to pack.

'We don't have time. We've got to go right now. Right this second,' said Kate.

Patricia tried to get up off the bed, but cried out when she put her weight down on her swollen ankle. The day, like every day, had taken its toll on Patricia Dubois. Andy helped her up. She was in her dressing gown and slippers. Andy in sweatpants and a tee.

He helped Patricia to get moving, supporting her weight on her weak side, holding onto her arm with one hand, his other arm draped around her for balance.

With every step Patricia grew a little stronger, and the ankle became accustomed to the weight. They left the room, Kate let go of the door and led them down the hallway to the stairs. There were no other guests in The Chanterelle. They were one floor up. No elevators. They took the stairs as fast as they could, Patricia holding onto the rail with one hand and Andy on her bad side.

They reached ground level. The bar, lounge and reception were empty. The front door was wide open. Kate could hear a large engine idling.

Eddie had told her not to use to front exit.

She looked around, but there were no signs for an exit other than the front door.

'We should get out the front while we can,' said Patricia.

'No, we can't go that way,' said Kate, breathing hard. It wasn't from the light running. Kate was short on breath because she was on the verge of panic. It was stripping down her strength – and stopping her from thinking clearly.

Shutting her eyes tightly, Kate swore, then dug her nails into her palms. She needed something. A jolt. A sharp flash to wake her up from this rising, nervous energy that took over her body and mind. Clouding everything.

It worked.

'Kitchen,' said Kate.

The Chanterelle only served one meal a day. Breakfast. With a choice of pancakes and eggs, or eggs and pancakes. They had both. On Thursdays it was waffles and bacon. Served in the lounge.

Kate took off down the hallway toward a door with a sign on it that read *Staff Only*. She tried the handle and the door opened to reveal a small kitchen. White tile on the wall, yellowed with grease, a grill on the other side of the stainless-steel island in the center of the room. Next to the grill – a fire door.

'Come on,' she said.

Andy and Patricia followed Kate into the kitchen, around the island, and Kate saw the bar on the fire door had been broken. She pushed it, shoved it with her shoulder and the door gave way to the outside. Kate held the door for Andy and Patricia. There was a step down from the kitchen to the back lot.

Once they were through, Kate came out and the fire door slammed shut behind her.

Andy and Patricia were standing there. Unmoving.

'We need to get clear of the building. There's . . .'

Kate's voice trailed off as she joined the mother and son. They were in a rear storage area for the hotel. Busted lounge seats, an old mattress and various cardboard boxes lined an area not much bigger than one of the bedrooms in the place, with the entire area caged off with a ten-foot-tall chicken wire fence.

There was a door in the fence, made of aluminum bars and chicken wire, with a deadbolt that went through the metal bar that was part of the doorframe. The deadbolt was padlocked.

'We can't get out,' said Patricia, gasping for air. The exertion was part of it, but she was scared too.

The padlock wasn't new, but it looked sturdy and secure. Kate looked around for something heavy, anything she could use to break the lock. There was an old gas cylinder, rusted to the ground behind some garbage bags but she didn't think she could lift it. An old paint can, but that wouldn't be heavy enough.

At the door of the fence they were maybe twelve feet from the building. Certainly not clear of it. If a bomb did go off, they were not safe. Not even close.

Andy ran past her and leapt at the fence. He climbed over, dropped down to the other side. Beyond the fence was an alley, with more trash and old boxes piled up.

'Andy, go. Get out of here. We'll be okay, but you need to go. We can't let anything happen to you,' said Kate.

'Go, baby. Get out of here,' said Patricia, tears glinting on her face in the moonlight.

Andy looked at Kate. Then his mom. He turned and ran down the alley.

Kate breathed out, put an arm around Patricia and looked back at the hotel. It was an old wooden building, and it would fall like a house of matches.

The fence was too high for her to climb. And even if she could get over it, which she doubted, she wasn't going to leave Patricia.

'Go on, you too. I'll be okay,' said Patricia.

'I'm not leaving you,' said Kate.

She heard something in the alley. Footsteps. Someone coming up on them in the dark. Fast.

She took Patricia by the shoulders, gently, and they eased back from the fence. Maybe it was one of the White Camelias, come to make sure no one got out of the hotel alive.

As the figure got closer, Kate took a great shuddering breath, and let it out with tears of her own.

Andy held a long, thick steel pipe on his shoulder. He dropped it to the ground. Wedged it under the fence door, and pushed. The door held, and Andy began to pump the steel bar up, using his legs and back, the bar resting on his shoulder, the other end wedged low beneath the door.

The aluminum bars that formed the door squealed and bent. Rust flaked from the hinges.

Andy began roaring with the effort, pumping his legs, trying to get the bar higher each time.

But the door wouldn't give.

CHAPTER SIXTY-EIGHT

HARRY

Harry closed his eyes, listened to Francis Edwards cry out. It sounded like something Harry had heard before. Humans can make a sound that comes from deep inside. It's part of them. Harry thought it might come from the soul. It's the sound of a parent who has lost a child. There's anguish and pain and something else in there. Something so profound it doesn't need to be explained.

Francis let his head drift forward onto the wheel, and wept. His shoulders pumping the tears and the sobs out of him.

'Now you know the truth,' said Harry, putting away his phone. He'd shown Francis the pictures of the paint flakes on the rope, showing that Esther was strangled and then hauled up into the air.

'They were starting a war. What they did to Skylar's body, it's significant for them. They place great importance on symbols and flags because it means they don't have to think about a real ideology. Makes it easier to hate if you're all wearing the same uniform and walking under the same banner. They tried to blow up some churches around here, but it failed. And then they got smart. Killing innocent people won't further their cause. What they wanted was legitimacy. For people to rally to them. The trucks coming out of your plant are ready-made catastrophes. All it took was someone willing to die. Gruber would've taught Skylar, so that was their way in – with you. He could reach out after she died, help you and your family. And then poison you and take away every reason you had to live.'

'They did that, alright. I bought all of their bullshit. Jesus, my poor girls.'

'The laptop and the plans made you look like their enemy. You were a crazed, commie leftist and they would've used you as their reason to recruit every idiot in this town. They've already printed their flyers for a march.'

The sobs slowed, Francis wiped his face with one hand, the other still clutching the phone. He leaned back in his seat and caught his breath.

'You ready for that drink now?' asked Harry.

He blew air out of his cheeks, wiped his face again, then leaned forward and picked up the glass.

'Did you put something in this? Something to knock me out?' asked Francis.

'I don't need to. You drink enough of this it'll put you on your back all on its own.'

Francis threw back the liquor, shook his head, and gasped.

'You're not a drinker,' said Harry. 'I can teach you.'

'No, thanks,' said Francis. And there, somewhere on his face, was the look of a man completely defeated by life, by loss, by anger.

'Thank you,' said Francis. 'Thank you for telling me.'

Harry watched Francis's chest beginning to move again, rapidly, in and out. The panic building.

'I know something too,' he said. 'I don't much care what they say about me after. I can't live like this anymore. I don't want to. So do me a favor and get out of the truck. I'll give you five minutes to get clear.'

Harry reached out a hand, slowly, put it on Francis's thick shoulder.

'You don't want to do this,' said Harry.

Francis shook his head. 'No, I do. I need to.'

His thumb covered the call button again, then rested upon it gently. Francis wiped his face and stared at the phone.

'You should get out, get away from here,' said Francis.

'I'm not going anywhere,' said Harry. 'I've got a bottle of bourbon in here that I haven't paid for, and no one else to drink it with but you.'

'I can't go on being . . .' began Francis, then bit his lower lip. As he panted, sweat blew off his lips in a tiny shower.

He grunted, moaned, and forced it out.

'I don't want to be in a world without my girls,' he said.

'There's no getting over this kind of pain. It's huge right now. It's in your face every minute, every second. But it won't stay that way. It will be there, always, but you won't notice it every day.'

Harry stayed quiet and listened to the big man crying. Harry poured him another.

Francis started nodding his head, coming out of it. He took another drink. Got his breath. But he definitely wasn't used to the bourbon.

'I think I'm going to puke,' said Francis. With the phone still in his hand, he pulled the door handle. The driver's door cracked open.

CHAPTER SIXTY-NINE

EDDIE

I could taste blood in my mouth. It startled me for a second. Then I realized I'd bitten through my lip. The sting only came with the realization. At first, I'd thought Edwards was going to push the button, but then he'd taken the glass on the dash, drunk it and talked to Harry.

Now it looked like he was working himself up again. Into a panic.

He had the phone in his hand still. Why didn't he put it down?

I heard sirens, turned, and two Sheriff's cruisers squeezed past the SUV. Shipley leaned out of the window as they went past, said, 'Get back!'

The vehicles formed a barricade across the street, maybe thirty feet in front of us. Leonard and two other deputies got out of the cars and used them for cover, immediately drawing their weapons and aiming them at the truck. Shipley popped the trunk of the cruiser and lifted clear a semi-automatic rifle with a scope.

'Don't fire,' said Berlin, walking toward them, his ID held high. He talked to Shipley, but I couldn't hear what was being said.

Then the driver's door of the truck opened.

Shipley pushed Berlin away, slapped the barrel of the rifle on the roof of the Sheriff's cruiser and took aim.

CHAPTER SEVENTY

HARRY

Harry took hold of Francis's arm, tightly. He had one foot out of the cab when he turned back.

'Give me the phone,' said Harry.

Francis bowed his head, looked at the small device in his hands, as if it was somehow unbelievable that such a small thing could trigger so much harm.

Harry had watched the local police show up. Probably tipped off by the feds and the chemical plant. Berlin was arguing with Shipley.

Francis placed the phone on the dash. Harry picked it up, waved it at the police.

'Maybe stay in the cab until they come get you,' said Harry as Shipley pushed Berlin out of the way, and then pointed that rifle at the truck. 'They haven't shot you because they were worried about hitting the truck. Stay in here,' said Harry.

'Thank you,' said Francis. 'Thank you for telling me what happened to Skylar and Esther.'

All four sheriff's deputies had their weapons aimed at the truck. Harry felt his gut tightening as Francis put two feet on the ground. He'd seen the deputies too. And Harry knew Francis had made a decision. The door of the truck kept the top half of Francis's body shielded from the rifles trained at him.

'Francis, come back inside. Please,' said Harry.

Francis shook his head.

'Who did this to you? Who got you into all this?' asked Harry, desperate to keep him talking.

Francis clutched at his chest. He took one step to the side.

'He called himself the Pastor—' said Francis, but if he managed any more words, they were drowned out.

Harry covered his ears with his palms, turned away. He couldn't look. The tension in the boiling air was suddenly cut with gunfire. Even with his eyes closed, Harry couldn't escape what was happening around him. His mind put images to the sounds. He saw the bullet holes sprouting blood roses on Francis's chest and face. When the shooting stopped, Harry was still covering his ears so that he didn't hear his own scream.

Then the door to his cab opened and Harry had no choice but to look. Berlin pulled him out of the truck and Bloch immediately grabbed Harry, took him in her arms and held him close and tight.

'Whoa, I'm alright,' said Harry.

Eddie hung up the phone, and within a minute Kate came running out of The Chanterelle's front door, and into another of Bloch's hugs. Kate's eyes blazed open in surprise, and she put her arms around her friend.

Eddie came back around the semi, walked up to Harry and punched him on the arm.

'What was that for?' asked Harry.

'For almost getting yourself killed. Don't ever put yourself in a situation where you can get killed. That's *my* job.'

They looked at each other for a time, as the relief ebbed into sorrow.

'He walked into those guns deliberately,' said Harry. 'He's a victim too.'

Eddie nodded, but didn't say anything. Not at first. He looked past Harry, at Berlin who was huddled in whispered conversation with the man who had driven the SUV – Anderson. Whatever they were discussing, Harry didn't want to know. Berlin was a dangerous man. By the look of him, Anderson was too. Harry looked down at his left hand. It was shaking, and right then he only wanted it to stop.

'Tell Berlin we need to talk,' said Harry. 'Kate and Bloch too. I asked Francis who put him up to this. It wasn't just Gruber. He said a name. I think it's a nickname for the leader of the White

Camelia. They pretended to have a Christian foundation, and there would be sermons at their meetings. He called him *the Pastor*. He didn't get to tell me his real name. We've got to find this man. I've got a Colt in my jacket that I'm itching to use.'

CHAPTER SEVENTY-ONE

TAYLOR AVERY

Taylor Avery couldn't sleep.

He sat on his porch, tea in his hand, the sounds of the Alabama night all around him. It was past midnight now and he felt tired. His copy of *To Kill A Mockingbird* had fallen from his grip half an hour ago as he dozed, and the yellowed pages called to him from the boards of his porch.

Where before there had been solace in that book, he could find none now. It was no longer a tale of people he didn't know, and a place that was strange. It was here and now. And he was one of the jurors. He knew what he should do. The evidence in the case against the Dubois kid smelled like horseshit. And he knew what that smelled like. You didn't need to be a lawyer to catch a whiff, farmers could smell it just as easily.

He heard the rumble of the engine long before he saw the car. The lights swept over the siding of the farmhouse as the car turned and stopped. The engine died, the door opened and closed.

He didn't hear Korn's footsteps. The man moved like he was part of the darkness. He stepped up onto the porch, papers in his long, thin fingers.

'Evening,' said Korn.

Taylor nodded, but didn't get up to shake Korn's hand.

Korn held out the papers. Taylor took them, and for a second, his fingers brushed with Korn's, and he felt the coldness of the man's touch.

'This is an application for compulsory land purchase. It includes the farm,' said Korn.

Taylor flicked through the pages. A company called Maxx

Development wanted a thousand acres. They were offering half of what the land was worth.

The last page had a space for a signature.

'Maxx Developments want your farm, Mr. Avery. I will see to it that they don't get it.'

'Thank you,' said Taylor. 'It's strange though.'

'Strange?'

'That they should put in a bid and application now, while I'm on this jury.'

Korn leaned over, put his hands on the armrests of Taylor's chair, their faces just inches from one another.

'I'm a shareholder in Maxx Developments,' said Korn. 'I persuaded the board this was a good investment, and that the county would be open to our application. I can shut this down, at any time. You bring home the guilty verdict in the case, and all of that goes away. You'll be left in peace. Your land protected. But have no illusions, if you fight me you'll be on the street in a month.'

Korn straightened up, and Taylor caught another whiff of something. Not bullshit. Something bad. Something decayed.

He watched the prosecutor leave without another word. There was no more convincing to be done. Taylor took the man at his word. He was telling the truth. Taylor knew what would happen if he defied him, and what would happen if he played along.

He sipped at his tea, looked down at the book on the porch.

It was a choice he never thought he would have to make. Principles have a cost. While Taylor was willing to pay the price, he didn't want his family to lose their home because he did the right thing. If doing the right thing hurt his family, well, was it really the right thing to do?

Rubbing at his forehead, he decided there was no choice.

He knew the other jurors on the case by name. They were part of his community, and it was clear they listened to him. He could get every juror to vote guilty. Of that there was no doubt.

Korn had picked the right man for the job. No juror would vote against him if he put his name to a guilty vote.

Taylor picked up his book, walked down the porch steps to the trash, threw the book on top of the garbage bags and closed the lid.

It was only a book.

This was the real world. He stared up at the window of his son's bedroom. The lamp was on. His kid was up there now, reading.

Avery swore, lifted the lid of the trashcan and retrieved the book.

CHAPTER SEVENTY-TWO

EDDIE

Kate had done her prep on Deputy Leonard. She was ready when Korn called him to the stand at ten o'clock that morning. She stretched her back, turned to a fresh page on her notebook poised to write down every word of Leonard's testimony. He would testify that Sheriff Lomax faithfully recorded Andy's confession.

There was a freight train of problems headed Leonard's way. It was clear Lomax had beaten the confession out of Andy before he had seen the report from the medical examiner. In the signed confession Andy stated:

My shift finished at twelve midnight, and I followed a fellow employee, Skylar Edwards, into the lot. I know Skylar. We have worked together for a while. She is pretty and I liked her. I wanted to kiss Skylar, but she pushed me away. I grabbed a hold of her and squeezed. She struggled and I made sure she stayed quiet. I didn't mean to hurt her. She stopped struggling and I squeezed harder. Afterward I felt real bad. There's a stretch of marshland beyond the parking lot, and I took her there and buried her so no one would find her.

The medical examiner said that Skylar Edwards' body had been burned by the sun. If Andy says he killed her at midnight, and then buried her, then she can't have been sunburned. Or Andy's confession is bullshit.

Kate was well armed, and she had written out some questions to bury Leonard in his lies. Man, she couldn't wait to get Leonard on the stand.

Harry didn't look so fresh. Neither did Bloch. There had been little sleep that night, but Kate was used to all-nighters. I had put on a fresh suit and tie and the management of The Chanterelle laid on fresh coffee for me that morning. I wondered if they would be as accommodating if they'd known Harry had helped himself to a case of bourbon.

I guessed not.

Patricia and Andy were about done. Neither of them had slept and Andy looked even thinner in that big suit. They held hands, like always. Only this time, there was a tremor in their grip. I couldn't tell if it was Andy's or Patricia's arm that was shaking.

Korn stood to address the judge. He buttoned his jacket, chin held high and his back straight. Like a man who'd already won. As if not a single thing we'd done mattered to him at all. I saw his witness, Leonard, fidgeting in the front row behind Korn and Wingfield. He had the excitable energy of someone about to take the stand. Deputy Leonard had combed his hair, trimmed his moustache and worn a shirt that didn't stretch across his stomach like he was about to have an alien burst out of it.

'Your Honor,' said Korn, 'the People call Deputy Sheriff . . .'

But he didn't finish his sentence. No one interrupted him. His voice simply tailed off as his gaze was drawn to the jury stand.

I looked over and I saw one of the jurors standing.

'Your Honor, I have something to say,' said the juror. It was Taylor Avery. One of the cool, rational heads that we were relying on.

'Yes, is there a problem?' asked the judge.

'Well, sir,' said Avery. Reaching behind him, he took some folded documents from the hip pocket of his blue jeans, and began to straighten them out. 'I've thought long and hard about this. I don't talk in public and I don't rightly know how to say this—'

'Mr. Avery, the jury is not permitted to make a statement. I want to stop you there, before this goes any further. You understand?'

'I can't say something?'

'No, a juror cannot say anything in court. If there is a question, the jury can pose a question, but that is usually written down and sent to me.'

Avery took a pen from his shirt pocket, scribbled something on the pages and made to hand them to the bailiff. The bailiff looked at the juror, then looked at the judge. It was Judge Chandler who said it was alright, he would read what had been written down.

The bailiff handed the pages to the judge.

'Your Honor, this is highly irregular,' said Korn.

He didn't look so confident now, and I had no idea what was going on. Judge Chandler didn't acknowledge Korn's statement. Not at first. He read the note, flicked through the pages and then placed them on his desk. He turned to Taylor Avery, and there seemed to be something passed between them in that look. Some kind of recognition.

'Mr. Korn,' said Judge Chandler, 'you are correct, this is most irregular. I have a question from this juror. He asks this – *why is Mr. Korn threatening to take my land away from me if I don't persuade my fellow jurors to vote guilty in this case?*'

I've seen a lot of things in my time in the courtroom, but I never saw anything like this. There was an audible collective gasp from the people in the gallery.

Korn smiled, waved a hand as if he was swatting away a ridiculous insinuation. The judge's attention drifted from Korn, to Avery, and then back to the district attorney.

'That is a ridiculous accusation. Where is his proof?'

'My word. I don't have any proof other than my good name,' said Avery. 'I'm telling the truth, it's the right thing to do.'

Judge Chandler nodded. I got the impression he believed Avery, but without proof it was one farmer's word against the district attorney. And that bird was never going to fly.

'Your Honor,' said Korn. 'There is something which has just been brought to my attention by Deputy Leonard. I didn't bring it up before because I have just learned of it and wanted to establish the facts. Now it appears appropriate that I should act upon this information. I am asking the court to declare a mistrial and for the bailiffs to place Mr. Flynn under arrest.'

This was Korn's back-up plan.

He'd been confident because he thought he had bought the jury. But Mr. Avery had refused. I got the impression that Korn was rarely refused anything. And yet this defeat, so public, and so shameful, had been in the works for a long time. People will only tolerate so much. At some point, one person will make a stand.

Avery looked more than uncomfortable – he was damned scared. And he had every right to be. And yet there he was. Speaking up. Not for himself, but for Andy.

Now that Korn's plan to strong-arm a guilty verdict had failed, he was pulling the plug on the whole trial. And he was coming after me.

'Your Honor,' said Korn, 'the only jury tampering that has gone on in this case was performed by Mr. Flynn. And unlike the spurious allegation made by juror Avery, I have proof, and I have a witness – the juror that Mr. Flynn bribed.'

Judge Chandler looked as though a freight train had just rattled through his courtroom.

'That is a serious, criminal allegation, Mr. Korn. Which juror?'

'Juror Sandy Boyette,' said Korn.

Judge Chandler turned to the jury. Sandy sat with her head down as he bellowed at her.

'Miss Boyette, stand up! What do you have to say about this? Have you received a bribe in exchange for your vote in this case?'

Sandy stood up, raised her head and looked at me. Some tears were forming in her eyes as she then turned to the judge. She swallowed, buying whatever time she could to find the right words.

'Well? Is it true? Have you been bribed?' shouted the judge.

'Yes, Your Honor,' said Sandy.

'Bailiffs, arrest Flynn,' shouted Chandler.

CHAPTER SEVENTY-THREE

EDDIE

Two court bailiffs stepped toward me.

'Your Honor, may I be allowed a moment. I think there's been a misunderstanding here,' I said.

'In what possible way has there been a misunderstanding?' asked Chandler.

'Your Honor,' interrupted Korn, taking an envelope from his pocket and opening it, 'I have here photographs of Mr. Flynn speaking with the juror in a chop house outside of town. These were taken by my assistant district attorney, Mr. Wingfield. To remove any possible doubt about the situation, here is a photograph of a leather bag, filled with money in this juror's apartment. Fifty thousand dollars in cash. Deputy Leonard took that photograph.'

Chandler was passed the photographs from the clerk. He examined them one by one.

Kate handed me a phone. I gave it to the clerk, told her the judge should look at the photos and the video. He took it from her, started swiping his finger across the screen. Then as he stared at the phone, and I heard the muffled audio from the phone's speakers.

'What is the meaning of this?' he asked.

'Your Honor, ask the juror,' I said.

'I can tell you exactly what happened,' said Sandy. 'Mr. Korn approached me privately and said he wanted to discuss the trial. He said we could help each other. I was scared and I didn't know what to do, so I spoke to Mr. Flynn, told him about it, and he said I should protect myself and be careful if anyone offered me money. His investigator gave me a pair of Minnie Mouse pajamas with a small video camera on one of the buttons. She also took the photo

378

you have there on that phone. It shows Mr. Korn walking into my apartment with that bag in *his* hand. Deputy Leonard was in on it too. Your Honor, I didn't want any money. I just wanted to do my duty. I took the video of my conversation with Mr. Korn in my apartment and I showed it to Mr. Flynn. He said I should ignore everything and just give an honest verdict and if I was asked about it, I should tell the court and agree to testify against Mr. Korn.'

Chandler studied the photograph I'd given to him. And it was clear as day. Bloch had taken the picture herself. There was Korn, outside Sandy's apartment, holding the leather bag full of money. And the video was perfect. There was Korn, in Sandy's apartment, giving her his speech, laying the trap for me. In Kate's divorce practice, Bloch's Minnie Mouse pajama cam gave them more incriminating evidence than they ever needed.

We'd flipped the script.

'Mr. Korn—' said Judge Chandler, but the DA was scrambling now.

'Your Honor, my assistant Tom Wingfield will affirm my version of events.'

Beside Korn, Wingfield stood and addressed the court.

'Your Honor, I'm afraid I have no idea what Mr. Korn is referring to. This is the first I've heard of this.'

Korn looked like he'd been stabbed. His mouth opened. Wingfield wasn't on video in Sandy's apartment, and he was distancing himself from Korn because he knew what was coming down the pike.

'Your Honor, I . . .' But Korn's words died in his throat.

Sandy was perfect. We'd suckered Korn into trying to frame me. I almost felt sorry for him.

'I don't want to hear any more from you, Mr. Korn. Bailiffs, arrest Mr. Korn and Deputy Leonard.'

Korn backed away at first, but then relented. Leonard fought the bailiffs at first, and then a shot to the ribs with an elbow took all the fight out of him.

'Before you go, Mr. Korn,' said Judge Chandler. 'I want you to hear this. I am dismissing this case against Andy Dubois, for clear prosecutorial misconduct. Mr. Dubois, you are free to leave. And please go with my apologies. You have faced an unfair trial, and for that I am truly sorry.'

The bailiffs escorted Korn, in handcuffs, through the courtroom to the side door, leading to the cells. He limped along, and as he passed me I saw his real face.

His slash of a mouth was twisted in anger, and his eyes were blazing. I caught his scent again. The smell of rotten flesh.

I turned away in disgust, and watched with Kate and Harry as Andy and Patricia disappeared into one another in an embrace that would last a lifetime.

CHAPTER SEVENTY-FOUR

BLOCH

Mr. Anderson pulled up outside 224 Calabasas Road. It was a run-down stucco house with paint peeling off the walls and rotten window frames. The lawn was high, and there were children's toys in the long grass, faded with the sun, as if they hadn't been used in a long time. If there was a poster for a home where the husband got the house and the wife got the kids after the divorce, it was this one.

The local radio was all about the attempted bombing carried out last night by Francis Edwards. The news confirmed he had been shot and killed on scene, and that local law enforcement were investigating. There was one other major news story, but it was getting buried under the attempted bombing lead. Last night, Hogg's Bar was robbed and the owner, Ryan Hogg, was shot and killed by the perpetrator who is said to have been seen leaving the bar carrying an automatic weapon.

Possibly an AR-15.

It looked to Berlin and Bloch like the Pastor was cleaning house. Professor Gruber had been reported missing by his mother. He had not been seen for two days.

Berlin led the way up the gravel path to the front door. He stood to the left side of the door, Anderson on the right and Bloch standing back. Berlin knocked.

Brian Denvir must've watched them walk up to the house, because he called out immediately.

'You are trespassing on private property. I am armed, and I will use deadly force to defend myself and my property. Leave now!'

'He doesn't sound too friendly,' said Berlin, then shouted back, 'Mr. Denvir, this is Homeland Security. Please lay down any firearms and step out of the house.'

Silence.

'You're trespassers! Get off my property. I'll give you to the count of three, and then I'm gonna start shooting.'

'Mr. Denvir, it is preferable that you and I have a conversation. I would like that very much. You are not under arrest.'

'One!' cried Denvir.

'Answer my question and we will leave you alone. We don't care about Hogg and any others you've killed. Tell us what we want to know and you're a free man.'

Either Denvir couldn't remember what came after one, or he was through talking, as a burst of automatic fire began shredding the front door. All three of them lay flat on the ground.

Berlin nodded to Anderson.

Anderson said nothing. He crawled to a side window to the right of the front door, quickly glanced inside, then ducked back down, shook his head.

Crawling to the window to the left of the front door, Bloch raised her head quickly, then dropped back down. She realized Anderson's problem immediately. The layout of the house made a frontal assault perilous. A wide hallway, with open-plan living room on the right and dining area on the left meant that Denvir could stand at the foot of the staircase and cover the entire front of the property with a field of fire.

He wore Kevlar body armor on his chest, arms, legs too. And a full combat helmet.

They heard a dog barking. A big dog.

There was a BEWARE OF THE DOG sign on the front gate, and the side of the house was secured with a seven-foot-high fence. Getting around back would be difficult. And the dog would serve as an early warning for Denvir, which would eliminate the element of surprise for that flank, thereby eliminating it from their options.

Anderson popped up at his side window, fired four rounds, fast. All four in under a second and a half, then dropped back down.

A burst of automatic fire in Anderson's direction answered the question. Bloch checked the window at her side.

The quiet man, Anderson, didn't strike Bloch as the type of guy to miss. She could tell by the way he held the Glock that he knew what he was doing. A bullet from that gun would find its target.

Anderson fired back. Bloch watched from her window and saw one round ping from Denvir's helmet. The rest would've found their mark, but in vain. Denvir was too well armored.

Bloch took out her cell phone, selected the camera option and placed it at the corner of the window, the base resting on the sill, angling it so that she could see Denvir on screen. She only needed a few seconds, and only a few inches of the phone were showing. Bloch got up on one knee, drew her weapon.

She looked at the phone, glanced through the window. Got her bearings as to where she was aiming in relation to where Denvir was standing.

Maggie felt heavy in her hands. She hadn't hit the range in a week now, and she was feeling it. Having chosen this gun specifically because she would only need to fire it once at a target, Bloch estimated she would need three shots.

One to calibrate.

One to adjust.

One to hit the target.

She squeezed the trigger and a plume of flame the size of a basketball flared out the barrel of the Magnum. Both Anderson and Berlin turned to look at her in surprise. The noise was deafening. Bloch was only aware of Berlin and Anderson in her peripheral vision. She was looking at her phone screen, and the cloud of dust, wood and carpet fibers filling the air three feet behind Denvir. There was a hole in the wooden siding of the house, and a hole in the stairs a foot to the right of Denvir's left leg.

Calibration.

Bloch adjusted her aim, squeezed the trigger.

The hole in the wall was lower, but close to the first one, and to the left.

Denvir screamed.

She had only needed two shots.

Bloch looked at her phone screen. Denvir was on his back, the assault rifle lying beside him on the floor. She heard glass breaking, and then Anderson was on top of Denvir.

Bloch retrieved her phone and followed Berlin through the window that Anderson had broken.

In the hallway, Denvir lay on his back, screaming in pain. He kicked at the floor with his right foot, digging his heel into the floorboards, his arms pumping.

His left foot was ten feet away, in the living room. The boot still attached.

There was a rack of assault rifles and two full bags of ammo by the door. Once she saw that Anderson had kicked away Denvir's weapon, and relieved him of a pistol from his belt holster, Bloch put away her gun. Blood already soaked through the floor. Anderson retrieved a curtain tie and strung it around Denvir's left calf, cinching it tight.

Berlin stood over Denvir.

'We can get medical assistance here in two minutes or twenty. It's your choice. I don't think you've got twenty minutes, Mr. Denvir. I think you'll be lucky to last five, even with the tourniquet. Couple of big arteries are pumping here. You don't have much time, so tell me who the Pastor is, and you just might survive this.'

'This is illegal! This is deep-state shit!' cried Denvir.

'It's not illegal because I say it's not illegal. Where were you going with all those guns, Mr. Denvir? I see there's a list on top of that bag. Are those targets?' asked Berlin.

'Fuck you,' said Denvir.

'Mr. Anderson, cut the tourniquet. Mr. Denvir is not co-operating—'

'No!' he cried.

Anderson bent down, flicked open a long, thin blade and held it to the curtain tie. It was the only thing stopping him from bleeding out.

'Last chance, Mr. Denvir. Who is the Pastor?'

'He'll kill me if I tell you,' said Denvir, through gritted teeth.

'Mr. Anderson will kill you if you don't. You decide which is the more immediate threat.'

'I'm not telling you shit. I don't care who you are.'

Berlin turned and walked toward the front door. As he did so, he said, 'Mr. Denvir is too stupid to stay alive. Help him out, please, Mr. Anderson.'

Bloch turned away. She followed Berlin through the front door, and as soon as she got outside she heard the sound of police sirens.

'Let's get to the courthouse,' said Berlin.

Mr. Anderson closed the front door behind him, used his key fob to unlock the vehicle. As he made his way to the car he threw the curtain tie in the long grass.

CHAPTER SEVENTY-FIVE

EDDIE

'I think you like it down here,' said Berlin.

'So you and Harry keep saying,' I replied.

We were descending the steps to the cells in Buckstown court-house about an hour after the court bailiff took Korn down here in handcuffs. Kate and Harry took Andy and Patricia back to the hotel to get away from the crowds in the courthouse and the reporters. And the FBI, who had descended on Buckstown in droves since the news of the attempted bombing had gotten out. They had checkpoints all over the town and the outskirts.

Berlin led the way down the stone steps, the silent man Mr. Anderson behind him. I followed Anderson, and Bloch was on my heels.

'Did Denvir talk?' I asked.

'I'm afraid not. If I'd had time and some privacy, things might have been different.'

'I don't like the sound of that,' I said.

The corrections officer on duty was a large man who looked like he'd eaten a slightly smaller man.

'Back again, Mr. Flynn?'

'Can't get enough of the place,' I said. 'We want to talk to Korn, if that's okay.'

'You his lawyer?' he asked.

'Depends. He has to hire me first. Let us in.'

The officer checked in weapons from Bloch and Anderson, gave us a cursory pat down, then took us down the familiar corridor, and opened the cell door. Korn was the sole occupant of those cells that day. And there was only one officer on duty.

'Let me know when you're done,' he said, and locked us inside with Korn.

He sat up on the bench, his elbows on his knees and his hands on top of his head. When he sat up, I saw a ring of blood staining around his thigh.

'Mr. Korn, my name is Alexander Berlin, this is Mr. Anderson. I take it you are already familiar with Mr. Flynn and Miss Bloch.'

'Who are you, exactly, Mr. Berlin?' asked Korn.

'Well, today I'm pretending to be with Homeland Security because that's who lent us our car. My precise role in government is not your concern. What *is* your concern is what I am here to offer.' Berlin had an electronic tablet under his arm. He brought it up, tapped on the screen, bringing to life a document, and then he gave it to Korn who began reading.

'This says I will serve five years if I give a full confession to prosecutorial misconduct. I'm afraid I can't sign that. I haven't done anything wrong. And I don't know you. What authority do you have to offer me anything?'

Berlin dialed a number saved on his cell phone. Whoever was on the line picked up, and Berlin said, 'Tell this man I have authority to make a deal,' he said, then handed the phone to Korn.

'Who is that?' asked Korn.

'It's the attorney general,' said Berlin.

His eyes widened as he said, 'The Alabama AG is on your speed dial?'

'No,' said Berlin, 'this is the United States Attorney General.'

Holding the phone to his ear, Korn listened. A minute later he handed the phone back to Berlin.

'My apologies, I had to be sure you had the authority to make me an offer.'

'I understand. You should think about it.'

'I already have. I told you, I've done nothing wrong.'

'Well, you see, the guy who ran against you in the last district attorney elections is getting ready to run again. I've arranged for some influential and wealthy backers to ensure he will win this election. You won't even be able to stand for re-election. Now for the good news. He's pro death penalty. The bad news is Mr. Wingfield will likely co-operate with me in exchange for immunity, and that means you will be convicted of fraud, perverting the course of justice and possibly the murder of Colt Lomax.'

Berlin let that last statement hang in the air.

'There's a witness who saw your car leaving the property, just after the fatal shot was fired.'

'What witness?' asked Korn.

'This witness,' said Berlin, pointing to Bloch.

She waved at Korn.

'You didn't think I brought Miss Bloch and her attorney down here just for show?'

I didn't think it was possible, but Korn seemed to turn an even paler shade of white. His Adam's apple bobbed in his throat. He was making calculations. The murder of a sheriff carried a certain penalty.

'You don't need me to spell it out, Mr. Korn. Imagine the new district attorney, taking your office, and strapping your ass into Yellow Mama up in Holman Correctional, five years from now.'

Korn was many things. A coward, certainly. But he wasn't stupid. I saw him straighten up. He had one last card to play.

'I won't ever admit to misconduct in office. I won those convictions. Those men were executed on my watch and I'm proud of my record. I won't admit to anything that would jeopardize my legacy. But there is something I can offer. Information has come into my possession revealing the real identity of Skylar Edwards's killer. He is the leader of a small white supremacist group. They call him the Pastor. I know his real name, and I have something to prove it all in court.'

Berlin looked at me. This was his play, but he knew I was concerned about the dozens of men on death row, awaiting execution, because Korn had cheated and lied to put them there.

'What proof do you have?' asked Berlin.

'I have a video. It's security footage from a gas station. It implicates the Pastor in the murder of Skylar Edwards.'

The small concrete cell seemed to suck the air clean out of the room.

'What do you want in exchange for this?' asked Berlin.

'Full immunity. We draft the immunity agreement right now, and we get the judge to witness it. I don't trust you, Mr. Berlin. I trust Judge Chandler. That makes it all official. Then I'll give you the Pastor, and you'll give me my freedom.'

I was about to say something, but Berlin had already made up his mind.

'Agreed,' he said.

It took another half hour for Berlin to amend the agreement, and for Judge Chandler to come down to the cells. He said nothing to me, Korn or Bloch. He spoke to Berlin and signed the immunity agreement using a digital pen, putting his name below Korn's.

As Chandler left the cell, he turned to me and said, 'You and Miss Brooks are good lawyers, even if you are unorthodox.'

'I'll take that as a compliment.'

The cell door closed behind him.

We fell silent, and then Berlin urged Korn along.

'So where is this footage?' asked Berlin.

'It's on a pen drive, in my briefcase, which the officer outside here has in my property bag.'

Bloch banged on the cell door, asked the corrections officer to bring us Korn's possessions. The keyboard that attached to Berlin's tablet had a pen drive. He inserted it and together we watched the footage.

'So when can I go?' asked Korn.

He had this in his possession while he was trying to convict Andy Dubois of the crime. I knew it. More than that, he was trying to have a death sentence passed. I couldn't look at Korn anymore. I left the cell, with Bloch and Berlin.

'Hey, we had a deal,' said Korn.

'We did. You give us information identifying the Pastor in exchange for your freedom,' said Berlin. He looked at Anderson.

As Berlin closed the cell door, leaving Anderson alone with Korn, he said, 'A deal is a deal. Mr. Anderson, set him free.'

Bloch couldn't look at Berlin, and at that moment, I didn't know why. But the expression on Bloch's face was dark enough to give me a hint. Right then, I suspected Korn would be leaving that cell in a body bag.

'So are you gonna get this guy?' I asked.

'Sure,' said Berlin. 'Soon as Mr. Anderson is finished, we're going to pay a visit to the Sheriff's Department.'

CHAPTER SEVENTY-SIX

THE PASTOR

Buckstown flew past the Pastor's window. His driver was pushing forty miles an hour, but they weren't going to get pulled over by the cops.

Not in the governor's car.

Besides, Sheriff Shipley sat in the rear passenger seat beside the Pastor. Of course, he didn't know him as the Pastor. He called him Governor Patchett. Shipley was required as a poster boy for the press conference, plus he provided additional protection. All that Patchett had worked for was so close to paying off. He checked his watch. It was almost four o'clock.

The press conference was at six. In Montgomery.

More than enough time to get there, but still, the governor wanted to be there early. He wore one of his best suits. The plain navy that he'd had made by a tailor in Mobile. It fitted him well, and the fabric allowed him to breathe in the heat. A white shirt with a pale blue tie complemented the suit. A flower in his lapel completed the ensemble.

A white camelia.

It didn't really matter that Francis Edwards hadn't detonated the truck. He had still threatened the entire town. He was still a terrorist. And now, the best kind of terrorist for maximum political capital – a dead one. He had put the fear of God into the people of Alabama, and that was all that Patchett had required of him.

The vehicle slowed on Union Highway.

'Why are we slowing down?' asked Patchett.

'Looks like the FBI are doing vehicle checks up ahead,' said the driver.

Patchett turned to Shipley, said, 'How does it feel?'

'What do you mean?'

'You know what I mean. How does it feel to be the hero who saved Buckstown from going up in a fireball?'

Shipley laughed, nervously, 'Not bad at all.'

'I think this secures you as our new sheriff,' said Patchett.

'It might only be for a few months though. I mean, there's an election between me and the office.'

'Don't worry about it. I know Korn helped Lomax. Now that the district attorney is in difficulty, we'll need all the good men we can get. I can pretty much guarantee no one will oppose you in the election. Not seriously. We might stand an opponent, just for show, and then get them to withdraw their candidacy a few days before the election. Makes it look fairer. Now, when we're at the press conference, I want you to smile, stand next to me, but don't try and answer any questions from the press. That's my job. Got it?'

'Got it.'

Patchett looked out of the window, saw that they had made little progress and they had crawled to a virtual stop. He twirled his FOP ring on this finger. A habit that he developed when he was on edge.

'Hey, why haven't you put on the sirens?' he asked.

The driver said, 'Sure thing, Governor,' and hit the sirens and lights on the governor's SUV, then pulled out to overtake the line of traffic.

'Alright, now give me a minute. I just want to go over my speech one more time,' said Patchett.

He had the pages for his speech in his lap. This was the most important speech of his life and he had done multiple drafts. Now, it was perfect. At six o'clock he would deliver it live on TV, and he didn't want to make even the slightest mistake. He put on his glasses and began to read.

On May 21, 1961, the Governor of Alabama, John Patterson, delivered a speech broadcast on WSB-TV News. He was responding to out-of-state agitators who had entered Alabama for the sole purpose of causing civil disobedience and violence. Among those agitators were the Reverend Martin Luther King

Jr. and John Lewis. Lewis was part of the so called Freedom Riders. Men and women, black and white, who were taking advantage of a Supreme Court decision that outlawed racial segregation on interstate transportation. In a time when the Jim Crow laws were still observed in Alabama, these men and women travelled together, to Montgomery, with the sole intent to incite violence in our peaceful city. And they were met with resistance. Governor Patterson appeared on television and he spoke out against Martin Luther King Jr. and the so-called Freedom Riders who were instigating the trouble.

As you know, we had an instigator attempt to destroy Buckstown last night. His name was Francis Edwards, and I am informed by law enforcement that he had further plans, including an all-out assault on the governor's mansion. Thanks to the heroic efforts of the local sheriff here, he was stopped before he could execute his plan which would have destroyed homes, businesses and cost hundreds, if not thousands, of lives. Edwards was part of a radical leftwing group associated with Antifa, a terrorist organization, who are hell bent on destroying this country.

I served as a police officer for five years, so I know the pressures that bear on our law enforcement personnel. That's why, given the unprecedented threat posed by these groups, I take strength from the actions of John Patterson that day in 1961. Tonight, I proclaim martial law in Sunville County. As well as the National Guard supporting our law enforcement officers, I have recruited a small tactical team of militia. Ordinary men and women – citizens of our great state – who will kick down doors, root out the instigators and traitors among us and deal with them by force. They are the Alabama angels. They will protect our homes as if they were the angel Gabriel himself.

Rest assured that I, as your governor, will take every action necessary to make our state safe, and to make it great again.

The vehicle slowed, and Patchett looked up from his speech.

'They're stopping vehicles here at the checkpoint,' said the driver.

A line of vehicles and men in FBI-branded tactical vests were blocking the road, checking every vehicle. The driver slowed and stopped as an agent waved them down.

Before the agent could say anything, two men approached the car. One was tall, wearing a dark suit, white shirt. The other was much smaller. He took off a panama hat as he opened the front passenger door and got inside.

'I'm Alexander Berlin, Homeland Security, good afternoon, Governor,' he said.

'What's going on?' asked Patchett.

'We've received intel on a highly credible threat of assassination. We will be escorting you from here. My colleague Mr. Anderson will be driving you to Montgomery.'

The driver's door opened and the man in the black suit waited while Patchett's confused driver exited the car. Anderson got in, closed the door and took the wheel. The roadblock cleared up ahead – the FBI vehicles parting as the governor's car was waved through.

'There's really no need for . . .' said Patchett, and then stopped himself. He couldn't play down the threat. He was relying on it.

'My driver was fine, and I've got the sheriff with me as security. I don't need—'

'You do,' said Berlin, looking into the back seat. Sheriff Shipley was behind him, and Patchett behind Anderson.

'Sheriff, how are you?' asked Berlin.

Shipley gritted his teeth, said, 'You don't have authority out here, Mr. Berlin.'

The man named Berlin turned for a moment to look around, and saw that they were on an empty highway, with no cars around. The traffic was still held up at the FBI checkpoint. They wouldn't let any cars through for another half hour, as Berlin had instructed.

He shuffled round in his seat, faced Shipley and said, 'Far as I know we're over the county line. One thing is clear here, and that is *you* don't have authority. Now, hand me your side arm. Slowly.'

Patchett felt his spine turn into a block of ice as he saw Berlin's arm come up over the back of his seat with a gun in his hand.

'You can't be serious,' said Shipley.

'The threat could be from anyone, Shipley. Even you could be the assassin. Now give me your weapon.'

Shipley's shoulders slumped as if he was pissed off at the bureaucracy of the federal law enforcement agencies, and that he had lost a pissing contest with Berlin. He slid his side arm from his holster and handed it to Berlin, who took the weapon, then pointed it at Shipley and blew his brains out through the back of the window.

'Jesus Christ!' cried Patchett.

'Calm down, Patchett,' said Berlin as he put his own gun away and trained Shipley's weapon at Patchett. Berlin noticed something then. He was sitting the wrong way on the passenger seat, his knees up, back to the windshield, facing the back seat. From this angle he had seen something.

With his free hand, Berlin searched the gap between the seat and the center console and drew out a pink iPhone.

Skylar Edwards' phone, which Patchett could not find in her clothes or her purse after he had beaten and strangled her.

'You almost got away with it, didn't you,' said Berlin. 'I just thought I would let you know that Denvir is dead. The people on your hit list are safe, for now. Here's what's going to happen. We went by the Buckstown Sheriff's Department, took the evidence found in Francis Edwards' house. Neither you nor anyone else will use his murder for your cause. The media will record his death as a tragedy brought on by grief, causing a mental breakdown. And that's all. There will be no political angle. Now, Shipley here, well, that's different. The FBI are going to find a lot of white supremacist memorabilia in his home. And a list of targets, too. You're on that list. In about three minutes this car is going over the Luxahatchee Bridge, into the river. Don't worry about drowning, you'll be dead already. Murdered by Shipley, a white supremacist. You're going to be a civil rights martyr, Governor. How does that feel?'

Patchett lunged forward, his hands clawing for Berlin's face.

There was the sound of a shot, and another, and another.

And then silence, and darkness.

CHAPTER SEVENTY-SEVEN

Eddie

The Next Morning

The diner on Main Street was pretty empty when I walked in with Harry. The big guy behind the counter, Gus, noticed us as soon as we came in.

There was no hostility from Gus. But there was no welcome either. He could barely look in our direction, and from the expression on his face it wasn't out of any malice toward us. The local media had reported Judge Chandler dismissing the case against Andy Dubois. Judge Chandler was a first-class asshole, no doubt, but the fact that he had apologized to Andy went a long way to changing minds in the community.

They no longer thought he was a killer. But men like Gus would not apologize. He was burning with the shame of it, and that was too much for him to deal with.

We took a table by the window, with four chairs.

I ordered pancakes and coffee from the waitress. Harry the same.

'I'm starting to like this town,' said Harry.

'You want to move here? Be my guest. It's about time you retired properly.'

'I'm not going to retire. Not yet. There's more work to be done in this town, but I think they can figure it out on their own.'

The chimes above the door rang out, Bloch and Kate came in and joined us at the table. A waitress who looked familiar came over with a flask of coffee and four cups. Sandy poured the coffee and asked Bloch and Kate what they would like.

'Did you get those expenses we talked about?' I asked.

'Yes, thank you. It means a lot,' said Sandy.

Berlin had authorized me five hundred grand for Andy's bail, and thrown in fifty grand for Sandy.

The newspapers were full of the news of the trial, the death of the governor at the hands of Sheriff Shipley, and the suicide of Randal Korn. He had been found in his cell, dead. The department of corrections made a statement to say that Korn had hidden a leather brace about his person, and that he had been found with the item tight around his throat. He had strangled himself sometime yesterday afternoon.

I had a pretty good idea what time.

Of the five hundred grand Berlin had authorized for Andy's bail, we had only withdrawn one hundred twenty-five thousand, and lodged it in the bail office, after we'd made it look like the full five hundred.

That left three hundred and seventy-five thousand dollars in that account, which I'd arranged to be transferred last night. Bloch had made the arrangements. The money went to a charity that funded appeals for death-row inmates. A nice lady named Jane was the vice chair. The first case on their list was a posthumous appeal in the case of Darius Robinson.

We ate mostly in silence, and then left the diner. The coffee and pancakes were heavenly.

We drove over to the courthouse, met Andy and Patricia. They both looked nervous.

'I thought the case was over, Eddie,' said Patricia.

'It is, there's just some paperwork to clear up,' I said.

We went into the court office, and Harry spoke with the bail office clerk. He came back with two pieces of paper in his hand.

'The bail clerk says she got a call from the bank,' said Harry. 'It seems when she deposited the five hundred thousand-dollar cash bail, they only counted one hundred and twenty-five thousand.'

'That's strange. The bail office must have made a mistake to lose more than three hundred grand,' said Kate.

'That's what I told her,' said Harry, brandishing one of the pieces of paper. 'Because we have a receipt for five hundred thousand.'

'True,' said Bloch.

'What's the other piece of paper?' I asked.

'Her phone number. She likes me. She's already spoken to the judge and given him my view on the missing money. I told her the late district attorney, Randal Korn, had enough money to blackmail jurors and that he could've taken Andy's bail money from the safe in the court office. The judge is writing-off the three hundred seventy-five, saying it was probably stolen by Korn.'

'Let's go to the bank,' I said.

We drove over to the bank, parked and went inside.

I went up to the teller with Patricia and Andy and said, 'These kind folks would like to open a joint account in the names of Dubois.'

The teller took their details, all the while Patricia giving me a quizzical look. She didn't know what was going on.

'We'll need some kind of deposit to open the account,' said the teller.

Harry gave me the receipt. I gave it to the teller.

'Here's a court order for the release of five hundred thousand dollars from court funds into the name of Andy Dubois. This is his bail money, which is being returned to him. That should cover it.'

On the way out of the bank, Andy had to support Patricia. She wasn't limping. She had fainted in front of the cashier.

By the time we got to the car she was feeling much better.

On the plane to JKF, I thought about all that had happened over the last few days. How close we had come. How lucky we had been. Berlin would bitch about the half million dollars in bail money not being returned, but he could hide the loss somewhere on his books. He was good at hiding things.

Before we'd left for the plane, Kate had made sure the narcotics case against Damien Green, the gas station clerk, was dropped by the acting DA, Wingfield. And she'd talked to Taylor Avery, put him in touch with a real-estate lawyer who would ensure that he kept his farm.

Taylor Avery.

All our courtroom tricks didn't really matter in the end. We told the truth. And it was thanks to Taylor Avery that Andy was free. He had listened. And he had stood up and used his voice. He spoke up for someone because it was the right thing to do. It wasn't political, it wasn't for money.

He had done the right thing, no matter how much it might cost him.

And if the time ever came when he needed me. I would be there. To speak for him.

AUTHOR'S NOTE

Between January 2018 and August 2020, fifty-seven people were executed in the United States.

Five of them died in the electric chair.

In the same time period, ten death row inmates were exonerated.

In states where the death penalty is still in use, it is reserved for the most serious crimes. District attorneys have sole discretion whether to seek the death penalty in such cases. Most do not seek the death penalty except for the most horrific crimes. Some district attorneys will seek the death penalty wherever possible. While writing this novel I stumbled upon research by The Fair Punishment Project (America's Top Five Deadliest Prosecutors: How Overzealous Personalities Drive the Death Penalty) which found that just five prosecutors were responsible for securing four hundred and forty death sentences between them, which is around fifteen percent of the total death row population of the entire United States. These district attorneys were so obsessed with the death penalty they sometimes broke the very principles of justice they had sworn to uphold, simply to send someone to death row.

At time of writing, the FBI and Homeland Security classify white supremacist terrorist groups as the greatest threat to national security in the United States.

The White Camelia were a real group who committed a number of atrocities between 1867 and 1870. When Governor John Patterson made the proclamation of martial law for Montgomery, Alabama, he really did identify the Freedom Riders, and Reverend Martin Luther King Jr., as the cause of the violence. Montgomery police stood and watched as young black and white, men and women, were beaten with hammers and pipes by the KKK and ordinary white citizens of Alabama. Representative John Lewis, the great civil rights activist and one of the original thirteen

Freedom Riders protesting racial segregation in the South, said in December 2019:

'When you see something that is not right, not just, not fair, you have a moral obligation to say something.'

While he made his proclamation of martial law on WSB-TV News on May 21, 1961, Governor John Patterson of Alabama wore a white flower in his lapel.

ACKNOWLEDGEMENTS

My thanks, as ever, go to my wife Tracy, because without her this book, and all the others, wouldn't exist. She is a huge part of whatever success these books have, and if you've enjoyed this one, or any of my books, then I know you will want to thank her too.

Thanks to Shane Salerno & all at the Story Factory, for all their work and guidance. I can confidently say Shane is the best agent in the world, and I count myself lucky to know him and to have his representation and friendship. My family thanks him too, every single day.

Thanks to Francesca Pathak and all at Orion for their patience, editing and publishing.

Thanks to Ali Karim for providing technical advice on BLEVE. Ali is well known in the crime fiction community all over the world and has been a supporter of mine for many years. I am glad to know him and to have his expertise and friendship. Thanks, Ali.

And my thanks go to you, the reader. I am very lucky to have you and I think it is important to acknowledge your contribution. Eddie Flynn survives because of you. And he is as grateful for you as I am.

Thanks for reading my books. I really mean that.

I hope the best of them are yet to come.

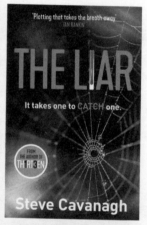

And if you just can't get enough of Steve Cavanagh, don't miss:

BEFORE YOU READ THIS BOOK
I WANT YOU TO KNOW THREE THINGS:

1. The police are looking to charge me with murder.
2. No one knows who I am. Or how I did it.
3. If you think you've found me. I'm coming for you next.
After you've read this book, you'll know:
the truth is far more twisted . . .

'A powerhouse thriller'
IAN RANKIN